CHRONICLES O

..Infinity collides with ...mortality

MARTIN JEREMIAH

Prologue

Classroom

"I think of it often. My Grandpa, use to say it a lot to my dad".

"They would spend hours together in his study, arguing over physics. Then, they would come to a point neither of them won the argument, my grandpa would look at my Dad, smile at him and say..."

"It's what comes next. Over and over he'd say it."

It's what comes next . Said the young girl smiling.

"My grandpa is very fond of my dad. They worked together at CERN for years. Grandpa was leading a project in high-energy physics and my Dad was his assistant. Mum told me a story when they first met. It was a bit of a secret. No one knew, no one suspected they were close, although my Gran said she suspected from the beginning. It was only a few years ago that my mum explained how it all began. How grandpa and my dad stumbled into something back sometime around 2013.

"Mum said it was the scariest moment of her life and a time she would never forget. She gets very emotional when she talks about it now. She believed it led to the kind of world we live in today and how I became the person I am now. I've started keeping a diary. I think it's the most amazing story of my family.

The headmistress studied the young twelve-year-old. *It's hard to imagine she is so young and yet so ...mature.*

"Have you started"?

"Oh yes! Miss, but it took a lot of questions and time with Grandpa Fletcher. At first, he wasn't so sure it was a good idea."

Dear God, this child is something else.

"Oh, why? The headmistress teased.

"He said the world wasn't ready. But I have it all down and have started writing."

It all started long before I was born, in fact before any of us were born."

CHAPTER ONE

The Judean Wilderness 29. AD

The desert was never a place to be when troubled with a tortured soul. It offered only utter isolation surrounded by endless emptiness devoid of humanity, an unfinished and forgotten part of God's earth, and therefore, an easy place to die.

Barely thirty years old, the son of a village carpenter, his lean body was beginning to weaken, all his native gifts no longer helped him. Gifts that came easily now failed him yet, as in his childhood he still possessed the gift of *sight*, seeing things others could not. Only now, in this desolate desert plateau he heard the taunts and mocking laughter carried in dry lifeless winds that swept across the arid landscape. The heat shimmer coming off the floor of the valley distorted the surrounding rock features into dancing and churning mirages. He faltered more often over the rough and craggy ground his eyes burning. Fever-racked and starving the pangs of hunger forcing him to seek shade from the relenting midday sun. This was how it has been for over 30 days.

Occasionally he stumbled and fell, his hands outstretched, cut to shreds by sharp and broken stones. His already bloodstained long garment rent from numerous falls was taking its toll. His body cried out for water to quench an indescribable thirst. The dry piercing wind gave no respite as tiny dust eddies clawed at his bruised and marked face. He marshalled his thoughts to assemble strength of mind. Thoughts of unimaginable fear and foreboding gripped him as he dwelt on what was to come. Steep and desolate walls of barren rock face gazed down indifferent to this troubled nomad's faltering steps along the narrowing valley. And then, there were the voices. They were real; he heard them reach deep inside his psyche something he had known since his childhood. He possessed the sight that permitted him sometimes to see his tormentors. The visions were always vivid; now they came from out of the night and taunted him as they had since he was summoned to the desert.

They spoke to him of friendship only to twist and confuse their meanings to torment him. Crying-out into the desert night for solace amid his tears of despair and hallucinations of mind and spirit. Sometimes there would be nothing only the sound of the night wind whistle through the ravines and canyons of the Judean hills. Then they would come, many of them with soft taunting tones offering comfort, only to laugh and mock him. Others appeared and stood before his glazed eyes deprived of sleep. Only this time they turned into creatures of grotesque forms that made him tremble at their hideous features. Each time with all the fervour left in his stricken soul he mustered the strength to repel their efforts and confront everything they imposed. During a respite from their evil taunts, he saw a cave partially hidden by fallen rock debris from above. He crawled his way painstaking slow each move drained what little strength was left. Once inside the relief from the frigid night cold was welcome. His breathing was laboured while his skin blistered raw from the unrelenting dry heat of the day. At night, heat was replaced with a coldness that made sleep almost impossible. With his arms wrapped around him lying in a near foetal position, he remembered his family. He intoned silent prayers to the God of Abraham to send him strength and hear his cries for sustenance. Then, within his slumber his senses sparked to life. A sound. An unmistakable rumble of stones broke the stillness of the cave. A sound rustling over rocks and getting closer. He raised himself slowly and looked towards the opening of the cave. His eyes widened with trepidation fearing the return of his tormentors and what might be in store for him this night

δ

CERN 2013.AD

For physicists to peel back secrets, to unlock mysteries, underground is sometimes the only place to be. Somehow buried deep beneath the surface of the Earth the tools of experimentation are often best served beneath the surface of the earth. Here it would seem secrets of the most fundamental forces of the cosmos are peeled back. The Large underground Xenon experiment for example, a huge water-filled tank lay fifteen hundred meters beneath Sanford in South Dakota seeks to understand sub-atomic particles interactions searching for evidence of dark matter. Places like Gran Sasso Underground Laboratory, buried under Gran Sasso Mountain in central Italy, studying neutrinos behaviour. A place where Muon flux radiation is studied and tracked. Or the Baksan Neutrino Observatory located under Mount Andyrchi in the Russian Caucasus.

Beneath the sweeping pastures of the Swiss countryside was CERN, home of the LHC- the Large Hadron Collider. A colossus of a machine spanning two Sovereign states with a circumference of twenty-seven kilometres that fired super-charged particles to within a hairsbreadth of the speed of light. Such great strides in scientific endeavours often fall upon shoulders of individuals who were moulded and shaped by their sense of destiny. For some in that rarefied space of quantum physics, they are compelled and drawn to the mysteries of some of nature's deepest secrets.

Alone and troubled one evening, such an individual gazed around his desk turning his pen endlessly fidgeting its small clasp. Around him neatly stacked papers full of theoretical models crammed with detailed equations and abstracts that very few on the planet understood. Yet, within the confines of his inner sanctum late that the spring evening, he stared at one single folder. Professor, Fletcher Du Pont was a man driven by science, a devotee of reason, freethinking, and logic. A man fascinated with the mysterious, but paradoxically loathed mystery or anything that led to unresolved cul-de-sacs. His entire moral make-up was defined by two powerful beliefs. Science will reign over all truths, and all religions were mythologies. He simply didn't believe or accept notions of a deity or God-ordained how nature worked. The folder sitting in front of him mocked everything he cherished and confronted every fibre of his being. Reaching gently into his pocket he withdrew a key. His touchstone, when confronted by unresolved issues. The contents of the folder before him left him speechless to the point of utter disbelief and assaulted all his powers of reason. Squeezing the simple metal key for a second almost breaking his skin and drawing blood. Then, in one anguished moment of pent up anger, he slammed it down hard on the folder in an act of brazen defiance.

CERN's Director General's office was on the second floor housed within a three-story donut-shaped glass concrete façade. With the least amount of fuss and the mastery of a magician, he managed to extract Felix Deveraux away from the departing group of visitors. The older man was taken aback at the sudden intrusion. None of the usual courtesies were present. Deftly and with slight touch of the hand Du Pont guided the Director-General of CERN into the small anteroom off his private office. Without preliminaries, he opened the folder and threw three loose-leaf sheets out onto the small coffee tabletop. His face barely concealed his anguish.

"You need to see this! I need someone to tell me I'm not insane." He hissed

"What's the matter? What am I looking at"?

"Take your time Felix, and see if this doesn't ruin a good night's sleep."

It took less then two minutes for the full shock to finally register with Deveraux and when it did, it almost took his breath away. Both men stood facing each other across the small desk. In the realm of pure particle physics what was before them bordered on the paranormal.

'This has to be a mistake! Fletcher this cannot happen! He shot his colleague a look.

"I'm serious. Quantum science doesn't permit this kind of thing!

"No, it doesn't Felix. But look at it again! I've sat on this for three whole days. What you're holding in your hand is the same image for the third time I ran the collision profiles. It's repeated three times already. Du Pont spat.

"The face of the Shroud! This is absurd. Deveraux shot back.

You've overlooked something!

"No! I haven't!

"You must have! Subatomic particles do not behave...

"Listen to me, Felix! Every possible test protocol and analytical tool at my disposal says this is real. I've checked over this result myself, rigorously. I've no answer why this happened". *Dear God, he thinks I'm losing it.*

Deveraux moved and locked the door, then began to pace back and forth never taking his eyes off the folder on the desk. His colleague looked haunted and troubled.

"I'm trying to imagine what kind of event caused this to happen and, I'm at a loss Fletcher. This cannot happen. I'm sorry dear friend, but you must have...

'What! After three days! I don't think so."

'This image...face is known the world over, and I have no explanation how in all that's possible, that it appeared from regenerated decaying quantum particles".

"What kind of high energy physics that we know of draws pictures? Deveraux said.

"Or regenerates decaying particles and draws a face.!

5

They let the remark hang. It had an edge that cut right through the silence. Both were friends for over ten years. This was the first and only time both men were confronted with something that mystified and disturbed both. The folder and its contents were so impossible their first instinct was to dismiss the matter entirely. Du Pont was Director of Accelerator Technologies and Applied Research at CERN's research complex, and a man Deveraux trusted without question. Du Pont's theoretical workings were outstanding with breath-taking ideas that started to display remarkable predictability as experimentation started to match theoretical equations. For him, it was a calling, a path and destiny seem charted for him to pursue a devotion and intense interest in Superstring Theory to decode physics at the most fundamental level. That was, of course, all before he met and married Claudine Burgoyne. Du Pont met a young student named Claudine Burgoyne a French national studying History and modern languages in Princeton.

He was 26 years with a Doctorate in Mathematical Physics, introverted, intense, and awkward when it came to women. She was the opposite, and only 23, with no shortage of devotees or admirers. Being French she bore a natural degree of poise and sophistication and flourished in her new surroundings that Princeton had to offer. When they met, there was nothing that each found appealing or attractive about each other. Some mutual friends lead to casual evenings, particularly in many of the debating classes that sprung up around Princeton during those years. Within 6 months, they were engaged, and within 12 months they were married and devoted to each other. She fell in love with all the things that kept him driven in his work. He adored her for the shelter, the shield she provided him from some of the life's intrusions, as he would see them. She was particularly adept at building a cocoon of privacy when he was nominated to become a Noble Laureate for his work in Particle Physics; he struggled with the fame and social engagements and politics that ensued. She had good instincts for people and wielded it when the occasion demanded to filter unwelcome attention towards her family. Yet, she complimented this protective cloak with a gregarious and personal charm that attracted people to her. Her fair skin and complexion with blonde straw-coloured hair give her a vibrant look that disguised her years. These were the positives in his life. He, on the other hand, was devoted to two mistresses, his wife, and his work. At 59 he had much to be thankful for even though his turmoil came about due to his obsession with his work.

It was inevitable that his path in science would lead to Switzerland. Then as is often happens fate played its hand. Becoming impatient with his efforts at Stanford, Du Pont turned away from teaching. He was at heart an experimentalist, a seeker, and no amount of money or creature comforts that a University post offered were enough. He made friends and collaborated closely with a French-born Corsican, Felix Deveraux a brilliant mathematician, and over eight years worked in an area of physics that brought both men closer. Quantum Geometry was gaining huge interest and funding into pushing frontier science into boundaries never before thought possible. Things were moving at pace in Europe and that's where the centre of excellence was going to be, as far as particle physics was concerned. His ability to push for excellence in bringing the best and the brightest minds in fundamental physics and funding to build bigger and more powerful machines made him the next driving force in European science. Within months, Felix Deveraux moved to boost an aggressive program of research to set about making superstrings the centrepiece for extending the Large Hadron Collider agenda. In quick succession, over a matter of months, the world's finest thinkers in frontier physics were attracted to pursue their life's work in Geneva.

"Who else knows?" Asked Deveraux

"Only two of us." Well, only two of us as far as I can tell. Not sure if my assistant might pick it up sometime soon. He processed the results and he is a first-class theorist. We need to consider his dilemma if he stumbles onto this."

"How do I explain an image with existential connotations? How do we do that? We need more time my friend, and absolute secrecy." Deveraux said lowering his voice.

"I have all of the event triggers and analysis from Euclid locked in a safe place. There are no copies. I've taken certain steps to keep this watertight. Du Pont said.

Deveraux reached to a cabinet and took out two tumblers.

"We need a strategy to handle this! He said opening a twelve-year bottle of malt whiskey. Du Pont looked at him directly.

"This is less of a physics event and more... of a paranormal origin, Felix!

He let the words sink in. Only this time, he held the stare as those dark hazel eyes absorbed the implications and tone of his words. Deveraux could see the crisis etched in his colleagues face.

"I think I'd like a better term then that, Fletcher".

"How about Quantum Aberration! How does that sound? Du Pont said reaching for the handle of the door and unlocked it. *I need to get out of here for a while.*

"If you don't mind Felix, I need some air. I need to clear my head. Do you mind if I...

"Of course! Of course, by all means, Fletcher. Take some time. But before you go, one question. Do you think this will any impact on Euclid?

Du Pont thought for a few seconds on the planned major experiment in a month.

Oh God, I hope not.

"Doubt it. This has nothing to do with Euclid".

Alone and walking briskly along Quai Gustave-Ador, Du Pont indulged in some self-analysis. Particles decay. Their arrival is brief and fleeting for a few billionths of a second. A brief instant of their sublime existence and then they're gone. Nowhere, was there any theoretical basis or evidence that they...reappear. It was beyond known laws that they regenerate, and yet...something that cannot happen in physics, occurred. Even more disturbing, sinister almost, quantum particles do not form and coalesce into any pattern that *resembles a face*. That was utterly impossible, and, particularly a face of a man with biblical origins. In his folder with absolute clarity was a haunting iconic image. The most fundament elements of nature he believed were omnipotent and behaved according to still unknown laws. Yet, locked in his drawer was a ghostly image that challenged all he understood about physics, including his utter contempt for anything to do with religious dogma. The memory was still fresh that faithful morning some days earlier. He paused and recalled how it all began.

He was alone at the time when his monitor a large 27 inch screen traced the particle debris like beautiful abstract art. Only in one brief moment when Du Pont's attention was focused on the refresh patterns- did a set of points coalesce into a form that almost stopped the scientist breathing. Its first appearance shocked him.

Peering through the tracer plots of decaying particles first was the formation of the lower jaw, followed quickly by the strong image of a forehead and then finally the complete ghostly image of a man's face emerged amid thousands of points on his screen. A face with unmistakable dimensions. A face recognised instantly by millions of worshipers around the world. On reflex, he tapped his keyboard and shut down his terminal. This was CERN's nerve centre where team teams of engineers and theoretical physicist's scrutinized colourful arrays of particle collisions form spaghetti lines across their screen clusters. Everyone here was also under his spell. Most, if not his entire group were devotees of Professor Du Pont, yet everyone referred to him simply as "Chief ". The command centre itself that morning was busy, consisting of a large open plan circular space. All test tracking display consoles were arranged in 6 different curved clusters throughout the floor area. It could have been a trading-floor in a major stock market location.

He's exterior was one of surreal calm, casual, almost disinterested, he could almost feel his heart pounding yet conscious of the folder snuggled under his arm. Nothing seemed out of place, abnormal or strange and if there were, he'd sense it. Nothing hinted of anything amiss.

"Do you have time to look at these with me Chief"? A voice said from behind him.

Doctor Paul Melrose leaned against one of the consoles, holding reams of paper, and clutching a cold cup of coffee looking like he slept in his clothes. He was Welsh by birth, his father was English, being a Member of Parliament who held the Conservative seat for New Burrow-Downs for over 10 years while his mother was Welsh, a schoolteacher from the Rhonda Valleys.

'Chief! Could we have a few minutes?

Du Pont froze. His mouth felt dry. He could hear heart pound inside his chest. His assistant Paul Melrose approached holding a large bulging folder. *Jesus, he knows.*

'Can it keep, till later Paul?

"Sure Chief, I'll leave them on your desk, maybe we'll catch up later.

"Would you do that? We'll go over them later- if that's fine with you"?

"Did you get any sleep; you look as if you need to?

"Sleep!

"Well, yes. Did you spend all night on this"? Du Pont asked

"Not quite." Shrugged Melrose.

'I did manage to grab a few hours around four am".

'You need to take things a little easier".

"Lunch then! Melrose said

Now what. How do I manage this?

"Tell you what, how are you for Thursday evening? Du Pont asked

"We're having some friends around for dinner, Claudine, and the girls are doing some new recipes of sorts!

Consider yourself invited", he said with a wink, and then headed towards one of the lifts at the far end of the floor. That was all earlier in his day, and now standing on the shore of Lake Geneva the anxieties deepened. Maybe this was all some absurdity, some meaningless anomaly that randomly came about. He rambled on for nearly 40 minutes towards the outskirts of Geneva itself. The evening was beginning to close in. The wind chill had sharpened and it was beginning to chop and churn the lake ever so gently. The light was fading and soon it would be dark. He fumbled his jacket for his cell phone only to realise he left it behind him at the complex earlier. He decided to head in the direction of the promenade of Quai Gustave Ador it would be a short walk till he made the old town. The overhead sky was beginning to show the first stars. At that instant, he made a mental note to check something when he got back at Sal Madere.

Moving quickly, he started down the promenade. As if to intrude into his thoughts he looked up against the darkening evening skyline. Almost reinforcing a simple message, the towering, and imposing shadowy Saint Peters Cathedral loomed over him. Its presence seemed to single him out and leer at him. He stared back defiantly challenging its very presence and all it stood for. His faith was in science, and wherever that pointed to he'd follow regardless where it led. The Shroud of Turin had no business with him or his beliefs or anything to do with his work. His mind was made up, this bizarre image was his to resolve, and resolve it he would. Nearly everyone on the planet had looked at it some time in his or her life.

Within twenty minutes he was in the centre of the Old Town. It was awash with a vibrancy that gave the city its power along with seductive energy. He fed off it. Energy was something he knew quite a lot about.

CHAPTER TWO

Du Pont's Residence - Sal Madere

For Claudine Du Pont, timing was everything.

Earlier that morning she checked to see her husband's car had moved off and was clear of the garden gates before turning to her two daughters sitting around the breakfast table. She smiled at both daughters. Her husband's birthday was something she loved to plan each year and always managed to surprise him every time. After thirty years of married life, the fire of love and deep affection still burned brightly between them. Moving to Geneva some years earlier had only reinforced their marriage and added a whole aspect to each other's outlook on life. Both were early risers, seldom in bed after 6 am.

He'd quickly shower, while she cooked full breakfast, and always with the early morning dose of, Johann Sebastian Bach playing low on the CD player.

They both shared a love of classical music. It washed through their home in the early mornings in Sal Madere as they and their girls gathered around the breakfast bar.

Not unlike many families at that hour of the day, conversations were often muted. That morning was no different other than she with her two daughters had a conspiracy to consider. A plan was being hatched. The plan was to have a surprise dinner-party for Fletchers 59th birthday, to ease him into the realization that he was looking down the barrel of turning sixty. The prospect bothered him slightly. He'd never admit that, but she knew otherwise. The intention was to wait till her husband had left before they discussed it.

"Does he know anything or suspect something, Mum"? Asked their youngest, Michelle. Claudine smiled at her daughter.

"Your father was born suspicious, my dear. Of course, he's suspicious!

"He probably thinks we're taking him out to dinner. That's what we did last year and the year before!

"It's not the same as his sixtieth, is it" Michelle said

"You know Dad, loves good company, a couple of friends around a table, plenty of good wine, music, and discussing ways of solving the problems of the world and he's happy as a pig in shit and stays at it till the sun comes up.

"OK, Michelle we get it", Said Claudine sharply, adding

'I was thinking of asking your uncle.

That brought a muted silence around the table. Both daughters exchanged glances.

"Why not! Uncle Francois would love it. It might be fun actually. It depends on who we consider asking to join us of course! She teased with a slight smile. All of them understood what that meant. They sat for a few moments letting the idea settle each with their memories of that occasion.

'Where were you thinking of Mother"? Asked her eldest.

"Here, at the house! Claudine said You two can help me with the list.

She said pulling a small pad towards her.

'Here! At home Mum you serious? Asked the younger daughter.

Michelle Claudine led the conversation around to who got along with whom. Finally, having picked a mix of personalities of friends and work colleagues of her husband, the list was cut and sliced into two groups. Denise and Michelle would host their own circle of friends while Claudine would handle a more conservative side of their friendships In all, it was down to forty-five who were by and large, those that Claudine felt comfortable with and valued as dear friends of hers and her husband- and all of them could keep secrets.

Claudine's picked up on something odd she chooses not to share with her daughters. It was a matter of instinct, but wanted to be sure to be certain before sharing with them. She detected it only in the last few days, a shift in her husband's manner around the house. There was a reserve. Some aspects of their conversations were more subdued more withdrawn. He seemed more content to listen to the banter around the table rather than mix it with all of them. Her husband loved chiding and goading his youngest daughter to provoke her. Instead, there was a withholding-the sparkle of wit and humour he wielded with ease and passion was absent. She'd bide her time and let her heart speak. It seldom failed her. But it was there, an unmistakable sense that something was amiss. *Funny, how neither of them picked on it. Denise is usually fast at noticing things like that.*

"I want both of you to take time. Head into the garden and get some flowers for colour. Can you do that for me sometime on Thursday? I trust you know which colours that would go well?

Claudine knew her eldest daughter adjusted well to Geneva, and the move to Europe came with certain difficulties. There were attachments back in the US that were hard to break. Severing ties with a college professor twenty years her senior was a problem for her, and her mother. He threatened to cut his ties to his tenure and follow Denise to Europe. Claudine Du Pont saw to it that never happened. The affair ended much of it in complete discretion without anything as much as a whisper ever getting to the attention of her husband. Her eldest daughter still craved the security of their home life, despite taking up a career in the public service in Switzerland. Now 4 years on, Denise Du Pont was a senior account executive for a large Anglo-Swiss Bank, specializing in funding trade agreements in developing countries in Africa. Unknown to her mother a new spark of romance had already ignited, but from a source no one expected.

"How long has it been since we had our beloved uncle stay with us? Asked Michelle casually.

She was already making moves to leave the planning to her eldest sister and mother. Michelle had more immediate plans that morning to finish a project in Art college and was already over twenty minutes behind. She stood up and glanced at her mother.

"Remember last time! She said, and started to leave for their garage, leaving the thought and memory linger behind.

Denise looked up at her mother across the breakfast bar. Claudine Du Pont's face was lost in the memory of the last occasion her dearly beloved brother stayed with them.

"Any second thoughts Mum?"

"No darling, none', then laughed off the memory.

"Besides your father enjoys my brother's company. It won't be boring, will it?

It never is! Added her eldest.

Claudine Du Pont thought about her older brother. She pictured him as if he was sitting across the table from her now. Slender build, sloping shoulders, and leathery face capped with a silver lined mane of hair. Father Francois Burgoyne was by any standards the nearest thing you would find approaching the term fundamentalist in Christian terms. A Jesuit priest, he was four years older than Claudine. Spent the best part of fifteen years in missionary service in the Far East, had twice been struck down with malaria, and nearly died. Then, one of the dioceses' he was serving came down with severe typhoid and the whole village population had to be quarantined for weeks before medical supplies reached them. Poor medical standards and inept logistics nearly ended his life for the second time.

His life was a vocation of service and devotion. The champion of the underdog, the firebrand cleric who went head to head with local chiefs and tribesmen and nearly risked the government's ire at the time for his confrontation with a visiting delegation of local politicians They were particularly unimpressed when this French-born cleric branded them inept, corrupt and a bunch of hooligans. All through his early years Fr. Francois Burgoyne wore his faith and beliefs as a battering ram. Challenging everything and everyone to be followers of the true teaching of Christ. Even to his superiors when he sensed they lost the way in matters of doctrine and orthodoxy. In every sense, he was a force of nature in both the practice and preaching of the gospels. Nor was he one to tone down, or modify his views in all things moral or ethical whether it was in the confessional or a pulpit.

A fervent fire of absolutism burned within. Claudine Du Pont lost contact with him for a number of years and scarcely recognized her brother when he returned from his missions overseas. His vocation seemed to have consumed him as if somewhere along his journey through the priestly life, her brother became someone else. Unflinching, uncompromising in all matters spiritual. He was a scholar of the Gnostic gospels and spent his first years in seminary immersed in scriptural doctrine and studying the life of St. Augustine.

Vows of poverty and chastity only served to reinforce his conviction of purity and absolute adherence to Gods laws and his commandments. And yet for all of that, was a man of great compassion, and warmth. He had a liking for the occasional malt and was capable of finishing a full bottle or two when the circumstances presented themselves. He was known to enjoy the occasional smoke and was seldom without his pack of Galois tucked away under his habit. By the time Francois Burgoyne was forty-six, he was called home, to pastures nearer his origins. He was given a parish of Dreux, just outside Paris. A diocese of over twenty-five thousand souls in much need of spiritual renewal. That's when Rome called. Father Burgoyne was reassigned. Unemployment and rising crime rates were sucking the life out of towns and villages around Dreux, local police efforts only managed to stem an escalating social problem that was getting out of control. A blend of mixed cultures of diverse ethnic groupings spawned rising drug usage and distribution into spiralling petty crime and regular violence. Little by little he led youth groups on weekends into the surrounding countryside and taught basic survival skills. Skills he developed elsewhere and proved useful in teaching the practical bushcraft to former gang leaders and petty criminals, and transformed them into hopeful and engaged youth leaders. He quietly set about over a four-year period in establishing a series of sporting clubs around Dreux and its parishes, including four separate football clubs and two promising rugby teams.

All achieved by the generous sponsorship from local businesses at the urging of a stubborn cleric, that many found hard to say 'no" to, or refuse. It wasn't beyond this man of God to use his pulpit to embarrass or name well-to-do parishioners into coughing up. Some felt one type of mugger was replaced by one wearing a Roman collar, as opposed to a ski mask.

In his later years he began to relax and enjoy life at a less frenetic pace and confined his pastoral duties to focusing on the elderly and the sick. When his sister returned from the States with her family to live in Europe he was overjoyed. He was thrilled at the prospect of spending more time with the only family he had left on earth. He adored his nieces, and in recent times reached out and started to build bridges to his only sibling sister and family. Theirs wasn't always an easy relationship.

When he considered his sister's, spiritual compass was off the Jesuit; rather then the brother was ready to offer direction to navigate her way back on the path, as he saw it. While never anything confrontational came between them, it put certain strains on their closeness over the early years of Claudine's married life. Both were strong-willed and forceful in their views. He believed in God's driving hand, she believed he belonged in the back seat. Both raised as Catholics, she differed in how she saw living out a fulfilling life was meant to be. Her faith was still strong, but life had a habit of changing perspectives and beliefs if they retained any. They needed to reflect the times we live in. Religion through the eyes of a child undergoes huge changes with adulthood, and many strayed or found other things to believe in. Such was Claudine Burgoyne.

Her brother was a different strand. He found solace in scriptural certitude and the need for personal sacrifice and obedience to the word of God.

His life was one of servitude and devotion, a pilgrim in an unholy world. By the time he was two years into the priesthood he was reciting all of the Commandments in Hebrew. It wasn't long before he mastered how to recite the Lord's Prayer in Aramaic, the very tongue, and the sound of how Jesus would have spoken it. Each consonant pronounced to sound as it meant to be. He was in every sense, a foot soldier to an ancient God.

For all that, each year's passing had a mellowing effect on Francois Burgoyne and he soon learned to keep his own council when he and his sister would touch on topics that divided them into moral and ethical matters. Both were diligent in expressing themselves to each other, and particularly in conversations between her brother a devoted disciple of scripture, and her husband, a committed free-thinker and a passionate advocate of scientific reasoning.

There was much that both men enjoyed each other's company and Claudine would often sit up into the early hours watching both men testing each other's standpoints and drawing each other out in areas when science and theology overlapped. Both were seekers of sort's, seekers of truths only both choose divergent paths to achieve it.

"No, you're right! It's never boring when your uncle is around. Claudine smirked to her daughter.

"And as you said earlier my dear, it depends on whom he is in company with, at any given time.

Denise DuPont stood and started to leave for work. It was just after 7.30am and traffic would be light. Her first appointment was just outside the city, a social introduction to a new client for the bank. Privately she thought her uncle and her mother needed to spend more time together, and it was a good thing for her uncle to visit as often as he could. For reasons she couldn't be sure of, Denise Du Pont found her uncle reassuring and comforting. His involvement in their lives and regular calls to the family would be good.

It was he, who first taught her how to use a fishing rod and fish in the nearby river. Taught both her and her younger sister how to swim and took a keen interest in their education, particularly in matters of faith and apostolic affairs. She'd smile to herself at the memories of uncle Francois, always cast in her mind as an Indiana Jones in a cassock and white-collar. Michelle Du Pont was the athlete in the family, and she would challenge their priestly uncle to tests of speed and agility. She would do handstands, and challenge him to match her skill. Many times, he did. And for every time she threw down the gauntlet to her uncle, he in turn, would challenge her to match his skill in tying intricate rope knots and so on it went. Summer days were always at their most exciting when visitors and friends alike enjoyed the company of this wily cleric who seemed to have stories that engaged many of the guests at the Du Pont's household.

Of course, it wasn't always like that. There were times, as his last visit, and certain friends of Denise from the banking world were present. It was a memorable evening and those who were present in the Du Pont living room would recall it with some unease. Much alcohol was consumed over the few hours, and conversations turned to politics and Third World needs. One careless banker well into the evening and well into a bottle of Cognac took on and questioned the Church's legitimacy in economic matters. Matters of great complexity with deep underlying factors were way outside the prevue of church interference. Everyone remembers what followed. The tirade and vitriol that descended on the unfortunate man from the Jesuit priest was a master-class in dismantling a person's self-esteem. It was one of the most vicious rebukes handed out amid of the gathering of friends and colleagues that anyone had witnessed. The entire mood of that particular evening went very chilly and many present made a mental note to avoid crossing this Jesuit brother of Claudine Du Pont. One person however who enjoyed the entire episode was Fletcher DuPont himself. From the moment the banker started to express his opinions earlier that evening, the scientist smiled inwardly to himself, knowing that a car crash was coming and was as good as any to end an otherwise mildly interesting evening.

A light rain started to fall over the centre of Geneva. Du Pont waved down a taxi and in brief broken French gave the driver his directions. The taxi drive took under an hour from the centre of the city to wind its way out to the rolling countryside west of Geneva rising through the curving sweep of the road leading towards Augnox and then on to Sal Madere. He was staring out at nothing in particular; oblivious to his passing surroundings until they had reached their destination.

'Mon Sur is this where you.... asked the driver sheepishly

"Ah! Of course, thank you"

He quickly paid the driver and thanked him and then watched the taxi down the driveway and disappeared through the gates of Sal Madere. He quietly stood for a few moments to savour the stillness of the evening. It helped just a little to clear his head, then slowly walked to the door inserted his key and went through into the open hallway. Claudine Du Pont came down the stairway and paused midway down. She had been watching him from an upstairs window and felt he seemed a little lost.

She came and took both his hands. Instinctively he took her and pulled her to him in a warm embrace. Her perfume enveloped him.

"I was worried you didn't answer any of my calls today". Everything Ok? She asked. Sure! He said smiling

"Just one of those odd days"

One look at her husband was all it took for her to notice the strain but always felt he was the architect of his own pressures. Many times, over the last few months even, Felix Deveraux quietly asked Claudine to try and get her husband to take things easy a little and to get a balance.

"Dinner will be in half an hour. It's just you, Denise, and me. Michelle is staying in town tonight, with one of her friends" She said.

"Drink?

"No, not just now Darling. I need to check something out. Won't take long"

He took off his coat and slung over a small chair, and headed towards his study. He stopped and turned.

"Maybe I'll have that drink. How about a chilled Merlot?

"Paul Melrose called, by the way, she said turning towards the drinks cabinet.

"You left your cell in your office, and he was a little concerned that you might have'... "Oh God yes! Paul, I knew I should have called him earlier. Did he say what it was? Anything wrong? *Dear God he's tumbled on to something.*

"Ask your daughter. She took the call. Can't have been that important? They were chatting for nearly twenty minutes, the two of them!

He thought he detected a note of mischief in his wife's demeanour.

And!

"Oh! Nothing dear. Go and do what you have to do. He is rather a handsome young man though. She said

"Speaking of my daughter, where is our eldest? He asked

"In your study!

Du Pont slipped off his jacket undid his shoes and strolled into his study to find Denise immersed on his laptop and taking copious notes. There were nearly twenty pages of handwritten notes piled in front of her. She looked up.

Hi Pops! She smiled.

"Hope you don't mind she said gesturing towards the laptop.

"Not at all pet.

He said bending down to kiss the top of her head.

"Research? He asked

"Yep! And not going well. I'm done". She said and closed the laptop.

"Would you mind checking out something for me while you're there?

Sure! What of?

Du Pont reached into his pocket and took out a piece of paper and the photocopy of the cover of a book. He moved next to her and placed it down slowly on the desk. He studied her expression while she glanced at his handwritten notes and the photocopy. Her face concentrated for a few seconds on the contents and then looked up.

"Really? You want to know more about this!

'Yes! If, you don't mind.

She turned to the keyboard and started to punch in details.

"Well, the best place to start with this! Is in Turin." She said to herself.

She keyed into the search engine tapped and waited. He leaned over and pulled up a chair and stared at the screen.

"I'll take it from here Pet if you don't mind. He said.

Denise stood and gathered up her notes.

"Thanks, Pops I'll leave you to it.

When she got to the doorway she turned for a few seconds.

'You know you could ask, Uncle Francois about that. If anyone understands this it would be him don't you think?" He looked up and wondered how'd his eldest would respond if she knew what was racing through his mind.

"Yes. You may well be right".

When he looked back at the screen Du Pont was confronted with the very ghost-like image that stalked him for the last few days. In just a few days the traces of that face had seared itself into his consciousness like an indelible stamp. The thought never entered his head that he was staring at an invitation of extraordinary proportions. He looked down at both pieces of paper on his desk.

"What in God's name is going on?

What's this about?

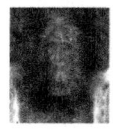

Screen Grab Image (Du Pont's Monitor) Photocopy.

Claudine appeared at the study door, breaking his thoughts, strolled into the study holding out a glass. She noticed her husband had a fresh glow about him as if he spent time outdoors. She walked around his desk handing him the glass without noticing his hands sliding the two sheets together. Deftly he placed his desk diary on top of the sheets. Before he moved to switch off his laptop, Claudine glanced at his screen.

"Has our daughter being doing more of her research? She said nodding towards the computer.

Turin Shroud, isn't it?

Before he could respond she placed the glass on his desk.

"Can I ask you something darling? And be honest with me? She said with a smile.

He leaned back, took the glass, and sipped the wine. *Oh, Christ, now what.*

"Sure! With a slight hint of tension in his voice

"I was thinking of asking my beloved brother to join us next week? Come for a few days and visit." She said trying to gauge his reaction.

"Francois! Since when do you need my approval regarding your brother"?

"Well, after the last time I just, wondered if perhaps you might have concerns?

Fletcher Du Pont considered Claudine's brother an enigma but one he found engaging and with some affection. Francois Burgoyne was always his own-man devoted to his world vision as, Du Pont was to his. On certain issues they were polar-opposites.

"Of course not my dear. I 'd look forward to it. When was the last time you two spoke?

"Oh! Nearly six weeks ago I think" She said.

Du Pont reflected on that for a minute. Then he eyed the screen in front of him. The Shroud image peered back at him from a long distance back in time. He considered how his Jesuit brother-in-law might view it entirely differently. Part of a sublime manifestation or a reminder if one was needed. All things scientific originated from a single divine source, plain, and simple. That's how his Jesuit family member would see this.

"Well. Why not, Claudine? I think it would be great to have Francois come".

He leaned forward and gently switched off the laptop. They both sat and chatted for about ten minutes, catching up on various gossip and some items from the States, and then finally emptied their glasses. As if on cue, Denise came through and announced dinner was ready.

"Why don't you call him, and tell him one of the girls will pick him up at the airport, on whatever day he arrives. Du Pont said as they headed to the dining room.

"Actually, I'd like you to call him! She teased.

CHAPTER THREE

The Boardroom. CERN.

A fortnight later and at precisely 9.15am Felix Deveraux sat in CERN's main boardroom in the Meyrin campus finishing his last mouthful of decaf coffee before the monthly review board got underway.

The meeting room was an oblong-shaped room and was dominated by a large Swedish glass-surfaced conference table that seated 18 places. One wall was completely covered with a walnut panelling from end to end while the opposite wall was a bank of four large plasma screens that could call up instantly any number of graphical displays at will. Only six board members were present. Seated to the left of the Director-General himself was Fletcher Du Pont, and to his right, Manfred Gruss, Deputy Director of Research a balding tanned face German. Next to him was Professor Miles Kingsley the most ascetic of them all, only ever seen in crisp immaculately tailored navy-blue suits? Along with two other Directors of Computing and Theoretical Development, the latter two were both women, Dr. Monika Reinhardt, a German and Dr. Carina Ambrosiana, a Theoretical Physicist from Bologna. Du Pont stood alone next to a coffee peculator. There was a slight tremble in his hands enough to cause the cup to shake as he tried pouring. The banter continued around him as the others in the room prepared for the meeting. A pair of hands came and took the cup from him and did the pouring.

"Having a struggle here Fletcher"? Said a smiling Monika Reinhardt.

It was no accident that six out of a possible full board of 18 attended this morning's board session. Felix Deveraux wanted to explore the issue that needed delicate handling, and he had a few kites of his own to float into this rarefied atmosphere. Du Pont fumbled his folder and sifted through several schematics until he came upon some of the more explosive material. No one took any notice except, Carina Ambrosiana at the opposite end of the table detected something in her colleague's general demeanour. Some light banter followed. His hands had stopped shaking replaced with a slight moistening of perspiration. Others while studying some of the documentation in front of them sensed a hint of tension. Felix Deveraux looked around the room trying to gauge this morning's meeting and the real purpose of their gathering. These were some of the most gifted scientists working within the CERN organization, all of which had substantial achievements in particle physics research. He placed his cup down on the table and calmly called the assembly to order. Everyone turned and looked at the Director-General. Reaching into his pocket Du Pont gently touched the small key in his pocket. Felt its metallic touch.

"Colleagues, friends, men, and women of science. Please disregard the agenda in front of you if you don't mind," He said.

"We will be discussing other matters this morning. Matters of a sensitive nature, and one where we are going to need each other's support if we are to understand the nature of what I am about to tell you".

The silence of the room was palpable. Everyone fixed their gaze on Deveraux sitting with both his arms stretched out on the table in front of him. Looking downwards at the immediate space in front of him Felix Deveraux seemed to age. He paused for a few seconds and looked around the room calmly.

'What is it, Felix. What's the matter? Asked Carina almost whispering.

"I must insist on all of you... No!

"I beg of you all here this morning to treat this entire meeting with absolute secrecy".

Du Pont punched a small control unit in front of him, and one of the large plasma screens sprang to life. Instantly, the screen turned on a series of powerful graphical displays showing a mathematical geometric dimensional of a curled-up space alongside particle-decay profiles. This was just the beginning.

Elsewhere on the lower floor of the building Du Pont's young assistant, Paul Melrose was studying a range of screens laced with complex collision traces. Something new was starting to trouble him. Something he found a little peculiar.

Inside the boardroom Fletcher, Du Pont was on his feet for nearly an hour pacing back and forth close to one of the large plasma screens. All present were still taking in and absorbing the information being laid out in front of them. The atmosphere around the table shifted into a suppressed sense of disbelief. No one was ready to voice their thoughts as to what was unfolding before them. Unease started to shape the mood around the table. Deveraux and Du Pont took turns to bring everyone through a set of results to explain how the recent events generated highly irregular outcomes. To bring matters to a conclusion, Du Pont kept the final piece of information until all had a chance to consider his findings up to that point.

'Let me stress. None of the particle images you are about to see was processed by human origin. These are as my Directorate received them in the manner that is generated by our computing infrastructure.'

He paused then picked up his hand-unit to activate the other plasma screen on the wall. Within a few seconds the second large screen bust in life and in nano-seconds began to filter and display a high-energy collision burst of coloured data. In vibrant and rich colour rendition, the screen began to fill from left to right showing a magnificent array.

"We are looking at images of particles my friends...that, should not be capable of detection with our LHC current energy levels. It is simply impossible...but yet look!

It took a few seconds for all of them to assess the data and when it did, a new sense of unease took hold.

"This is unbelievable Fletcher! Remarked, Manfred Gross adjusting his glasses.

"This is not possible even theoretically with what we have here at present?

"Not even remotely Manfred. Du Pont said

"Then... *there is this*"

Du Pont adjusted the image of the graphic slightly to change the resolution and then began to rotate the graphics a few degrees clockwise so that those seated around the boardroom table could identify how the pattern on the wall changed orientation a few degrees, and then it stopped.

A few seconds of silence passed as the cross pattern of intersecting traces froze into a stationary position. Everyone looked and stared, not wanting to believe what there were looking at.

"Good God! Miles Kingsley whispered.

Slowly, Carina Ambrosiana stood and moved around the table towards the screen and stopped in her tracks. Transfixed as she took in the Turin Shroud image clearly defined.

No one spoke for what felt like an eternity. The room almost emptied every ounce of oxygen as they took in the ghost-like facial outline embedded in the pixilated screen. Du Pont pressed another button and immediately a second image appeared next to the first. Except the second image was a copy of the face associated with that of the image of the face of the Shroud of Turin. The mere comparison showed the first image of particles seemed to have coalesced into a near-perfect copy. The whole room was electrified everyone sat speechless. No one looked around. Everyone became consumed with the two nearly identical images.

Everyone, except Felix Deveraux that is. His attention was focused on each of his associate directors, and wondering if his gamble had paid off. This was his moment to try and harness the considerable talent in the room to deal with this. Or would it fall apart and descend into major crises for the organization and him personally. Each of his colleagues took a minute to comprehend what they were faced with. Monika Reinhardt remained seated in her chair turned and stared at her hands as if in deep meditation saying little avoiding any effort to make eye contact with either Du Pont or Director-General. Each of the group gathered their private thoughts. All appeared shocked at the impossible set of images on the wall.

"Is this the reason why a full board wasn't called? Monika questioned looking directly at the DG. " Why was this information not shown to us before now?

The room went quiet for a few seconds. An air of crisis gripped the group as each of them studied Monika Reinhardt. Felix Deveraux fixed a steely look towards her.

"Well, given the reaction in this room right now, what do you think Monika? We show this to the entire board. Word would leak out and before we know it, we'd be reading about it in every newspaper and technical literature in the land. He paused.

"Until we begin to understand what this is, it stays in this room. Is that clear to everyone? No one, not associate Directors, senior Researchers, anyone in the theoretical dynamics, personal staff, and dare I say this, family members also. No one! This stays here in this room".

Deveraux fixed each of his team one by one established direct eye contact; each knew what was expected. All nodded their assent without saying a word.

"Thank you. Now if you please, I'd like to go around the room for analysis and your thoughts. I know this is somewhat disturbing, but deal with this we will." He said.

Then looking to Du Pont.

'Fletcher! You're thoughts?

Du Pont glanced around the room and sat back down in his chair. *They're going to dismiss this as a system's mishap and move on. I can see the cynicism already. Can't say I blame them, this was a mistake to bring them in on this.*

"Does anyone here think this might be a hoax of sorts, a prank of some kind? He asked casually. No one responded for a few seconds.

"We can't rule it, Fletcher. Said Manfred Gruss finally.

"Manipulating an image into the collision results might be difficult to do, but not entirely impossible, but fabricating the neutrino ghost particles emerging from our existing energy levels, well that's entirely something else. And as for this image..." Leaving the sentence unfinished.

Du Pont looked at Monika Reinhardt.

"Monika?

She leaned forward placing her elbows on the table looking very subdued. She fixed him a look.

"I don't know what to think, Fletcher I really not sure what we are dealing with here". She seemed lost for words. This was her domain. The entire computing system and grid network was her baby. It provided some of the most advanced computing power on the planet. Now it seemed, it was playing games with them. Carina Ambrosiana studied Du Pont for a few seconds.

"Fletcher, for these proton particles to appear like this what kind of energies would it take? Within our theoretical workings, where are we'?

Du Pont studied his hands for a few seconds. *This, is where all this becomes absurd.*

"Somewhere nearer, 21 TeV range. He replied

"At least that! Added Miles Kingsley.

"That's way outside our current capability of 14 TeV. That's simply incredulous! Are we absolutely sure of data content here? Carina asked.

Another 30 minutes passed as each of the group worked their way through everything they could consider. Felix let the discussion roll-on, listening to each of the directors go through everything. Carina Ambrosiana studied the images on the second screen with renewed intensity. A germ of a notion had started to form in her mind. She let her thoughts circulate a little, wondering if any of her associates connected any of the dots. Absurd dots, if she was being truthful she felt. As a practicing Catholic, she was shocked as any of them at the very presence of the similarity in the images fixed on the large screen.

"Felix! She called out breaking the silence.

"Yes, Carina, what is it?

"There might be a connection here that we are overlooking". She allowed herself a nervous laugh, for what she was about to add to the deliberations was a little off their turf. She looked around the table and then addressed herself directly to Du Pont himself.

'You all understand that I am Catholic, yes? She hesitated for a few seconds.

"We have long believed that the Holy Shroud was a secret artefact from biblical times. The face on the Shroud for many of us believes it to be that of Jesus. Some are uncertain but for many, it does represent Jesus because the whole image of the holy shroud includes markings consistent of a man crucified on a cross. There has been numerous research works carried out on the veracity and authenticity of the cloth itself and its date of origin. In recent times, carbon dating techniques have proved beyond a reasonable doubt, that it is as old as we think it is and is consistent with the linen fabric used in the time in Judea and his life"

"Much has been written also as to whether it was a forgery, but the techniques to create a forgery of this order of the image pattern shown here was simply not possible then'. Everyone considered Carina Ambrosiana carefully taking in the import of what she might be suggesting.

"Please go on Carina", added Du Pont gently.

"There is still divided opinion in our Church, in the scholastic circles on its true authenticity, and more so, as to whom the image of the man is. My faith tells me it is that of Jesus Christ. The area however where there is much discourse is what caused this image to embed itself into the fabric of the cloth in the first place. Again, many views and arguments suggesting alchemist of all sorts attempted to create religious artefacts and make forgeries. These were considered valuable and all sorts of disreputable practices were widespread. These arguments were well understood in the Catholic Church hence even today our church neither denies nor endorses the image of the Shroud as that of Christ. It does bestow on it a certain divine significance, and for the moment is happy to leave it at that... She stopped to collect her thoughts.

"For others of us in the church- our faith tells us that this is truly the image of Jesus and his countenance of his face showing severe trauma and injuries, and the formation of his image was caused by the extremely high energy of light. To us this was his Resurrection; a source of tremendous energy of light transfigured his death like image into the shroud fabric"

She stopped and reached to pour a beaker of water next to her. Then slowly sipped the water watching her colleagues ponder her last few words. No one said anything for a few seconds letting her remarks settle. Deveraux leaned back and studied Carina Ambrosiana for a few seconds.

"So that takes us to what, Carina?

"Well, Professor, perhaps this is not entirely a coincidence, this image of the Shroud was perhaps created from a source of light energy of an order of power and origin that is beyond our level of thinking. Does it not strike anyone here that it turns up here like this, almost bizarrely? In the midst of one of the powerful man-made energy sources here in CERN. Is this some monumental cosmic coincidence that both images separated by nearly 2,000 years of history has *energy*, as its common linkage?

For the second time that morning everyone looked at the Italian and then back at the two ghosts-like images staring down at them from off the wall. Fletcher Du Pont felt his mouth go dry as he assimilated the very suggestion that his fellow scientist was making. Felix Deveraux noticed that everyone sitting at his board table sat upright taken at the suggestion from the other end of the table. Carina sat back and took another mouthful of water reflecting on her own words. Du Pont also leaned back almost slumped into his chair and carefully looked at the images on the wall then glanced sideways at Felix Deveraux. His face remained passive.

He's the first to break the silence.

"That's quite something to consider Carina, Ecclesiastic and scientific overlaps. There is an enormous gap here; you're asking us to consider that there is some mystical coincidence at work here. That's a lot to..."

"Do you have any single scientific explanation for this"? She cut in.

"May I suggest Felix, after this meeting we meet with Doctor Reinhardt and check if my system is the only one affected by whatever this is. Monika you'll have to handle this personally for an obvious reason for security"? She nodded.

The meeting quietly concurred. Deveraux stood up and looked around the table to his group content that he had their complete confidence.

"Thank you all. May I stress my earlier comment for the need for complete silence on this matter"?

With that, the meeting ended and each of the group stood up and filed out of the room. In turn, each of the members shook Felix Deveraux's hand offering a few words of appreciation and support as they left.

Within ten minutes each of the senior directors filed into Du Pont's office and closed the door. Du Pont's desk was in two parts resembling two horse-shaped segments facing each other. Monika Reinhardt entered the room. All were present. She quickly set about getting to work. Immediately she took up Du Pont's chair and keyed into his terminal and started to trigger of rapid serious of queries. She then asked him to indicate which file structures he used to run Euclid. A few minutes passed rapidly as her fingers danced across the keyboard at speed. The two terminals on the desk fired up in succession responding to her commands. No one knew his or her way around CERN's computing monolith like Monika Reinhardt. Her fingers glided across the keyboard barely touching, almost caressing each key. She was in commune with the world of binary processes. Code that spoke to other code, which in turn spoke to more code to unlock keys to large file clusters.

The numbers were spellbinding as she cruised through a whole hierarchical structure that took decades to assemble. She was engaging the assistance of complex file filters buried deep inside the system to respond to her delicate touches. Hard drives began to purr in rapid succession followed by a cascade of graphics. One by one-new files appeared on the screen. As she stopped to read something, she muttered something in German to herself, and started again, a flurry of hand movements issuing commands and commanding responses.

"Will this take a while, Monika? Asked Miles Kingsley

"It will take as long as it takes Miles!"

It took less than a few minutes and all of Euclid File data was ready for viewing. She turned to DuPont and extended her hand

"Can I have the file time stamps when the image first appeared here Fletcher, if you please?

He quickly complied and passed her details. Stillness descended around the desk. It was like they were engaged in a secretive hacking exercise to a highly secure government location. She took the sheets studied them for a few seconds, memorized the contents, and then with deliberate ghost like touches entered the data and pressed ENTER.

There was a purr from the hard drive and then nothing. The 27"screen remained blank for seconds, and then it just materialized slowly in front of them, a mass of tracer lines of divergent colours with a rich speckle bust array of the proton beam collision profiles. No one said anything but stared again for the second time that day in utter amazement to see it occurred as Du Pont saw it the first time. The particles commenced their decay and fade but as they did the image itself started to appear. First, it's just one side of the face, and then the right eye closed appeared. It moved down and began to define an elongated male face and was completed in a matter of seconds. Monika, stared at the screen silently then turning to group around the desk.

Each struggled to grasp the implications or provide any rational explanation.

"My God! Fletcher what have you done to warrant this?

All stared at the impossible ghostly image begin to emerge across the screen. Seeing it for themselves only served to heighten their disbelief.

"This cannot be happening! Gasped Manfred Gruess.

"Now we go to your access Miles, and see if this would have occurred on yours? You're code password, please.

He quickly complied, and she immediately turned and keyed into the access protocol. Instantly the screen flickered and went hunting. Professor Kingsley's terminal address appeared, on the screen.

Similarly, as in Du Pont's, she brought up the identical file and data sets for Euclid, paused and waited. Everyone watched with anticipation no one saying a word. Silently, the graphics came to life again, repeating the same sequence as before. The group imperceptibly leaned closer, the identical formation as before traced across in front of them only this time there was no new ghost particle decays. They continued staring, waiting. A few brief seconds passed.

"Where is the image? One of them asked.

Each of them sat and slowly it became clear. There was no image.

"Let's try yours, Carina please.

The mood remained subdued. For the next ten minutes, the Director of Computing worked the keyboard over and over for each of the remaining scientists. In all cases nothing. The only terminal that seemed to be affected and displaying the anomaly, was Du Pont's own terminal. He finally stood and began to pace back and forth slowly feeling that the eyes of everyone in the room were on him. He cast a searching look towards his close colleagues. His grey eyes turned icy cold as he started to process his thoughts, and his fears.

"Thank you, Monika. First-class piece of work" How would you describe this Carina"? Mystical, or paranormal?

She slowly stood up and folded her arms and cast a furtive glance around the room. She thought for a few seconds.

"I'm nowhere near, being able to answer that question Fletcher, and might I add, nor is anyone else present'.

The room was quiet for a few moments, assessing the possible implications of their little exercise.

"I, for one believe in neither!

It was Monika's turn to make her point of view known.

"We are all scientists here. We only believe in facts, data, and logic. There is no room for superstitions or beliefs or hunches. We must deal with these as rational beings"

Du Pont moved to his window and stared out at the distant Jura peaks. He was immersed in crossfire of conflicting issues, and somewhere between scientific absurdity and evangelical nonsense, lay the truth. *This is now an issue for all of us, and no one has mentioned Euclid, not yet. Dear God, lets hope there's no connection here. How could there be?*

"Let's leave this for the moment, everyone. You all need some time to reflect on this. For the time being we should just consider how the formation of these ghosts Neutrino's particles showed up in experiments'

Everyone got up feeling a little lost unable to offer any kind of reasoning or new insights. They nodded to each other and agreed that each would give the matter a few days further thought. With that they left the office and return to their own spheres of work with an additional preoccupation to ponder. Miles Kingsley turned to Du Pont as he left the room.

"If it's any consolation Fletcher, I couldn't sleep if I had this around my neck. If there's anything you need, just ask."

" Thank you, Miles.

'One other thing Fletcher! Ghost particles we can try and figure out. This other matter of the image, I agree with Carina, none of us are ready to answer that one' He said, leaving Du Pont with his thoughts.

φ

Four days later the complex went into high readiness counting down towards the next Euclid beam-run. None of the senior members met with each other to discuss informally what they now knew. Preferring privacy some retreated into their disciplines and spheres of activity trying hard to focus on the upcoming Euclid run. Others coped well with the information, while some simply became distracted and a little distant from their key staff. Keeping secrets, particularly ones like this proved to be deeply distracting. Later walking briskly down the main hallway looking every bit the woman with purpose, Monika

Reinhardt stopped by a coffee vending machine feeling the need for a shot of caffeine. She saw Paul Melrose and then caught his attention.

"Good afternoon Paul. Have you a few minutes to spare? I'd like you to explain to me some of the finer points of Euclid. Are you free to talk? She smiled.

CERN's canteen hall in the Meyrin campus is a large open space area to cater for a large staff of scientists. Off in one of the corners of the hall, Melrose and Reinhardt huddled over sandwiches and freshly brewed coffee. She listened noting the intensity of his pale blue eyes as he took her through Euclid's underlying theoretical basis.

"...The quantum world simply resonates with vibration the music of all known matter is played out by billions upon billions of strings. All of them vibrating with an infinite amount of frequencies and resonances, and by some still unknown mechanisms deep within the quantum world, the music of these vibrations creates all the known particles that make up the matter in the entire universe." He finally paused.

"Do you think we will ever get to observe them directly?" She asked

"Well our constructs predicted that if we could compress our protons way beyond what we normally do, we just might begin to see traces of...

"I'm not sure I get what you mean, *compress protons more*, I thought we did that in our accelerators."

"Yes, we do, but limited up to energy levels of around 6TeV. Now, with two counter-rotating beams inside our tunnel, we manufacture combined energies nearer 14 TeV inside our LHC. We vaporize matter particles that arrive into our detectors. Our accelerator technologists have designed to do this very efficiently. I might add that Professor Du Pont is one of our most foremost experts in this field, along with of course Professor Kingsley".

For nearly an hour he outlined all the expectations they hoped from Euclid. She studied the young mathematician for a few seconds taking in everything he said. She shifted her position in her seat. She thought back to Du Pont's office and the board meeting earlier that morning. Finally, she picked up her cup finished the last of her coffee and smiled at Melrose.

"Paul thanks for taking the time with this. I'm starting to realise; I need to spend more time with my brethren here and appreciate the work. It's truly inspiring, she paused, and then added,

"Can I ask you something else?

'Anything, shoot!'

'So far, with the Euclid program, and these induced magnetic pulses that compress our bunches have there been any new developments, anything worth getting excited about yet? She asked nonchalantly.

He returned her look, and saw those intensive grey eyes peer at him.

"Well, as a matter of fact, there might be".

CHAPTER FOUR

Paris. Society of Jesus Provincial Residence.

The building used to be a safe house during the Nazi occupation and survived numerous attacks from the French resistance over its life. It stood on a relatively small plot of ground just fifteen minutes from the Arch de Triumph in the centre of Paris. It was an unimposing two-story building. A modest garden, surrounded by wrought iron railing did little to attract attention unless one had a reason to visit. On its northwest corner of the building was a large spacious office, furnished with minimal trapping. Its walls were oak panelled and smelt of recent varnishing. A small desk sat in front of double windows with a plain faded brown rug occupying the centre of the room. Brother Alphonse Sienna S.J, was sitting behind the desk with a large manila folder open in front of him. He glanced at the clock on the wall; it was just after four in the afternoon and was expecting an old friend.

As Father Provincial of the Society of Jesus, he pondered how his visitor would respond to his request. He swivelled his chair and stared out the window recalling past missions where both of them gave service together in places that took their toll on lesser men. Then as he poured himself fresh tea, a tap on his door and an elderly nun entered.

"Brother Francois Burgoyne for you Father Provincial!

He jumped to his feet and came around his desk, to greet the striding Francois Burgoyne entrance into the room. One glance told him everything he needed to know. The wiry but powerful movement of his brother Jesuit spoke volumes. They quickly embraced.

"How are you dear friend,' He said smiling to his visitor.

"I am, my doctor tells me, to be in very good nick, Father Provincial". Burgoyne joked.

"Please Francois, no formalities here, not for two old campaigners like us. You look good my friend. Druix must be good for you. Let me look at you. Lost a few pounds I think!"

Francois Burgoyne guessed his old friend was well up to date on all that went on in his parish. 'I still make time to stay active. A little cycling around the parish is good for body and soul'.

'It suits you, my friend, come take a seat. Sister Claire some fresh tea if you would please."

Both men moved to the desk, Burgoyne sat down and noticed the pile of folders spread across his friend's desk and one in particular. Even from his side of the desk, he recognized his own photograph staring out amid loose leaves of pages. The Father Provincial also noted that his friend still chooses to wear the distinctive black cassock, a robe that wrapped around the wearer and tied with a tincture coupled with a Ferraiolo, a cape that added to the presence and aura of the Jesuit.

"They seem to be keeping you busy", he said nodding at his friend's desk."

"Yes, they do dear friend and it isn't always in matters ecclesiastical I might add".

After a few minutes of light banter and some reminisces of times past, the tea came. Sister, Claire had added some croissants with freshly made jelly for both men to nibble. As the tea was poured a silence settled.

"Troubling Times my dear friend. Our world is in turmoil. We stumble from one crisis to another from the lowest levels to the highest levels of our society including our churches moral leadership is nearly none existent. References to scripture are only in passing at some ceremonial events. Never as part of what we are as humans. Some parts of this planet, religious fervour is used and debased. Teachings from our Bible, the Koran, and others get perverted and used as a precursor to inflicting destruction on others. Willful disobedience to the laws of God. You've seen some of these evangelical events in the States, preaching love and togetherness in mass halls and stadiums. Some of these new so-called religious churches are shameful fabrications of the teachings of the gospels. Their motives are business and the accumulation of wealth. Not scripture!

A few seconds passed, Burgoyne sat back and stretched his legs.

"I agree with you Alphonse, but there is also great thirst and capacity to follow the right path. Human beings are only waiting to follow the right path provided it's authentic and has purity to it. All truths possess it. To be authentic is to seek access to bedrock principles and may I say, old friend, that's our work. We provide the source of wisdom that's descended from Divine Intelligence, knowledge, and deep adherence to scripture. Besides, is this in some way connected to the reason you asked me here? Am I being defrocked? He asked with a smile.

The senior cleric thought for a moment and leaned on his desk and studied his old friend.

"I need you to run a series of seminars for us. Apart from being a Scriptural Scholar, you're also eminently suitable to be authentic given your missionary work, your parochial work, and the achievements in your parish.' He paused

'I've looked at others, Francois, but quite frankly you are the most seasoned within this provincial community. " He said gesturing at the pile in front of him. He smiled at his fellow Jesuit and leaned to open the bottom drawer of the desk. Rummaging briefly, he produced a bottle of a Benedictine Liqueur and placed it on his desk.

"Perhaps we need to give this some thought eh, He added with a smile.

Some hours later they had talked into the late evening.

"Stem cell research Francois is a pathway that leads us into the abyss. I need you to look at where current medical ethics is headed. My instincts tell me one thing, my prayers tell me troubling things." The Father Provincial confessed.

"Will you take up this challenge? Look at the present ethics and see what is driving this research and see if it conflicts with the teaching of Christ himself. The Holy Father has ordained that our order takes the lead in putting the Church's position to all medical efforts in this Stem Cell matter. Our theology in Rome is…a little circumspect here Francois, and in my view also very suspect"

Burgoyne fingered the chain holding the silver cross around his neck and looked at his friend for a few seconds. Then nodded his consent.

Within a matter of days, the inner circle of the leadership team within CERN went into crisis management footing. All recent experimental recitals remotely associated with the Euclid programme were isolated and quarantined. The secrecy edicts from the Director-General went into effect immediately and retrieval protocols within its computing system were frozen. This was followed by a top-down screening process across its entire data capture ecosystem for anything that remotely looked sinister or anomalous. There were also human weakness issues at stake. One slightly puzzling aspect to all of this why did it occur only on Du Pont's system file.

"Fletcher! Miles Kingsley said, strolling into Du Pont's office.

"Something to think about. It might not need a spontaneous burst of energy to …

"Leave it for now Miles. I need time to think if you don't mind." Du Pont said cutting his colleague off.

"Sure! Let's talk again. When your head is in the right space. Kingsley said, adding,

"It may not be always about the level of energy my friend. We may need to rethink our entire notion of *matter*!

Then, he quietly turned and left Du Pont to his thoughts.

Paris 1.15am

The last embers of the log fire were slowly dying as both Jesuits sat in two large armchairs. Both were relaxed but troubled by events taking place within their church and events outside it. It was just after ten o clocks at night. It was beyond their normal retiring time but much was discussed, and it wasn't certain when the opportunity to meet again would arise. They had eaten a meal prepared earlier by Sister Claire and two other sisters before retiring earlier leaving both men themselves for the rest of the night.

'How is your family? Don't you have a sister here in Europe? Asked the Father Provincial, moving the conversation to more personal matters?

"Yes, in Switzerland. Very much settled here now I should think. Why do you ask?

"Do you get to see them much? Enquired the older cleric.

"Yes, we do now. Hasn't always been the case as you can imagine. My sister has her family and a husband to cherish. Life is good for them. She used to teach in the States before she came back here. Married to a wonderful man, a man of science actually, and two beautiful daughters. Funny you should mention it, but I am travelling in a few days to stay with them'.

'Where in Switzerland'? Asked the Father Provincial.

'Geneva! My brother in law is a Senior Fellow with CERN. A Physicist, and a Nobel Laureate I might add. Really lovely man. He is also a seeker Alphonse, like us. The older cleric studied his friend. The flickering flames of the fire casting an eerie glow across his visitor's face. It made him look grey in the low light of the study.

"Do we seek the same things, do you think? The older man pressed mildly.

Burgoyne drained his glass savouring the taste of the liquor fire its way around his throat and thought about it for a few seconds.

"He seeks to find truth also my friend but he seeks it in different places to us. He has no belief of course. There is no need for the Almighty in his life. My brother–in-law seeks answers only in numbers, in equations. He seeks to understand how creation in all its magnificence and form, in the symbols of Mathematics"

The older man thought he sensed a reserve in his friend. A withholding of some judgment towards the scientist.

"There are many paths to truth Francois, as long as they all lead to the same source, does it matter. He whispered.

"It matters if there's no humility! Burgoyne shot back.

"To inspect the workings of creation and not wonder with awe at its curious existence. Humility before the awesome power of nature is often missing with these men of science. They decode some small nuances of our world and assume much. Take this Stem Cell Business! It's a prescription that leads to a new morality. Just, because we now have begun to understand the DNA structure of a human being. Where is the humility, Alphonse? We race ahead to understand how to use this knowledge without ever asking if we should. Human tissue that's sacred becomes a commodity.

Both fell silent for a few moments, letting the crackle of the fire interrupt their thoughts. Finally, the elder man asked.

'Is this man of science, your brother in law, a man of any faith?

He's a man of conscience and great principle that's beyond question, but that is not what you asked is it? '

No! The other replied smiling.

"I said earlier he was a seeker of truths, I 'm not sure he'll recognize it. Not with equations that is. He may find simple truths without ever seeing the greater truth. Francois said

"Maybe that's how he'll get there in the end. Said the other

'If you don't mind Francois, I 'm no longer able to stay up late as you are. I will retire now. We will talk further in the morning. He poured the last of the liquor into his fellow brother glass and then quietly left the study to his fellow missionary.

Meyrin Complex. CERN

Despite walking at a brisk pace his heart was a steady 103, Du Pont felt that he could handle another twenty minutes if the mood took him, but not this morning. Other things beckoned. His preference was casual and only when formality demanded did he choose suits. Within five minutes both he and Paul Melrose sat opposite each other in Du Pont's Office. Melrose placed the fresh coffee mug in front of his boss while placing his own on a small side table. He tried to settle and composed himself.

"OK Paul, talk to me!" His tone was direct and to the point

"Chief our work on Euclid is, as you know is tasked at CMS. We've created models to test if the radiation signatures behave in any unexpected patterns and certain energy levels in the 12TeV to 14.6 TeV range. Our models predicted some unusual particle appearances."

"Did anything emerge from your models?

Melrose leaned over and placed a sheet of printed data on the desk

'These!

Du Pont scanned the results of a computer-generated particle decay pattern.

"Lead ion decay?

"Yes, Chief. We modelled it on lead ion mesons emerging with quantifiable lower than expected energies than is the norm. Of course, experimentation might prove this is nonsense!

Du Pont's inner demons were already at work. No amount of theoretical workings could explain ghost particles coalescing to manifest what was locked in his desk drawer.

"What else have you got there?

"This bit is intriguing, Chief it's the results from beam runs on the 16th Euclid 4beta-7- just after 14.46 pm." Melrose said sliding another page across the desk.

"We think this is new…it's a particle we've never seen before, it has a mass of 132 GeV" Du Pont glanced at the page instantly recognized the data and graphic contents. It was an identical copy of one of the data profiles he had. He felt a mild throbbing in his temples.

"We suspect it could be an exotic quark-anti-quark type meson showing up just at these energy interval levels. Nothing extraordinary, but not quite normal either if you see what I mean."

"Do we have a theoretical model that permits this at this energy band level? Du Pont asked.

"Funny, you should ask, Dr. Reinhardt asked me the same question a few days ago. It was connected to the way Euclid bunched proton clusters. I didn't go into too much detail. It's something we may need further work on.'

"Chief is there anything here that we need to talk about? Some aspects you need me to follow up on?

Du Pont shut his eyes a few seconds wanting to share with his senior analyst but that decision was not his to make.

"No! Not for the moment Paul. Thank you. You know your theoretical work might be onto something though. Why don't you consider..."

"There is just one little thing here, Chief, I'd like you to take a look at.

Melrose stood and came around the desk. Opening his folder containing an array of particles energies overlaid with tables of known values from their Standard Model. Du Pont reached for his coffee and sipped. He ran his finger along the diagrams taking in values and gauging the range of energies and decay rates showing up on the data, some were known and then his finger stopped. Reading for a few seconds then put down the coffee. Melrose had his arms folded; his expression blank.

"A particle that decays and then...mysteriously regenerates itself into something completely new! Du Pont whispered to himself.

His heart rate quickened. *A particle with imbued intelligence! What if...it was responsible for... Dear God!*

Melrose leaned on the desk.

"Chief, we're looking at something new here! Particles of unknown origin lurking in some zone of energy levels. They seem to regenerate from what appears to be complete annihilation from collisions then- miraculously re-emerge and transform neighbouring particles altering their properties... that are impossible! Miraculous almost.

Du Pont studied his assistant. The *miraculous* reference threw him.

"A messenger particle, like nothing we've ever seen? He whispered.

"Like nothing, we've ever contemplated beyond the Higgs field, Chief?

Neither spoke for a few seconds both letting the moment settle. Du Pont sat back in his chair and fixed the other man with a stare. The haunting image appearing from nowhere a few days earlier upended any known laws of nature or physics. Now, an exotic particle turns up that seemed to disrupt his whole understanding of how messenger particles behave.

"This is somewhat irrational Paul. A particle that seems to decay, and then reverse itself, then re-emerge to alter other particles in the same energy field. What kind of quantum mechanics is that?

"It's a strange one Chief. It's a particle that not only has the characteristics of a messenger but also possibly has some process to determine which particles to charge or select and imbue electroweak values to neighbouring particles!

"This, is all lead-ion exchanges here, yes? Du Pont asked

'Yes!

Du Pont put down the pages. They knew it wasn't the Higgs Particle that was clear, and yet, this was something quite extraordinary.

It's like this suggests, *intelligence*!

"I thought of that also Chief, like American football, the quarterback calls the plays works out the moves and quickly decides the pass. A choice made instantly based on options that open and close amid the field of play. Our little friend here is playing God. It first transforms itself from decay, and I have no idea how that happens, theoretically or otherwise. It's the *Uncertainty Principle* gone daft.

Du Pont's face remained impassive. The messianic image on a sheet sitting locked in his drawer was tearing his mind in half. Is there a law at work here that bestowed Intelligence? An organizing agent that decays, and then somehow undergoes a dramatic change in its properties in turn, fine-tune other particles.

"Chief, may I bring up something niggling at the back of my mind.

"Of course!"

"Let's for a moment consider something a little non-scientific something that crosses my mind when I'm working on my models. I look at our symbols in our equations, and what they represent. At best they are descriptions of the workings of nature at the most fundamental level. Particles that have mass, or carry forces: the very essence of what we all are.

"Stardust my boy…Stardust! I'm with you. Go on."

"With nearly 200 of us working on Euclid. Just think of all of that intellectual effort and where it's focused. Pure intent. What if our thoughts are..? He hesitated

'…Our thoughts resonate at a frequency that is detected at the quantum level. What if our own thoughts that are intent on finding out things, are summoning an unknown law that we are aware of. We are unwittingly calling into existence these sublime messenger particles with properties that fall outside our Standard Model. They emerge spontaneously and respond to our thoughts."

Du Pont sat up in his chair

"The intelligence particle, we spoke earlier. It's somehow... He paused

"Thought sensitive! Melrose Whispered.

At some frequency or vibration level during our collisions, an event that responds to the very thoughts we have, causes a new type of particle to emerge with intelligence. It tries to match the frequency …*of our thoughts*.

Stillness settled in the room. Neither men spoke. Du Pont rotated his wedding band realizing his hands were moist with perspiration.

"How long has this been in the back of your mind?

'Last two weeks, Chief…ever since we finished 4 Beta 6 and commenced working with lead-ion beams on Beta-7.

Du Pont picked up his phone and tapped the direct extension number. Immediately Felix Deveraux's voice came through. He spoke quickly and listened for a few seconds, nodded and replaced the phone. He then reached into his drawer and withdrew a large cream-colored manila folder and dropped it on his desk. Melrose stood and glanced at it. Du Pont smiled.

"Relax, just need you to join me for an informal meeting with the D.G. Come you'll find this more interesting than you think.!

'Chief, please if I stepped over the line here. I'm sorry if I'…

"Nothing of the sort Paul. Now relax, the DG welcomes new ideas. I think this one is going to grab him by the balls! Let's go!

Five minutes later both Du Pont and Melrose strode into the office to find Felix Deveraux pacing in front of his desk. He greeted both of them and beckoned them to sit. He glanced at his Director of Accelerator Technologies.

"DG, Paul here, has put together most of the theoretical work on Euclid and has extracted a lot of the experimentation data, and carried out extensive comparisons between the predictive models and results.

Instantly Deveraux shot Melrose a glance and then back to Du Pont.

"Am I going to enjoy this?

"Intrigued, I'd say is more the word, Felix".

Deveraux settled back into his chair taking the pages of data from Melrose. Then listened for the next ten minutes as Melrose took both senior physicists through his entire theoretical reasoning, he inlaid into the Euclid Programme. He stopped occasionally to handle some questions from the DG who was leafing page after page through Melrose's notations. He slowly raised his hand signalling Melrose to stop talking when he came to section. A silence followed that seemed to last ages. Deveraux's face became concentrated, absorbed the content of the page. Du Pont nodded to his young colleague to proceed and placed the manila folder on the on the DG's desk. Melrose looked puzzled at both men. A moment of awkward silence crept into the small space. Deveraux came around his desk holding the manila folder and handed it to Melrose.

φ

CHAPTER FIVE

Director General's Executive Suite

Paul Melrose felt the silence around the room consume him.

Each of the others stood around the large spacious office. Hardly anyone spoke, they merely studied the younger man seated by a small desk. In front of him was a series of particle images and one of an iconic facial image of the Turin Shroud. Miles Kinsley rested in the corner; Monika Reinhardt stood beside the desk. Melrose stared in disbelief at what was in front of him. Carina Ambrosiana paced around in small circles. Felix Deveraux sat motionless at his desk.

"Without having seen this a few days ago, what you're suggesting now Paul, would have me on the floor laughing. But this is what we are dealing with."

"This is unbelievable! This is a joke! Melrose muttered.

'I have no possible...! No.! There cannot be any possible construct of known physics that, that explains this. It's not experimentally possible to reproduce this...this image"

"That's our understanding as well, said Miles Kingsley

The flight took just over an hour as the Easy Jet touched down at Geneva International Airport at 2.36 pm. The reverend Francois Burgoyne felt relaxed and looking forward to seeing his sister and family again. Within minutes, waiting at the arrivals gate, Michelle instantly picked out the unmistakable black-robed priest. She rushed to him smiling and waved her hand and caught his eye, and then in jest, stopped in front of him, made an impromptu curtsy. He swept his black biretta hat, and equally made a sweeping grand gesture, then they both embraced causing strange glances from nearby passengers. She grabbed his baggage and whisked him out into the nearby car park. The cleric had hardly had gotten a word in as his young niece rolled off a string of tasks she had to complete various projects, and of course the preparations the following evening for her father's surprise birthday dinner. She pushed the Golf through the gears with ease and was soon heading out sweeping on the route de la Vorge onto the autobahn.

Director-General's Suite

The group was now increased by one. Du Pont and, Paul Melrose were the last to leave then headed straight back to Du Pont's office.

Du Pont calmly closed his door slumped into a chair. Melrose looked shaken and agitated. His mind preferred structure, where the disciplines of an ordered mind saw the world in precise terms. Explanations always required understandings and in order to make sense of these understandings, one needed to have a solid grasp of causation. It was the bedrock to rational thinking and analysis. What he now knew unsettled him deeply.

"They must think I'm certifiable! Chief! Quantum mechanics doesn't permit elemental particles to form into images. This *image thing* is so absurd!

"I know we've discussed messenger particles emerging with some type of intelligence, but this is... disturbing. It's paranormal!

"It just seems that way, Paul. If, we just look for a moment. Some unimaginable intelligence at the most fundamental level of known physics may be at work here. Something outside parameters of our understanding. We simply do not possess the theoretical mindsets to grasp everything that this might represent. Young man, listen to me! You may well be the only one here in this entire complex to suggest that sub-atomic particles detect and exhibit sensitivity to human thought! Never for one minute have we ever considered, other dimensions to energy...or its origins!

"Chief! There's no known mathematical framework or equations that permit particles to converge into a human facial image and worse. ! It's not just any face, is it. This is simply way outside any rational. It's fucking lunacy! And then, it's only on *your* terminal. You of all people! Someone that doesn't subscribe to any... He left unfinished.

"So, what's left? What are we left with? Du Pont asked.

'I'm not sure?' 'You saw the way they all looked at me. They must think I'm on something".

"Let's head over to Cessy to the CMS. Just you and me. We can talk on the way. Du Pont urged.

Reaching the car park in less than five minutes they find Melrose's Morgan. Both jumped in for the short journey into France. Site Five was a few short kilometres on the other side of the 27-kilometer huge collider ring and home of the large CMS complex at Cessy.

"Next Beam Run is in three days. That's correct yes," Du Pont asked.

Melrose nodded as he drove the Morgan steadily through a network of small roads or short cuts to the other side of the complex. The CMS –Compact Muon Solenoid represents one of the most powerful detectors added to the Collider system. The structure is a massive 12,500-ton cylindrical 15.0-meter diameter barrel-shaped tube. It contained a series of layers of super-sensitive technology to detect collision events within millionths of seconds. It sat inside a massive underground cavern carved out of the earth one hundred meters beneath the surface of the French countryside.

"You know Paul this has other dimensions to consider."

"How so Fletcher? Isn't it complicated enough as it is"!

"Only to us my friend, only to us, it's complicated. Du Pont said entering the lift.

"What do you mean? *Only to us*!

"This is about information Paul. All particle behaviour at the subatomic level is about information either in determining what constitutes matter or one that carries a force. Either way, it's information. Our understanding of particle behaviour how it ordains the quantum physics may be suspect. For information to exist there must be intelligence and consciousness, and that last piece, consciousness, is something you may have just touched on young man! Du Pont snapped

"Let's head over to the command centre. Let me ask you something else, Paul?

"Do you subscribe to divine intelligence? Yes, I do, as a matter of fact. Melrose shot back.

He stopped walking and fixed Du Pont a look. "Chief! You don't. Why are you raising such an idea?

"It crossed my mind that you're a practicing Christian, and I just wondered. I only ask that's all. You know I don't share in any of that thinking.

Yes, Chief. That, I do know!

They reached the command centre where twelve to fifteen people seated in front of an array of large wall displays. It was a spacious open plan room cluttered with desks and an array of control room workstations. This was the very serious end of the Large Hadrons Collider. Melrose stood next to Du Pont still holding the manila folder. Something from inside this enormous behemoth of a machine conjured up an image contained in the folder he was holding. He felt deeply unsettled. A loud klaxon alarm went off in the background breaking into their thoughts. Just then Melrose's mobile went off. Glancing down at the unit he quickly fumbled to switch it off. Turning, he excused himself to a private area. He fished out the mobile and thumbed a single button and waited.

"Sorry, my love! Was in the wrong place just then. Yes…eh. It was your father'.

Café C'est La Vie!

Stephanie Morgan began to fidget and noticed her friend's soup was getting cold. She could see her through the large glass windows, still clutching her mobile and pacing with her usual animated hand gestures. She guessed all was not going well. Denise Du Pont finally returned to the table saying little nothing for a few seconds.

'Men! She scowled. Or maybe its just Welshmen!

"Well? Did he go through with it?

"Course not! He chickened out. It's about the fourth time he tried to do it…and guess what?

"I think you're being very hard on Paul. It's a man thing. Give him a break for God's sake!

Denise Du Pont sulked into her soup letting her oldest and dearest friend poke fun at her.

"He promised, Stephanie. He said he would do it today; he'd pick his moment when he and Dad were alone. "No! He left the moment slip. He was even with him when I called. Alone, both of them. God, Men!

Stephanie Morgan reached out to her friend and held her hand.

 "You love him, don't you? She asked gently.

Denise's eyes filled with joy and contentment.

"Like no other man Stephanie". She whispered.

"How long has it been, since you two got close"? Must be a while from your emails.

"Four months, two weeks... and three days   Denise replied

'Jesus! How have ye managed to keep it so quiet? Who else knows?

"Apart from you, just Michelle. She even knew before me. I think my Mum suspects something, just not sure. Michelle thinks she doesn't. The restaurant was beginning to fill with more diners.

"Let's order the main course, I'm hungry. Said, Denise

"You know Denise it must be quite difficult to work for a guy like your Dad, and at the same time, be in love with his daughter. That's got to be tough. Come on babe cut him some slack".

"Do you know how many times we rehearsed? You've no idea. Paul is brilliant at what he does, but in these matters, he's lost!

'Can I ask if it's the real deal? Are you guys serious? Why bother your father with someone whom you're just dating?

"I've told him, more than once, the longer he puts it off the odder it's going to look with my father. He is in awe of my father. Would never do anything to …

"What? Bed his daughter. Come on'!

"I never said anything about our sleeping together. What you are talking about?

"Oh right! So apart from being a brilliant physicist, his in training for a life of chastity. Give me a break girl!

The young waitress appeared and quickly took the order. No of them spoke for a few moments.

'Do you feel he needs to know, your father I mean?

'Yes…Absolutely!"

Why?

"I intend to move in with Paul soon, to his apartment on the other side of the lake near Les Charmilles.

Oh, Denise, I am so happy for you. You do look very happy. I'm there for you. You know that?

"I've never been more in love, Stephanie, and this guy is so special."

Tears filled her eyes and looked over at her friend…her voice broke

"I 'm also a little scared". Stephanie understood her friend well. The secrecy aspect was somewhat delicate but manageable or so Stephanie thought.

"My advice, Denise. Both of you. You both tell your Father, together. Keep it, simple babe!

"It's not that simple Stef. My father is..."

"I know your Dad too Denise. He's a super guy. Come-on! He might be taken aback a little. You're building this up in your head into something it isn't. Chill!

Their main course came. Both women started their meal, and then it was Denise's turn. For the next forty minutes, they talked about their work. Careers were discussed and both women took the time to understand the issues affecting their respective lives.

"Isn't corruption still an issue in some of these places"? Asked Stephanie

"You should ask my uncle Francois about some of these unbelievable stories."

"Tell me about your Uncle. Is he staying with us also"?

"Oh Yes! Francois is a Jesuit. Wait till you meet him Stef. Now there's an interesting man". He arrived yesterday. You'll meet him tonight.

After they finished lunch, Denise decided to give her friend a tour of Geneva itself. Stephanie was enthralled and instantly fell in love with some of the beautiful architecture and characters of Geneva's buildings in its Old Town

"It's stunning! Denise, I had no idea how magnificent it was here.

'Yes, indeed it is. Denise replied.

"For me, it's become a magical place.

CHAPTER SIX

Claudine sat on the living sofa in Sal Madere finishing off a text message, some last-minute instructions to her daughters, while waiting for her brother to come and join her. It was Spring and Sal Madere was already showing its richness of green foliage all around its lush garden setting. He wandered in refreshed from his shower and gave his sister a peck on each cheek, picked up the glass of scotch sitting on the coffee table.

'Must say, Francois you're looking better now. Cheers!

Slipping into an armchair he stretched his legs and savoured the mild breeze that gently blew the drapes around the windows. The combination of the shower and the hint of garden fragrances filled the room offering a soothing and comforting presence. He cocked an eyebrow and gave his sister a mischievous look

"Does Fletcher suspect anything? He asked,

"Don't think so, but you never know with Fletcher. Likes to think he's ahead of the game in everything."

Claudine always considered her older brother to be good looking in a haggard kind of way. No longer in his traditional black, he wore a light grey polo shirt with a cream pair of slacks and matching sandals. Michelle strode into the living room. She checked some arrangement details with her mother then poured herself fresh orange juice.

"Francois, I 've set up the chessboard in the garden".

"Aha! Think you can outsmart an old man'. He teased

"Want to find out? She laughed

He put down the glass and, on his feet, and in one swift easy movement followed his niece out to the board. Claudine just laughed to herself. He rubbed his hands and cracked his fingers

"I'll have both your Bishop's in fifteen minutes!

"Dream on Uncle! Michelle scoffed

Claudine picked up her cell phone and dialled a number. The voice on the other end was a dear friend.

"If you can manage to get him here to Sal Madere around 7.30 pm that would be great.

Bientôt! Felix! She said ticking off the final item on her list.

The final detail of her planning involved getting her husband home just at the right time.

Master Command Centre- Large Hadron Particle Accelerator

Two hours passed quickly. Fletcher Du Pont straightened up and smiled at everyone clustered around the command control master-board. Miles Kinsley was anxious to ensure all his team within the Dynamic Entanglement Group set thresholds to detect any anomalous particle behaviour. Du Pont strolled over and joined him.

"Fletcher, just look at it! It's a Camera. A very sophisticated one, grant you. How in God's name did *that* give us those results of an image?'

Paul Melrose joined them and gently touched Du Pont's elbow.

"Excuse me Chief, I am going to slip down into the main hall for a while."

"You go ahead. Catch you later!

Melrose quietly slipped away and headed towards the gantry lift. Stepping inside the doors hissed and he descended to the hall floor of the LHC Tunnel.

100 meters underground.

After strolling for thirty minutes he found a small workshop where some of the fabrication team planned routine services to the collider infrastructure. In every sense he was alone to think. Opening the folder he spreads the documents and sheets out in front of him on the floor.

Over the next hour in complete privacy, Melrose reacquainted himself with each of the data sheets going over and over the facial image-captured pixilated on the single sheet.

It peered out from amid the mass of particle tracings of pure radiated energy. From the back of his mind his personal life intruded. He promised Denise he would sort matters so it was time to focus on getting that done. Turning he moved towards the east end and began to head back along the tunnel. Moving along the ring going from west to east, in an anti-clockwise direction. After strolling for nearly twenty minutes his head started to clear when he noticed the tunnel lighting had been switched off at intervals over 100 meters. Then glancing at his watch realised how late in the afternoon- it was five twenty-three in the evening. It was time to head back.

Outskirts of Geneva

Late evening traffic was building up and Denise and finished showing Stephanie the last of some of the sights along the lake drive. She was also becoming agitated. Stephanie sensed the annoyance and tried a little reassurance.

"He's probably sitting in a pub with your father. Leave it a bit and let them get on with it." Denise looked at her friend and smiled. She gave it no further thought, made a wisecrack then gunned the car out on the autobahn and headed back towards the hills and Sal Madere.

He called out twice in either direction, to see if working crews on the system were present. His voice carried and echoed in both directions. He quickly became aware of the silence.

Then for an inexplicable reason the tunnel became quite cold. Noticeably colder. The temperate dropped quite rapidly His most immediate thought was that the beam pipe was being replenished with liquid Nitrogen but then dismissed the notion, given that the tube was a hermetically sealed unit along its entire length. He managed to travel no more the three hundred meters when he first heard it. He stopped and turned to look back, straining to hear. Absolute stillness, not even the faintest sound. Looking back he saw in ever-progressive steps the lights in the tunnel began to fade one by one into darkness. Slowly the lighting started fading in a creeping menacing progression of darkness closing the distance towards him. Unconsciously he tightened his grip on the folder and as he did, a stream of frigid air rushed past him that caught his breath as its icy fingers plucked at his breathing. He called out to no one in particular. Suddenly from the depths of the tunnel, a groan-like sound filled the entire space. A sound with enormous presence almost human in origin deep inside the tunnel reached out towards him. A further few seconds elapsed, and then from nowhere a further gush of ice-chilled air passed by him chilling him to the bone. He started to back away, and as he did a deeper sound emanated from the darkness.

It felt and sounded like a deep breath was exhaled wrapped within a deep rumbling sound causing his body to shiver. From the stillness, something disturbed the air like the progression of a shock wave only this was matched with the unmistakable rhythm of a beating heart. He stumbled backward against the curvature of the wall and despite the plunging temperature his body began to perspire. Turning he started to move away gripped with a haunting sense of not being alone, he dropped the folder. The contents instantly scattered around the tunnel floor. His hands trembled and fumbled to grip something. The energy rapidly began to drain from his body, and slumped to his knees and began to experience vision distortion. Tunnel walls around him expanded and warped as though concrete became malleable. The entire curvature of the tunnel seemed to oscillate in rhythm to relentless steady cadence. When he stared at the floor some of the sheets from the folder were in full view.

His eyes then fixed on one single sheet. It shimmered and appeared to bend and reshape in front of him. Fear now took hold. An image of particles stared back at him. An image that had dominated his psyche over the last few hours confounding everything he believed in. Except for the eyes of the face are no longer closed. They stared straight at him and then within his distorted vision, the face began to fade into a cluster of points that no longer had any recognizable pattern. The last conscious process his brain performed before he passed out was, ghost particles reaching out as... *if responding to human thought"*

$$\Phi$$

With just twenty minutes left in their journey, Felix Deveraux, opened a small compartment in the back of the Mercedes as it sped along the autobahn and took out two small Waterford Crystal tumblers.

"What were your instructions, Felix? Take me around the Jura's a few times and then what?

"I don't know what you're talking about. Your wife merely asked me to get you home in time for us to have a small drink before we meet my wife, and then we go out for dinner. Simple"

"Besides, it's my birthday tomorrow, Felix. Why wouldn't Beta 8 deliver some interesting new material?

The banter continued until the sleek Mercedes sedan finally slipped through the gates of Sal Madere a little after 7.35 pm

Celebrations. The Party.

It was just after midnight, and Sal Madere rocked to the music of Elton John's Saturday Night while the guests danced and swayed to the rhythms that filled the residence. Guests mingled and broke into various mixed circles. The entire house was bathed in a glow of soft lights a blend of yellow and light blue lighting accentuated by a set of candles placed about the hallway and at the bottom of the stairwell. In large lettering hanging from the ceiling was the number 59, under which earlier in the evening Claudine waltzed her husband in close embrace to the sounds of Tony Bennett. Fletcher Du Pont soaked up and enjoyed the enormous rapturous outpouring of goodwill to those who swarmed around him that evening. The food was an assortment of dishes set up on two long tables, along the sidewall of the conservatory overlooking the garden.

The ambiance was relaxed and convivial as various members of their circle of friends got acquainted. With some prodding and teasing from his youngest daughter and aided by his brother-in-law, Du Pont eventually made his mandatory speech, holding a glass of Bollinger Grand Annee Vintage in one hand, and his arm around Claudine. As the evening progressed Stephanie Morgan moved around the ground floor of the residence trying to catch sight of Denise. She was nowhere to be seen; her absence unnoticed by most of the gathering. She quietly mingled and drifted from one grouping to another seeking to find her friend. Du Pont himself, Francois Burgoyne, Felix Deveraux, and four of the more senior colleagues of Du Pont retreated and sought refuge to the front of the large open fire and refilled their glasses and sank into the circular set of seats around the fire. As she passed the study, Stephanie saw the light. Moving closer towards the door she heard the familiar voice. She gently pushed the door of the dimly light study to find her friend sitting on the edge of her father's desk.

She held the phone in one hand and thumbed through her father's personal diary of telephone numbers. They were his direct dial numbers to all that mattered within CERN. The one number she had dialled over and over throughout the evening remained silent and unanswered. Denise looked up at her friend, her face distraught with worry. She had gone through over twenty other numbers. No one had seen, or spoken to, the one person that mattered to her. Her smile was gone; her colour had turned pale replaced with uneasy look panic

"I can't reach him, Steph"! Something isn't right!

Across the hallway amid more tranquil settings, Du Pont reached over with the Cognac bottle refilled each of the glasses of those sitting around him.

'Well! How about our birthday-boy here, any special insights on getting older Fletcher?

It was Manfred Gruss. At sixty-eight he was the elder in the group. Before Du Pont could respond Marco Andresen, a neighbour of the Du Pont's and a local politician, moved the conversation into more engaging territory.

"It's interesting when you think gentlemen that we live on earth for what? Maybe eighty years' and yet think we can understand the cosmos. That's what, ten or twelve billion years old. Are we not crazy to think we can do that?

That brought a chuckle from the group.

"At least we can try Marco. Said Du Pont casually

"Yes. But Fletcher, look at the challenge. We have only limited time on Earth what kind of knowledge do you think we can gather or accumulate in that time. To think we can have answers to something...that is much older than us. We're just here. New arrivals. In the history of the universe, it's got a massive head start on us".

"Are you suggesting some kind of arrogance on our part, my friend? Asked the Jesuit quietly.

"Perhaps Father. Just a little naïve on our part. We ask too much of ourselves and there's futility about it also. Marco said

"Futility. Wow! There's a word! You think our work in physics research is futile? It was Carina Ambrosiana who was sitting relaxed and becoming more bemused with the politician. Marco sat back paused and considered the company sitting around him. He was about to say something.

"You are in the company and presence of some of the world's finest minds in physics. One of which is a Nobel Laureate. You might want to think hard about suggesting futility! Claudine teased

"I'm sorry Claudine, Fletcher I mean no disrespect, please. But I know how much work goes into what you do here in CERN.

It's amazing what it is you do... Its just so, speculative!

The atmosphere in the living room became more defined by the crackling of the wood in the fire while in the background the tempo of the music seemed to be more muted. Miles Kingsley slipped next to Claudine and found a spot next to a small piano. Claudine moved over to him and refilled his glass.

"Had enough of the floor Miles? She teased. The normally impeccably attired professor appeared somewhat dishevelled from his antics across the hall.

"Do you think it was futile to decide to travel to another planet in the '60's at a time when computing technology was primitive by today's standards? Kingsley baited the politician.

The politician eyed him.

"I do, as a matter of fact. It was an act of political expediency and scientific blindness. It was almost an accident that they got there and back. They were lucky! "

Almost everyone glanced at the only American in the room. Du Pont merely smiled

"Hindsight! Marco, it's a wonderful thing. Its perceived wisdom in reverse"

He looked at him and wondered if his socialist views approved the 6 billion Euros the CERN alone consumed each year.

"Futility is not really the issue is it? Francois smiled.

"It's how we use this acquired knowledge for the good of humanity and there my dear Fletcher is where we as humans fall short. Profit and its pursuit lead to greed and massive concentrations of wealth in the hands of the few. When the benefits do flow to humanity- it's nearly always at a price to those that can least afford it. The intention, while noble in itself, is not matched with outcomes."

Miles Kingsley casually tossed another log onto the fire and turned to the priest

"Scripture is rather silent on these matters, Francois isn't it? It doesn't say very much on science"

Oh! It does my friend. And it's quite simple. It says all truths emanate from a divine source." He put down his glass and sat upright and smiled over at his sister.

"Please, everyone this is not the place for me to give sermons, it's a time of celebration.

"No! Please, father, continue." Urged Carina Ambrosiana.

Francois Burgoyne put down his glass and turned to his brother in law. Du Pont smiled

"You heard Carina! Go on?

"Well, for me, it's always been and always will be, a matter of faith. You are men and women of science and it's a matter of facts for you. What the facts say or don't say, that is your truth. Now that's all fine so long as you're facts or, more importantly your acceptance of these facts to be truths in themselves. That they do not conflict with truths from Christ. There are great natural laws that defy human understanding. Laws based on infinite wisdom, and when we as humans seek out truths it's important to hold deep in our hearts that these workings that you study, your simulations and equations are merely our means to peer inside how divine intelligence exists. If something cannot be proven with facts, it's not real for many men of science. There is a danger my dear friends that in holding to things we perceive to be true, or false, we miss the bigger truth. Science is incapable of making value judgments on things it measures. The orderliness of your world of subatomic physics is a majestic and wonderful mystery to me and permits me to reason that is it inconceivable to believe in the existence of a watch, without the existence of a watchmaker. It's simply an article of faith for me.

Miles Kingsley studied the Jesuit

"Faith is an unusual attribute, Francois. It requires the reliability of our sense perceptions. One has to believe our senses are trustworthy enough to get a true picture of the universe and enable us to understand the orderliness we observe. This faith, you speak of, can be ephemeral perhaps. The truths we speak of as scientists- are observable. Is that not a valid proposition that permits us as men of science to accept as real? Provable, without our senses or perceptions getting in the way?

Burgoyne raised his glass towards the scientist.

"That's an interesting observation, my friend"

"There is nothing inherent in science that guides men towards the application of the discoveries they make. You, or any of your intellectual colleagues believe that given enough time man will understand everything in how our universe works. You talk of a Theory of Everything. Science says nothing about how nuclear energy can be employed to destroy cities or cancer. This is a judgment outside the scientific method to determine. And remember, Professor, our God is not only our creator but also sustains. "He is before all things, and in him, all things hold together" (Colossians 1: 17) "...The universe would fall apart without his sustaining power. Even if man understands and explains everything, he still needs God. Knowing how the universe works are not the same thing as sustaining it."

He paused and sipped his malt for a few seconds,

"Humility is a valuable virtue for any scientist. He teased.

Du Pont leaned forward

"Francois. You mentioned a larger truth. We see some things but miss the bigger picture." What is the larger truth, then?

The Jesuit leaned back and smiled.

"The greater truth is that we are all pilgrims, my friends. Pilgrims placed on this earth to fulfil and lead lives that glorify God. Simple as that. Now, how we each choose to meet that challenge is part of our personal salvation. Priests, like me, men of science, and people in public service, people who work the lands and in our huge factories, in all walks of life can only be fulfilled if we place our divine creator God at the centre of their lives. Of course, there is the question of naivety to consider. He continued.

"Do you know Fletcher, many of us deny, not only the very existence of God but also the pervasive presence of evil. The devil, the Diablo himself!

As he spoke everyone noted how his voice changed. It became more elevated revealing an edge to the priest. He seemed to recall some more disturbing aspects of his work as a missionary.

"To witness the presence and manifestation of evil is an unholy experience that no one should experience my friends. To sense the presence, to smell the arrival of creatures that take possession of people, to occupy their bodies and have them commit unspeakable acts of depravity. These forces are evil and everywhere and powerful. I have seen this first-hand. Mortals are utterly powerless against their influence. I have experienced the power of their mockery and their strength... He paused.

"Go on Francois, urged Miles Kingsley.

"I have been lifted off my feet and held against my church door, by a young twelve-year-old girl. Repeatedly pounded against the wall, till my spine nearly snapped. Worst of all, the face was transformed before me from a beautiful innocent little child into a snarling unrecognizable face of a demon..."

Suddenly, from outside shouting, and the unmistakable sound of broken glass shattered the stillness of the room. The door burst open and Denise rushed in. Du Pont looked up and instantly knew something was wrong.

What is it, sweetheart? What's wrong?

Her voice quivered trying to keep some composure.

"It's Paul! It's Paul Melrose, Dad. He's...!

Du Pont was on feet and over to his daughter.

"He's... He collapsed. He was found in the tunnel, had some kind of an attack. He was unconscious and he...

"What!

"He was in spasm when they found him, convulsing and shaking violently" whispered Stephanie.

Everyone in the room stood, the mood changed in seconds

'Where is he now? Du Pont asked

"Reached the Hospital Barthes-Sant-Jovanne some time ago. No one seemed to know what happened to him or how. Some technicians found him alone, almost unconscious."

Slowly Du Pont straightened himself and looked around the gathering in the room. Thoughts of the impending Euclid run and the more recent happenings. He looked at Felix Deveraux and caught the unease on his face. Deveraux picked up his cell and quickly summoned his driver to have the car ready to move quickly. He turned to his fellow scientists in the room and suggested they call it a night. He would take Du Pont and head for the Hospital. Du Pont and Deveraux quickly organized themselves, within five minutes and were ready to leave to the waiting Mercedes in the driveway. Du Pont quickly went around the house and thanked everyone for the evening. He apologized and was out of the hall door.

'I'm coming with you! Said Denise.

"And so am I, professor, if you please. Said Stephanie Morgan.

The men looked at them both. Du Pont glanced at his wife she just gave him a nod, and that settled it.

"You realize it's 2.30 am! Turning he gave Claudine a close hug and kiss. She looked him straight in the eye and squeezed his hand gently.

"OK ladies! If you must, let's get going. Felix, lead the way." Du Pont said.

CHAPTER SEVEN

When the call did come in, it was a high speeding ambulance announcing its arrival within ten minutes. It's just after Midnight. Details were dispatched from the ambulance and the emergency stand-by team had been duly noted of the incoming patient.

Male Patient - Mid Thirties - 185 Lbs. Found in agitated and convulsing condition. - Elevated Heart Rate-No apparent physical trauma to the person – BP 180/ 85. No external signs of injury- erratic breathing – Patient Slipping in and out of consciousness. Paramedics note: Patient exhibits symptoms consistent with someone has undergone severe emotional trauma and in severe shock   Name Paul Melrose (Scientist) /CERN. Time: 12.33am

Sixteen kilometres to the west from the centre of Geneva in the surrounding hillside Stephanie Morgan sat upfront with the driver, as the Mercedes purred noiselessly through the side roads while Denise sat between her father and Felix Deveraux in the back. They made good time. It dawned on Du Pont that he hadn't seen his assistant all evening. Now guilt took hold. He should have been more aware even if this was his night.

"How well do you know, Doctor Melrose Denise? Deveraux asked casually.

"He has been around to Sal Madere a few times. Of course, she knows him' Replied Du Pont.

Denise caught her friend's eye in the mirror, both surprised at the casual remark.

Hospital- Emergency ward.

Four of them stared for a few moments and watched the young man tremble and shake and then stop and slip back into restless sleep. Two of the nurses had carried out a preliminary examination. The young junior doctor- a Swiss national was in his second-year internship carried out a detailed physical check on the young scientist. All were satisfied no evidence of any kind or marks of trauma physically was present. He was completely unmarked and yet he'd undergone severe shock. The other was one of the paramedics who brought him in.

"He did a lot of groaning and shouting on the way here".

"Well, some shouting as well. He said.

'What kind of talking? A voice from the door behind them called out. They turned and saw the senior registrar standing in the shadows of the hallway. He had been standing taking everything in.

Sal Madere went quiet very quickly after the last of the guests had left. It was well into the early hours, but no one was tired. Claudine went and sat by the fire with your youngest daughter and poured herself a drink.

"Denise is taking this news rather poorly do you think! Francois said

"She seemed quite upset. Does she know him well?

Michelle looked across at her mother.

"They're very close Francois. Have been for some time. Claudine said

"In fact, they are both deeply in love, and now she has to deal with it"

Michelle shot a look at her mother.

'You knew!

Oh! Yes dear, for quite some time now. It was only a matter of time, unfortunately, not this way. Hope Paul is going to be OK. This is going to be difficult for her."

Claudine also knew this would affect her husband. In recent days he'd retreated into his study and stayed well into the early hours. The Euclid project was important, but something was lurking in the background. She could almost touch it. Francois sat forward

'I see and does Fletcher...?

"No, he doesn't, at least we're pretty certain he doesn't. Claudine said.

Barthus Sant- Jovanne.

Just after 2.45 am the Mercedes saloon pulled up outside the main entrance at Barthes Sant Jovanne Hospital. They quickly made their way inside and after making the necessary preliminary inquiries they were directed to the second floor on the east wing of the three-story building. After a brief set of introductions, the young doctor led them down a small hallway off the main corridor into a pleasantly furnished waiting room. Tasteful pictures of Geneva's lake views graced the walls, and a series of soft armchairs were placed about the room. Du Pont and Deveraux asked the young Doctor when they could see their colleague and if he was able to see them.

"Father, might it be better if we let the doctor explain a few things first. Denise said

"Eh! Yes of course madam, please excuse me. Before we start, none of you are family members, no!

Deveraux stepped forward close to the young doctor.

"Do you know who I am?

'Yes! Professor, I do know. It's just we have certain protocols to follow you understand I'm sure.

"Of course. Deveraux said.

"Please, take a seat and I will tell you what we know. He gestured towards the chairs.

'So, in our view, he experienced a seizure of sorts. There were hardly any physical marks on him so, we focused on identifying if there was any head trauma, and there wasn't.

'How is he now Doctor"? Denise asked

"Is his condition serious? Is it life threatening? Stephanie reached out and clutched her friend's hand.

"As far as we can tell, his condition is not physical. It's emotional. Our most senior clinician is presently seeing him right now as we speak.

"Can we see him now Doctor. Asked Deveraux

"Yes of course, but I must warn you he is not in a condition to answer questions the young Doctor added.

They all followed the doctor back out into the corridor and proceeded down until they came to a flight of stairs. They came to a door, which the junior doctor tapped on and entered. It was the noise that jolted them first, followed by an unmistakable sound of somebody involved in some sort of struggle. The room was almost completely darkened except for a small bedside lamp that illuminated a patient lying on the bed. The figure jerked spasmodically like a caged restless creature, and only then as they moved closer did they see the restraining straps. Even in the dim light of the room, Melrose's whole appearance shocked them. His face looked pale and his hair was limp from sweat. The hospital clothing, a light blue cassock was saturated with perspiration.

A series of tubes dangled from an overhead monitor into one arm that was secured to one of the bed's tubular pillars. His upper body began to shake, causing the whole bed and surrounding equipment to vibrate violently. Without warning he jerked upright to try and sit-up only to be held back by the restraints. He gurgled and tried to speak but the words were indistinct and garbled without meaning. Denise gripped her father's arm with alarm. Du Pont and Deveraux were speechless.

"Is there a clinical explanation for this? Du Pont asked

"Not one that fits this patient's particular condition" A voice came from a dark corner in the room.

Everyone turned, and then noticed a shadow of a figure sitting in an armchair recessed in the corner of the room. The voice carried presence and authority deeply accented and seemed to have been sitting there for some time. Slowly he rose and moved out of the shadow towards them to merge into the dimly lit circle of light around the bed.

"Forgive me, good people, I am Doctor, Benjamin Alexander Mochti he said extending his hand. He took his time in deciding how to choose his words and how they might respond. But first, he let them absorb the patient's outward condition. It was Deveraux who spoke first.

"What do you mean his particular condition? What the hell does that mean? He asked. He was about to add something when Mochti raised his hand to silence him, and then looked at the prone patient. With his hand still raised, it was like a command for silence he leaned till he was only inches from the patient mouth- listened with an unusual level of intensity. His eyes burned with rapt attention lost in trying to make sense of something. He listened further for a few seconds and then relaxed

"You all obviously have questions, so how can I be of assistance"? He asked with a slight bow.

"Are there any head injuries doctor"? Du Pont asked

"I gather you're all work colleagues of this gentlemen yes! Mochti asked politely.

"We are indeed Doctor. Now, what can you tell us about his condition?

Mochti paused before answering. He was certain of some things and, uncertain of others. But he was willing to share his thoughts, well at least some of them.

"He has all the characteristics of someone who is suffering some kind of trauma, stress-induced trauma. He either experienced or saw something that affected him deeply. We are monitoring all of his vital functions. And in that regard, he is satisfactory. He needs constant observation and that he will get, but he also needs complete rest. We've given him a mild sedative to bring down the level of agitation you have seen. The straps are a precaution.

"We also took blood and tested for drug use. He says calmly gauging the reaction of the two women of his last remark. Happily, that proved negative, in fact, his test revealed that this young man is in remarkably good physical health so, we have to consider family history."

"Such as? Asked DuPont

"Well, for a start, mental illness in the family, perhaps episodes of Epilepsy.

"Paul Melrose is a senior member of my staff Doctor. He would have gone through a rigorous medical before joining CERN." Mochti considered that for a few seconds and looked over at the bed where Melrose seemed to rest more peacefully.

"What else can you tell me Professor about this young man's work? What exactly does he do for you?

Du Pont casts a side-glance at Felix Deveraux, who hadn't taken his eyes off Melrose.

"He is part of our theoretical group. He is a mathematician. He works on complex models in the sub-atomic physics. He designs experiments. Now, how this is connected to...?

"And languages Professor. Is he proficient in many? Mochti asked.

"Wha, what do you mean? Du Pont asked

"Fluent in French, and passable in Italian, and some German, said Denise quietly from behind them.

Her intervention caught them off guard.

"I see, Mochti said.

'A man of ability then and one who works long hours, yes Professor?

"Well yes, Doctor. My assistant is a very capable scientist. What of it? He speaks a number of languages as well. So, what?

Du Pont started to feel he is being crossed-examined.

"Indeed, Professor and, how long has he been speaking Hebrew"!

A chill invaded the small ward for a few seconds no one moved or said a word.

"*Hebrew!* Du Pont finally said.

"What are you saying Doctor, has he spoken?

"Well, not when he was conscious, if that's what you mean. Mochti replied

"But he was, speaking in a Hebrew tongue while he's under.

Felix Deveraux remained silent. Now another bizarre episode was adding to an already troubling set of events over the last number of weeks. Mochti broke into their thoughts.

"It's late good people and it's been a bit of a difficult evening. The next twenty-four hours will be crucial and our patient needs rest, I suspect you all do. Why don't you all go home and I will contact you should there be any change".

For the first time since they met, Doctor Benjamin Mochti showed warmth and gentleness that was absent up to now. Everyone nodded in agreement and took one last look at the Englishman and then turned to leave.

"May I stay Doctor? Denise asked.

He looked at her with renewed interest.

"Certainly, I will go and see what we can do to make your stay somewhat more comfortable" He was just about to leave them when he turned to Denise.

"I must ask you, young lady, if the patient starts to speak or appear conscious, no matter how peaceful he is, you must summon me at once. I will be just across the hallway in my office". Is that OK with you"?

His handshake to both men was firm but held Du Pont's hand for a few seconds.

"If I were in your position gentlemen, a question that would preoccupy me would be, what kind of physics frightens someone like that?

Mochti bowed and left them to their thoughts.

Once outside, Mochti walked down a dimly lit corridor that led to the second floor of the hospital wing. Then he headed for a door that was nearly always locked. He took out a key that fitted. Within seconds he was outside completely hidden and private. Standing out on a small-unused balcony he gasped in the night air. The words and the manner of the speech from his patient simply shocked him. His own personal history was complex, part man of medicine, and a part-man steeped in ancient studies. Troubling still was the sheer coincidence of what occurred. *His* particular hospital, the evening when he was on duty and his ability to understand and recognize a dialect of obscure origin and, most unsettling of all, what was spoken.

Within ten minutes both Du Pont and Deveraux were speeding westward towards the rising hills into the darkness of the night. The first order of business would be to have a thorough review of the events that gave rise to this matter and establish what was Paul Melrose working on or what circumstances gave rise to this most disturbing incident.

Du Pont thought Doctor Mochti's preoccupation with his assistant's ramblings a little odd rather than in his clinical state, but that was another matter. Still, he found comfort that Melrose was stable despite the deeply disturbing trauma of it all. Back on the third floor of Barth Sant Jovanne, Denise and Stephanie found some extra chairs and cushions and settled into the available confines of Melrose's room.

It was just after 4.00 am, Dr. Benjamin Alexander Mochti finished his last consultation down in the emergency department, then wearily headed for his private quarters on the second floor of the building. A quick coffee, *regular*, from the canteen in his hand he threw himself down at his desk and sat back. He selected a slim pen and pulled a large yellow pad towards him pausing to gather some thoughts and tried to remember the words. Broken phrases in a tongue that hadn't been spoken for quite some time. He began to make notes. Writing with deliberate care stopping occasionally to reflect on some detail that played in his mind.

The flow was broken and the pronunciation poor, but to a trained ear, the meanings were real even though the patient was trance-like and almost completely unconscious. When he has finished his notes he had nearly two full pages of detail along with his own comments. Rubbing his eyes he was feeling tired, and the coffee's effect was wearing off. He was about to dispense with his writing and put down the pen then, in a single moment amidst his musings a fleeting thought came to him. And when it did, it registered with the force of a whiplash.

He stopped instantly and looked up. A piece of an obscure phrase connected with something deep in the recess of his memory caused him to gasp inwardly as his mind raced to connect something he had missed up to now. A sudden rush of adrenaline shot through him. He stood and walked to his small desk.

Boardroom 606, CERN.

The wall clock read 2.37pm the following day. Both men sat around a large boardroom table quietly digesting the brief findings of a report. After spending several minutes going over its contents neither were none-the-wiser to Paul Melrose's accident. The document in front of them referred to the matter as the *Melrose Incident*. In summation, two technicians carrying out routine inspection found him seemingly unconscious, in the tunnel section no more than 100 meters from the main CMS detector Hall. He was physically shaking and covered in perspiration. Paramedics on the site were summoned. Basic first aid was provided by one of the technicians until the medical team arrived within twenty minutes...after which time an ambulance was summoned. By 12.15 Melrose was attended by paramedics and promptly whisked away to the hospital in the centre of Geneva.

"How is he doing now? Asked Deveraux.

"He had a settled night.

"Do we know if he can talk, to tell us what happened?

"We should know something later this evening- I am meeting that Doctor we spoke to last night, Doctor Mochti. Du Pont replied.

'Good, perhaps you might keep me posted, Fletcher."

"Was there anything amiss, or out of the ordinary over in that section where Paul was found? Anything unusual? "

As far as we can tell, absolutely nothing. This has more to do with Paul, I suspect".

Then Euclid can proceed? Deveraux pressed.

"Yes, of course, Du Pont replied.

ϕ

Stephanie Morgan had finally got her way and persuaded her friend to leave the hospital and Paul, in the hands of the medical professionals. By midday, they were heading back to Sal Madere and to try and get some much-needed rest. Denise remained subdued and said very little.

"You want to stop somewhere, have something to eat?

Denise hardly heard her

"Yes, why not. You pick a place'.

Back on the second floor of Barthes Sant Jovanne- Mochti reviewed the clinical notes from the previous evening. He checked a small recorder to ensure its tape was functioning.

Dr. Benjamin Mochti was born in Odessa just after the end of the war, the only son of Russian Jews. His father was a musician who taught music, while his mother was a gymnast. This brought certain privileges under the new soviet socialist era that swept across central Europe and the Balkans. They lived a relatively prosperous lifestyle well into the mid-seventies, then their first, an only child and were born, Benjamin. The young boy was raised in the Jewish faith and thrived in school until new soviet policies emerged and the state took more than a passing interest in the Jewish population. In mid-eighties, after much wrangling and some political connections, the family uprooted and finally moved to Israel. In the ensuing years, young Benjamin grew up and adjusted to his new life with ease. He found study easy and decided to study medicine at Tel Aviv University. Along the way, Benjamin Alexander developed a keen interest in ancient history and artefacts. His father himself was a self-taught expert in all things of a historical nature, particularly dealing with early Judaism. Mochti's medical career was interrupted for the mandatory military service, and in which his interest in matters of deep historical significance blossomed. He read everything he could lay his hands on.

Journals, ancient texts, geographical notes, maps of the ancient worlds and civilization were consumed with vigour. He did this, amidst the turmoil of broken bodies and dismembered limbs from car bombs and suicide bombers that walked the streets and lands of a place that is called Israel.

In that process, he became a warrior soldier. One who has seen death up close, one who inflicted death in equal measure? *Cometh the hour, cometh the man.* He entered service as a boy and emerged a man. Returning to civilian life he went back into medicine specialized in trauma emergency victims. It was no longer a profession for him, but more of a calling. He decided to spend the rest of his days healing broken people. Entering the corridor that morning he heard a barrage of raised animated voices from the end of the hall. He recognized Melrose's voice.

It was raised almost screaming. He rushed through the door. Three nurses and a junior doctor were over the bed struggling to hold him down; No one in the room understood what he was saying. The difference this time, the young man was now fully awake and alert and deeply agitated with everyone around him. He saw Melrose's eyes are fully dilated and sharp. Raising his voice Mochti shouted a series of words in *Hebrew,* which instantly had a reaction on the patient. Melrose stopped instantly as if the words stunned him into immediate obedience. None of the medics understood the wording or the language. An awkward moment lasted a few seconds then, Mochti merely nodded to his staff, and moved calmly to the side of the bed and studied his patient for a few seconds. Then Melrose fell back while both his arm fell limp to his sides. Mochti reached out and removed the small microphone from the pillow after making sure his patient was relaxed and completely subdued. Satisfied, he withdrew and headed back to his own study. He took out a card from his pocket and noted Professor Dr. Fletcher Du Pont with a direct dial number to call.

News began to circulate across the European scientific community of the upcoming Euclid project. On the second floor of the main CERN executive building. Felix Deveraux sat around a large teak table. Around him sat Du Pont, Miles Kingsley, Monika Reinhardt, Carina Ambrosiana, and Manfred Gruss. In two days time all would be ready to inject lead-ion protons into the Large Hadrons accelerator. There was much at stake. Du Pont looked across at the youngest of the group Monika Reinhardt. Her gargantuan computing infrastructure was CERN's awesome computing arsenal. Her skills would be vital. Her prodigious analytical powers were going to be crucial to Four-BETA 8 run.

"Grid protocols in place Monika? Du Pont asked.

"Of Course! We're in good shape Fletcher. She said.

For the next hour, the group covered the steps involved. There was also something else. Lying deep inside his psyche Du Pont felt something he never experienced before, an irrational fear. Was there a link to the haunting ghost image and that of his young assistant? He was also unaccustomed to entertaining doubt. Such things were corrosive to one's sense of purpose and, if left to linger would and fester would destroy self-belief and, in some cases undermine authority. He'd never permit that to happen.

Sal Madere.

The book-lined study was where she chooses to share what she knew. Brother and sister sat opposite each other, no words were spoken. One by one silently she passed each of the sheets across the desk to him allowing time to absorb each page and what it represented. They were sitting in Du Pont's study. He studied each image absorbing all it implied, his face remained impassive. Both the Jesuit in him and his family coalesced into a single intensity. The unsettling feedback on Paul Melrose's condition along with what was in front of him was eerie. Added to that, his brothers-in-law handwritten notes scribbled all over the sides of the piece, spoke volumes. Francois gave his sister a questioning look.

"How long ago?

"About two weeks give or take. That's when I started to notice things"

Second Floor - Barthus San Jovanne Hospital.

Dr. Mochti rummaged for over an hour putting a series of sheets together in some form of a sequence. He selected certain passages and then placed them side-by-side. Each page was a transcript, typed single-lined text as best as he could muster from the recordings. In such things, he was clinical and precise but now something very mysterious started to draw him in. Something began to emerge that defied his rational thoughts.

Asher Mochti at eighty-four, still lived alone in Ein Kerem on the fourth floor in a modern apartment block in Jerusalem. Since his wife died three years earlier he lived a solitary life, but past his most of his days reading and absorbing everything he could on ancient Judeo–Christian antiquities. A passion he maintained for over sixty years. His only connection with the outside world was with his son, a senior medical professional in Switzerland.

They had their regular weekly calls, part of a bond between father and son that was more akin to two best friends. They shared everything. It was over 24 hours since they spoke. The conversation with his elderly father left Benjamin Mochti with little doubt. What lay in front of the younger Mochti was quite remarkable. It was one of the last phrases in the first recording that clinched it for him. Thinking that the ramblings were the results of poor diction making recognition difficult, but by slowing down the speed of the tape, the sounds and the dialect became clear. For all his training in medicine, his exposure to severe trauma during military service- how the human body handled the shock, something ominous was at work. The whole neurological fallout that lingered in humans who had undergone severe stress was familiar to Benjamin Mochti. Nothing however prepared him for lay before him. He'd been meticulous and thorough in everything with patient number 241.

On his desk, lay a white cardboard box he had brought from his apartment. In it several carefully wrapped picture frames. In all, they were six. Each one was wrapped in a fine cloth to protect them from scratches. They represented his most prized possessions he had given to him by his father. Collected over many years out of deep interest and passion. Each picture frame contained fragments of ancient texts. Texts of another age, that described secret meanings and told stories with buried truths within. One by one he removed and laid them carefully on one side of his desk. He needed to demonstrate to his guest, certain peculiarities with patient 241.

CHAPTER EIGHT.

At first, it was the smell of disinfectant, then a perfume. Someone leaned close to him and gently rearranged the pillows. He felt hands around his shoulders and then a soft voice. A second voice and then slowly became aware of blurred images in front of him. A single image came closer enough to see a face, a face of sallow skin.

"Paul! The hand squeezed his hand and Denise leaned closer followed by a perfumed fragrance he knew well. Sitting up he gathered himself for a moment taking in the surroundings.

"Chief! Denise! What's going on? Mochti moved closer to him and smiled.

"Paul! I am Benjamin Mochti. It's good to see you looking well. How do you feel?

Melrose looked at Denise and took her hand.

"I feel good Doctor...Indeed, I feel very good!

"How did I get here? Is everything OK? What's happened?

Then in one effortless movement, he kicked off the bedclothes and wheeled his feet to the ground and stood. Du Pont and Denise moved to steady him.

"Now hold on Paul, you're going nowhere. Du Pont insisted.

"Darling, please! You need to rest now. Demise said. Resigned, he slumped back into the bed oblivious to anything that occurred.

"I'm not kidding, serious, I feel great! Now if someone would tell me...

"You were found unconscious Paul, not far from the CMS hall two days ago, and no one knows what happened to you".

"Two days! You're kidding" Mochti moved closer.

He had his own questions. Pushing back his spectacles on the bridge of his nose he folded his arms and studied his patient. Melrose looked at Denise and then to his superior trying to see if there were signs of disapproval in what was now very obvious. He was in love with his daughter, and this was not how he planned to tell him. Du Pont sat in silence. Mochti allowed the young man to describe for the next ten minutes all he could remember.

"That's all I can recall...I'm afraid. He said finally.

No one spoke for a few seconds. A disturbing story. Unexplained phenomena in a highly sophisticated complex, the world's largest of its kind, with one witness. Or, a most disturbed and troubled young man suffering from exhaustion and undergoing some form of the delusional condition. Mochti studied his hands then turned to Du Pont.

"Professor, can we have a moment together. Perhaps leave these young people alone for a while. My study is just down the corridor"

Du Pont stood looked at Denise, and Melrose, winked, and followed the physician out into the corridor. When they both get to the small study, Mochti closed the door behind them and offered Du Pont some coffee. He went and sat behind his desk.

"Well doctor, is he fit to leave hospital?"

"He's physically in good shape, Professor. But that's not what you are asking, is it?"

"Well, I need to know if my associate is suffering delusional after-effects. His psychological condition. His mental health?"

Mochti quickly ran through a summation of the kinds of symptoms that trauma victims suffer. Explaining how some patients show remarkable capacities to overcome their own first-hand experiences of trauma, while others undergo deep and long-lasting effects for just having witnessed traumas inflicted on others. Lasting effects were hard to determine. In more serious cases the shock and trauma were so deep, that some part of our neuro-defences shut down memory functions completely. The victims simply have no recollection of the primary source of the trauma. It's a psychological blackout.

Du Pont listened sensing there was more to come.

"You mentioned, or enquired about languages?"

"Indeed, I did Professor!

He reached down and removed a large folder- dossier from a drawer and placed it on the desk in front of him. Slowly and with deliberate care he removed a series of typed pages and placed them to one side. He needed to share his thoughts in a clinical and precise manner and at the same time thread carefully with his information and its portent. He had to calibrate how the man sitting opposite him, preeminent in his field, a scientist who worshiped and knelt at the altar of science would respond.

What he was about to share with him had little to do with medicine or science. He studied the physicist. Matters that remained outside the boundaries of scientific inquiry. Matters that required great depths of intellectual honesty and an open-mind as well as heart. Other wisdoms that defied mathematical treatment or descriptions. It would never occur to him that some laws operated in dimensions that had yet to be charted or not meant to be charted at all.

"I can tell something now Doctor, Paul Melrose, doesn't speak Hebrew. You can dismiss that idea."

"Do you know that for a fact, Professor?

"Yes, I do. Why is this relevant anyway? You were talking about trauma!"

Mochti choose his words carefully

"It's not my experience Professor that victims of trauma pick up and acquire new skills or abilities. And as a mathematical physicist, you will appreciate the odds of acquiring certain abilities here in this instance are...well, incalculable. I have something here to show you, and then I will explain. Please allow me".

Du Pont stirred uneasily in his chair. Mocthi produced a small recorder and explained how he positioned a small microphone to record the sounds that came from his patient in his bed. Given the forcefulness and of his actions Mochti tried to make sense of the language he was speaking. His dilemma was this patient was a physicist and Welsh yet managed to record what he could then carefully transcribed the pieces onto paper. It was broken and random and difficult to make any coherent sense. But then a few pieces rang bells. Mochti recognized phrases that mysteriously switched from Hebrew to something more obscure. He reached over and played the recorder for a few seconds and both men listened. It was unmistakably the anguished voice of Melrose; it was laboured breathing and plaintive. The language was a complete mystery to the physicist; even its sounds were not remotely like anything he heard before. As they listened, Mochti held up a transcribed sheet of his typed text and ran his finger along the line. The translation was sparse in places.

"...Ye seek light and truth...but will. Be withheld...until he puts all under his ...My wisdom and my truths will be revealed in.... a time ...that is fitting for ... (a) man to receive such wisdom.."

A second page is picked up as the recorder went on this time Melrose's voice was weeping and sobbed in anguish, which truly started to unsettle both men as they sat dumbfounded.

Come to me! ...And be righteous in heart and spirit and (he)... my father WI. (All). shine. A...light into things ...whe (re) darkness reigns... A pause, and immediately the voice became commanding, strident almost, a complete change in tone. *"Let this moment... be told, for if he is righteous and worthy, he will see...anew things tha.. were obscure.*

It went on for a further twenty minutes. Both men listened while reading the translation that Mochti had taken great care to be as precise as the recording permitted. Du Pont became absorbed and speechless. Mochti leaned and switched off the device. He then took out of his drawer a set of picture frames and handed each of them over to the other man. Du Pont saw inside each frame tattered discoloured yellowish parchments with very dated looking mid-eastern text. He gauged they were items of significance and precious.

"What am I looking at here?

"They are over two thousand years old, my friend. Mochti whispered.

"Ancient Hebrew? Du Pont asked as he studied the writings

'It's not Hebrew, my friend. It's *Aramaic*! And it hasn't been spoken on this earth for quite some time. Well, until yesterday by your young assistant."

Du Pont's head shot up. Not sure he heard correctly. His mouth went dry.

"You were correct Professor, that young man of yours does not speak Hebrew. But he was most certainly speaking a more ancient tongue. He was speaking Aramaic, Professor The language of your Jesus, if I am not mistaken"

Before Du Pont could gather his thoughts Mochti reached out and took both Du Pont's hands in his.

"There is more! Mochti said calmly.

"Each of the words in the recordings, are all Aramaic, and each of the passages that I have shown you on the typed sheets, are exactly what is written in those two parchments you were holding in those frames Mochti reached across and picked up the last sheet of typed text that he had transcribed. He showed the page to Du Pont there was a single line... Eloi-Eloi...Lama-Sabachthanni

"This was the last thing our patient uttered late last evening. Do you know what it means, Professor? The physicist just shook his head

"It's Aramaic also, and translated it means: *Father, Father...why have you forsaken me.*" Du Pont sat frozen.

"It's some of the very last words, Jesus of Nazareth cried out two thousand years ago. Mochti whispered.

Nearly a full minute passed then Du Pont got up and leaned over the parchment frames on the desk, and simply studied the handwriting of the texts itself. He tried to imagine the hand and the person two thousand years earlier acting as a scribe.

"What does any of this mean?"

'I have no idea, Professor. None. You've no idea how much of a relief this is, Professor to share this."

Mochti gathered himself then stood and faced the American.

"We are dealing with strange unnatural circumstances here, Professor Du Pont. What do you think the odds are here? A young physicist undergoes some trauma in a huge physics laboratory here in Switzerland. He becomes delirious and semi-comatose and commences to speak a very ancient language, brought to *this* hospital where, a person like *me* who is Jewish, speaks Hebrew, and holds in his possession unique *set of texts*, that mirror the words this young man speaks of. There are no actuarial tables for this my friend. This is way off any set of charts I know of."

Du Pont moved to the desk and stared at the recorder.

"One more time Doctor if you please. I'd like to hear this again."

He asked using his handkerchief to wipe his face. They both sat and played the tape again as they did, they follow Mochti's typed sheets that match the haunting broken words from the machine.

"Benjamin, what texts are these? He also noticed a tremor in his right hand.

"They are extracts from very old Scrolls, Fletcher. These are from the Book of Mysteries, also known as the Insightful. Their origins are somewhat obscure as is who the original authors were. These form the very genesis of Judean–Christian beliefs. These were mystics who scribed their beliefs in secret. Some believe angels inspired their writings. He hesitated.

"Go on! The American urged.

"These are works going back thousands of years. They're accounts that in some respects conflict with the gospels, as you know them. Some predate the gospels themselves. What Paul Melrose was reciting were incantations from the Gnostic gospels and all of them in Aramaic, a most ancient of languages. Scholars of these ancient texts are to this day, still working on them and their source of authenticity.

"Dear Jesus! Du Pont shuddered. Incantations from an unknown language. Mysterious ghost particles that possess properties unknown, or outside current quantum physics.

"What is it, Fletcher? Mochti asked.

"Nothing, Benjamin. I just...need to... consider some things."

Just after midnight, Du Pont, Denise and doctor Mochti stood on the front steps of the hospital in the cool night air. It felt refreshing. Both had their own perspectives on what all this meant. A reality, that would taunt them both and bring them closer then each could have imagined. Denise left them and walked to the car. Mochti remained quiet. The American turned to him.

"You'll let me know if there is any...?

"Yes, of course, Fletcher. Give me another twenty-four hours. Then he's yours. Just a precaution"

Du Pont nodded and walked to the waiting car. Denise sat in the driver's seat with the engine running. He got in and glanced over at her.

"Let's go home, babe."

He picked up his cell there was a missed call from Felix Deveraux.

"Dad! There is much I need to explain, and up to now there has hardly any opportunity to..."

"You and Paul! Even in the muted light from the dashboard, he smiled.

'Yes, I know, Denise." He reached out and squeezed her hand,

"And that's fine too. What matters is that he recovers and is back with us safe."

Following day. Du Pont's Office.

A little after 10.30 am Du Pont's Phone rang on his desk. The receptionist in Barthus Sant Jovanne asked if he would take a call from Doctor Mochti. He was put straight through and recognized the familiar voice.

'Benjamin! Good Morning"

He listened to the voice at the other end then picked up a pen and started to jot down some notes. His face became quizzical as he listened further.

'Yes, I intended to pick him myself. Is that still in order"?

Listening further he sat forward and scribbled a cryptic note...Riemann.

He stared at it for a few seconds. 'That's very good news, Benjamin, and yes I will come and see for myself."

He returned the phone to its cradle, pondered on the brief conversation, and then picked up the scribbled note, studied it briefly, and then tucked it away in his pocket.

Two hours later he pulled his car into the hospital car park and made his way briskly to the entrance. He went up the granite steps and straight into the main reception area. The place was thronged with people; medical staff in green and white tunics traversed the main concourse. Denise came from nowhere and grabbed her father's arm.

'He is in here Dad"!

They went through a set of double doors into the hospital discharge lodge to find Paul Melrose bending over a desk signing what appeared to be his discharge papers. Denise had brought him a complete change of clothes. He appeared alert and fully recovered. Without any preamble, he turned smiled and then began to speak in rapid succession

"Chief, how are the Euclid preparations going. I have some notes for you to look at. It's amazing! I have been looking over some of my background calculations and you wouldn't believe Chief". Manifold projections with tensor...!

"Ok! But you need to take it easy now. Let's wait till we at least, get you outta here " Du Pont caught Denise's eye and pulled her aside.

"Is he OK? He seems... a

"Little wound-up' She replied.

"Before you leave here Dad. Would you go up to his ward, please? There is something you should see."

He nodded and then saw Melrose coming over to them. Du Pont smiled and reassured Melrose that everything was in hand, relieved at his apparent rapid recovery. Then watched both of them head off down the steps of the building. He turned and went back inside.

Two minutes later Benjamin Mochti met him on second the floor. They shook hands "Thanks for coming Fletcher. Come this way." He gestured. Neither men spoke as they made their way down the corridor.

"This may be nothing, Fletcher. But before we change everything. I thought you might find this interesting."

Then he pushed the door open and gestured to the American to enter. Du Pont walked straight in and moved to the centre of the room, and stopped in his tracks. A scene of utter chaos confronted him. It looked like the room was ransacked. Symbols and handwritten notes of a demented soul were scattered everywhere. Most of the windows in the room were covered and festooned with sheets. As were the two adjacent walls, all completely covered with masses of sheets and pages. Everything was completely covered with complex equations, in green, red, and blue markers. Sheets upon sheets of abstract notes and mathematical symbols carpeted the complete floor around the bed. Some areas of pane glass were covered with mathematical notations, all interspersed with the words *Riemann*.

The bed was almost invisible, blanketed with piled-up sheets of some of the most intricate equations coupled with drawings of curved space geometry. There were days of work, sitting on the floor alone. The level of reasoning extended to the walls themselves. It was graffiti on a grand scale.

'Dear God Almighty!

He gasped, moving slowly toward the window he studies the complex iterations intertwined with calculations. He scanned the neighbouring sheets for continuity. Force field equations meshed into quantum depictions of mass and energy. The entire scene was an explosion of work that was prodigious as it was complex. He focussed turned to the references around Riemannian mathematics. Mochti's voice broke his concentration.

"Does any of this mean anything to you, Professor"? Du Pont didn't move for several seconds.

"Benjamin, if you would let me have the room for a few minutes, please. Mochti nodded and moved towards the door.

"I'll leave you to it, Fletcher! This, whatever this is, isn't over. Is it?"

"Nope.' It most certainly is not. Du Pont muttered to himself.

Later that Evening, Melrose's Apartment Denise poured him his second glass and sat back to take in how the man she cared for deeply, was feeling. It was just after 8.30 pm and both were finishing the meal she prepared earlier. Lamb served with honey-crusted sauce, with a selection of fresh vegetables, fennel, finished off with dauphine's potatoes. His right hand ached, from writing. She then went and took his hand and led him from the table, and went and sat on the rug, in the living area of the apartment.

"Where is the Morgan by the way? He inquired.

Safe, and where you can't drive it, for at least a few days.

She moved closer to him, and snuggled into his arms and stared at the flames relieved that he was himself again. She was glad her father was on side also with everything there was between her and Paul.

"Darling, did you feel threatened that night in the tunnel?

The question unsettled him a little. His last immediate recollection near the CMS was a mix of sensations and a vivid recall of haunting human sounds.

"Not in any great detail my love, it's was just something maybe just fatigue. He said dismissively. He leaned and wrapped his arms around her waist and pulled her to him.

"What I need is some form of therapy. Something that you won't get in hospitals" He whispered

"Yes, I can think of some things that might work if you'll let me."

"You are trespassing you know." He whispered in her ear.

'Oh Really!

Yes!' You have trespassed into my life, and have taken my heart, Miss Du Pont. And for that, I love you, more than you know.

Twenty Miles northwest of Geneva. A small farmhouse in the hills.

Doctor Benjamin Mochti retired into his bedroom tired and near exhaustion from seventy straight hours at work. The next three days were his, and his alone. He went upstairs changed from his working attire and then stepped into the shower. Afterward, he towelled himself off and changed into a light cotton blue robe He went and poured himself a glass of white Shiraz and then went out into a small garden. Reaching for his briefcase he took out the recorder and carefully opened a small wallet size pocket in the case and extracted a spool tape. He sat turning over in his mind his reasons for withholding details held in his hand. For the fourth time in the last few days he slipped the small tape into the recorder and pressed the rewind button. He pressed the play key, adjusted the volume just so he could hear the tape began to whirl into the life. Paul Melrose's voice cried out intruding into the stillness.

This time was different. The voice was gripped and seized with fear, almost a disembodied voice broken, tearful, and pleading.

Only now, entirely in English. He listened to it again.

*"Oh no. Please, these particles cannot do this for pity sake, not Fletcher. Change Euclid, please alter the magnetic...^^^^^**** He cannot survive its ungodly. Warn him; warm him, before the be...m swop. No Euclid. Please, No Euclid. It will kill him, for God sake please doesn't let him.... We forgot "Oh no, not Fletcher, stop him...stop!*

He finally flipped the off switch. Then he thought of Du Pont himself recognising the type of character that lay behind those questioning eyes. Formidable and objective dominated his thinking. Mochti saw that, and more in Fletcher Du Pont. He saw certitude of purpose and absolute belief in himself.

"... For pity sake, not Fletcher ...for pity sake, not Fletcher!

He reflected on why he withheld this piece of information from the eminent scientist. He had come to respect the American in ways he didn't expect. He opened the box he brought from the hospital and removed all 6 frames with their parchments. One by one he returned them to their places on the wall above his desk. Reaching over he unfolded a small cream-colored rug, placed it on the floor. From a tabletop, he took the book and opened it. It was rich and steeped in sacred words.

The Torah had its usage stamped across its battered and worn cover. Its pages ruffled and discoloured having endured the brutality of war in the Golan, and the Baaqua. Wrapped inside his military backpack it sustained him in the bleakest of hours. Now as many times before, he turned to the prophetic books. Each containing God's teachings. Instructions to the Jewish people. Carefully and with reverence, he slipped past the Five Books of Moses to the section on the holy writings and lamentations. Dropping to his knees, his face in his hands and commenced to recite a private prayer in Hebrew. Then he opened to the Ketuvim, and paused and recited a selection of sayings from a psalm. Slowly, turning to Moreh Ha-Nevukhim a guide to the perplexed for souls seeking answers. He rose and looked up at one of the frames, held it in his eye line, raised his hands, bowed his head and began a low chant. In the intimacy of his room, Mochti summoned his God to his presence. When finished, he stood for a moment in contemplation and for answers. Finally, as the sunsets, he picked his favourite narrative Divrei-Hayamin, the Book of Chronicles. He lifted the leather-bound tattered book and held it to his chest for a few seconds then headed to his study. That's where he decided all things.

A little after 8 pm and getting late Du Pont was still in his office. A desk lamp cast a warm glow around the office. All the working sheets from Melrose's ward were neatly stacked to one side, along with his own observations. His head ached to try to follow Melrose's equations and how he would try and coax them to reveal their secrets. They were mere models of encoded information that contained subtle laws that governed the physics of nature. There was, however, just one last thing he needed to do. He picked up his phone and called Carina Ambrosiana. A few minutes later she knocked on his door.

"How are you Fletcher, how is Paul?

"He seems to be in remarkable shape, considering. Thank you for dropping by. That's why I wanted to talk to you, Carina. There's a... little more to it then everyone knows. She cast him a curious look.

"Really! How so"?

Du Pont tried to settle in his chair to get more relaxed.

"Do you recall, how you explained to us in the boardroom you're thinking on the whole image thing, and how as a Catholic, your faith suggested that..."

"Yes, I remember Fletcher. It still keeps me awake at night. Why? What is it?

He could see that the Euclid beta 7 episodes played on her mind as well.

"I don't mind telling you it still troubles me, Fletcher. It's not physics, and it bothers the others as well. Is there a connection with that, and Paul?

"I'm not sure Carina, in fact lately I'm not sure of a few things. But I want to share something new with you. I know you as a friend and a first-class theoretical physicist. You hold strong convictions in matters of faith also, and that's why I need to discuss…

'Oh, God! You think there is a connection?

"Well, I'm not sure".

For the next ten minutes, he took Carina through everything in the hospital. Leaving nothing out, including the whole exchange with Doctor Mochti, the tapes, the transcripts, they're meaning. Then he covered the unsettling use of Hebrew or Aramaic, and its bizarre twists as Mochti outlined them. He left nothing out including his own worries as to what all this meant. Added to all this, was Melrose's description of his experience near the detector hall and the near hallucinations that followed. As he spoke, his colleague's face became more drawn.

Her expression turned to disbelief. Finally, he pointed to the pile in front of him.

"And then there is this!

Pulling a mass of sheets and diagrams and pushing them over to her. He opened his mobile and showed her photos he took in the hospital ward. Then she took the pages, and sorted through them quickly, just scanning, but noting the manner the formulae, and cryptic equations were dispersed throughout the entire bundles of sheets. She reached for the phone and went one by one through the photos of calculations that were strewn all over walls of the ward.

She said little as she went over the calculations and began turning from sheet to sheet. Her face frowned. Du Pont allowed some moments to pass. The silence in the room lasted an eternity.

"Apart from what I've told you, anything in there that disturbs you?

She shot him a look.

"Are you kidding me, Fletcher? This just keeps getting worse!

They sat for a few more seconds, while she studied the scribbled mass of notes and calculations.

"Most of this is new! The workings are different from anything he has been working on. There is rigor I haven't seen before. There is a lot of abstract work on Riemannian geometric calculus that's new. He moved some of these workings to Fourier transforms, wave functions and then completes a series of calculations that extended into 5-dimensional analysis using tensor extensions! He kept scribbling notes on the side on wave-particle duality. Here in this section, he employed dimensional analysis, but has substituted a numerical constant, the Hamiltonian (h) operator in these equations with a new factor (-b) altered possible space-time geometry". This is all new Fletcher. It's nothing we've being working on. She said mystified

"Well, Carina, that's what I think too. All of this is off the charts!

Carina got up and poured herself a glass of water.

"Before I respond to all this, Fletch. Why did you ask me about my religious beliefs earlier? He stirred uneasily and stated to remove his wristwatch

"Does any of this strike you as being metaphysical in some way? Is there something here that we need to consider? Some unnatural things seem to be occurring, and I was wondering if...

"I might have some extra insights. Are you asking me as a practicing Catholic, or as a theoretical physicist? She replied

'Both. I'd like you to balance scientific insight, with alternative intuition. Your beliefs on matters that defy scientific explanation?

It became clear to Carina how all of this was beginning to impact on him. She reached out and touched his hand.

I think you're asking me if I believe in miraculous happenings? Do I subscribe to divine interventions"?

"Well, something like that". He said softly.

"Firstly, I think we should hold off bringing any of this about Paul, to the DG. Euclid beta 8 commences in 24 hours, let's get that underway. Then, when the time is right, we'll bring him up to speed.

"Perhaps you're right. We'll keep this under wraps for the moment. Thanks for listening. I'm grateful Carina."

"You're welcome Fletch! We should do this more often. She added softly.

"Now as to my beliefs on the miraculous. I'm nowhere ready to answer that. They are matters here that are beyond anything I've known".

He smiled knowing how direct she could be."Fletcher, might I make a suggestion!

"Sure! Go ahead."

"You might consider exploring issues like this with...

"Who, could I possibly talk to about this whole mess and its whole mystical?

"Isn't your brother-in-law someone? The Jesuit!"

Fixing him a curious smile, she turned and headed back her own office.

"Give *that* some thought," She said over her shoulder.

After a few moments he stood and picked up his large square briefcase and gathered up all the Melrose notes and schema sitting in a pile. Lifting his phone, he dialled his wife.

Sal Madere- Du Pont's Residence.

Du Pont opened a small cabinet in his desk and took out a bottle of single malt and planted it on the surface. Francois sat opposite him sensed his brother-in-law was in the midst of some kind of crisis. Both tumblers were refreshed and the bottle was returned to the drawer. Then, like his earlier encounter with Carina Ambrosiana, he systematically recounted details in the precise order and their impact completely unaware of how much the Jesuit already knew. He recounted the hallucinogenic parts of Melrose's language and its supposed origins. The Jesuit sat back and lost interest in his drink and listened. The more he heard the more his face masked his disbelief. He mentally took note of certain details.

"How do you know; it was Hebrew or Aramaic"? He finally asked

"I didn't. I was told, by this Doctor Mochti"

Du Pont became uncomfortable and decided to change subject, preferring to focus on recent issues regarding the troubling Facial Images leaving out the finer points of the physics.

"Particles decay Francois, it's a basic law a product of quantum behaviour, and they don't regenerate. What I'm going to show you next, is not science, its not physics. It's something else!

Francois ran his hand over his crucifix.

"We refer to it amongst ourselves as the... *Aberration!*

He passed the image of the pixilated face over to the priest, followed by the photograph of the Shroud image itself. Then settled back, took his glass and waited for the reaction.

"Aberration eh! Interesting choice of words? Burgoyne replied.

"Is there any connection with all these calculations here from young Melrose, and what you are telling me now?

"That's equally puzzling Francois. This work is so original and all new! Very interesting in many respects, but it's completely out of the blue. It's all unstructured, but it maps out an alternative view on how Space-Time geometry could exist and how it may be unlocked".

Burgoyne studied his brother in law.

"Paul Melrose produced all this? The Jesuit picked up the image with the unmistakable face. The bone structure, evidence of distortion in places caused by unknown physical force, despite the grainy resolution the identity left little to the imagination.

"I have no answers for this Francois. It's becoming a nightmare of unimaginable proportions. No one has slept well since this manifested itself. Nor is anyone in a position to offer any kind of rational, scientific, explanation of how this came about." The hour was getting late. Neither man felt ready to retire.

"This is most peculiar, Fletcher. More so when we relate what took place in the hospital with Paul and where it came about in the first place. The Beam tunnel!"

"Yes, Francois. Lots of questions? No answers.

Tomorrow's big event, *this Euclid*. Is that highly experimental? The Jesuit pressed "They're all experimental, Francois. That's what we do here in CERN, we push boundaries. Tomorrow and over the next few days, we'll soup up our collision energies, to levels never attempted before. We're not going to put anything on hold if that's what you're thinking. It's about what's next! We came out of the cave, and climbed over the next hill"

"And at what price do we pay for doing that? Francois quizzed.

"Well, sometimes the price is we answer some questions only to find they're replaced with even more difficult ones. And then, we hit something like these. He said pointing to his desk.

"Tell me a bit about this Doctor Mochti? The Jesuit enquired.

'Why.?

"Well, because he has introduced a dilemma. Perhaps not so much to do with pure physics as one of metaphysics! For what it's worth, maybe these things have to play themselves out. Leave matters as they are. See how they evolve without forcing answers.

No? Not in my world. Questions demand answers, Francois. Problems are merely gateways we navigate through to get to deeper insights and knowledge. It's the way of the universe my friend, all knowledge comes with a price, or at the very least, requires perseverance and determination. Nature *will* surrender her secrets, but only to those worthy of such efforts."

Du Pont nodded and reached for his glass. His brother in law was always good at helping others exorcise ghosts. Then he remembered Benjamin Mochti's parting remark in the hospital.

"Whatever this is, it's not finished, is it?

"Francois, may I ask you something?

"Of course, ask."

"As a man of conviction and belief, do you believe in Supernatural events?"

The Jesuit smiled to himself and sipped his malt. "I believe in divine purpose. If that required some act on the part of our Creator to cause something to occur, well then so be it. Of course, a man like me wouldn't refer to something like that, as an Aberration!

"Oh! How would you see it then?

"Perhaps, and depending on the events involved, I might consider such things as miraculous. Why would a man of physics ask such a question anyway? Lost your way?

"If I appear lost dear friend, might be because something keeps messing with the signposts"

"Maybe, you need to learn how to read them" Du Pont smirked across at his relative. "Perhaps Francois.

'But I'm very indifferent to things you refer to as miraculous! Du Pont sipped his whiskey, glancing at his watch. It was getting late.

"We do some extraordinary things tomorrow Francois, and in the coming days, our LHC is going to answer many questions for quantum physics. It's truly a great time for us here in CERN. It's quite a moment for everyone. Some have waited years to test out theories".

Francois stood and picked up a large sheet of mathematical equations covered from edge to edge of the page. He scanned all the notations and the work involved in trying to fathom the secrets and seals behind the symbols. Truly remarkable he thought, how one approaches and views Creation in such sterile terms, and yet for all its complexity, the ingenuity of science to find ways to compress the workings of our universe and physical reality into these abstract numerical constructs. How ambitious he thought, that man could garner into a set of mathematical devices the wonder and awesome magnificence of Creation. Compress the transcendent power that sustains all living things into a string of symbolic appendages. Can such things be done he thought? Du Pont leaned against the bookcase watching him, trying to guess this Jesuit's view on what all this meant.

"Do you know something Fletcher? Isn't it remarkable in all the holy books ever written, all the ancient books handed down to mankind, nowhere was any of God's laws transcribed in symbols or equations like these? Did you ever think, perhaps, that we are not meant to know such matters"?

The American said nothing for a few seconds

"Maybe it was meant to be that way so that we could discover them for ourselves. We grapple with the workings of nature Francois in the most imaginative ways we can think of. We portray the beauty behind the forces that make our existence real. That's what our equations depict. They're elegant. They help us understand what makes our reality work. Burgoyne walked around the desk.

"And the images, the re-emerging Ghost particles in your recent trial. Your young assistant speaks Aramaic in a trance of some kind. It gets most unsettling in what he says in this tongue. A language he has no knowledge of. Then new particles with strange properties?

This is not the stuff of equations Fletcher or particle physics, is it?

Du Pont stared hard at the priest for a moment...

"Well, what the hell could they be?

"Perhaps something else. Something, you all missed. Replied the Jesuit.

"Like what?

A Warning! Maybe it's a Warning, Fletcher!

CHAPTER NINE

CERN: Central Control - April 5th

The atmosphere throughout the sprawling control centre that morning was expectant tinged with muted excitement. Among the gathering were visiting scientists from other physics laboratories around the globe. The large Hadrons Collider along with the pre-boost rings was primed and ready. Within the hour two super beams of protons and ions would be generated and focused into counter-rotating directions within the LHC itself pulsating around the 27 kilometres ring, 17,000 times each second. Paul Melrose was happy to be back, Otto his mechanic had just returned his serviced Morgan to him that morning adding to his upbeat mood.

"She purrs like a pussycat Paul' He said handing him the keys.

Felix Deveraux and members of the Directorate sat around a large table in the centre of the centre absorbing the sense of occasion the Euclid Programme represented. Others were busy elsewhere. Monika Reinhardt sat at one of the dedicated systems management consoles. Her team scanned the entire systems running rapidly through levels of systems readiness. With a simple set of keyboard strokes, she activated a large plasma screen into life, displaying a massive map of the Hadrons' ring.

Over the public address system. **Readiness Alert- Proton Beam initiation in 15 minutes.**

The large plasma screen showing the entire LHC system turned Green. Designers, along with all the technicians now focused on their respective roles. Beam luminosity, Magnetic field synchronization, dipole magnets, cryogenics systems, and Linac Ion generation, radiation shielding-all cascaded through a battery of readiness conditions, one by one. Elsewhere, standing in the stillness against a blackboard in his inner office, Fletcher Du Pont ran his eyes over the symbols spread across the board. He copied the last segment of the work from his assistant's sheets onto his pad. Finally, Euclid Beta 8 was in countdown mode. He went and checked himself in the mirror. With only four hours of sleep he still looked remarkably fresh. His skin had a fresh glow and he was feeling good. Today was going to special. He brushed his hand over the dark blue polo necked cardigan and ran his hands through his hair. Then he checked his watch.

It was time.

Reaching for some chalk he quickly wrote in bold lettering *Spontaneous Release of Energy* on the blackboard and then left and locked his office.

Over 30 scientists crammed into the control centre. All the walls had large monitors showing a large graphics display of the inside design of the CMS. It had all the appearance of a large onion with its tightly arranged internal layers. An overhead announcement told all that beam initiation was 5 minutes away. All safety locks and procedures would be underway shortly. A klaxon overhead sounded

Attention: - Ionization Sequence in 3 minutes –

The Suburbs of Jerusalem, Israel.

That morning the early sun, rose over the ancient city of Jerusalem, the sky was clear radiating a vivid blue and already the temperature was heading into the mid-twenties. Spring had firmly given the city a vibrant look as palm trees swayed in a fresh morning breeze. Ein Kerem, was an elegant suburban part of the city where traffic noise was minimum and well away from the normal tourist bus routes that traversed the city with sightseers. The phone call that morning was unexpected but was always welcome. Since his wife had passed away three years earlier to a stroke, Asher Mochti looked forward each week to contact and trading stories with his son in Switzerland. Even at the age of eighty-four, he kept a schedule. He loved cycling at the start of each day around the suburb for a brisk 30 minutes. Then, on his return to his apartment, he would cook and eat breakfast. His strict self-imposed regimen included reading all the daily newspapers he had delivered to his apartment, then he'd spend the rest of his day alone, reading and indulging in his passion for history.

The call that morning lasted fifteen minutes. He put aside his morning papers and listened with intent, exchanging opinions and mixed reactions with the younger Mochti. Both tone and content told him something not to be taken lightly. Strange happenings he thought as he listened to his son's voice. He was troubled, yet the analysis and his son's attention to detail as always were impeccable.

"Never dismiss such things! Benni. You did right to call. This sounds very strange indeed my son, particularly if it's from *the Recitals*.

He listened further.

"Before you do, let me do a little research son. We'll speak this evening. My love to you."

Then the phone went dead.

The Compact Muon Solenoid Detector - 100 meters down

All 9,000 dipole magnets fired into life energized to the tune of 8.5 Telsa, over 100,000 times the earth's magnetic field. This enormous concentration of power produced a powerful electromagnetic field that marshalled two beams of pure energy into circulating the 27 kilometres. Then, as they entered the large super ring, magnetic forces bend and curve the beams pushing them to 99.9% of the speed of light. Conversations became muted as the finest minds in physics watched as mighty forces were unleashed, corralled, and harnessed by technologies designed to peer inside the most fundamental particles of nature. As both beams pass each other in opposite directions, they enter the massive CMS detector, the 30,000-ton colossus 3-storys' high. Their plans, hopes, and designs orchestrated by Du Pont and his team. At one console where the luminosity of the beams was tracked Du Pont watched with his colleagues as a series of large plasma screens told their own story. With equal elegance, multi-layer software algorithms were at work. Ingenious powerful algorithms converted and reconstructed these into visual graphics that permitted physicists to see the events unfold.

Du Pont, Carina Ambrosiana, with Miles Kingsley along with a few others kept their own vigil. Each watched a set of displays as the events inside the detectors progressed. Paul Melrose, along with Felix Deveraux and some guests studied the entire process from the main control block. Over at the Cessy Detector site, the cell phone in Du Pont's pocket rang. He glanced down and recognized the number.

"Benjamin! May I call you back in an hour? Bad timing I'm afraid. We're into something here. Yes, of course, Benjamin. I will. Goodbye for now".

Du Pont closed his phone and thought for a second. He looked up at where Carina and Miles Kingsley were standing. Attention now seemed focused on one specific screen cluster. Miles turned to him,

"We are now approaching an interesting phase. Significant velocities Fletcher. Come take a look"

Du Pont nodded. All in the room around him wanted their equations, their years of insight and theoretical reasoning to mirror reality. To verify and prove their view of the hidden quantum universe. Euclid was running for over an hour and already omens emerging were promising. He moved over to one of the vacant workstations and quickly punched in a series of codes. Instantly multiple particles decay images appeared with a high density of curved patterns. High-energy particles with significant mass were appearing and this- at only 80% of the energies the LHC was capable of. As if reflecting his thoughts, a klaxon sounded in the background

100% Energy Beam in, One minute...

In rapid sequence, display screens changed colour to signal the beams hurtling around the Hadrons Accelerator were now at full tilt. Over the next 10 hours, billions of particles would be contained, stored within a frigid cryogenic tube, surfing along a pulsating enormous electromagnetic field. As they raced in a circular path, they emitted a massive amount of radiation brought about by the bending influence of powerful magnetic fields. Du Pont gazed at the reconstructive graphics working to replicate events being tracked inside the huge compact Muon Solenoid Detector. A hushed silence settled in the centre. Everyone stared into their screens. Images of particle decays began to reveal streams of new characteristics not immediately recognised. No one spoke, hardly able to comprehend the new images, or what they meant. Inside the central control, Felix Deveraux along with his fellow physicist's looked at the same graphics.

Their excitement started to mount, as spectacular more exotic subatomic particles began mysteriously to be detected. Du Pont slowly eased himself up from his console without taking his eyes off the terminal. Without attracting any attention he quietly wandered over to the large glass viewing area and stared out at the marvel of engineering at the large steel Detector structure in front of him. If what he was thinking was possible, they were witnessing something truly spectacular. His mind retraced all the equations that he had gone through earlier.

Extracts of Paul Melrose chaotic number crunching, the Riemann models describing the warping of space-time geometry then,

"Super Particle partners! My God! There you are! He whispered to himself.

Deveraux allowed the images to play out, assessing everything and where these results were headed. Superstrings just got that little bit more serious as the emerging new images began to appear. Glances were exchanged throughout the centre as the results were starting to sink in.

"Get Professor Du Pont! Paul. Ask him to join us. Devereux said.

For Fletcher Jameson Du Pont, from the age of 20, he had but one ambition, to unlock secrets. A self-belief anchored to the certainty of leaving a legacy in experimental physics and a destiny that would be his. To be the one to force nature to surrender it's hidden truths. It was written and codified into his being that days like this would happen- as news spread quickly that something truly marvellous was finally emerging. Super-partner particles, that elusive but compelling piece of quantum physics had finally made its appearance on the stage. At that moment he placed his hands on the glass as if to reach out and sense its power, to experience an inner peace that comes with knowing what was taking place a few meters from where he standing. Fletcher Du Pont closed his eyes and tried to summon the ghosts of those that went before him: Bohr, Planck, Rutherford, Feynman, and Albert Einstein. Giants. If they could just see how far they had come, and now this. Then the cell pinged inside his jacket and disrupted his thoughts. A text, he stared at.

Need to talk Fletcher. Can you give me a quick call? It's important. Mochti

At first, it was a mild sensation that started at the tip of his fingers, and then pleasantly gave his hand a warm glow from the glass surface where his hand rested. A mild vibration resonated directly beneath his feet followed. He stepped back awkwardly caught completely unaware. Suddenly he became distracted and disorientated. He stumbled and caught the edge of the glass frame. Amid the noise and clamour behind him and despite the confines of the room, no one noticed. He reached out and pulled a swivel chair towards him and sat down. Then the vibration stopped but his fingertips began to tingle more. Just as he attempted to call out his voice faltered unable to make a sound. Now all over his body, he began to experience a powerful calming sensation, accompanied by a gradual sense of fatigue. Starting with his arms, and slowing progressing up to his chest, he began to feel a great drain of his body's energy, almost like an instant sleep beckoned him. His body started undergoing a powerful drain, like nothing he had ever felt before.

The sound of him crashing to floor startled everyone. In seconds, everyone turned and then saw their colleague slump to his knees. They rushed and grabbed him to an upright position. From their expressions, Du Pont felt an instant disconnection from his surroundings. He experiences only silence and utter calm. He saw only panic in their faces. Paul Melrose was only inches in front of him. He appeared to be shouting at everyone around him. Du Pont leaned back; the life force seemed to be disserting him as he stared upwards at the ceiling. The room began to bend all around him. Things that were solid seem to turn into fluid images that ran like water down a glass surface. Silence.

He saw bedlam but felt only serenity. He saw everything with great clarity acutely aware he was the source of the calamity all around him, yet he seemed to be present, but not part of it. He began to hear himself think.

So, this is it. This is death, or what seems to be the end. Strange, it's all very peaceful. Very orderly in fact. Wonderful. Wonder why I can't speak or talk to them. I feel fine, really. They all look very frightened. I just feel like I need to sleep. So tired, so very tired, that's all.

Maybe it's a Warning, Fletcher. He heard from somewhere.

"Can someone get the medics here? It's bloody urgent! Yes! He is still breathing" Melrose screamed.

They lifted him onto two joined desks and grabbed some cushions and got him into a lying position on his side. Five minutes later the door burst open and a paramedic team rushed in. Two guys followed by a young female doctor. In almost no time they were all over the senior scientist who appeared semi-awake but looked completely helpless. The entire atmosphere in under in those brief minutes went from excitement to shock. No one could answer any of the rapid-fire questions from the paramedics. Miles Kingsley lost his colour and composure, deeply distressed sat next to his colleague clutching his hand trying to keep some kind of dialogue going. Paul Melrose knelt at Du Pont's head with his hands on his shoulders.

"Did any of you see what the hell happened? The young female doctor yelled

"His pulse is good, BP is low, and breathing is very steady. One of the paramedics answered.

"He needs to get to a hospital", Melrose shouted

"No Kidding! She snapped

One of the older male paramedics looked at the young doctor, who was no more than 24 years old.

"We've summoned the ambulance! It will be here in..!

"Forget it! I want the chopper. Now!

Melrose reached out and touched the young doctor's shoulder. She saw fear in his eyes.

"Don't lose him doc, please!

"Not on my watch soldier! She said.

No more than two meters away, Du Pont's cell phone lay under a small swivel chair with a small text message in its display.

When Felix Deveraux finished overseeing the medical activity around his friend, he stood and gathered his thoughts. His top senior team circled around him. Some were shaken as they surveyed the small group of medics worked feverishly around the prone scientist. There was nothing he could do now. He summoned all his reserves to impose a sense of business. Then quickly convened an impromptu meeting with senior heads to an adjoining room. The first order of business was to ascertain what caused the incident. No one could tell. One minute Du Pont was focused as any of them were on the events playing out on displays, the next minute they heard a crash and that was it. He then went around the room. Each of the specialists in their own fields gave cryptic analyses as the performance of the machine and where the status of Euclid 4 beta 8 was up to that point in time.

Satisfied that they were in the midst of something new, Deveraux issued instructions to maintain the proton beams for a further three hours. As best as he might, he related the last piece on Du Pont's condition to his colleagues. The only word that registered with everyone in the room was 'uncertain." No sooner was the emergency flight in the air clearing the Meyrin site when the medical team responded to an immediate change in the scientist's condition. Twice in flight, the young female doctor initiated defibrillation procedures to revive him. What started as an emergency process under control, descended rapidly into medical crises. By mid-afternoon, the entire campus of CERN was talking about just two things: Super partner particles and their existence, and the sudden departure of Professor Doctor Fletcher Du Pont airlifted from the Meryin complex to hospital in Geneva. By six-thirty that evening all major experimental physics research centres worldwide would be salivating with the latest news out of Geneva all heralding a new chapter in particle physics. Little did anyone know of the drama, which unfolded in the skies over the countryside earlier that morning?

Trauma Unit- Emergency Wing

Over four hours later inside the emergency unit of, Clinique Generale Vallence hospital a team of doctors was slowly coming to terms with anomalies of their most recent patient. When no physical damage was apparent, the team immediately went to work to determine if there was evidence of internal organ failure. They had worked on him for over two hours. No surgery procedures were contemplated until his condition became stable. No other medical intervention would be considered for a further 24 hours. What stunned everyone however, was his *appearance*.

Earlier that day, Claudine Du Pont's first taste of what was to come confronted her at the bottom of the stairs in Sal Maldere. Returning from a garden centre with her youngest daughter, Michelle, she stopped. Standing in full Jesuit regalia with his ferraiolo cape, her brother, Francois his anguished expression was all it took. Before he could utter a word. She moved cautiously towards him.

"What's wrong Francois? Reaching out he took both her hands.

"C'est Fletcher, Mon Amour!

Two minutes later, they were speeding out the large metal gates of Sal Madere, Claudine at the wheel her youngest daughter sat in the back struggling to contain her tears. Francois sat upfront, one hand clutching the overhead handgrip, the other clasping the small crucifix around his neck. Claudine said nothing as she pushed the saloon through the narrow winding roads. Her face a steely mask of concentration.

Inside a meeting room in the centre of Geneva, Denise Du Pont practically kicked back her chair and threw her cell phone into her bag. Amid a stunned group of business associates around the table before anyone could respond, she ejected herself from her seat, and shot out of the room leaving a wake of sheets and notes scattered on the floor. Thirty seconds later shoes in hand; she raced across the car park to her car.

Inside the Directorate suite of offices back at CERN, Felix Deveraux stood at his desk, a phone in one hand, and writing a rapid set of notes with the other. He listened to the attending physician on the other end. Dr. Joseph Heinz relayed the known details of Du Pont's condition. The call lasted ten minutes, and from what he heard, Felix Deveraux's mood became sombre. On the inbound autobahn, 402 he pushed the Morgan to its limits, jumping lanes and prompting open hostility from surrounding autobahn users. Paul Melrose steered his 2.5 liter sports car past inbound traffic trying to get to the hospital before the rest of the family. Lying on the passenger seat was Du Pont's mobile phone he found earlier on the floor of the control room.

When they eventually entered the ward, it was very still. The lighting was subdued and laden with unease. There were already four of them standing almost in a semi-circle gowned up without the facemasks. They hardly spoke and then one of them came towards them and invited them with a simple hand gesture to draw closer. Positioned in front of them was a surface, more like an operating table. Du Pont's figure lay completely still with a series of electrical connections and a tube inserted into the side of his mouth. He appeared to be asleep. On closer inspection and somewhat more distressing, his eyes remained open staring almost lifeless. No flicker of recognition. Nothing.

Claudine stood transfixed at the sight before her. Her daughters moved closer to where their father lay. Francois Burgoyne drew closer and blessed himself. Paul Melrose reached out and took Denise's hand, awestruck at the image in front of them. Both daughters gasped. The alteration to the appearance of their father, mentor, and husband shocked each of them. The skin had sunken in around his face severely accentuating his facial bone structure. It had a greyish tinge making him appear to age almost twenty years. His hair was nearly grey and noticeably grown longer. His overall body mass had atrophied to an alarming degree in a matter of a few hours wasted from rapid weight loss. The overall effect that of a homeless vagrant picked up off the streets and brought in. A mere shell of the vibrant human that was an hour earlier, now wearing only a hospital blue gown. One hand rested on his midriff, the other hung limply over the edge of the bed. One of the doctors turned to them.

"I'm Doctor Peter Schultz, and this is Doctor Joseph Heinz. I can only imagine what's going through your minds. Please pull up some seats".

François Burgoyne chooses to stand. He then walked around the figure and extended his hand and placed it on Du Pont's forehead. He paused and closed his eyes. He had witnessed many things in his pastoral life and strangely, he felt no fear. His composure brought some calmness to the room.

"What can you tell us, Doctor? Claudine extended her hand touching Schultz's arm.

"Is my husband going to live? Francois removed his gold chain from around his neck, and then leaned over his brother-in-law and placed the chain around him. Then, with deliberate purpose and grace carefully positions the crucifix on Du Pont's chest. Bowing he recited a silent prayer.

BOOK 2

CHAPTER TEN

Another Realm of Time. 29 AD

As with all dreams with vivid images, Du Pont's felt them reach deep inside causing his body to shudder. As strange as it was, it danced and dazzled him with such vivid places and faces. Faces of people, friendly and absorbing in every way imaginable. Wonderful colours surrounded and enveloped him, and whisked him effortlessly with ease along a ribbon of majestic gold that twisted and flexed into more twists before being transformed into newer things. Memory was purged of all familiar things while recollections of identity and previous existence were banished from his mind. All sense of location or orientation became absorbed into white light and his sense of place was if he was part of an enormous murmuration of birds that moved silently through a tapestry of shades and hues of colour beyond description. Awakening from his dream-like place, revealed a plateau overlooking a vast plain of ochre-coloured desert.

His physique jerked spasmodically awakening him with a start he felt the coldness of the night. A sound of distant animal howled to a lonely sky. He turned and twisted on the unyielding ground trying to settle and reach some measure of comfort. His muscles taut and tense- such were the realism of his transition. Without question, his conscious mind seamlessly accepted his altered new reality and its surroundings without any recourse to what had gone before. An awakening deep within his very being permitted his consciousness to accept what is, without recourse to what was. The setting, the place, his altered clothing of a Shepard became as instinctive as breathing. He adapted without question to the mystical reality unfurled around him as the fabric of an alternative existence unfolded. He was now a being without a history of any kind, unburdened with a past only driven to seek new things. He fumbled his small bag and wrapped it around his shoulders and started to move. The Sun would be up in a matter of hours, and he'd face the heat of the wilderness. To him, everything was as it should be, oblivious to processes that now shaped the reality he'd entered. Places and scenes began to unfold that radiated with texture, warmth, and a gentle breeze completed his alternate reality as the landscape of rock and hills opened up before him.

Everything he saw or touched, smelt, or sounds materialized around him with unquestioning certainty and substance. His awareness of dimensional shifts meant nothing. All that surrounded him was real as the steep canyons of barren Judean wilderness looked down, as was his own physicality or what appeared to be. He then saw something that inexplicably drew him towards it.

A small opening came into view on the opposite side of a cliff face. Beneath it, a large mound of loose stones was piled. A cave. Someplace he could rest up in safety. He changed direction and crossed the short gap in the canyon and started to make his way straight for the stones. When he reached them, he pushed his small pouch around his shoulders onto his back and slowly started to climb, carefully making sure not to cause loose rocks to come crashing down. He summoned his strength and commenced to climb. Halfway up he paused and heard the howling sounds echoing around the rocky valley. He pushed and pulled harder hauling his body upwards. As he did, loose rock from beneath him gave way and started to roll away from under him. His efforts became a struggle, trying to grab bigger stones for purchase. As he did, he gripped a small angular sharp piece that cut into his palm badly, forcing him to cry out, and release. Almost close to the top amid grunts when he started to lose his momentum and began to slide backward down the mound. With both hands scrambling to find a solid grip amid the rocks, a hand reached out from the darkness and gripped his.

Instant terror took hold with the touch of another human. The grip was strong and powerful. A hand that knew physical work. With one effort and strength, he was lifted up over the edge and on to the floor of the cave entrance. He rolled forward and then adjusted himself away from the edge. He froze as he saw the shape and outline of a large man in the shadow of the cave. The figure didn't move for a few seconds and then slowly advanced towards him. Again, the hand came towards him, this time it's holding a small cloth and then placed it into his wounded hand. A gesture of a friend.

He took it gratefully and placed it over the wound. The figure emerged further from the shadows knelt and slowly reached out and took his hand. The face still masked in darkness. He felt the stranger's hand rest against his cut and bruised hand, then his other hand clasped itself to his. Instantly he felt the warmth. Before his weary eyes, he felt the warmth turned to a surge of heat around his hand. He gasped and tried to withdraw, but the hands around his were like a vice grip, powerful and unyielding. Then, he heard the whispering voice from the darkness utter something as the glow around his hand emitted blue light as pure as he has ever seen and lasts briefly. Then it began to fade.

The hands released his. Cautiously he shuffled into the corner of the cave never taking his eyes off the shadowy figure. Nothing was spoken first, moment's pass, and then the movement. A gesture to sit followed by.

"You have travelled far, rest now. You can shelter here "

He glanced up and looked across the small opening between him and the tall figure sitting in the corner. He was about to respond when the figure moved to the mouth of the cave and dropped silently to his knees. Against the night sky from the east, he could see the powerful build. His hair looked thick and fell to his broad shoulders.

Geneva. 2013 AD

Each of the doctors was a specialist in their field took time attempting to explain, what was inexplicable. Claudine listened trying to control the trembling as did the rest of them to every word, every nuanced answer from the four men sitting around them in the privacy of the room. Regardless of the patient's alteration in appearance, each of the men in surgical attire gave answers as best they could.

"Madam Du Pont, we're not entirely certain to the underlying cause your husband's condition. What you see is a form of catatonic state. We don't believe he is aware of anything' and neurologically none of us here has any idea what is taking place inside his brain at present. We intend to submit him to an MRI scan later this evening to look at motor neuron activity. After that, we will form a better idea of what we're dealing with".

"Will my father will have brain damage doctor? Michelle sobbed.

"Hard to say before we scan, young lady. I'm sorry. If it's any reassurance I've seen many patients exhibit this condition, and then, just come out of it.

"There is obviously something wrong with him Doctor. Just look at him! Melrose snapped.

"How long?

They looked at Claudine.

Pardon?

"How long could my husband stay like this? She whispered.

Over by the bed, Francois listened. As the tone and direction of the conversation moved despairingly towards the end of the session, he went and knelt placing his hands on Du Pont limp left hand and held it, bowed in silent prayer then gently lifting the scientist's hand and rested it on the other.

Without warning, trickles of blood began to stain onto the blue gown. It was also on his hand. He looked down and gasped in shock. The others turned as the priest stood back and saw his own bloodstained hands. Doctor Heinz came quickly to the bed and took the Jesuit's hands, his fingers covered with dark stains. Worse, there was no cut or wound. The others quickly surrounded the bed and checked the life support systems. One of them reached and examined Du Pont's left hand. A gash nearly 27 mm in length appeared along his palm, around where the blood is beginning to congeal. Quickly, another doctor picked up some clinical towels and disinfectant and began to clean the almost lifeless hand. As he did, others instantly saw something else. As the stains were cleaned away the whole hand appeared torn and scratched. Marks covered the hand including the fingers, roughed over, as if the scientist had dragged his hand over a ragged surface. The gash was deep and was going to need stitches.

By instinct, the Francois reached and turned the other hand over. The one resting under the crucifix that he had placed. As with the left hand, it bore scratches all along its length and some bruising of the skin. No one spoke for a few moments. Doctor Peter Schultz then turned to Claudine.

"Claudine, girls, let me suggest something if I may. Your husband has no apparent injuries of note, but it seems he may have experienced as we spoke earlier some form of a neurological episode. That was some time earlier today as you know now. As we can all see his neurobiological systems have experienced some kind of systematic failure? After we complete our MRI scan, we can start to think of some strategies and steps we might consider. We may have to consider some life support mechanisms."

Then there was a loud bang, with a small stainless-steel surgical dish crashing to the floor scattering small utensils. The young nurse jumped up and stepped back knocking over the small chair. She gasped and threw her hands to her face. Paul Melrose was first to cross to the bed. The others quickly stand and looked. The nurse looked like she had been struck. Doctor Schultz moved quickly and saw where the nurse was pointing to the hand she was tending. Melrose reached and lifted the prone scientist's hand, and stared at its condition. There was no longer a wound or scaring. It was clean, without any sign of the wound. Not a mark, not even the signs of scratches moments before. There was silence.

Francois lowered his head. A shell of the man he knew well, broken and empty, discarded by some unknown force that seemed to have reached in and stolen his life force. The questions would come. He also knew, as this got worse; they would turn to him for explanations. In their despair and anguish his sister would confront him, and all that he held sacred. A vengeful God would be thrown in his face. The sheer scale of change in Fletcher's appearance and its progression over a few hours was unnatural.

"It's always highly experimental" He remembered. Lost in thought he felt a hand on his shoulder.

"Come and sit with us, Francois. It's too much to take in". Melrose said.

"He looks so, changed, so un-Fletcher." Francois whispered.

The ward door opened suddenly, and four figures quietly entered. Felix Deveraux, Miles Kingsley, Monika Reinhardt, and Carina Ambrosiana said little as they cautiously made their way to the bedside. Each came and touched Claudine's shoulder and moved towards the bed. The effect was immediate on each of them. Deveraux's face was one of horror and disbelief. The rest stopped in their tracks, speechless. The Italian physicist looked for a few seconds then closed her eyes. Moving silently, they gathered around the bed. Each of them took-in the horror of the scene. The change in the man was so rapid and striking, that each of them took some minutes to absorb the extent of the physical changes to their colleague. Felix Deveraux reached and took the listless hand and gently squeezed it. Everyone in that room that spring night felt they had been summoned to witness something deeply disturbing and surreal. Never in their normal experiences did they encounter or contemplate such changes in physical appearances were possible in such a short time frame. Most of them were people of science, men and women of deep insights into biology, physiology, and physics. Mortals used to dealing with complex processes. Men of vision, accustomed to peering beyond boundaries of normality as defined by conventional wisdom and human knowledge. As of that moment, they confronted something that no training, or experience prepared them for.

"I'd like the room to my family if you all don't mind, Claudine asked quietly.

She had issues with everything she saw. The sequence of events that led to this. No clear ideas from anyone what caused this in the first place? Now his condition, and again no one sure what were the reasons for his appearance. She had issues with some of those in the room, although that could wait. She needed to have time alone with the man she loved, uncertain if they would ever talk or comfort each other again. There were things she needed to say to him directly and alone. She gathered her strength.

"I need to speak with my husband" She faltered.

"Now if you all don't mind.'

Doctor Benjamin Mochti sat in a battered old armchair in his study on the second floor of the hospital wing, holding a folded newspaper in one hand and a mug of coffee in the other. It was just after 4.30 pm. His eyes were drawn to the last part of the article again. His eyes fixed on a tail article in the science section that followed events out in the CERN complex in Meyrin.

The news is still very sketchy, as to the circumstances of the scientist's condition. Sources close to the Directorate of Theoretical Studies stated that one of their senior staff, an American, Professor Du Pont was taken ill suddenly. His condition is not life-threatening. It appears that Dr. Fletcher Du Pont is a key...

Mochti stared at the wording, letting the content sink in.

There were no further reports on his condition going to print, our reporter understands that what started as critical but stable condition, now...is more serious than first thought... Scientists at CERN remained tight-lipped as to the ... "

He put down his coffee then slowly removed his glasses and glanced at the blank wall opposite him. Then back to the article *Professor Du Pont was the key architect and chief exponent of until, only two hours into this phase of experimentation. When he suddenly collapsed...*

Mochti reached for his phone and dialled a number, waited a few seconds then heard Paul Melrose voice answering service. He left a brief message. A small tape recorder was lying on a bookcase in the corner. He scanned the article again. Suddenly his phone rang. Almost by reflex he reached and grabbed it.

"Mochti!

"Doctor! It's Paul Melrose.

"Paul! Thank you for calling back."

"I know what has happened. Could we meet? I have something that may be important. It might be nothing, or it might be everything. We need to meet Paul". The other end of the call stayed silent.

"Doctor Mochti something horrific and disturbing has happened to Professor Du Pont! Nobody seems to have any answers. We're all... It might be a question of time if he survives this." A few seconds passed.

'What do you think *this* is Paul?

"I have no idea. He is changed. Altered physically and it's continuing. Almost by the hour. Why did you call doctor? Is there a connection between my recent episode and this?

There was a long pause from the other end.

"Yes Paul, I do. We should meet, and might I suggest, you bring Denise with you.

In an hour then! Mochti said.

He then gave the young scientist directions to a small village on the outskirts of the city on the south western side of the lake and a route that offered a shortcut that avoided the city traffic. The journey would take no more then half an hour.

Meanwhile, three senior physicians moved to a darkened room studying a series of magnetic resonance brain images of Professor Fletcher Du Pont. Each of them said little. The set of images appeared on the laboratory monitors. They were on the second floor of Clinique Gerealle Valence hospital. Dr. Eugene Cary, Dr. Peter Schultz were top neurosurgeons, the third was Dr. Joseph Heinz a specialist in brain trauma. Over several seconds, additional images appeared that showed multiple images of both hemispheres of their patient's brain. They were looking to see if key brain motor functions showed signs of degeneration or worse, no functions at all. Segments of brain tissue were depicted with colours that showed various neuron activities. None of the images revealed any evidence of trauma, instead, the entire upper left-hand quadrant of the epilistus part of the frontal lope pulsed in a series of purple glows as if the brain was immersed in some hypnotic trance. Dr. Heinz stood transfixed at multiple brain scan images. He had observed and studied countless similar scans of the human brain. This was something entirely new.

In the stillness of the ward at the other end of the wing, alone for the first time, with only a small pilot light barely showed her husband's face. She lifted his weathered and battered hand and held it to her face.

"My dear husband" she whispered. If you can hear me, if you can sense and hear my voice, please somehow let me know my love. Fletcher, I am here with you."

Her voice faltered with everything she was looking at. His hand felt chilled and his face and pallor were a washed-out grey and cold to touch. The silver tinged black hair was no longer smooth and trimmed, but now lay ruffled and lank. It looked ragged and had grown longer, and had almost transformed her husband into a much older and different human being. His breathing was laboured with its cadence faltering intermittently. In every manner of appearance, this human was in the last throes of life. Life was slowing leaving his body and no answers as to why or how his physical alteration in such a short time could be explained. She started to sob. Clutching his hand, she tried to intertwine her fingers with his. Suddenly the realization that his fingers were rigid and un-flexing and rigor mortis was beginning to take effect.

"Oh, God! Please don't take him now, please! She cried out.

The trembling stopped, and the horror that gripped her since they arrived was replaced with something remarkably different. Getting to her feet she pulled over the chair and sat down and leaned back. She felt for her bag and finally found what she was looking for. A small miniature bottle of liqueur brandy. She quietly finds two small drinking glasses then with a strange degree of composure, she emptied the contents of the bottle into the two glass containers. She stood over her husband and placed the glass into his hand, and wrapped his fingers as best she could around the tumbler. Like a sentinel standing over her husband, she stared down at his emaciated frame leaned over and kissed him.

"Now my love, we are going to try and get to the bottom of this, she said gently in his ear.

Turning, she returned to the chair.

"We are going a have a three-way conversation, and I want some answers" She turned and looked up at the ceiling, and cradled her glass in one hand in a gesture of defiance.

"I know of a vengeful God. I've heard it many times from my brother, you're devoted and misguided servant on this Earth. I even heard him tell that you will not be mocked. For all your divine wisdom you are still a fucking mystery to us. We seek you in our prayers in our private moments. We seek and ask for your aid in times of trouble and, what do we get? What do we get back from you? Your charade! You neither acknowledge us, as weak, or fragile, but on just a whim you dish out retribution. Vicious, and vengeful, you careless and unthinking thug! Take your eyes off my husband your feckless creature! And just for once show us that you care! She screamed. ...

"My husband is one of your creative human beings on this earth, in what he does and to his very being, he seeks to understand how this magnificent world functions and, now you bring him harm! You're nothing but an enigma, a mystery to all of us. And maybe he's right after all. All you are is an irrelevant myth. Nothing more! Just this once! She took one gulp and finished the drink. Why don't you show us you're caring and loving nature? She slumped back into the chair and sunk her face in her hands.

It was just a little after 8 pm and dusk had arrived.

A hand reached out and touched her shoulder. Her brother stood in the shadows and put his arms around her shoulders. Her youngest daughter, Michelle knelt next to her and took her hand.

"You have issues with God dear sister. All I ask, all he asks, is that you trust him. Place Fletcher's life in his hands. Have faith in things we can't fathom or understand right now" Francois whispered.

She looked up at her brother standing over her.

"*Your God*! Not mine! She spat.

"My God would not inflict this on us! She hissed with bitterness and barely concealed contempt. She stood and leaned closer to him.

"Your God is a blasphemy! His divinity is an absurdity, and a fucking ambiguity to me, and my family right now. He's nothing but a vengeful thug! On a whim, he strikes down good people. What's that all about Francois? She sneered.

Taken aback at the venomous taunt, he pulled back and looked towards the bed. He moved towards it struggling to fight the rage and anger he felt towards his God well up inside him. His powerlessness seemed to sap his energy.

Just a little after 9.45pm that evening a light blue Saab pulled into a small side street and parked two hundred yards from the hotel entrance. The hotel was small by normal standards but was well appointed and tastefully decorated. Within five minutes Mochti looked up and saw Paul Melrose and Denise Du Pont standing at the reception. When they joined him both of them look completely distressed and shaken. He noticed Denise's eyes are dark and Melrose looked ashen. A few seconds of awkward silence followed.

"How have you been Paul? Getting plenty of rest.

"I'm fine Doctor, thanks for asking.

"And you Mademoiselle, how are you doing? He asked

"I'm really not so sure how I am, Doctor. We're all very...She left unfinished.

"And your father, I am shocked as anyone when I heard of his accident. I understand he is getting the best care there is. I know both the attending senior people over there; they're the top men in their field. Mochti said.

"Please, take a seat. Do you feel like eating something, I'll order something for us? I will pray that God keeps your father safe". Then turning to Melrose

"Can we talk a little about *you* for a moment?

"There are some things you need to hear and then understand. I hope you didn't mind coming here. But I feel we needed absolute privacy to discuss recent events, as well as your father, Denise. Paul, your recent episode you were under my care. There were things around your symptoms and your condition that was somewhat unusual. Now as far as any clinical issues are concerned I am happy that you made a complete recovery. That being said, there were other matters went outside the normal course of treatments that we had to deal with.

" Such as? Denise asked

Mochti stirred uneasily in his seat. He leaned forward and lowered his voice.

"Well, there's no easy way for me to explain any of what happened other than to be as factual and truthful as I can be. During these episodes, I am pretty certain, that you experienced some form of neuropsychiatric disturbance. These presented themselves in the form of hypnotic outbursts. You began to utter sayings. That these were completely out of context, quite frankly to say that they were extraordinary, is putting it mildly. Most of what you spoke was very old. And apart from being from an ancient past, they were mainly old sayings, recitals, some were chants. Sayings that emanated from another age, from a time where deep spiritual truths were written down. They were...scriptural in origin, expressions of a profound nature. These were considered sacred texts, and even by today's standards, these writings divide scholars of their origin and authenticity.

You also... He hesitated

"Used a very rare and seldom spoken language during these episodes. I am referring to truths laid down in a bygone age. Aspects of knowledge that relate to not only our physical world, as we know it, but to other levels of existence. Great spiritual leaders Mystics, who understood the multi-dimensional nature of man. These truths enshrined in mysticism were well known and understood by our ancestors, and there are some, who hold these laws to be immutable today, as they were in former times. My own father is one such person. He is a scholar of sorts, of all things ancient, and a life-long student of some of the oldest known texts, in both Hebrew and Coptic scripts. During some of your episodes, well that's our medical term, I believed that you experienced, or underwent a connection, a channel of some kind and specific recitals with certain meanings were expressed."

Mochti's interest and passion became obvious.

"Do you believe in things that lie outside normal scientific or medical science? Things that belong or behave, in accordance with more, ancient laws? Knowledge that pre-existed our present level of understandings!   He paused. Melrose felt a slight chill.

"Let me show you something, and then I'll try and explain.

Melrose became tense. Denise on the other hand never blinked but stared intently at Mochti who seemed to possess a strange aspect about him, one she was uncertain of. With that, Mocthi opened a beautiful leather briefcase with an oak finish and placed it on the table between them. Effortlessly he moved his fingers around clasps and released them. He removed some parchments and notepads, and then took a small chrome metallic tape recorder, and placed them on the table. Melrose glanced at Denise, uncertain where all this was leading. "Do you believe in things that "*lie outside normal scientific or medical science*?" Got his immediate attention.

For the next 30 minutes, Mochti went through a description of Paul Melrose's episodes during what appeared to be trance-like outbursts. In parts, he switched on the tape and kept the volume so nobody within their proximity could hear the plaintive outcries of a troubled and tortured patient. Occasionally interjecting Mochti traced the ancient parchments that match the young Welshman's outbursts. Melrose and Denise sat rapt in their seats looked spellbound at the small recorder, mesmerized by all they heard.

Then Mochti opened some of his notepads, which contained photographs of the sheets computations of complex calculations that littered the Melrose's ward.

Professor Du Pont was fully aware of these events Paul. He and I tried to piece this whole set of events together then we tried…

"Stop! Please stop doctor. Melrose cut in. Mochti paused and studied his former patient

"What's the matter? Melrose sat upright.

"I remember in the tunnel that night. Funny, how I didn't think of it till now. It was just a few days before Euclid would commence. The breathing in the tunnel it began to sound like it was breathing, and the sound that came from deep inside the whole ring. It seemed to…come alive. Then the walls shifted and a language that didn't mean anything… Mochti and Denise remained silent.

"Doctor, is there more you wanted to show us? Denise asked

"Yes, there is. This last piece no one else has heard, and why I think there is more to all of this then we think… "May I?

He pressed the button on the small recorder one more time. A few seconds followed then the unmistakable voice of Melrose's voice of anguish fills the intimate space around the table.

Oh no! Please, these particles cannot do this for pity sake, not Fletcher. Change Euclid, please alter the magnetic…^^^^^**** He cannot survive its ungodly. Warn him; warn him, before the be… swop. No Euclid. Please, No Euclid. It will kill him, for God sake please doesn't let him. We forgot "Oh no, not Fletcher, stop him. Stop! For pity sake, not Fletcher …for pity sake, not Fletcher…

Mochti leaned forward and replayed the tape again. This time Mochti took some of the parchments held inside clear transparent sheets and showed them the Aramaic texts that matched some of Melrose's earlier plaintive utterances word for word. Finally, after a minute switched off the device. By now most of the other tables in the room are nearly empty, and they are almost alone. No one said a word. Melrose stared down at the table. Denise's had a ghost-like an appearance clutching a tissue.

"Something deep inside your trance-like state reached out and foresaw an event that impacted on Professor Du Pont himself." Mochti whispered

He slumped back and allowed both of them to digest everything.

"May I ask do you have any recall or any imagery in your memory that might match these words? It sounded like a warning! Anything at all?

'Doctor Mochti I'm lost here. What am I doing speaking this strange language old Hebrew, or something!"

"Aramaic! Well now my friend, that's an even bigger mystery to me?" "Is there any connection with your work? All of this seems that it was intimately connected with this Euclid project'. The tension changes instantly at the mention of the project. Melrose ran his hand through his already ruffled hair. He glanced over at Denise, then back at the doctor. It was Denise who spoke first.

"My father was very preoccupied lately. Something at work seemed to be troubling him a lot. He became a little aloof. He spent a lot of the last few weeks locked in his study. Something he kept private. A few times when I walk in on him, he would scramble some of his notes in a way, I know he didn't want me to see or notice. It was almost secretive in the way he did it. Oh God! I'm sorry. It's so, not my father. He was open and he always shared his love of his work with us at home. But this was entirely out of character. Whatever it was, I also know Felix; I mean Professor Deveraux knew about it as well. I'm pretty certain. And there's something else. I think my father discussed what happened to Paul with my uncle and possibly what was troubling him".

"You're Uncle! Mochti asked

"Yes. Uncle Francois. My mother's brother. He is a priest, a Jesuit in fact".

Mochti leaned forward and studied both of them for a moment.

A Jesuit! That's rather interesting. Is he close to the family?

"Yes, he is. He is very much part of our life and a very devout man. He, my sister, and I are very close. He is a wonderful man and right now we are so grateful that he was here.'

"Is he close to your father?

They have their occasional little battles, but my father greatly admires my uncle. They are good friends now.' My father is an atheist."

Mochti's expression remained impassive. He knew about the work of the Jesuits and their order. He encountered some of them when he was a soldier in military service in Lebanon. His overall impression was fearlessness. They were warrior priests.

"Does any of all of this mean anything to you? He asked.

Melrose appeared distant and became uneasy with Denise speaking out. Those particular memories were very sharp. The ghostly Shroud image that convulsed the inner sanctum at the top of CERN. Was there some ominous logic to any of this? Glancing at the parchments sealed inside their pouches an ancient language he does not know of, and a piercing outcry, a warning to his mentor.

"Doctor, we need to keep all of this…

"You can call me Benni. Mochti said

"If its secrecy and confidentially, please be assured these stay between us. But let's be clinical for a moment. All the most recent events in the tunnel, your resulting episodes, and the trauma, are in some sense random. Very strange granted but confined to you, and only you. Now this unfortunate accident with Professor Du Pont the connection is, that both of you are in high-energy physics. You both worked closely and are in the middle of this breakthrough, Euclid.

"You suspect something don't you Doctor? Denise whispered.

CHAPTER ELEVEN

Benjamin Mochti stood to stretch his legs and noticed the restaurant was empty, and they were the only ones left. He caught the waiter's eye and quickly ordered coffee and a mixed assortment of sandwiches. Turning he sat down and wondered how he'd respond to such an open question.

"Yes! I suspect there is a link. I think you, and the work you do is somehow tied into some mystical issue. And, if I am honest, I think there are some aspects here that Paul is keeping to himself. I can fully understand that of course. But, if I am to be any help I need to try and deal with aspects surrounding your work. Whatever this program you and the Professor worked on, may have created events that triggered very abnormal incidents."

Denise looked at Mochti.

"Mystical issues! What's that to do with any of this?"

"I am not sure Denise, but I sense something here and I'm sure Paul does as well. Coffee and sandwiches arrived but neither of them felt hungry.

"I'm not the physicist here, but are there links in your work in theoretical physics, and these recent events. I wondered if... some exchange was going on? Mochti paused.

Melrose gave Mochti a fearful look.

"I'm not comfortable with this any of this Benni. Look if you don't mind, we need to go away and think about this a little more. We need to go! He said and reached and took Denise's hand and stood.

"Very Well. I understand, and I'm truly sorry for any inconvenience to you."

Mochti said standing. Denise stood. "Yes, Doctor. Perhaps we need time to think on this?

She said reaching for her bag.

"Please, Denise, let me take care of the coffee. Mochti said. Denise took a step towards the Doctor. She took his hand surprising him.

"I'm very grateful for everything you have shared here with us Benni. I want to talk again soon. I share your thoughts about, well, everything! There is more to this? She held his stare and then at Paul.

"Thank you. You've been very kind. There is something I need you to do for me, Benni. There were tears in her eyes.

"Of course! Whatever".

She picked up her belongings and took Paul's hand.

"I 'd like you to meet my uncle, and soon".

"The Jesuit?

"Yes. I want you to go through everything you shared with us this evening with Francois. Can you do that for me? She hesitated for a few seconds. Everything Benni. Tell him everything we spoke of here this evening."

Melrose looked uneasily at her. He shook hands with Mochti and then headed towards the door.

"Tell me, before you go! Is there such a thing as a Messenger particle?

Melrose stopped caught off guard by the question.

"It's a loose term we use occasionally to describe particles that are not yet fully understood, or behave in ways we cannot describe. Why?

Oh! It's nothing. I'm doing a little reading on the subject of physics and I came across an oblique reference to it. That's all! He said.

"Good night to you both, let's stay in touch".

Then he was gone.

$$\beta$$

Over the following two weeks, both the Claudine and her family took it in turns to maintain a bedside vigil at Clique Gerealle Vallence hospital. Du Pont's form continued to show slow but gradual signs of changing as if undergoing some unexplained aging process. He was now isolated in a single ward on the second floor in the neurological wing of the building. Only a limited number of hospital staff had access to him, along with his family and immediate senior colleagues from CERN. Each day took its toll on the family and those closest to him.

Felix Deveraux showed the most strain, unable to shake off the feeling he was responsible for pushing his friend to unreasonable limits. Then there was also that other issue that only the key people around Du Pont knew about. Each of the inner circle began to entertain their own personal demons while trying to keep stringent protocols and procedures to watch for any further anomalies tuning up. Carina Ambosiana, in particular, became deeply disturbed by her colleague's physical deterioration. She was haunted by the notion of an uncontrolled set of forces they had unwittingly unlocked unleashing a set of conditions beyond their grasp. In secret they all met in the evenings in the conference room adjoining Deveraux's study to review the new results from Euclid and its implications. They needed to get to grips if this new emergence of particles was in some way a factor in Du Pont's accident. Staff was on a need to know basis and no notes were kept. The triumph of the Euclid was now subsumed into full-blown crises in the making. CERN's inner functions continued as normal, but within the inner sanctum of the organization shocking and disturbing events were beginning to unravel. Each of those huddled around the conference table that evening harboured personal fears. Their colleague's physical alteration since the event was deeply disturbing. Felix Deveraux had a pile of sheets in front of him. All eyes around the table noticed how haggard and drawn he looked. The conference room was lit by a single lamp casting a low yellow light around the room.

"Until, any of us, understand what's happening here Felix, this stays in this room. Miles Kingsley said.

Deveraux's furrowed face hardly registered if he heard him. He looked up and scanned those around him. Something was stirring within the realms of particle physics. Some new set of laws was emerging, and it seemed these forces were imposing an alternative version of reality. He had no model or framework to build any understanding of what was going on. He rested his chin on his interlocked hands and studied each of his trusted fellow scientists sitting around him.

"Does anyone here, think this image, the shroud event, and what it represents, Paul Melrose's recent episode, the emergences of these new mystery particles, and what has occurred to Professor Du Pont think these are not connected? He asked

No one spoke for a few seconds.

"Impossible to say DG. Miles Kingsley said Up to now Felix, I would have said no. But I'm not sure anymore. Further silence.

'Something very abnormal is at work here! Manfred Gruss said.

Deveraux had his eye fixed on his Italian colleague, Carina Ambrosiana but he turned to Monika Reinhardt, the youngest in the room.

"Monika, are you happy with the integrity of the data so far? He asked. She hesitated for a second

"Yes Chief, to the data question." She said, adding

"There is a connection here. Fletcher himself was convinced of the existence of messenger particles. I think we are dealing with an alternative set of physics beyond our theoretical horizons."

The mood around the table was muted. Deveraux managed a smile and nodded. Taking his time, he fixed his gaze at Carina, who seemed absorbed in her own forensic thinking. He saw the conflict in the eyes, the struggle within between science and belief. Paradoxically, if anyone mirrored his inner conflicts more often than not, it was she. She looked up.

"I am afraid to say, what I'm really thinking chief! She said with some defiance.

A few eyebrows were raised towards the Italian. Deveraux's political radar was alert to the potential consequences and fall-out from everything that had taken place. He had chosen to leave the last word with the slightly fiery and passionate Professor from Bologna, knowing that if anyone would be the first to think the unthinkable, she would be the one.

"There are no boundaries here Carina. Please! We need to hear what everyone thinks. Manfred Gruss said.

She gave him a piercing penetrating gaze, then towards the others.

"We are either witnessing something very special, or, we are being summoned.

I am now certain that the image face, was created by these messenger particles and we are all part of some miraculous intersection between science and higher intelligence. Forgive me, everyone...I know this is not what we do here, but in my heart in my very being, I know we are being sent a message to prepare for something. I think Fletcher is part of it. I think he is in no danger. I saw peace in his face."

No one said a word. The air in the room became unnaturally still, laden with doubt and a sense of foreboding.

"This might be a bell ringer for us! She said.

Jesuit Aumonerie Rue De Planage. Paris.

Father Provincial Alphonse Sienna listened intently to the voice on his phone. It lasted over an hour. His evening meal prepared for him earlier, lay untouched. His head bowed rested in his free hand as he tried to assimilate everything he heard.

Alone in his study reading when the call was put through. He was a man of the world well accustomed to life's upheavals and no stranger to meeting difficult issues both in church matters or substances that affected his flock. The call, when it came was like nothing he'd expected. It was the second call from Geneva, only this time as more intimate and graphic details emerged did he become apprehensive with the tone and nature of the conversation. The agitated state from the other end the call was palpable with some aspects nearly had his head spinning as he took in everything on the call. The flow of revelations was measured to allow the full ramifications to take hold. Outside, it was late in the evening while much of Paris was enjoying a balmy night and the first early signs of spring were well in evidence. He didn't need to make notes only to lock into every detail his brother Jesuit in Geneva was relaying. The more he heard, the more he began to fidget with his chain and cross.

"Yes, of course, Francois! He will be in our prayers."

"Are you sure? The face of..! He interrupted the call for a moment and laid the phone down on his desk for a few seconds and stared at a picture. A simple wooden frame held the image of their orders founder, Francis of Assisi. His fellow Jesuit brother laid everything out down to the convergence of miraculous occurrences. Brother Burgoyne left nothing out in the details

"Francois, listen to me very carefully my brother! This must be handled with great care and sensitivity." He paused. Before you go! Were the recitals, the Aramaic passages? Did they suggest?

He stopped.

"I see, Dear God! Were you able to discern if there was..?

Finally, when the call finished the leader of the Jesuit Order in France replaced the receiver back in its cradle and spent a few minutes assessing events in Switzerland. Standing, he decided to retire to his private library to his books, and spend the rest of his evening and perhaps the best part of the night there. There was a select set of volumes that required some careful reading and study. It was going to take some time, but he knew what he was looking for.

In a Realm, Beyond Physics

Early morning light poured into the small crevice where he was lying, startling him from his sleep. He slept fitfully, full of strange things, people he never knew passed before him yet they seemed familiar. Faces filled with kindness. Then as his eyes began to flicker and slowly open, began to adjust to the figure and build of a tall man, broad frame shoulders with a long garment running the length of a powerful physique. He had thick brownish red hair that fell just to his shoulders. He slowly sat up without taking his eyes from the man in front of him. He looked strong and powerful and yet there was weariness about him. Then the stranger reached out his hand in a gesture to assist him to his feet. Taking it, he pulled himself up to his feet and looked straight at the face and brooding eyes. The stranger held his grip almost menacingly, and then released it. The face was marked showing signs of blistering, and covered in sand and grit. Yet through the grim and dried sweat, the most piercing radiant brown hazel eyes stared back at him almost into the depths of his soul. The garment was stained and marked from the desert, and in some places, the clothing was ripped as if slashed by something sharp and the unmistakable marks of dried blood covered his sleeves.

Then he noticed the rough and callused hands. Hands, that had seen much physical use.

"Who are you, good friend? The stranger asked

Then without any warning and in one easy movement his left-hand reached up and gripped the other's shoulder. The power stranger's touch was forceful. Then with his eyes closed, he spoke with an intense whisper to himself. It lasted a brief few seconds then the other looked into those eyes again, only this time a flicker of intense concentration. There was an unsettling intensity in his haunted countenance. A face that knew things, knew about things, yet to happen.

"I'm not sure who I am. I can't seem to remember how I got here"

"Don't harbour any fears, my friend. There is nothing here that will bring you harm. Just have strength". The hint of a smile crossed his worn face.

"Walk with me, Traveller! The stranger said.

At that moment his identity undergoes change. He became the "traveller", a voyager across a chasm of unimaginable dimensions leaving all four dimensions of time and space behind, venturing into a new realm existence. To him, the fabric of one reality was crossed in a blink of an eye akin to a dreamlike state where everything was real and everything became possible. The physicist of one age dwelt in a place where only the dead come to stay. In this new sphere of reality, his old knowledge of his identity was curtailed. He retained only a spark of memory of his former self, and any recollection of events that led to his new presence was diminished. Willingly, Traveller accepted the notion of a walk. Without further talk both helped each other to leave the small mountainside cave down a sloping mountain pass and through a deep narrow canyon shaded from direct sunlight that crossed a great boulder-strewn plain, heading north into the sweeping hills of Judea. Traveller fell in behind the stranger as they commenced to walk a winding series of paths across the rock-strewn terrain, bleached ochre under the anvil of a relentless sun. The stranger walked with his shoulder red cape wrapped like a hood to shield his head from the blistering and suffocating heat. There appeared no urgency in the pace. Traveller followed, instinctively trying to conserve his energy and match the figure in front of him. He noticed the certainty of his leader's steps, and despite his own pace, a gap began to open up between them. They are now a couple of hours into the canyon as it bends and moulds itself into the contour of this rugged and unforgiving landscape. Once through the canyon, they faced into the open plain of the desert. Their journey was in some parts torturous over broken stones that simply had crumbled in time with unending heat and little rainfall. They had been moving for over five hours.

The Traveller started to feel tired the strain of the pace pushing him to limits beyond what he thought was possible. He needed rest and shade. Just as he is about to call when from nowhere, he felt something changed around him? Something unseen. He paused and looked around. From nowhere and without any warning he was brushed by an abrupt and rapid movement of cold air that almost knocked him over. He stopped dead in his tracks and then felt a powerful sensation of air that blew almost instantaneously around engulfing him. Invisible energy shook him forcing him to grapple and hold on to a nearby rock. The frigid air was a shock to his system and it spun everything from small stones to scrub and whirled into a powerful vortex. His frame was gripped and shaken like a small rag doll by some unseen hand that began to weigh down on him forcing him to his knees unable to resist this merciless invisible force. It's a sensation of drowning in the air that wrapped itself around him like a vice grip. The experience lasts in intensity for no more than a few moments. He held to the rock fiercely and crouched to shelter himself from the dust storm. He cried out to the figure in front of him, only to see nothing of his companion.

Then, without warning, the air began to lose its chilling bite to be replaced by an invisible force draining his energy. Sleep almost consumed him accompanied by an inexplicable sense of weight or unknown force pressing down on him. Slowly the noise of the air subsided and became settled with a strange calm. His breathing was forced and rapid. At first, he thought it was a whisper that's barely human. Then a further silence, before a soft whisper called out to him.

"Your presence here has a purpose. This purpose and your presence here will cause you no harm. Be calm and be at peace. No harm befalls you here. I am a friend"

Then nothing. Regaining some measure of composure he looked tentatively around. Utter calmness. Not even the whisper of the slightest breeze. Then for the second time:

"I am a good friend. There is nothing to be afraid of. You cannot lay eyes on me yet, but all in good time. I am your friend. I am your guide".

The timbre of the voice had power. A few seconds of silence pass. Traveller sat terrified. The voice possessed tranquillity and warmth to it, a voice that spoke from the rocks of the wilderness, the Judean wilderness. A fear and rising panic took hold as the enormity of his isolation was compounded with menacing ghostly voices

"Please, for pity sake! Who are you? Why can't I see you?

The shimmering heat from the desert caused a vast shifting mirage of images that transformed the landscape into shifting ghostly rocks. Then from the emptiness of the wilderness and carried in the winds, the voice:

"On the Oath of the highest. I promise you will come to no harm. Let me show you".

With that, the immediate ground in front of him started to shimmer and distort. A swishing sound welled up around a patch of the ground like an invisible suction that seems to soak the very air around the spot in front of him. In seconds a small hole began to appear on the stony surface, and started as a small depression, opened out into a crater and as if with some invisible process, the hole deepened and slowly became a dark stain in coloration. Then after a brief interval, a first trickle. The hole rapidly began to fill with more water. Quickly it filled. The traveller looked on aghast if his eyes were playing tricks with him. The voice whispered

"Now, dear friend…Drink! And then rest for now. I have much to explain."

First, a rumble filled the air causing the air around him to amplify a wave of vibration that shook the entire canyon. Its deep resonance emitted a mild sonic wave that progressed towards him almost knocking him over. Slowly a cloud began to take form above him casting a shadow over the place where he knelt. It cast a massive shadow and grew in size slowly shielding him from the rays of harsh and merciless sun. All his basic instincts scream as he realised some powerful entity was stalking him. The air seemed to move in obedience to whatever power now moved about him. Then abruptly a peace followed by a calmness that settled over him. Now, shaded from the burning sun he leaned over and began to scoop handfuls of water over his face, drinking in gulps. It's coolness and refreshing taste surged through him drinking as much as he could. He slowly crawled to refresh his face, leaned over, and saw his own reflection staring back.

A few moments pass while he stared into the small well of water, his face suddenly stiffened as he began to recall things. Faces of people, he saw lights on ceilings that floated in and out of his mind. Gradually all cognitive and reasoning powers along with his native intellectual powers return, permitting him to reason, but without recourse to memory or his earth history.

"May I begin if it pleases you?" The voice called out.

Now in those few moments instead of the fearful and nervous pitiful nomadic traveller, he became more composed with strength and courage that felt different.

"Yes, if you would. Can you tell me who are you? What are you?

Nearly a full minute passed.

"It is indeed right and proper that you ask for who it is that speaks to you. You may refer to me as, Messenger for it is with that purpose that of bringing you the knowledge I have been chosen to be your guide and inspiration" The voice paused.

"I will also tell you, from whence I come from, and who I am, for it is just that you ascertain these facts for yourself. Then silence.

Without warning, the air stirred. Something was very close- he could almost hear breathing. Then in the gentlest and soothing voice.

"I am one of God's Truth spirits. One of his highest of Spirits in his Dominion, and I come to you, with a purpose, and to impart knowledge. You are much favoured. There is much for you to learn and, to see!

'Is there a purpose a reason to all of this? He finally asked.

The cloud rumbled with a crackling sound and began to change colour started to descend towards him. Then the cloud resonated within itself as if an invisible source of power was present.

"All contact with the material creation has a purpose. In this case and circumstance, it is in accordance with the divine will of our Creator. But first, let me acquaint you with your true identity and nature. You must know also, that all contact and all processes, which you have seen here before you conform to laws unknown to you as a mortal, but in keeping with everything that exists in the universe. There is nothing in existence that does not conform to the great seals that govern both the physical reality of your world or that of the ultra-mundane. Our divine creator is order and beauty. All living things in existence have a purpose. The cause and true purpose of the material world has a divine purpose. There is nothing taking place here that will cause you harm but will progress in accordance with the will of the Higher one".

Put away your fears dear Traveller, you are also greatly loved for you have stored up great blessing in a higher place."

Traveller moved and sat on a large rock absorbed in what was being suggested. He picked up some small stones and started to fidget nervously, his hands still shaking.

"My name, my identity you said you would tell something about who I...

"If I were to reveal your entire past, Traveller and the roles you played in them, you would be struck speechless with horror. But it is not my purpose here to show these things. I will, however, speak of whence you came from in this sphere of existence. In your age of mortality, you are a man of great learning. You have acquired great knowledge of the nature of substance and matter. Your life has been devoted to curiosity, to seek answers to the workings of how the material creation functions.

All the processes that govern laws that support life in its wonderful richness on the earth. You are a man of science, you are a seeker of truths and so, it follows that I am ordained to impart other truths to you if you choose to accept this offer? It is entirely of your choosing."

Traveller stirred and looked around for a few seconds. Glimpses of another time came to him; fleeting images flowed through him then like a sharp pain.

"Drink, one more time from the well"

With that, he sank to knees and scooped up water with both his hands from the well. It was cool. Its refreshing and luxuriant feel coursed through him, and as it did a surge of images filled his head. Looking down at the water surface he was startled to see it transform from its crystal-like clearness to blue colour cloudiness. Then, images began to form. Faces of loved ones, women, with fair skin smiled from the mist. In quick succession, other images appeared of two younger females floated into view. Others of men followed, and at that moment traveller felt a powerful connection to the images. Abruptly these were replaced with a series of light circles moving about a small object in its centre, a symbol that instantly looked familiar, yet he was unable to give it meaning or context. Deep within the recesses of his mind a connection with the images of the women and the others. He closed his eyes and allowed the images of those faces to dwell. A deep attachment and a bond without knowing why he felt tied with those he saw. Then from somewhere very near him, the voice said.

"These are your loved ones whom you will see again soon. Does this help answer your question or shall I continue?

With a few strides, he climbed onto a large ledge that looked out across the vastness of the desolation of rocks trying to find his mysterious companion with those piercing brown eyes

'You call yourself, Messenger? If I am to listen and, take your wisdom. Then show yourself to me. It's only right that I know to who speaks to me from the winds of this desolate place. You said you were my friend that I had nothing to fear.!

"Well then, show me! Let me see you".

No sooner had he spoken, when the atmospherics around him shifted and the ground beneath him shuddered and again he felt with an invisible pressure on his body forcing him backwards. Then a cloud began to form into a rotating shape. It swept everything around him into an enormous whirlpool of air as it did, he felt his knees buckle. The shaking began to decrease, but as it did the light around him began to fade and daylight seemed to be surrendering into the cloud forming in front of him. His eyes struggled to cope with the luminosity of an enormous figure that began to take shape.

A figure and stature nearly twice the height of a human. A powerful white light emanated from all around it. Every rock and stone about the ground began to vibrate beneath him. Then, wings that glowed a bright orange-gold colour began to appear. A magnificent aura of power flowed outwards with an intensity of light that almost blinded traveller causing him to drop to his knees, shielding his eyes. The Light radiated outwards and bathed the immediate area in a powerful afterglow. It lasted seconds, and then the light diminished and the powerful forces attending the event subsided. Traveller stared at the towering resplendent figure now standing over him. It's clothed in a long flowing robe to its feet. Long flowing hair fell to its shoulders. It's face, a vibrant luminous texture, of flawless perfection. Its countenance looked down at him, was that of great nobility, it studied him for a few seconds, and then without any warning, it smiled. Then its huge span of wings closed behind it, it reached out and extended one arm towards traveller. Then raising his face upwards.

"In the name of one of the highest, I am honoured to have to be chosen for this great task". He then looked down at Traveller.

'*I am from the highest of places of creation. I am Messenger!*

CHAPTER TWELVE.

The Hills of Southern Spain. Andalucía Region.

High in the Andalusia hills, basking in a glorious midday sun the small village of Canta Maria Dela Rosa a tiny rural community lived out its daily life much to the charm and delight of tourists who found their way to discover its beauty. A mere collection of rustic white-stone buildings set back into the hills looking southwest over the broad Atlantic, complete with the traditional reddish tiled roofs. It sat amid the lush green oasis of orchards dotted around the circumference of the village with strong Moorish influences of its buildings. The entire setting nestled on a gentle slope on a large embankment nestled into the granite and limestone terraces of the surrounding hills. Its origins dated back the Roman Empire, founded as settlement; an outpost garrison to keep trade routes open running from the Atlantic coast northwards into the heart of Spain. Now it flourished as a small tourist diversion and populated mainly by native Spanish of Arabic descent.

It had a small circular centre; a focal point where its weekly fruit and vegetable markets eked a living from locals and frequent passing tourists. Sitting off to one side is the Church of Saint Augustus, a petit building those seated no more than 40 at a time. Perhaps the only remarkable feature within the entire structure sat high above the altar itself. A curved wall wrapped around the altar creating a natural reflector that carried the sound and the celebration of the mass without the need for amplification. Hidden beneath for nearly two centuries of dirt coated grime and neglect, and, only accidentally uncovered after a minor earth tremor shook the small hamlet in 1766. This caused much of the plaster behind the old altar to peel away. The semblance of a set of figures with faded colours emerged from the dust and debris.

On the upper section of this curved wall, laid a spectacular full-length copy of Leonardo's Last Supper fresco. More intriguing still, not one member of the parish had any recollection or knowledge of who the artist was. Suffice to say it was over nearly 300 years old, and given the relatively dry climate, the work remained in reasonably good condition. Other than every four to five years the local pastor, Father Miguel Sebastian a man of small but wiry stature nearly at the end of his seventh year, set about to garner up enough funds from the populace to have its entire surface cleaned with great care. It hadn't been touched in nearly five years. Now it was time. The elderly cleric had stashed enough funds to give his beloved church and its glorious mural, a timely makeover. Today, he paced back and forth outside his church looking towards the lower slopes, watching to see the van making its approach while barely concealing his annoyance. The cleaners were seldom good to their word, and nearly three hours late to begin work on the mural.

It was Monday and the work was slated to take over four days in time to unveil the new piece for the following Sunday's mass. Eventually, the cleaners arrived and under the caustic stare and gaze of Miguel Sebastian, work commenced on the painting. It would be worth the wait.

CERN. Some Time later.

That evening behind his large oak desk Felix Deveraux drummed his fingers against the phone, consumed with guilt. The latest news from the hospital was the same as the previous few days. No significant change to the condition of his friend and colleague. Worse, none of the medical team seemed to be able to pinpoint precisely the nature and depth of Du Pont's alarming condition. Their prognosis was vague suggesting they simply didn't understand what triggered his abrupt and profound changes taking place in his body. A series of red folders marked Classified lay on the desk. All the data that was classed as 'remarkable" from Euclid, included the medical report and findings of Paul Melrose episode, also included Professor Du Pont. Then there is the Shroud image itself, perhaps more troubling of them all. Added to what is neatly laid out in front of him, he began to assemble details that disturbed him further. Transcripts from Doctor Mochti of some remarkable revelations that emerged from Paul Melrose's condition while in care. He picked up the phone, and punched four digits and waited a few seconds. Carina Ambrosiana voice answered. He needed to have a conversation.

"I need to take a walk. Would you join me? Just the two of us. Ten minutes in my office. Grazie." Then hung up.

The walk was inside the Large Hadron Collider tunnel, a place often quite peaceful, although it was never empty. Work was always ongoing. Super cooled cryogenics, to near-vacuum conditions; to the enormous dipole magnets ensured an army of engineering and technologists worked to keep this colossus in good working order.

Carina expected his call. Her intuition was always tuned into Felix Deveraux moods and sometimes even his thoughts. Theirs was a comfortable relationship and he respected her as a first-class theoretician. He also knew, Carina Ambrosiana held deep beliefs about her faith and matters of conscience. She never forced or imposed her beliefs on any of those around her, but never reluctant to express her thoughts either. Now alone in the depths of their setting, he looked at her sideways trying to pick the right moment.

"Let's talk about this Shroud thing for a moment. Bear in mind, while I am a religious, but not a practitioner. He said.

She smiled and gave him a wry look. *He looks so drained; so vulnerable.*

You're not thinking of converting are you Felix? He just looked straight ahead hardly aware of her mild rebuke

"How in God's name does an elemental particle in a moment of decay manage to coalesce into a human face, Carina? Answer me that! Does any of your theoretical reasoning, even with these new messenger particles, even in our abstract constructions of elemental physics, has anything remotely suggested they create an image such as we have seen? What did you mean when you mentioned at our last meeting, this might be a bell-ringer?

Carina looked down for a few moments then glanced in both directions of the tunnel. "Where do I begin Felix? Firstly, there is nothing in any of the physics I know explains the image turning up on Fletcher's screen. We shouldn't be looking for a smoking gun. Some mathematical logic that explains how the image and face of Christ turned up in our data! She moved closer to him and held his stare. "When no science that we know of explains what any of this is, then perhaps it's time to consider another meaning"

"And how do you suppose a man of my background takes that on board?

She smiled at him for a few seconds

"Well, you could start, by keeping an open mind to...other possibilities!"

Just as he is about to respond, the clatter and sounds of a series of walkie-talkies burst into their conversation. They turn to see a series of small-mechanized golf carts come around the bend towards them. There was some shouting as the crackle of walkie-talkies was moving with speed to some location within the tunnel itself. On seeing the Director-General, the lead cart pulled up. One of the senior technicians, a French national jumped out recognizing Deveraux and spoke rapidly in French.

In a series of quick-fire questions and answers the two exchange comments, and then he looked anxiously at Carina. Something was off. She picked up some of the exchange something over in K section of the tunnel. Deveraux quickly nodded and grabbed Carina's hand and jumped onto the back of one of the carts. With that, they moved off again with pace in convoy around the tunnel with still a lot of crackle from the handheld radio units. From the agitated state of the driver and Deveraux's face, she knew it wasn't anything good.

The cart's electric motors hummed silently and raced off along the curvature of the tunnel. Somewhere deep within the complex a klaxon echoed.

"What is it, Felix? What's going on?

"Markings Carina! Markings in the tunnel". He said

In just over two minutes the cart slowed down and came around the bend to face a large group of technicians standing in a group clustered around a segment of the tunnel wall. A few small strobe lights were set up and directed towards one particular patch. When the carts slowed to a stop, the group parted. The most senior of the group immediately approached Deveraux and quickly the two spoke for a few seconds, again in French. He asked to be shown through the small gathering. They walked over to where the lights were set up and then stopped dead in their tracks. A silence fell as they all allowed Deveraux and Carina to move closer to what they were looking at. Sheer bewilderment spread within the group.

A large set of markings covered the entire wall and stretching up to the curvature of the tunnel ceiling itself. There was shock as seconds ticked away while everyone took in the large-scale markings etched into the very structure of the tunnel itself. Scored into the concrete almost completing the full arc of the wall curvature, a dark singular line etched interspaced with unknown symbols. It was highly symmetrical possessing precision and no more than sixty-five millimetres thick. Carina broke the silence.

"Those were made by heat! Look!! She said, pointing to the brown heat stains around each of the markings. They stretched some 10 meters vertically on the curved tunnel wall. The group studied the marks for a minute. Deveraux stood speechless. All eyes shifted from the wall towards him. He stood and gazed in utter amazement at the form and manner of the alignment. His mind raced and quickly made an on the spot decision. Turning he beamed at everyone with a disarming smile.

"So, we have some people with a sense of humour here, eh. Techno Art ! Perhaps. He laughed.

This lightened the tone momentarily and brought a few bursts of mild laughter from the group. As the group dispersed, he turned and gathered the more senior techies over to himself and Carina. He waited till most of the others were well out of earshot. He looked at them with steely eyes.

"This is a potential Security issue here. I want all roster records of shifts on my desk in the next hour. We will review all access rights to the main tunnel chamber. All staff who have access passes to the collider, I want to know how many, and any video footage that is available." None thought for a second the Director believed this was a prank done in bad taste. His demeanour however, suggested he was ready to vent someone's spleen over it. When the last of them left and they were alone, Deveraux walked to a small housing unit and sat and just looked at what was staring at him from the other side of the tunnel. He glanced over at Carina, who seemed distracted with her own questions.

"Do you think this was the work of someone here? She asked Walking a little along the wall she extended her arm. Her outstretched fingertips touched the markings.

"These are symbols of some kind, and this took a great amount of heat to generate these marks." She whispered.

Finally, Felix stood and took in this new twist that had imposed itself into his domain. He studied his surroundings for a few seconds as if marshalling all his intellectual capacity to deal with this latest piece of fantasy. Events were crowding into his world and distorting every perspective he held dear.

"Carina, we are going to have to create a whole new strategy about our work here". His face reflected a man in turmoil. Events were beginning to take on a sinister and troubling aspect.

"I don't know if Fletcher is going to make it. Carina. Now, this! I've no answers to any of this? What's next?

The Italian saw the strain. She was beyond any strain because she compartmentalized all her scientific reasoning into boxes of logic. Known laws, things that were fact, theoretical models, mathematical certainty, and what was left was a matter of personal belief and faith. Somehow, she was less perplexed than any of the others. She was also highly creative in her thinking, with a mind that permitted nonlinear assumptions. She walked over to Deveraux and took his hand.

"Just days before Fletcher's accident he called me to his office and shared much of his concerns, and confided his inner thoughts, Felix. He was convinced that everything that has occurred here in recent weeks is connected somehow. In fact, he was also quite fearful" Deveraux leaned back against the wall. He glanced around at the scene and tried to imagine what kind of aberration of energy and heat could have created such scoring.

"Where do we go with all of this? This madness. Carina. Where?

"I think there is someone who can help us get through this. She said softly

Andalusian Hills.

The work was completed ahead of time and the results were better than he had wished for. He gazed with a mixture of pride and satisfaction. Pride, because the result was superb. The images of the apostles were resplendent as they gazed down at him. Satisfied he was able to cut ten percent off the price for the complete job. Only the light from a few flickering candles added a warm glow to the inside of the tiny chapel. He took great solace and meaning from the work and what it represented, those final hours before the passion of Christ. He stood and cast his eyes in appreciation at the wall and its magnificent painting. He knew it well, had looked upon every day when he celebrated mass, he held in great awe. There was one other that he knew of, that surpassed this. Michelangelo's original in the church of Santa Maria Delle Grazie in Milan.

With a simple genuflection to the Altar, he turned to head for the small side door. He moved a few feet then paused in his tracks and turned one more time, and glanced up at the piece. He hesitated, his eyes focused with renewed intent at something that caught his attention, shrugged for a moment then reached for his small cane and shuffled for the door. As he made his way down the small aisle, in his head began to count.

"Uno, Dos, Tres, Trece! He stopped and turned, with faltering steps, he moved back down the centre aisle his eyes now firmly fixed on the old mural. As he did, he began to start from the left and count off each of the apostles sitting around the central figure at the table. Something was odd. He moved until he stood almost directly beneath the piece. With its renewed clarity of detail, without the years of dust, the figures were well defined and sharper. There was something peculiar. Something he missed or hadn't noticed before. He took his time to study the work. Its colours, though faded, still held a power. The entire edifice of his Christian beliefs and his life as a man of the cloth were enshrined in those events over 2,000 years earlier. All his articles of faith in his church were ordained and set in stone at that table.

"You will do this in memory of me..." This is my body.... Before the cock crows twice..." the setting of those seated in that room were to herald a cataclysmic shift in human history.

This image was different. He looked hard again in the poor lighting. Then, with a sharp intake of breath, it finally struck home. Thirteen Apostles!

Father Miguel Sebastian staggered back for a second and recounted everything for the third and fourth time. Dismay along with shock gripped him. Briskly he moved back and a stepped over to his alter and lifted one of the larger altar candles and lit it and struggled to keep his arm steady. Carefully, he manoeuvred and managed to stand balancing with his candlestick for extra lighting. Now, with the painstaking care, he got up close and studied the fresco in more detail. His gaze going from the image of each apostle one at a time, each one with their own part in that last of suppers. As he moved across the scene, each one familiar to him, each whose gospels he spent his entire priestly life studying and teaching to his flock. Peter, Andrew, and Mark he moved with care keeping his candle steady. With each one, he would utter a sentence to himself in Latin, then with a slight nod of deep respect moved to the next one. Each one had some meaning for him, even that of Judas Iscariot, then he came to a point, and stopped. His eyes squinted, and then his face froze and looked at something he had never seen before. His jaws dropped as he studied the image. Father Miguel Sebastian eventually made his way back to the seat and sank into it, gazing upwards completely mystified at his beloved mural. A face and image of a thirteenth apostle.

It was spring, the weather had shifted bringing changed with it cold fronts that moved in from the southwest, wet and windy weather with bursts of torrential rain over the Jura's. Inside CERN'S large conference centre over two hundred physicists sat through a presentation on the recent Euclid beta 8 experiments. The absence of Fletcher Du Pont brought a sombre note to events. Many present were deeply indebted to Du Pont's influence on their career paths. His absence only served to make the entire event more intense. Du Pont's team remained subdued aware his life hung in the balance. It was up to Deveraux, who eventually brought the session to a close. His own mood darkened by the unwelcome and sinister appearance of markings in the LHC structure.

Elsewhere at Sal Madere, the mood was akin to a haunting. Almost everything was on-hold. The house normally exuded vibrant energy, now it became a refuge. Claudine retreated into a world of solitude and personal isolation trying to avoid entertaining her worst fears. Around her, their two daughters sat, both reading trying desperately to find a distraction from their private fears. Paul Melrose and her brother Francois Burgoyne sat in Du Pont's private study. The near shocking images of her husband and his condition almost sucked the life out of Claudine. In Du Pont's private study, the mood was more sanguine. Paul Melrose sat cross-legged on a large circular rug on the wooden floor surrounded by sheets of some of his own work and data from Euclid. In the corner, the Jesuit sat at Du Pont's desk immersed in some notes he had scribbled. In front of him lay the contents of a folder that Claudine had shared with him sometime earlier. Disturbing things that heightened his sense of foreboding for his brother in law. He paused his reading, and lowered his glasses and reached and picked up the folder then took a bundle of sheets, and selected the image of the Shroud and studied it. He glanced down at the younger man sitting on the floor, noting how restless Melrose was.

"Paul, there is something I'd like to ask?

"Sure Francois, go-ahead

"You've been pre-occupied with those sheets; I couldn't help but notice and I wondered if they were important some way that connects everything. Those are yours aren't they, your calculations. This is the material you produced in the hospital if I'm not mistaken".

For a few seconds, the mood became tense. Francois knew it troubled the younger man. Something was eating at him and the older man sensed it. Melrose got up and moved to a chair and sat.

"Some of these calculations Francois, are totally new derivations. There are equations here that defy anything I have done before. I don't know how I came to produce them!

"Really! That is very strange.

'Much of these Francois are of a higher order of complexity, beyond anything I have done to date. Beyond even the finest minds in CERN. I've no idea how I managed any of it.

Francois removed his glasses and laid them on the desk, leaned back in the armchair.

"What exactly are they about. What do they suggest?

Melrose pursed his lips.

"This work goes beyond Riemannian thinking. It's a concept that deals with space-time geometry. Curvature. Space and time were seen as a single unified field. It encompasses more than 3 dimensions of space, possibly much more, and then Time. My calculations here, suggests how some new elements can be proven. More dimensions exist buried deep within the atomic nature of matter. What these calculations describe are almost…

"Almost what ? Burgoyne whispered.

"Existential, Francois.

Both left the idea linger for a few seconds.

"Sounds remarkable! When you say curvature. Is that what I think it means. Space and time have a shape?

"Yes, but we still have to find a formal treatment in equations. It's still an abstract idea. If I can follow where some of these equations are going, space-time curvature can be proven to exist in reality in certain conditions. At a very deep level there is the force-carrying particle that may exhibit a characteristic that…

He stopped, unable to say out loud what he was suggesting.

"Exhibit what? I promise I won't laugh."

Melrose relaxed and smiled. The conversation acted as a welcome distraction.

"Well, it might just be possible, that there is some new class of particle. One that carried force. This is not unusual in experimental physics. We have identified certain particles that transmit force. But now, there may be some new mysterious particle that we've never imagined existed in nature…*A Receptor*! He whispered.

Francois said nothing trying to understand what he was hearing.

"What does that mean?

"A Receptor Particle, Francois. Something, which has never been heard of. However, if you piece some of this material here it suggests the existence of some unknown elemental entity buried deep within atomic physics that responds to a frequency that is extremely delicate and almost impossible to detect. In other words, my friend, a particle, we have never dreamed of that responds to human thought".

"*Responds to human thought*! Francois whispered

"Yes, A particle so exotic with a property to pick up on human brain frequencies expressed as thoughts like a receptor and if that were true, well…

"A strange notion my friend coming from a physicist. It sounds very bizarre.

"You'd be stunned, Francois how bizarre the quantum world of particles is. Everything is a flux of probabilities. Uncertainty rules the roost. Particles are often not what they appear to be at that scale. Yet, at our reality and scale the world and everything about it is normal. It's highly deterministic and yet at the sub-atomic level nothing is absolutely certain. It's a highly probabilistic place"

"That's… unbelievable Paul!

"Within some of these equations, there are new derivations that prove that not only do we exist in a curved space dimension but also even time itself gets distorted".

He lifted one of his sheets and folded it into a "U" shape.

"Some of this work here Francois formalizes in these equations an explanation of how this can be proven. You know what that means. It means linear distances become irrelevant in curved space-time. Not only would it be possible to travel to places of great distance in our cosmos, but also experience alternative time dimensions all through curved space-time geometry.'

The Jesuit leaned forward and picked up the Shroud image and held it. He reached and pulled the computer-generated a graphic of the same image found on Du Pont's terminal.

"Do any of your equations explain something like this? He asked holding up both images.

"Not a chance! That's entirely off-the-map. It's a complete mystery, Francois".

Just as the conversation moved towards more penetrating aspects around the image, the mood is broken by a gentle tap on the study door as Denise stuck her head in.

Paul, it's the Centre. Professor Deveraux for you. She said holding out the phone.

"Professor! Melrose said

He listened for a few moments then looked at the priest. His face turned serious.

"When was this discovered? Section! His face became taught.

"Caused by heat. That's impossible that's just not. That cannot happen! "I'm on my way. There in less than an hour."

He pressed the terminate button and looked at the phone for a few seconds. Then he turned to the Francois.

'Francois, you asked a lot of questions on what we do in CERN. Well, here's your chance. Fancy a ride into the heart of physics. I am going to the complex right now. Want to join me? I think you'd find this incredible.

The Jesuit sat up.

"Well if you think I might be of...

"You might be the only one left around here with some means of dealing with absurdities. Melrose retorted

He moved to leave quickly bundling all his notes into a single tidy pile. He turned to the Jesuit.

"Francois, I don't know why I am saying this, but I am deeply glad you are here. Come. I'll explain on the way' He said, reaching for the keys to his Morgan.

It's a little over an hour by the time they reach the CERN complex. It was just after 4.15pm when they reached their destination. No experiments were running, and none were scheduled for the next 10 days.

Once underground, it wasn't until they moved closer into the circle of lighting did the enormity of the situation became apparent. Teams were still carrying out checks to the surrounding walls.

"Good God! The Jesuit said. He stared at the walls and turned his head to follow the complete impact around the circumference of the tunnel wall. Melrose stood with his hand on his hips absorbed in the almost surreal scene. Francois removed his raincoat and left it to one side. He cast a strange, if not misplaced figure his black habit and silver chain and crucifix. Melrose stared quietly taking everything in. The markings were nothing short of mesmeric, spanning the entire arch of the tunnel wall. The scorch marks were a series of constructs that suggested form and purpose.

"Does this suggest any kind of scientific context to you? Francois whispered

'This has to be the mother of all absurdities, Francois". Melrose gasped

The marks were precise in shape with sharply defined angles. The dominant mark comprised of something approaching a U shape with symbols superimposed within a structure. Each of the others was disjointed shapes. All were and aligned in a semi-circular pattern from one side of the tunnel wall up across the ceiling and down the opposing side. Melrose walked to the wall and looked closer. He recalled what Felix Deveraux mentioned as to the origin, seemed to be undoubtedly heat. From what he was looking at there was little doubt heat was the cause. Francois moved to the other side of the tunnel. Everything he saw and the reactions of others, told him sinister forces were at work.

Melrose then noticed something that wasn't initially apparent. Just below where the line ended and barely noticeable, was a symbol. They both leaned closer to see the detail, his eyes adjusted to the light. What he saw made his blood run cold. He stared almost transfixed at a symbol he knew well, encountered it much of his theoretical work and as famous as any symbol in the whole mathematical arsenal. The unmistakable symbol for infinity ∞ stared back at him.

"It's the same Paul, on the other end of the line on the opposite side. Francois said.

The young Physicist climbed over the small railing to the other side.

"Is this serious, as I suspect it is?

"Yes. Melrose barely answered. This is no mishap or accident, Francois! There is some guiding mind at work. There is precision here, it's a puzzle. We're dealing here with a collection of marks, that's all tied into what's happening elsewhere. He struggled to maintain some composure.

"You can't be sure of that Paul. Now relax."

"Look, do you see these two symbols at each end of this whole arc - they're perfectly aligned opposite to each other. These infinity symbols have a special context in my work, and now they are positioned in this tunnel exactly in positions that line up in polar opposites to each other."

"Are you serious! How can I relax? It's all too...ordered. Francois. It's almost as if they're arranged. His agitation was starting to grow. Reaching out he griped the Jesuit's arms.

"Listen to me, Francois. Listen to me, please. This is becoming sinister! This is not science this, is. *unnatural*. There is some malevolent force at work here"

Francois looked and saw panic. His own demeanour remained calm yet saw enough not to dismiss anything. Things here were indeed strange. There were no disputing matters that were anything but normal. 'Right! I think we have seen enough for now. Let's go somewhere where we can think' He said.

Reflecting on what he had just seen, he glanced over at the face of the troubled young man sitting next to him. He looked tense.

"You think this is all quite amusing don't you, Francois. Melrose said casting him a glare

"Well, only some parts. I think it's wonderful what you do here. Really. To see your work with your equations, your experiments, your deep theories, such as these particles, and how they behave and yes even your curved what? Space...

"Space-Time geometry. Melrose replied

"Indeed! It's marvellous at the ingenuity of people like you. To see things in a more penetrating way. To view this world of ours as... How was it, you explained in the study with that piece of paper and it's folding of space. Marvellous! He said.

"It's because we follow on from the work of great minds from the past, Francois. Brilliant minds. Men who made that inspirational step into new ways of thinking'

"Like this fellow... Riemann. Francois joked. "See! I do listen even for an old priest.

"That's right Francois, like George Bernhard Riemann a Mathematician. Great thinkers of their age.

"And these places, where we are now. These are the new Temples. Temples on which the alters of science pay homage' He teased.

Melrose smiled back at his companion.

"Are you poking fun at us again?

"Not at all! Merely an observer. Science can stand the occasional critique. Even if it's from a man whose beliefs go back to another age. Seriously young man, these are the new temples of science and exploration. Look at this place even your churches are curved into rock. Everything here is curved, a tribute no doubt to this chap Riemann or whatever.

Melrose laughed at the subtle way the man sitting next to him challenged much of what he stood for. For all of that, the cleric possessed great charisma and charm and found intriguing ways to poke fun at some of the most abstract aspects of theoretical physics. As they arrived at the elevator. The Jesuit looked about and stopped. Melrose sat in the cart, almost motionless, fixed with an expression on his face. There was no longer humour but a face full of intensity. There was composure but he became deathly quiet.

"What is it? What's wrong? He asked.

Melrose stood. Slowly he got up and moved toward the older man.

"What was it you said? Everything here is curved.

Jesus, Francois.! Those markings.! Whatever there meant to depict. They're on a curved surface. The tunnel itself is curved. The choice of location- to have these appear maybe no accident, but a pointer to something that connects to Fletcher! Melrose's voice became elevated. We need to study these markings more. It's a message Francois! This is some kind of message which helps explain all these happenings here!

"I don't follow. What are you talking about?

'These bizarre calculations of mine in the hospital were mainly in Riemann's field of Space-Time curvature, an area I am not familiar with yet I produced these derived equations. Now in this very tunnel where we stand markings appear in some strange context that happens to be played out on a curved structure. Arranged with some level of precision, of which curvature seemed to have significance. This is way beyond chance. Everything about Riemannian geometry dealt with space-time as a warped curvature. I think... these markings... No! I know, Francois. These markings and their location have meaning. We have to figure out what these are? What do they mean?

His voice betrayed the strain that has been building up inside. Paul stared at the older man. Was he the only one who was starting to assemble a picture within which might explain some of the disturbing events? The return journey back to Sal Madere was less frantic though the mood in the car was subdued. The Jesuit allowed the journey time to give them both the chance to digest all that Melrose was suggesting. He was a simple priest, not a physicist, but from what he knew already coupled with what he saw earlier in the LHC tunnel did not bode well. More relevant was what the young man next to him was thinking. The choice of location with its curved setting along with these markings all linked to a perverse logic. Riemannian geometry aside, the whole convergence of events was deeply troubling. Even sinister. Melrose looked across at his passenger and felt somewhat sorry for him. He knew that tensions between himself and his sister were far from comfortable. Denise on the other hand worshiped her uncle; he was like a spiritual anchor to her in particular, despite his unflinching stance on scriptural teachings.

"I understand you speak a little Hebrew, Francois? Melrose finally asked.

It caught the older man off-guard. He smiled. He could guess where this was going.

"Yes, a little. Just enough to get by, if I am ever stranded in Israel.

"Denise mentioned you also speak a little of the more ancient tongues?

The Jesuit glanced over at him.

"Indeed. I speak and read a little Aramaic. Why do you ask?

"I just wondered if you had heard any of the tapes from my... He left unfinished.

"Yes, I have. I think Fletcher may have heard only a small portion. Francois smiled

That's it". Melrose quipped

"Any thoughts on what was on it?

"Lots! All of them questions. A most unsettling set of events, my son."

Melrose' mind returned to the markings in the tunnel complex. He reflected on their structure and alignment on the curved walls. Four distinctive marks each with its own particular structure, and position. As he assembled the images in his head, somehow each of the individual marks had a connection with each other. The first set of markings were more intricate. They possessed geometry. U-shaped structure depicting again, a curved form. Then when he considered all of the others, each with a simple alignment of intersecting lines, all-encompassing 3-dimensional axis. An idea was beginning to take shape. The intricate patterns suggested a hidden or obscure message that carried a clue. In isolation these markings meant nothing. However, he could see all five images within a single framework. Problem was, what they meant. Curved space-time and its possibilities were well understood by the young physicist.

"You're Anglican, Paul yes? Francois asked

"Yes. Not practiced for some time.

Why do you ask?

Do you know what these words mean, as a matter of interest? "...Eloi, Eloi, lama Sabathtani! He enunciated with reverence.

Melrose stared ahead, slowly mouthing the sound to himself. "Fraid not Francois! Sounds Arabic or some sort. What is it"?

"Well, young man for what its worth. It's not Arabic. It's an old tongue, not spoken in nearly two thousand years. It's Jewish in origin, but its neither Hebrew nor Yiddish for that matter. It's Aramaic".

Melrose looked sideways at his passenger.

"Is that from one of my tapes that Doctor Mochti recorded?

"Indeed, it is, and what's interesting is the choice of words. What it represents?

Melrose shifted gear as they made their way through some small sharp bends through wooded hillsides and twisting narrow lanes. A silence settled until they moved onto a less demanding stretch of road.

"Go on Francois. Don't stop now. I know I'm supposed to have said these words but it means nothing.

"Yes, yes! I know Paul. Don't worry. I'm not giving you a hard time."

A few moments passed.

"Those words are almost sacred to us Christians. Someone, not much older than you, uttered them in the depths of despair and agony. They mean *Father, father, why hast doth forsaken me.* They're almost the very last words spoken by Jesus Christ, moments before his death, impaled on a wooden cross"

Melrose's face appeared pale as he took in the tone the man sitting next to him.

"Yes, my son. Words that you pronounced with near-perfect diction some weeks back when you were ill. And, as you can imagine not only did you not speak this obscure language, but given its historical context we were all spellbound."

Melrose remained quiet for a while. "Francois, there is one more thing I need to mention. Denise and I would like you to meet with someone. My doctor, Benjamin Mochti, and I think it would be a good idea if that happened soon.'

Francois sat forward. They would soon be arriving at Sal Madere and he had a feeling that this was not something dreamt up on the spur of the moment.

"Any particular reason?

"It's a feeling Francois. I'm beginning to think there is some kind of convergence taking place here. Something that's beyond the boundaries of our thinking. None of this is coincidental and I'm getting more fearful with each passing day Francois. And it's not just me.

Moments later after parking his Morgan at the residence, Melrose, and Burgoyne find their way to the living room. Claudine was coiled up on one of the settee's trying to get some needed sleep. Denise was elsewhere drumming up some food. She walked into the living room when she heard the men's voices. She went and took Paul in her arms and then kissed him gently. Turning she went to her uncle and hugged him.

"What was the big emergency about? Anything serious?

"Well, we're not sure? We should get some rest first. Francois said.

Melrose enquired if the was any fresh news from the hospital.

"His condition was stable, but no change, Denise said

After some further comments on medical bulletins from the medical centre, they settled down and munch their way through a plate of sandwiches and a fresh pot of coffee. Melrose then excused himself from the family and retired into Du Pont's private study. He sat and began to reproduce all the markings he saw in the tunnel. Recalling his attention and eye for detail, he carefully sketched each one of the markings on a separate sheet. Meanwhile, in the living room, Francois paced around bringing his niece up to date on events back at the CERN complex. Claudine turned and twisted on the settee, but remained asleep.

"You look tired Denise."

"I'm not like Mom. Francois. She can switch off. I can't!

"Has she slept long?

"Just restless fits and starts, but she is remarkable. She has great strength, like you."

She stood, and moved to cover her mother with the wool blanket over her shoulders and then went and kissed the top of his head, and excused herself. When she entered the study, Melrose was sitting on the floor absorbed with a series of his drawings spread around him like someone reading a set of tarot cards. He got up and gently wrapped his arms around her. They held each other closely letting each other's body contact ease the stresses of recent events. She gently took his face in her hands and kissed him longingly.

His body responded as he felt her respond to him. Then he pulled back and looked deeply into her eyes seeing nothing but adoring love and something else.

That look of uncertainty. He never saw that in her before. Their love was deep and any doubts he had as to their future was gone. He simply adored Denise Du Pont, and nothing would ever change that. She just filled his whole being with completeness and joy that he thought only existed in romance novels. He gently moved her over to one of the armchairs in the study and sat down. She moved and sat on his knees and draped her arms around his neck. She looked at him and smiled. With gentleness and delicate touch, she traced her finger across his face covering the contours of his cheekbones letting the moment of intimacy envelope their closeness and bond. He took her face in one hand and ran his other through her short hair.

"You're not about to propose to me, are you? That's my job".

"Do you love me? She whispered. The smile was gone.

The uncertainty was there again. He took both her hands in his and held them tightly and returned the stare for a few seconds.

"With all my heart. I love you; Denise Du Pont and I want to spend the rest of my life sharing it with you. He said

"*With us*!

He was about to respond, then stopped.

With us my Love. She repeated slowly. Then she wrapped her arms around him and whispered in his ear.

Us! You will spend the rest of our day's together sweetheart. 'I'm pregnant"

112

CHAPTER THIRTEEN

The Wilderness of Judea.

The event lasted no more than ten to fifteen seconds in duration. The release of hidden unnatural disturbances forced the very fabric of the space in front of him to part like a curtain that suddenly ruptured out of nowhere. The manifestation of the creature of sublime beauty was like nothing the scientist could have imagined. Traveller gazed on the impossible scene as an explosion of colour of white light erupted from nowhere and engulfed his entire surroundings with a glow of energy. He tried to cry out. He staggered backward and braced himself against the large outcrop of rock. The powerful radiant light that consumed the creature's entire stature began to subside. A surge of energy briefly passed outwards and touched everything in its path. Traveller felt its energy pass through him and then the light gradually faded. Then the spirit entity altered and began to transform itself and gradually assume human form. Within seconds it stood only some feet away standing in height similar to him. In one simple movement, he moved towards him and extended his hand.

"It is, so good to greet you, good friend. I am greatly honoured for this task.

Traveller slowly extended his hand.

"I am a simple man. I know nothing of all of this? These mysterious things!

As soon as their hands touched, a great surge of power passed through him, followed by an enveloping sense of comfort, a peace filling him with courage.

"I am one of God's great Spirits of Fortitude. I instil and fill you mortals with great Courage, and Belief in all things. There are a great many of us in our realm, we are endowed with gifts to bestow to all you mortals".

He then extended his arm toward the surrounding rock and a luminous blue light of such intensity emanated from his arm and formed a small rectangular shape on the rock surface. Followed by a pulse of heat around that part of the rock causing the stone face itself to ripple. An act that suggested the entity had accessed and summoned unseen power that pulverized rock. Traveller raised his hands to shield his eyes.

"You will begin to learn new things Traveller, new Truths for your age. Truths that will shake your world to its foundations. Behold the great Book of Seals. The work and history of all Creation, you are indeed, truly favoured in this task.

As the entity spoke, a great shape began to form surrounded by an effervescent- golden light of great purity. A book began to appear. Pages began to flutter, cream-colored parchments, and then with great speed, all the pages started to fill with text in silver and deep red as written by some mystical and powerful scribe. Its cover then began to manifest a series of gilded gold-leafed wings. In an instant Traveller's eyes are drawn to this image that he knows. From deep inside his being he stared at the shape of an image that defined his past. His mind raced to connect this simple single image that draws him to the past.

A past that started to emerge within his consciousness. The symbol ∞ traced itself across the cover of the book and into his memory. His sense of time is uncertain while the passage of time itself became meaningless, he fell into sleep.

A fire burned amidst a circle of stones and he then heard footsteps draw closer. A figure came from the shadows carrying a small basket. He placed them near the fire. Reaching into the baskets he took food, some assortment of bread, and fruit. In another basket, he smelt the aroma of cooked meat, goat meat. The baskets were laid out on the ground in front of him, and a gesture with a friendly face.

"Eat, my friend, you need nourishment"

It took Traveller a few seconds to recognise the man. The apparition seemed to possess the ability to take on the appearance of a mortal with all its normal attributes. He reached into one of the baskets and grabbed one of the portions of bread and some of the pieces of meat. He began to eat, allowing the time to compose him and try marshal some level of awareness of what was unfolding and try to assert himself with this stranger who calls himself ‚Messenger.

His appearance is one of great bearing his clothing was immaculate. It consisted of a long cream-colored garment tied in the middle by a brown leather belt. His sandals are of the finest animal skin, laced with strips of woven animal hair. Most striking of all is his face and skin. He appeared to possess flawless olive skin almost ebony in colour and radiant grey eyes that seemed to exude great warmth toward him There was also a knowing about him. Finally, when he could feel at ease, Traveller reached out with one of the baskets and offered the other some food. Messenger smiled his entire face blossomed into a glow of delight. A bridge of trust began to open up. He took the food and thanked him.

"Talk to me Traveller! You must have questions?" He asked gently.

It was then Traveller noticed sitting on top of one of the rocks a beautiful leather-canvas covered thick book nearly a full meter in length. He got to his feet and walked slowly over to the rock. Its cover was covered with symbols wrapped inside a circle of overlapping wings. Large gold-embroidered Angles wings formed a circle over the entire surface of the cover as if enveloping the symbolic images inside a cocoon of knowledge. He traced his fingers with the barest of touches almost as an act of reverence. Running his hand across the infinity symbol sensing the power it represented.

Messenger studied him watching his reactions and allowing his companion the moment to himself. Little was said. Traveller fixed on the symbols noticing numerous smaller scripts with objects, circular in shape, intertwined into connecting other objects represented by circles that were interlocked with more circles. Looking across the fire he saw the other study him with some compassion.

"The Book of Seals? He asked. Similarly, the markings on this book had a familiarity. This man opposite him had spoken earlier of his past. A past that defied every effort to recall yet this creature mentioned a past from another realm.

"Tell me Messenger, who are you? I need to understand".

Messenger stood and walked to the fire.

"I will explain my friend but first let me show you".

Without any warning- over the flickering flames of the small fire, a mist began to form. As if by magic it hovered just out of reach of the tips of the flames. The mist began to condense into a small bright sphere that spun at high speed around him. Quickly an aura of light formed about the small sphere circulating in an elliptical pattern. Within seconds a second elliptical pattern formed and similar to the other its speed gathered momentum till its speed appeared like a continuous burst of energy. The image is quite small but sat over the fire. Both elliptical paths began to alter their pattern till they are tilted as polar opposites encasing the tiny sphere in its centre. Traveller gasped as he instantly saw something he recognized. The powerful icon of the atom and its nucleus take shape.

Its familiarity shocked him. Emerging from the shadows of the rocks was his missing companion. His haggard appearance caught him off guard. He was about to say something to break the silence then stopped. What happened next was completely unexpected. Messenger turned and in one graceful gesture turned towards the other figure and bowed before him. It was an act of obedience from one to the other. Traveller paused, uncertain of the significance of what he had just witnessed. His companion's entire face was covered with dry perspiration like a man in the depths of some mortal dread. There was anguish, his body shook and trembled, his eyes dilated with near panic.

'What is it, my friend? What's wrong? Traveller said

"You will help me, yes? The other trembled.

"Yes, of course, I will help you. Why are you so frightened?

"You will keep true to me, my story. He asked

"Keep True! What do you mean? Keep true to what! Tell me?

Seconds passed.

"My tormentors are everywhere. They invade my every thought. I have no peace. It's nearly forty days. They have almost taken my soul and they mock everything that I hold precious. It hasn't stopped even during daylight. Taunting me with unspeakable tongues. At night I can see them. There are many of them. Each taking turns twisting untruths and false meanings from my own beliefs and always-different images. Horrific ungodly images"

Traveller stepped back and gazed at the tortured soul in front of him.

"What kind of tormentors? What images?

From nowhere deep inside him, some semblance of familiarity began to register. The fleeting image of a face that he has seen before. The expression was a face that felt everything within the human character. A face, which saw potential in all mortals. Now, he has become one of them also to feel and know fear .

"My face! You have seen it before?

Then Traveller hesitated and noticed his companion's attention shift. He followed his gaze. Turning slowly around- he froze. Nothing could prepare him for the scene that unfolded behind him. Standing some distance away but towering over them were a group of winged creature's part human part animal. They seemed suspended as if held from making contact with the ground by some mystical force. They were devoid of skin tone or colour. Their faces lifeless, but their eyes were large and completely round like birds of prey. Their upper part of their skull was exposed, wherein some of the creatures a single horn protruded from the top of the head.

Others held a grimace that revealed fangs curved teeth that ran down outside a deformed bone structure. On one, a large set of ribbed tailbones extended out of their backs on which animal fur grew the full length of its back. As they opened their mouths their grotesque appearance became more pronounced as the nostrils filled with toxic stultifying acrid smoke. Then in unison, they leaned forward and stretched their upper bodies like birds reaching out from a perch they hissed a stream of sounds. Sounds of voices that have lost all human origin. It's a screeching mixture of animal baying and words barely audible.

"Look! It's the delusional one. He is powerless. He is purposeless. He is abandoned! He is consumed by fantasy and without authority. He is a mirror of an empty ego. Useless!"

Just as one of them moved to advance to get closer, a powerful sonic rumble ripped through the surrounding air. A figure began to materialize into space between them. A powerful angelic creature appeared. With one sweep of his arm, a bolt of light arched outwards across the ground in front of them scorching and vaporizing the very air around the creatures. Amid screams of sheer terror, the dark entities recoiled as they see the arrival of one of the most potent of all spirit beings of the realm. The epitome of everything they feared most, an Archangel.

A towering winged creature carrying a lance of pure gold, attired in silver breastplate covering all his upper body. Rather than flowing long hair, a gold band ran around his forehead and his dark hair was tied into a long-braided ponytail. The entire terrain, on which the two lonely mortals sat, shook violently as the debased creatures become engulfed in a blinding radiant light.

He stood with complete authority over everything he gazed upon. Traveller had counted up to twenty of the creatures, now huddled together. The lance was raised, and as if summoning a hidden power, he spun it into a complete circle. Almost in an instant, the anguished cries of the entire group of hideous forms erupted into jolting convulsing screams of terror as their grotesque bodies crumbled and began to dissolve before the intensity of the light attended their destruction. Everything physical in the immediate area resonated and vibrated as the energy from this warrior being washed over them before abating. In seconds the fusion of light intensity became suffused and finally dimmed to a glow around his physique.

Then to the amazement of the near stricken Traveller, the being standing before them did not speak, but in one single gesture turned and faced his nomadic companion next to him. Raising his lance in one outstretched arm he bowed down in an act of great respect and submission. He placed his other hand across over his breastplate and then made a gesture as if bestowing and honouring someone of great importance. His countenance looked upward and closed his eyes, began to dissolve and dematerialize before them. Traveller slumped to his knees dumbstruck letting the moment pass, then gave his companion a look. He noticed the trembling has stopped. Now he knew something else. Nothing appeared to be what it seemed. Never did such things cause him to consider his cave companion nothing more than a wandering nomad. A man nonetheless possessing a strange power of presence an unspoken authority of powerful physical strength yet, vulnerable.

His weakness cloaked something else. Possession of sharp intellect shown through hazel brown eyes concentrated now all their intensity on him across the flickering flames of the crackling fire. Shadows danced across the gaunt haunted face staring at the flames. The eyes soften.

"What is it you wish to ask good friend? He asked softly

"What were those? Creatures! Where did they come from?

"They're not of this world, but a darker place. His companion said.

"They come from the Abyss. From the very depths of the Abyss.

Regaining some degree of composure Traveller leaned forward and stared at the man sitting across from him.

"Abyss! What is that? Before you tell me anything my friend. Who are you? What do I call you? The howling of distant animals ceased and quietness of the Judean night settled about them.

"I am known as *Yeshua*. I am a craftsman from a village north of here in Galilee".

Traveller simply nodded knowing this was no nomad. He was in the presence of a man who was an enigma, and his interest in his companion took a whole new dimension. Looking carefully he tried to discern anything about him that suggested someone with a secret. Having witnessed with his own eyes the arrival of supernatural beings with unearthly powers and angelic forms that could transform themselves and wield unnatural forces. Powers that could harness and cause light to melt and dissolve solid rock at their command. Yet, they viewed and responded with great deference to the one before him. Then, there were the hideous ones who taunted him with such venom and utter contempt

"These creatures from this Abyss? What are you to them? Why do they cause you so much fear?

"I will tell you more my friend if you will travel some of the way of my journey with me. We have much to learn and understand each other. Remember what I said to you when we first meet. I asked that you be strong, and have some faith".

Traveller noticed the night mysteriously started to fade as the first light of the new day began to fill the sky to the east.

"What do I call *you*, my friend? Do you have a craft? He asked Traveller.

Traveller became wary and anxious. His companion was held in great esteem, and one of immense mysterious authority. A simple man, but there was more, much more to this most mysterious of men.

"I can't remember what it is, I do. He said. Standing, he nervously moved a few steps away and gazed into the Judean landscape. A vast sea of sand and rolling hills opened out before him.

Without any warning, the space-time conjecture moved in new directions for the physicist of the 21st century. Now wrapped within an independent existence he morphed into a reality that appeared normal to him. Everything he touched, heard and tasted, told him unconditionally that he is a nomadic traveller. He took everything for granted.

In reality, an uncharted fabric of the space-time conjecture enabled him to experience a four-dimensional existence wrapped and folded inside an alternative dimensional space that now permitted the notion of Time to be compressed and elongated in ways known only to beings of a higher realm. To allow some appreciation of his circumstances and lift some of the veil that cloaked his memory, sudden images exploded in his head.

At first, a colossus of a cloud rising and reaching into the heavens in the shape of a mushroom. Then faces of people with different attire and clothing flashed across his cognitive senses. With his eyes closed other images of another time stalked his memory. Symbols and numbers float past, along with shimmering faces. Out of nowhere in the near distant horizon, something strange unfolded. At first, it appeared like a mirage that caused the entire landscape of barren wilderness to ripple as if its composition was no longer a substance of solid matter.

Instead, as far as his eyes could see the landscape began to do something that mesmerized him. The distant horizon rose up and began to fold and bend by some unfathomable power. It slowly reshaped the immediate rocky landscape and commenced to rotate, causing everything within the fabric of the land stretching outwards for the horizon to begin to distort and ripple like the surface of the sea. Then everything around his immediate location shifted and began to move off in the direction of the horizon as if the entire physical reality was being folded and rolled into a colossal tube. The scene crackled and resonated by a powerful sonic rumble as the fabric of the entire scene transcended any known law of nature.

It was if the essence of all physical reality ruptured within an invisible vibrating plane. A voice suddenly called out.

"Behold the workings of all Existence and the *Material Creation* my friend."

The man of science spun round to see the enigmatic Yeshua, standing some distance behind him. His ragged appearance contrasted with the dramatic alteration of their surroundings. Standing to his right was, Messenger, head bowed in a posture of silent meditation and submission. A peel of thunder rolled across the tapestry of the entire space ricocheting off in all directions causing entire surface of the desolate wilderness to tremble and contort. What was once the distant horizon now rose hundreds of feet upwards into the heavens. As they took in the vision unfold all around them, a spark of white light erupted from a tiny prism that floated in the emptiness of the void, spewing light of thousands of colours outwards extended beyond the limits of their visual senses. Instantly these colours fused and took shape into a beautiful orb that slowly turned from its golden sheen, into a deep blue sphere. It began to shrink in the middle causing both the upper and lower parts to expand rapidly outwards and recreate a total transformation of one reality into a vastly different vision.

An alternate reality unfolded. Exploding outwards in a vivid show of white light, revealing *himself* standing deep inside a tube of light of great intensity. A wall of mathematical scripts emerged and passed before him, with certain symbolic constants glow to suggest some obscure importance. A diagrammatic image burst open showing an intricate geometric object that unfurled revealing an inner-structure, which collapsed into a single undulating surface that began to stretch with immeasurable speed. Traveller witnessed a vision. Within its vortex he sees himself centred within multiple rings of light. Followed quickly by a shocking emergence of a much younger man vaguely familiar to him convulsing amid scripts of writing. It lasts only seconds, to be replaced with silence, and then an image of a man, lying on a surface, surrounded by men. The image moved towards him unhindered to float and contour itself around where they are standing. His gaze was drawn to the face and instantly recognizes an almost mirror reflection of himself. Awestruck, he stared at aspects of the imagery as it started to mirror events his mind began to understand.

Deep within his consciousness sparked a recognition that ignites his faltering memory. His transference from a place in time to another is conveyed and replicated with startling clarity and power. Following rapidly, he saw the unlocking of pages containing secrets from the Book of Seals. By some unknown authority he had survived to glimpse into the miracle of creation. He turned only to stare into the face of his companion. Then, as if time froze the features of his companion facial image burned into realisation. It's a face that that has haunted him from another time.

A face of a dead man. The fog of memory began to lift. Time restoration began to reconcile stored memories of the past to the new reality he found himself. Several minutes passed as Du Pont sat gripped with searing anxiety. Slowly his thoughts and tears struggle to find reasoning with the circumstances of his altered existence. He shook uncontrollably unable to speak. Messenger sat next to him. As a powerful spirit, he commenced exuding all his power to strengthen and infuse his friend. Within seconds Du Pont experienced an overwhelming stillness throughout his body.

"Everything you have witnessed has a purpose. Messenger said.

His personal history, his family, and his former existence slowly began to reassert themselves. The realisation of his circumstances unfolded and the full impact of his transition to an alternate realm dawned on him.

Oh, dear, God! This is death! Is this what it feels to die. He gasped

Purpose! What purpose is served here? I don't belong here. This is another age! What am I doing here? I call you Messenger! How is any of this possible? His voice quivered

"You are not dead my friend.

"Please! What name do I call you? Du Pont pleaded.

Without warning, Messenger raised his hands out wide and commenced a transformation into a stunning manifestation into his former incarnation. Morphing into the towering creature as he first appeared, light emanated around his figure, large gold-coloured wings extended out and his entire form radiated a power outward causing a shivering sensation pass through the man of science. He stood transfixed at the magnificence of the creature before him. There was also no longer any fear only assurance.

"From all I know… we'd imagined you must be an Angel. Is… that what you are?

"Indeed Traveller. I am a Seraphim. I am one of God's good spirits. I am, Etaanus. I am also the keeper of the Book of Seals, the source of all wisdom.

The physicist just stared across the barren wilderness. Etaanus clasped in his arms around the Book of Seals.

"This transformation from your world and your altered existence is not permanent, so be not alarmed. I might mention also, during your transformation to this state, we altered some infirmities within your mortal body. We Seraphim's are the alchemists in the higher realms"

Du Pont noticed something that escaped his attention up to now. It intrigued him. He could hear clearly what was been said, but the Etaanus lips or mouth hardly moved. Then after a few seconds the full realisation of what was happening dawned on him. Etaanus, the Messenger in his full manifestation was communicating directly to his thoughts, through telepathy. This powerful spirit made himself understood by an extension of his thoughts demonstrating a remarkable existence where speech was unnecessary.

"What of my companion, Yeshua? Is there a purpose as to why is here? He asked

"You may well ask such questions. My task is to fulfil and bring you knowledge. Your companion my dear Traveller, is an Incarnate."

That took a few seconds to sink in. Incarnate!

Du Pont gazed towards the figure sitting on a rock.

"He is the highest in all creation. The most powerful in perfection and intellect. But as a mortal, all memory or recollection of his former existence as the most powerful being in existence is, expunged. Be gentle with him Traveller, he carries a burden. One he was destined to carry. And one that ends in his martyrdom.

The physicist picked up a small twig and started to scrawl on the dirt.

"Am I going somewhere with Yeshua? Am I meant to be with him?

Just as he was about to move a tiny trickle of water started to break the surface and swirl about his feet. Within seconds became a small pool of crystal-clear water. It flowed like a spring in a circular motion around him, extending itself about him till he is standing amid a small pool with a small fountain giving a cooling and refreshing sensation that quickly washed over him. He tried to move but is held fixed to the spot. Staring down he saw the water raise to his knees soaking the lower length his garment.

Etaanus moved to a higher position above him.

"Traveller, you will from now on only hear me in your thoughts. I will guide you and explain matters of great truths to you, but without always seeing me. Go now, you will feel refreshed physically, but what's to come, will refresh and nourish your soul.

Then there was silence. A hot breath of air swept up from the surrounding canyon floor brushed over him almost sucking the air from his lungs. A parched dry wind swept across the forbidding landscape of the Judean wilderness sweeping like an unforgiving furnace of hot air. His companion, Yeshua approached him. His movements were sluggish and drawn, a man haunted by demons and an unyielding sun. Yet the image conflicted with what he had just learned. How, in all that was sacred did this nomadic figure be any more than some lost soul, abandoned seemingly marooned living in such a pitiful and lonely existence? Then he remembered messenger's words *be gentle with him, he carries a burden that ends in his martyrdom.*

ψ

For the next three days, they moved across the wilderness with little to sustain them. No food and very little water. Slowly Du Pont came to terms with his circumstances. Some deep inner strength and energy burned within. His memory began to assemble images of another existence. The veil over his identity began to lift further. A fog in his intellect, his history began to clear. Physics, experimental trials, atomic structures, symbols, and numbers and energy field equations start to take hold. Temporal time became clearer. Within this awakening glimmer of faces that slowly looked familiar. Emerging from the mists of consciousness the realization of his predicament hammers home like an anvil. His nomadic companion, no more than fifty paces ahead of him was no ordinary figure. Yeshua, while a deeply troubled soul, aloof, enigmatic and haunted by horrific creatures, possessed a physique used to physical work and laboured effort. There was also a formidable temperament and boldness as well as sharpness of mind, and most disturbing of all, an innate ability to sense and read the mind of others. For all of that, there was warmth in the companionship between them.

They crossed through a series sloping hills with little or no vegetation, just dried and scorched scrubland stretched in all directions. The effects of dehydration and near starvation began to take its toll on the Nazarene. His steps became a struggle and regularly sunk to his knees from heat and exhaustion. Du Pont caught up and lifted him to his feet draping one arm over his shoulders to raise his weary companion. Their garments were soaked with perspiration.

"Yeshua! Please, we must rest. You need to stop! We need to find some food. You are very weak. Let's rest here for the night".

The Nazarene looked up at him and eased himself into an upright position. Leaning on Travellers' arm for support he managed a smile at his companion and pulled him closer to him.

"You are a good man, Fletcher. You have a pure spirit" He whispered hoarsely.

Du Pont froze. Before he could say anything, the Nazarene lifted his hand and placed his finger on the other man's temple and held it there for a brief few seconds. There was a trickle of energy then stumbled backward. Dropping to his knees he rolled over onto his side while something quite unexpected stirred deep within the recesses of his mind. Lying limp for a few seconds he slowly sat up.

"Fletch...Fletcher!! He whispered

Sal Madere

It was the same feeling she had over the last few mornings. Dizzying nausea, hot flushes, and empty retching. Everything was a struggle even getting five hours sleep did little to shake off a dampening sense of dread. It was just 7.15 am, already the bright early morning light filled the room with a pale golden glow. Still, she fought off any temptation to return to her bed. After a brisk shower, she tried to muster a sense of urgency into her morning start. There was purpose to her movements despite the emotional upheaval of the family. Denise Du Pont always ensured she looked her best. Her complexion and colour looked radiant, regardless of the toll events had taken on each of them. No sooner has she reached the bottom of the stairs when that sudden empty feeling and sickness gripped her. Ten minutes later she was back downstairs. Claudine and Michelle were at breakfast, both tried to read newspapers to distract them from their demons. Very little was said or spoken. She hugged her mother and kissed her gently, then similarly with her younger sibling.

"You heading to the hospital now? Michelle asked

"Yes, want to spend some time with his Doctors."

Claudine sipped her coffee still in the grip of uncertainty fighting the strain that seemed to have shrunken her. Both daughters knew that was just appearance. Inside a deep and smouldering anger simmered beneath the surface. Another day of challenges and vagueness lay ahead, medical cul-de-sacs without answers. A steely resilience to seek answers from those who stood over her decrepit and emaciated husband.

Outside Denise moved towards her car and stood and fumbled with her keys for a few seconds. Before she started, she reached for her cell phone. Scrolling through a series of numbers and then finds the number. She pressed and waited. Eventually, Paul's voice responded from his answering machine. Hesitating for a few seconds she decided it would wait, there was no good or bad time for this she thought. Switching on the engine and some decisions taken, she slipped the gears and in seconds passed through the gates of Sal Madere.

Paris.

Just over four hundred kilometres to the northwest in the middle of Paris two deeply troubled men sat and finished the last cups of coffee from a freshly brewed pot. Temperatures outside are already high for that time of year. The library itself sat on the ground floor of the Provincial Residence. Both had sat for over two hours already pouring over everything and exploring the implications of events in Geneva.

Despite their friendship and history, the mood in the room was tense. A large reading table dominated the rectangular room, its ochre-coloured walls ornate with a series of faded paintings of various saints, all depicting scenes of redemption or damnation. A small dossier lay on the table; its contents and personal notes were strewn about the surface. The more senior cleric had assembled a selection of works from his private research, along with extracts and copies of scholarly papers he dug out over the previous few days. There were no answers within those sacred texts offering any explanation or meaning to events in Geneva.

The Brother Provincial was more an administrator and scholar than his contemporary fellow Jesuit. The other man was steeped in spiritual certitude that held deeply that all truths and utterances within the gospels to be literal. Sitting quietly, he pondered events like a forensic scientist. Assembling the pieces in chronological order, still racked with grief unable to fathom events surrounding his brother in law. Played out in his mind was his sister's gut-wrenching display of open hostility to everything he held sacred, including his personal turmoil to contend with. The Brother Provincial was an eminent theologian in his own right, found all the evidence before them unsettling. Miraculous occurrences were something that the Catholic Church historically approached with extreme reservations and caution. But everywhere both of them looked, they were confounded and challenged at every level, spiritually, theologically, and scientifically.

No single explanation from current research that he examined or historical artefacts handed them a single clue to the events contained in the dossier before them. Church politics aside, there were obvious enormous human issues at stake here. Historical overtones hadn't escaped either man for that matter. Right down through the ages, both church and science clashed over matters that dealt with that most elusive and divisive issue of all. Truth. Or more to the point, the mere perception of truth. For one group, truths are handed down, for others, truths were discovered, proven, therein laying seeds of turmoil and intractable mutual suspicion.

"What does your heart tell you, Francois?"

"Do I trust my heart even though it speaks to me with great clarity?"

"Well, what is it saying, and should you listen to it? The brother Superior said.

Francois Burgoyne leaned and sunk his face in his hands, fatigue and uncertainty ebbing at his being. A conflict of soul and intellect filled him with doubt and foreboding, which he knew would pass once he could reach some sense of understanding.

"None of this is neither accidental, or coincidental. None of this! He whispered.

"Ask yourself, Francois, whose will is served by these events? Is this, an act of God's will? Or, is there a more sinister aspect to these events. Evil has no limits to prey on human weakness."

Francois Burgoyne straightened himself.

"I spoke with Fletcher only days before this happened. I suggested to him that this might all be some kind of warning"

The older man shot him a look and began to pace around the table.

"A Warning!

"Yes, Alphonse. A warning or a series of messages that heralded something of significance. A marker of some sort."

The most senior member of the Jesuit Order began reflecting the import to what he was hearing. He knew his fellow Jesuit for over fifteen years and had never known or heard him sound so adroit in his pronouncements. He paused and then walked over to a small folder lying at the end of the large table. Lifting it he gently emptied two A4 typed sheets onto the table. Also, a small section of a newspaper clipping for a Spanish publication fell on the table.

Quietly he gathered and sorted them and strolled over to his friend.

"Perhaps you also need to see these, my friend"

Burgoyne reached over and took the papers and studied the contents. He stopped and glanced at the newspaper clipping from a Spanish *El Correo de Andalucía* of which had a coloured picture. Half a page contained an article of a small village on the southern coast where there was local and regional excitement around happenings inside a village church. He read on and then stopped to look at the attached picture. It took a few seconds for his mind to absorb the picture itself, and then his eyes are drawn to the source of the entire piece. Looking up at the older man who was standing over him then reached out his hand holding a large magnifying glass piece. Burgoyne took it and laid it over the picture and held it for a few seconds. No words were spoken. Holding the piece, he gasped at the clearly defined face of a loved one. The effect almost caused him to drop the glass. He stared incredulously at everything in front of him. Thoughts raced as he tried to comprehend what seemed to confront every rational essence of his being. The face staring off the page was an identical near-perfect image of his beloved brother-in-laws face as he looked days earlier. After what felt like an eternity and the initial shock had passed, both men sat for a few private moments for reflection and prayer. Stillness settled in the library. Neither were strangers to turmoil or anguish; both having travelled different paths to reach their present state in life. Both took comfort in each other's company finding it easy to express their own spiritual strengths, and frailties to each other. When they could, and time allowed, they heard each other's confessions. Now it acted as an anchor to their friendship and their faith.

There was a tap on the door and Sister Claire interrupted the silence of the room, entering with a tray of freshly brewed coffee and some light sandwiches.

"Holy fathers, I thought perhaps you could do with some refreshments". She announced in a motherly fashion, providing both men with a welcome relief from their deliberations. As quick and efficiently as she entered placing the tray between them, she withdrew to leave both men to themselves.

"Let's assemble certain facts Francoise on what we know. Your dossier seemed to have all the troubling pieces. Let's take them and lay them out here on the table. Starting with this. He said holding up the image of the Holy Shroud.

Working slowly and deliberately saying very little, both began to rearrange the contents of the dossier in roughly the order each event took place. Photographs of Paul Melrose hospital ward with all the equations covering most of the walls. Next pictures of the pixilated particle images that emerged from the displays on particle decay and its ghostly appearance within the CERN control centre. This was followed by the markings on the Hadron tunnel itself, ones that Burgoyne and Melrose witnessed the following week.

Then came the troubling transcripts of Paul Melrose trance-like utterances in Aramaic along with pictures of some parchment documents lent to them by the attending physician Doctor Mochti. There were some personal notes from Du Pont himself. They contained some of the scientist's inner worries that started to haunt him and the emergence of mysterious particles that showed up in conflict with all known laws of physics. They laid the documents lengthways and width ways creating a cross arrangement of intersecting lines of paper. Next came close circuit image pictures frozen in time of that moment Du Pont collapsed in the large control centre. Lastly, and more forbidding of all was the image of an emaciated aged figure lying on the table in a hospital many kilometres to the east. Then the final puzzle.

Newspaper clipping placed down on the table at the interesting point of the spread. They stood and took in the array of papers laid out in front of them on the rectangular table. It was mere coincidence that their arrangement formed a cross, but its symbolism wasn't lost on both men. Finally, the Brother Provincial leaned over the documents taking in a sequence of events. All concentrated around a close circle of people. Eventually, he nodded almost to himself.

"I agree with you Francois my friend.

"How?

"None of this is by chance dear brother. Not now!

X

When Denise Du Pont reached the hospital grounds and managed to find a convenient spot in the hospital car park, she sat for a few moments considering the unthinkable. Her father may not ever speak or see her again. He may not make it. He would leave here in a coffin and she would never hear his voice again or feel his warmth and laughter around their home. Such a thought struck terror in her. Yes, she had Paul whom she cherished and loved deeply, but her father was her bedrock. She shook herself and pushed it from her mind. Staring up towards that part of the Hospital wing, she picked out the window where he lay clinging to a fragile thread of life. Within five minutes she headed down the cream coloured hallway and then through a set of double doors to the isolated section of the intensive care unit. As usual, the roster was now full of all too familiar faces.

Rather going straight in she paused and braced herself. Again, she felt nausea swept over her momentarily. She grabbed the door handle and took a moment.

"Hello, Denise! Good morning. He had an uneventful and calm night. All his vital signs are steady. A nurse said.

Would you like some time alone with him?

"Yes, that would very much be appreciated. Denise smiled

Then slipped into the darkened room. His bed was dressed and immaculate, sheets were draped over her father's prone physique. The only sound was a series of purrs and clicks from the equipment punctuated the otherwise sedate calmness of the room. His breathing still sounded laboured and heaving as if each breath was a life-death struggle. Hearing it again still unnerved her. She moved to his side, and bent over and kissed his forehead. She took his otherwise limp lifeless hand in hers and gripped it in both of hers. Bowing her head, she did something she hadn't done in a while.

She whispered a prayer. Moving closer to him she studied his almost lifeless face.

"Pops, if you can hear me, I miss you now so much. I love you, and we're not giving up on you. Tears welled up and ran down her pale cheeks.

"It's not your time. You have still so much to do, with us, with Mum. Please come back to us Dad. We all need you. I need you. I need you now, more than ever before because... You are going to become a granddad, Pops. Your first grandchild is on its way. I am pregnant and we are going to need you".

She closed her eyes and tried to recall her most cherished memories as a child growing up back in the States. Good memories, glorious moments that came flooding back to her in this very surreal setting. She took out a tissue and dried her eyes and smiled at him.

"You'd have to do some things all over again with your grandchild, Pops. That's why this is not your time, do you hear me?

She remained by his side for the next hour just holding his hand trying to recall those last moments they had alone. Her little secret and her love of his young assistant. All those anxious moments, often-missed moments to tell someone very close how special they are. Her life was good and fulfilled and she owed much of it to the person lying before her. Then, from nowhere the tiny little sounds hardly registered till at that moment she heard it again.

Breaking into her thoughts she became distracted by a sound very close and somewhat rhythmic. It registered as being out of place, the tiny sounds of dripping water. Snapping out of her thoughts and childhood memories Denise intuitively looked upwards at the ceiling, seeking to connect the sound of dripping water with some loose connection somewhere. Slowly she stood and looked around. Unmistakably the sound of water was present when it shouldn't be. Not only was the sound of water, but there were also sounds of drops contacting with water. Moving away from the side of the bed she moved around to the other side. As she did, she felt the surface of the floor became slightly slippery. Looking down, a small pool of water was forming at the end of her father's bed. Startled, she looked around to see the source and as she did her hand touched the covers where her father's feet rested. The cover was soaked and creating a darkened stain at the bottom of the bed.

She almost jumped back in shock. Then carefully she reached out and lifted the soaking cloth off her father's feet folding the whole section of the covers to one side. She covered her mouth in disbelief at the sight that greeted her. Both her father's feet are quite wet as if there had just been washed and left to dry. Beneath the bed, a large pool of water has formed as water still seeped from the prone figure's feet. Gathering her composure, she reached and touched the wet sheet. For a few seconds she stood to take in the strangeness of it all. Then while remaining in the same spot she noticed something else, her father's feet. In complete contrast with the rest of his body his feet were radiant, complete with a healthy glow and colour. The skin condition and tone were immaculate. His feet to his calves were those of an athlete in peak condition. Then in one of those peculiar moments that defy easy explanations, Denise mustered a nervous smile and stepped quickly over to her father's side.

'Dad, you can hear me. I know you can. I believe everything is going to be OK! She called out. This was a sign. She began to sob, but not from despair but unadulterated joy. She leaned over and kissed his forehead, her tears falling over his dried skin.

"We need you home soon, and wherever you are, please don't stay away for too long more."

She smiled at him reaching out to caress his forehead and brush his hair. Removing one of the towels adjacent to the bed she knelt and soaked the towel in the pool of water. Then standing she returned to the head of the bed where she began to gently and carefully wash her father's face with the cool water. Over the next ten minutes a ritual of love and deep joy she tenderly ran the soaked towel over his arms and around his eyes. When finished, she tidied the area around the bed removing and soaking up the remaining pool until there were no traces of water left. She moved to her father, kissed him one more time.

"We all love you Pops, please come home soon." After a moment, she squeezed his hand then stood and left the room.

CHAPTER FOURTEEN

Judea.

The realisation of where he was, and more importantly, with whom he was with, took some time. Sitting upright with his arms wrapped around his knees, Du Pont gazed over at the man trying to garner some sleep. Nearly all his faculties were restored. Immersed in his thoughts, measuring and calibrating some form of logic that explained how Time itself could be understood or explained. He was past all the emotional trauma of his circumstances. That might come later. Now, he was reliving his last conscious memory in CERN. That defining moment when they pushed past boundaries of known quantum mechanics and what he felt as he went through that unforgettable sensation as his own being became liberated and unbounded by any physical limits. There was a momentary thought that this might be death and if it was, well there was nothing to fear from it. Ironically, he never felt more alive. More profound questions stalked him now.

How, or what triggered space-time rupture from one dimension of time to another that permitted him to experience an alternate almost duality-type existence. Amid these questions he called out his own name quietly *Fletcher*, then shifted his attention over towards the figure sleeping peacefully. It began to chill down. Looking around thinking of ways to start a fire he saw small twigs and dried-out brambles of scrub lay strewn about near them? He still had questions, troubling questions. Then he remembered, Etaanus. It was he that he must direct his questions.

"That is correct Traveller. It is I, that is to impart certain truths" A voice called out

"Be at peace. I am with you at all times, even if you cannot see with your mortal eyes. Now, if you will gather as many sticks as you can find and place them over by the stones".

Du Pont quickly got up returning carrying both arms full of scrub pieces. He saw a small circle of stones arranged close to them. No sooner has he placed the sticks into the circle, a spark from nowhere ignites the brambles and a small fire starts. The man of science smiled to himself enjoying the sheer simplicity of how forces of nature were harnessed with sublime ease. As if reading his thoughts, Etaanus responded

"Indeed, my friend, if only you could command the order of all things to your wishes. An act of will, Traveller. God's Will."

Du Pont instantly got to his feet. Defiance and anger gripped him.

"If that's true- if that's so easy. Why is Yeshua enduring such anguish?"

At this stage a warm glow emanated from the now fully burning fire giving off a welcoming comfort from the chilling landscape. Etaanus's voice broke into a mild chuckle almost playfully.

"Is it going to be your intention to challenge me in everything I tell you, dear friend, Yes, it is his to endure. As it is with all mortals, life's vicissitudes weigh heavily on each of you. It is only after you have exhausted all your own native efforts to overcome obstacles in your

lives, will our creator intervene to supply support and relieve you from these burdens. And so, it is with your companion and, my Lord. Once he succumbs, having used all his native powers, then will great powers be provided?*

Du Pont stood his ground.

"That's absurd! Yeshua is almost completely drained. You can see he has endured a great deal of physical and mental anguish. What more must he do, and to what end?

"Yes, that is so. It is almost over; he has endured all for nearly forty days. It is his task as part of Redemption. One that takes place in accordance with divine will. Watch, and soon you will see mighty things, but do not be afraid. Recall what he asked of you when you first encountered each other. Be strong, and have faith

Then there was silence again, only broken by the crackling of twigs burning quietly. That night, his dreams came alive and reached out to him. Without warning, he woke with a start. Woken by the sound of a plaintive voice in the distance. It cut right through the night. Distinctive and decisively the sound of a voice in distress. He jumped to his feet and instantly saw he's alone.

"Yeshua!

As he picked up his robe, he heard the unmistakable sound of a raised voice coming from somewhere above him and to the left. With the athleticism of a man half his age, he scrambled sure-footed up a sloping wall of solid rock. It was still dark but his eyes adjust quickly to the night as he headed towards the sound. After climbing upwards for nearly three hundred meters he reached the top of the dome-shaped hill and stopped to catch his breath. His physical ability surprised him. Again, a voice rang out in the night. Last few steps he took with deliberate care. Then a slow realization crept over him. Forty days in the wilderness, the taunting, and harassment- flashbacks to the stories he remembered as a child. Great images of biblical sagas much he relinquished in later life from both old and New Testaments. In the great stories of New Testament sprung to mind in particular "how the angels lead him into the great wilderness"

He hesitated as he recalled how that all ended.

"Oh, dear God! He gasped.

Picking up the pace he started to follow a narrow ledge that slowly curved around the rock face and upwards. His breathing became harder as he pushed himself frantically as the gradient becoming acute with the wind chill biting into him. Then, from nowhere a piercing howl of an animal, a large animal, only this time not so distant. Eventually, when he could no longer stay upright with the steepness of the rock, he began to crawl. Then he heard the sound of panting and rustle of something moving over the surface very close to his path. As his efforts became a strain, he reduced his pace still shielding his face from the harsh coldness of the night. He paused again to listen for sounds. Then from the surrounding rocks and crevices came a deep gut-wrenching growl that filled him with terror. It seemed almost on him. It's the sound of an animal or beast. He was being stalked.

A few steps forward, he listened again, all his native instincts for survival sharpened. His breathing became harsh. Then, to his right on a large rock outcrop loomed a distinctive shape of this enormous animal stood like a sentinel, his nostrils displaying its breath in the chilling air. Du Pont stopped dead in his tracks. With unusual composure, he reached down and picked up a rock that just fitted into his hand. Without a second thought he mustered all his strength, hurled it straight at the shadowy animal. The rock fell short and smashed into the surrounding walls with noise quickly sending the animal scurrying off its perch and faded into the darkness. With all the remaining reserves he could muster he pulled himself upwards and climbed that last steep section which started to level off. Without realizing it, his climb had brought him close to a summit. The wind howled around him as he came near the top of the mountain. Then, despite the dust-flown wind, he saw it. The scientist in him rejected what his eyes showed him. Darkness gave way to two figures just far ahead to make out the detail. One figure kneeling, bowed over almost crouching and limp. The other was a tall figure much broader and much larger stature stood looming over the other. Neither was in contact with the ground. Suspended completely separated from the surface- both images held in suspension just a meter from the ground.

A purple glow radiated outwards from both figures. The taller of the two held both arms outwards, and it was then Traveller could see that the proportions of his limbs were wrong. They were nearly as long as his full height. Then as he stumbled forward, he braced himself. He knew what he confronted. The manifestation before him was the epitome of Evil itself. Towering over his companion was a creature of horrific appearance. He wore a cloak that blew outwards in the wind, just enough to reveal two deformed spikes protruding from his back, and his skull part creature, part mortal. Just as he started to run when a gentle unseen force took hold and pushed him to his knees. Suddenly a thunder peeled out across the entire valley and like a floating mirage, a whole landscape of cities and capitals appeared right across the sky. Then he heard the booming voice of the creature speaking in a tongue that was unknown to him. The creature waved his arms about and caused a cascade of visual scenes of great mountains and lakes appeared before them. The air felt heavy, accompanied by the odour of acrid sulphur. It's choking and stultifying mist spread out across the ravine.

Du Pont was unable to move held by some force. He finally cried out with all his strength towards his companion. At first, there was hardly any response. It's a sight of great misery pity and horror. Ominous sound of howling wolves that seemed to travel on the wind encircled them. He stared helplessly unable to move only witness what was playing out in front of him. Then in one single gesture, his Nazarene companion stretched out his arm and stood and pointed into the distance. Without warning his voice echoed across the entire mountaintop, and valley walls, reaching into the canyon below them. The whole mountainside fell silent and the wind in obedience, fell silent in a matter of seconds. Dust ghosts that danced around them earlier with such fury and menace slipped away into the darkness of the Judean wilderness. The dust slowly cleared accompanied by an unusual stillness in the air despite the high elevation of the peak, leaving one figure slumped to his knees

Yeshua, then raised his head and looked toward Traveller. Neither moved. No more than a mere hundred meters apart, facing each other, one completely drained while the other felt restrained. Traveller started to get up and move toward Yeshua. Slowly the air between them gave a gentle rumble very faint, and then a glow of light began to form, as it did, a cloud of dust rose up from nowhere. Within seconds, a sound peeled into the distance like one blown through a horn and light started to glow and intensify and began to envelop the figure kneeling in front of him. In a matter of seconds, clouds began to form into eight distinct formations, and as it did a pulse of heat rippled outwards casting a warm glow that wrapped both of them in a blanket shielding them from the freezing night chill. Awestruck Du Pont sat up and gazed as each of the clouds began to materialize into shapes. Quickly they transformed into creatures of great beauty similar in tone, colour, and radiance that he had seen before. Both males and females appeared carrying nourishments. Gathering around the Nazarene, and with great care and compassion began to attend his physical wounds, and offered him nourishment. Then two came towards him then quietly attended his physical wellbeing and offered food. He drank, but it was unlike water or wine he had ever tasted. One came over to him and knelt and extended his hand. Du Pont immediately recognized, Etaanus who reached out.

"Come, my companion. Eat with him".

Again, Du Pont noticed the effects. The closer to these powerful entities approached a corresponding drain on his energy. He felt its effects as he slumped to the ground. In his head hears a now familiar voice.

"Now my Traveller be rested and within your sleep, I will reveal some matters of great consequence.

Etaanus extended his out-stretched arm and a light that passed through Du Pont's body causing him to shake briefly and then complete surrender of his body's life force. All eight Spirit beings stood guard over Yeshua, each gifted with powerful telepathic and mediumistic gifts. Each in a precise order passed outstretched arms over him as he eat and gathered his strength.

As Du Pont slipped into sleep, he heard a voice that spoke as if part of a dream.

"In keeping with divine laws and wisdom, Yeshus Ben Yosef had passed the first such trials as a mortal, and had endured all the mental and physical ordeals over the last number of days in this wilderness. Each of these Spirits you have seen here plays a part within divine wisdom, to fulfil certain tasks, my friend, depending on his chosen gifts, offers necessary gifts towards Redemption.

A task of enormous consequences for this, the most powerful spirit being ever called into existence. Such were the difficulties to be overcome that the work of redemption is a task only for a High Spirit Being to wage a battle against the forces from the Abyss. This battle was to be a defensive one only and one to be waged on Earth. But first, this chosen one had to assume a mortal's existence, and with all such steps- in keeping with divine laws for which there are no exceptions, this chosen spirit loses all recollection of its former existence and glory. All memory, all knowledge of his identity my friend is expunged; hence it is a task of the utmost risk that the work of Redemption is undertaken. So it was, over the last forty days in the wilderness chosen. Spirit Beings begin to reveal matters of great importance to this incarnate mortal known as the Nazarene. The task of Redemption is about to commence.

Geneva.

None of the three men standing in the ward was particularly emotional nor for that matter excitable. Theirs was a profession of clinical focus and training. Men who practiced medicine and brought comfort and meaning to many of their patient's lives. Each had his specialty, along with his humanity and medical expertise. They performed it with great care and compassion and today was no exception. Except, this patient was different. Neither spoke for a few seconds but stood silent looking at the man lying in front of them. When they were contacted some hours earlier, it was just after 3.15 am in the early hours of the morning. Two were sleeping; the other was at the Airport waiting to board a flight. Each came at once when summoned by the hospital's main switchboard.

No other persons were contacted. The ward door was closed and absolute privacy was insisted upon. Careers over the decades of years of intensive training and specialties did little to help them understand the true nature of this most troubling clinical presentation. Some hours earlier they had inspected and catalogued the status of vital signs of this patient. This process put in place conformed to the most stringent medical ethics and protocols, and yet now they were standing over one of the most perturbing paradoxes in human medicine. A complete enigma. Something that simply confounded all their collective wisdom. Finally, the most senior of them, a neurosurgeon let out a sigh.

"We need to summon the family, first thing in the morning, Professor Peter Schultz said. "Do we even have a prognosis for any of this? Asked his colleague.

"Prognosis! Said the senior of the three.

"We don't even have an explanation for this new development. After such cell degradation and DNA destruction. Now this!   Replied another.

"In the meantime, we should commence a complete clinical and medical chronicle of all that has occurred here. Photographic records, physiological, neurological tests, and a complete chronological record of the physical changes.

"Gentlemen, we need to brace ourselves for what might come next."

There was a knock, and two young nurses and a junior doctor enter the ward without saying a word. The senior clinicians moved to one side. Then, after making sure he was secure they moved back, taking in the changes in him in the last twelve hours.

"Thank you, the senior physician said

"Perhaps we can also collect the hair, yes!

Just a little after 7.30 am the phone rang in Sal Madere. It is picked up by Michelle Du Pont, who is about to leave and start her morning run. She listened for a few seconds and quickly dropped the phone back in its cradle. The summons did not go into detail, but the hospital requested the family to come as soon as it was convenient. There were some positive developments with her father, and nothing further was said. Within twenty minutes Claudine Du Pont along with Denise was already making their way to leave. Claudine quickly called her brother in Paris and informed him of the call. He would get there as soon as he could catch the next available train or flight to Geneva.

Within minutes all three women were heading at speed towards the northbound A41 autobahn. Denise did the driving, while Claudine and Michelle sat for the most of the journey quietly expectant. Traffic was heavy on a Saturday, so it took Denise just under an hour to reach the outskirts of the city. At precisely the same time, two other parties became equally absorbed in what was in front of them, both in entirely different settings.

One was Paul Melrose sitting in a small corner of CERN's canteen. Sitting in front of him was Carina Ambrosiana, both nursing their coffee quietly going over Melrose's notes. The other was, Benjamin Mochti. He was off-duty and resting at home in his study. With a phone in one hand, his father on the other end and mail he received. The conversation had grown intense. He held a photocopy of one piece of faded parchment sent to him from Jerusalem the previous day. The call from Israel was timed to allow his son the opportunity to receive the copy before they spoke. The timing of the call was not unusual, this was normal on Saturdays. What was unusual was the subject of the call. Asher Mochti even at his advanced age was a persistent man, and disliked unresolved issues, particularly when it affected his son. Doggedly over the last number of days, he immersed himself in his passion for ancient writings and those of Gnostic origins. He was captivated by something he discovered and anxious to speak with his son. The piece in question came from a recital contained in one of the ragged and faded parchments coded and transcribed from the so-called Mystery of Secrets.

The meaning was open to question and scholars had come down on the side of one version of its meaning. Not so Asher Mochti, he along with the other enthusiasts sought and studied the linguistic tone, along with idioms within Aramaic script. It came down to the interpretation of one or two significant words. What made this all so perplexing was these were the words uttered by the young scientist who was struck down recently and treated by his son in Geneva? Words that sounded and spoken either in dread of some event or, those heralding some an announcement.

"Listen to me, Benni! " Just listen! Let me read what I believe it means!"

Benjamin Mochti closed his eyes and listened with exasperation to his father. The voice down the phone switched to old Hebrew. Listening to his father's punctuation and familiarity with the ancient tongue he remained quiet, then finally his patience wears thin.

"In English! Father, I cannot get what this means, please! Can you just explain"?

A pause on the other end, as the older Mochti sat for a few seconds trying to convey the proper translation and context.

"This piece at first glance seems to say the following" *And lo one will come on foot and witness all of this age, a new wisdom and carry on foot a great learning that diminishes all force and power upon the earth. A traveller of timeless wisdom will consume new knowledge with all before him.*

"Well, that's not how I would interpret this piece, Benni.

"What's that all about father? Something about carrying wisdom on... foot?

The old man came back sharply.

"This is a typical apocryphal narrative son, but the words are not translated in the proper context. The true context, and remember Benni this is what came out of that young patient of yours with its proper idiom and diction.

133

And Lo one will arrive as a witness of an age and new wisdom on a light of learning that comes as a force beyond earth, a traveller where time is nothing, who will possess the knowledge to render the earth new beginnings...

"Written back then in another age Benni. This seems to be an announcement about some event, some traveller or, it could also mean, warrior into the future comes to a "light of learning" as a force, and where *Time is nothing*.

Benjamin Mochti listened, and then bolted upright. Pieces of a puzzle obscure and meaningless began connecting dots. Something snapped into place. CERN! The capital of physics, a place that describes how time exists, the inter-changeability between energy and matter, all achieved with beams of high energy. He took the phone and spoke briefly for a further few minutes with his father. Thanking him they said their farewells then returned the phone to its cradle.

∫

The canteen began to fill. Carina Ambrosiana reached out and touched Melrose's hand.

"If I may say, these Riemann workings are a little off the wall, if you don't mind the pun.

"You know Carina I don't know how I did all this? It was as if all the theoretical stuff coursed through my head. It was relentless. I could imagine and see space-time geometry being wrapped and stretched, and the Riemann equations came spilling out trying to force my head to absorb it all."

Carina studied him stirring her coffee endlessly at the same time intrigued at his complete ignorance of the underlying complexity and depth of thinking it contained.

"I don't know which frightens me more Paul, your stuff, or these new markings in the Collider Hall. Much of your graffiti stunt in the ward is beyond me. However, there is something in the material that struck me as being a little weird. She said bemused.

"Really"!

"Yes, Riemannian workings aside- inside the abstract calculations, guess what was lurking in there?

"Go on.

"*Soul's Theorem*! She said. Enjoying the irony.

Soul's theorem! My God that old chestnut! He whispered

"It's all in there, submersions, and manifold structure. I thought it was a bit odd given the term. She teased.

"You have any further thoughts on these markings since we last spoke? He sipped what was left of the cold coffee.

"Yes, I think there's a link. They're all out-workings to do with Riemannian geometry, and those markings seem to hint or suggest some symbolic representation of…

"What!! Are you proposing that there is a mathematical basis or structure for these heat marks? She said.

Carina Ambrosiana was one of the best in her field in chaotic systems, but over the last few days she put her best minds in her department on it. No one found anything absurd or ludicrous. Some equations suggested the existence of dimensions beyond anything understood in current thinking. Its formal structure was quite baffling. They both exchanged some of the photos' that Melrose took at the time when he first saw them in the presence of the Jesuit.

"Fletcher himself thought there was something to them, she said.

Just then his phone rang.

"Melrose! He listened and then nodded, looking a little tense.

"OK! Let me know as soon as you can. Then I will inform the others.'

He put down the phone.

"There's been some positive news with the Chief He said.

Carina pulled out her cell phone.

"I will let the Felix Deveraux know. Are you intending to head into Geneva? She asked

Both of them left the canteen and headed in different directions.

The Saab saloon pulled into the first available space they found just after 8.35 am and within five minutes they were met by the medical team in an ante-room at the other end of the corridor. All three of the senior team looked tired. They stayed most of the night completing all the necessary medical protocols that they deemed important. Greetings were brief and pleasantries kept short. All three of the women were offered seats.

Doctor Schultz the most senior of the three quickly summarized the present status of the patient. That took no more than a few minutes, then he prepared them to what awaited them. A quick walk down the hall with very little been said. When entering the room, they saw the scientist was still lying in the bed but noticed some of the tubing and electrical connections to his head were removed. Moving closer towards the bed they were confronted with something they least expected. At first, they thought they had strayed into the wrong ward. In front of them lay a man, completely bald. All hair was absent. On closer inspection, the scientist's skin colour was changed. Instead of the worn and emaciated figure of an old man, with a haunted near death-like mask, was replaced by a picture of a regenerated physique. Both face and arms were tanned, almost sunburned, the face radiated a glow of inner health. The face exuded a fullness that was completely at odds with its appearance twenty fours earlier. His entire appearance contradicted everything that preceded recent days.

The hands had some calluses and forearms displayed well-defined muscles. Also, there was his breathing. Gone was the laboured struggle gasping for every breath to be replaced by a steady strong respiratory action. Claudine reached out and took his hand. A tear ran down her face. Both girls approached trying to believe they were facing a turning point in their father's nightmare. A mixture of relief and joy took hold as they both gazed at another version of a loved one, almost afraid to believe what they were looking at.

"What have you done to him. What's happened ? Claudine asked mystified.

"Absolutely nothing, Claudine This, new development is beyond anything we've done here.

Such changes disturbed the three medical men who felt they were consigned to mere observers. The fact no one knew or understood why was ignored for the moment. The next step was to determine if the physical alteration was matched with his neurological condition. Denise turned and for the first time since this entire episode began, she saw the effect her father's condition had on all three Doctors. From her contact with Dr. Mochti she knew about the toll some doctors endured with their patients. Claudine pulled over a chair and sat. She felt some spark of joy despite her private outburst some weeks earlier in that moment of despair. Her anger while understandable was harsh. Now she wondered if her pleas didn't go unheeded, and perhaps this was a response from a rebuked God.

"Doctors, could we have some time in private with my father? Denise asked.

"Yes, of course! Take all the time you need." One of them said

"Thank you for being here for us Gentlemen. You must be drained by all of this." Claudine said

TGV /Paris -Geneva

The reverend Francois Burgoyne S.J sat in carriage 6A on the 2.15 pm TGV as it cruised east just over an hour out from Paris. No more than fifteen people shared the same car. Most of them reading while a few listened to their music as the French countryside glided past in majestic silence. It would take be less than four hours and gave him some much-needed time to think. The priest stared out hardly noticing the passing spectacular landscape. All personal beliefs that defined him as a Jesuit were absorbed in thoughts that started to consume his spiritual strength, while fuelling rising moments of doubt. Mentally he ticked off the iconic face of the Shroud manifesting itself inside the workings of particle physics, unleashing utter disbelief to those close to it. Troubling and unsettling as it was, the appalling alteration of appearance to his family member was devastating in the extreme, and tested his own reservoir of faith. If there was room for doubt this was abolished with two events.

The entire Melrose episode was truly disturbing coming as it did only days before his brother-in-law's catastrophic mishap. The mysticism of ancient authentic utterances suggested some kind of intersection was taking place. A strange and unsettling convergence between physics and a metaphysical was upon them. Then, those surreal markings within the Hadron tunnel almost reflective of cave markings of earlier man he thought. Primitive signals of life and intellect. Sinister markings with embedded meanings perhaps cloaking truths that linked everything. Was it conceivable that a knowing intellect was at work, laying down in sequence- clues to the meaning and purpose to everything he witnessed? Purpose! He recalled his private moments with his Father Provincial, *Are these events an act of God's will, or some evil portent. What purpose is served here, with all of this?* Burgoyne leaned back and shut his eyes, silently he asked and prayed for insight. What was the significance of Paul Melrose's trauma in the tunnel, and those episodes in the hospital? All those equations that no one either dismissed or understood. How did they connect things that dealt with very abstract notions? What was it, Space-Time distortion and geometry shifts? How did any such stuff have relevancy to speaking Aramaic. Then of course, the precursor to everything, the mystical almost apparition of a pixilated face of the Holy Shroud?

He tried to remember those soft lights in the tunnel when he was brought there recently, and how Paul Melrose whole reaction after he considered the significance of, not only the markings themselves, but also their location. Curved surfaces suggested some kind of alternative way of looking at time and space and how they seemed to be intrinsically aligned. He felt tired. Much of this was beyond him as a priest. His entire being was about the teachings of Jesus Christ. How we saw or envisaged our saviour was everyone's personal journey and salvation. Even if one used the image on the Holy Shroud itself helped in that process, that was fine.

Outside, the countryside changed as the sleek high-speed train veered south onto a southern path towards Switzerland.

Burgoyne sat back in his seat immersed in deep thought. Each human journey through life was an opportunity to build a relationship with Christ. To know him and to experience his...

Abruptly he opened his eyes and sat upright. A strange notion quickly formed. All the images of recent events both in CERN burst into his consciousness like an avalanche as a series of connections sparked a deeper reasoning. Slowly an alternative view and realization began to dawn. A startling idea took root in his mind. He dared not think or suggest what was emerging. A theme that lay in front of them throughout all that's was happening. *Time!* Historical time, relative time. This experiment that his beloved family member was involved in, Euclid, was to test or prove some dimension in quantum physics that hinged on our notion of Time. And, if in response to that quest, some mystical power had responded. He leaned forward and clasped his silver crucifix in his hand, and stared into the sweeping beauty of the surrounding countryside. Reaching down to his briefcase he rummaged through some papers. Something he saw and noticed in the study back at Sal Madere.

Then he found it.

Written on a yellow page he slipped out a sketch that Paul Melrose drew him in explaining how the markings were remarkable in their layout. He stared at it

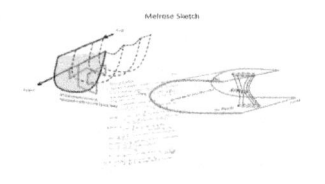

Melrose Sketch

Recalling how he'd sketch Time as an elastic fabric in space-time at least that was the theory. This was beyond him, but within the sketch, there was something that referenced time that physicists were preoccupied with. He sat back and considered just for a moment, what might have happened to his brother in law. Dare he think, the unthinkable? He wasn't thinking science anymore, his instincts were been corralled into contemplating certain mysteries. Mysteries that served as a backdrop to his entire life as a priest, maybe beckoning him to reach into his soul to confront a new reality. He needed to rest for the remainder of his journey, but ,if what he was starting to think was true, it was unlikely he'd get any sleep that night . Quickly took out his cell phone and dialled a number.

Ten seconds later, Brother Alphonse Sienna's voice answered sitting in the back of a taxi, heading for the airport. The call while always welcome was unexpected. The Father Provincial adjusted his glasses and put down the material he was reading. He listened to his fellow Jesuit for a few minutes and then leaned forward and slid the glass partition in front of him closed. What he heard over the next fifteen minutes caused him some dismay. He said little but knew enough of the facts that he found all he heard to be compelling. It also complicated his journey now. He was making his way to Rome. This matter needed to be brought very discretely to a higher authority. Someone both men knew within the Roman Catholic curia that needed to be kept informed. As far as both men knew, there was little or no media interest in events in Geneva. However, what he heard from his colleague was both breathtaking and astonishing if any of it were true. He also needed to think. Great issues were at stake. He had decisions to consider now and a matter of trust was needed particularly with the man he was going to meet.

Francois Burgoyne ended his call and sat back to his seat He would welcome some coffee, although he would have preferred something much stronger.

In Geneva, Paul Melrose had made it into the hospital a little after three-thirty in the afternoon. He had a few hours to think about Denise's text earlier , and while welcomed, he knew her father's life still hung by a thread. The story CERN put out simply stated that the scientist was suffering from exhaustion and making steady progress. He would return to his post when his doctors were happy with his condition. Once he parked his car, he made his way towards the now familiar ward. A crowd had gathered in one of the corridors when a familiar face caught his attention. Benjamin Mochti was standing amid some 'white coats' professional colleagues deep in some clinical discussions. As soon as he saw Melrose, he broke off from the group and sauntered over to him smiling.

"Paul! It's good to see you again. You look great! How are you keeping?"

"Under the circumstances, I'm good Benin, and you? This is not your part of the world, is it? Melrose smiled.

"No, it's not. I'm visiting a fellow college student from Tel Aviv. How is Fletcher Paul? The warmth faded as his eyes bored straight at him. Just as he was about to reply, a voice from behind them.

"He is stable" Denise said softly from behind them.

She moved and embraced Paul, then turned to Mochti.

"Benni, would you like to see my father? She asked.

It caught Melrose off guard. There were a few seconds of awkwardness then Mochti smiled and bowed.

"Yes, Indeed Denise. I would if that's all right with your family?

All three turn and walked towards the intensive care unit and led towards Du Pont's ward.

Inside, Claudine and, Michelle are sitting in two armchairs by his bed. Slightly startled both of them stood. Then Denise turned and introduced Mochti to her family only to find him standing behind them fixed to the spot. Standing back from the group, Mochti was almost hypnotized by what he saw. After a second or so, he came forward smiled towards Michelle. Then with a simple gesture reached out with both hands and took Claudine's hand and held it.

"Madam, I wish and pray that Almighty God will bless you all in this most difficult hour. He said.

Gently he moved away and over towards the bed and stopped short. Bowing slightly, he whispered a few silent words in Hebrew. Then gathered himself, he made some gesture with his hands, then turned and approached them. His face ashen with disbelief.

"May God hold him close… and return him to you all".

Claudine instantly warmed to the man, managed a brief smile "Thank you, Doctor, you're most kind. I understand we're also grateful to you, for this young man's recovery"

He held her stare for a few seconds then turned and gazed at the bed without saying anything. He absorbed everything before him. No one said a word. Melrose was unsure if this was a good idea to have Mochti present. Then, in the most measured tones, Mochti turned and looked at all four of them.

"May I equally pray that the same outcome comes to your husband?

Then with an effortless movement, he crossed over to the bed and stared down one more time at the figure of a man he'd come to greatly admire. Standing for a few seconds then quietly bowed his head. For a moment nothing was said while he took in the whole transformation before him never once looking at any of clinical dials on displays. Melrose was about to step forward and say something when Denise squeezed his hand. She guessed the good doctor's presence was no casual thing.

"My husband spoke well of you, Doctor when he was…" Claudine left unfinished

"If there is anything, I can do to assist any of you" He hesitated, searching for the appropriate words.

"I would like to help with everything. Both medically…or otherwise"

CHAPTER FIFTEEN

Magdala, fishing village. Sea of Galilee

The rocking movement from side to side was deeply soothing and rhythmic with the occasional sloshing of water. It made for a pleasing and restful feeling. That coupled with a warm but cooling breeze and the smell of salt, added to the sense of contentment.

Then there was the sound of laughter. People, seemingly enjoying them. Male voices. The sound of male voices and further laughter interrupted by the odd sound of clapping. The rocking seemed to ease and there was less lateral movement. The man of science slowly managed to open his weary eyes to see a large reddish-brown slightly torn sail. It took a few seconds for the brain to register that he's no longer on land, but on something that swayed. A boat rocking and moving on water.

His mind quickly assembled all the sensations as he slowly gathered himself to new surroundings. For a brief few seconds, he thought he was dreaming. However, both image and recollection fade with the realization that he was captive within a surreal reality. Gently leaning up on one arm he gazed at the scene before him. Gone is the stark empty wilderness of undulating hills and canyons and scorching sun. Before him spreads a sea of azure blue sea gently rocking the vessel he had been sleeping in. The boat was over fifteen meters in length, made entirely of wood, creaking in tune with the gentle rocking action of the whole vessel. The sky was a clear cloudless picture with a refreshing breeze that was soothing on his skin. Then he saw them at the other end, five of them pulling in nets. All wore beards and stripped down to their waists. Two of them were quite tall, easily over six feet the others were average height nearly all with their hair tied back in ponytails. All are quite muscular all working with their hands and in this light; they looked like men in their late twenties. Fishermen, he assumed. He sat up to get a better sense of his bearings and absorbed his completely changed surroundings. With a single gesture, they all stopped and looked his way. Curiosity was clearly their focus.

Then one of them dropped his rope came forward stepping over a large pile of fish still flapping on the deck. Up close he is every bit a powerful man as he was tall. He asked Du Pont something with his hand stretched out and laughed. The language and tongue were unknown to the man of science. He gesticulated with his hands for a few minutes not making much sense until he gestured with his hands the action of eating and his mouth. Du Pont stood and smiled appreciating none of these gestures were threatening. There were the actions of simple folk offering food to a stranger. Then the big fellow looked beyond Du Pont over his shoulder at someone. He turned to look behind him only to see the lone figure of a man in long clean brown robes staring at him.

Yeshua. From an imperceptible nod from his friend, the large fisherman bade him sit and backed away and back to their nets. Du Pont had no idea how or when he got here but pleased they were no longer lost in the wilderness He gathered himself and stood nearly falling over trying to find his balance.

Immediately he noticed the difference in his companion. Sitting composed and rested he looked like a completely different man. He smiled, got up stood and came and embraced his friend. It's the first time Du Pont recalled ever seeing him stand upright and surprised at how tall he stood. He guessed he was as tall as the big fellow at the other end of the boat. The boat suddenly rocked unexpectedly and caused Du Pont to lose balance and stumble but not before Yeshua caught him with both arms and steadied him.

Then raising his voice, he called to the others something that sounded like a caution. "They're fishermen but not good navigators sadly, He said with a smile.

Du Pont studied the man for a few seconds and tried to summon the confidence to address him in a manner befitting who he really was.

"Yeshua! What is…happening?

"Yes, my friend what is it? Speak. He teased.

"You're a Carpenter, aren't you? Not a fisherman! I do know this.

The other man came closer and looked him straight in the eye.

"And I know you're not just a traveller lost in a wilderness"

He retorted with a menacing look. Du Pont felt an immediate panic as if he was about to be accused of some major deception. Some truly disturbing offence and exposed.

"No! Please, Yeshua, I didn't mean to suggest!

"Suggest what? The Nazarene asked.

A frosty moment lingered for a few seconds.

"Speaking from the heart isn't always easy is it dear friend".

Still, with a menacing stare of indignation and then without warning, he burst out laughing at the way Du Pont was getting unsettled.

Yeshua reached out and grabbed him in an embrace and shook him in a bear hug and laughed. The haunted look that permeated his entire personality over the last number of days was replaced with vibrancy and charm. His whole face lit up and exuded great personal charisma. There was sharpness of wit coupled with an attractive engaging personality. There was also a force of intellect. He noticed Yeshua examining some of the structural sections of the boats flooring and checked how some sections were showing wear. He also examined sections of the large rudder beam used to steer the vessel with great attention to detail. It dawned on the man of science that as a carpenter his friend must be skilled in the workmanship in boat construction. There was studied attention to how the creaking noises he heard earlier might be cause for concern. Yeshua spoke rapidly to the others in a tongue he didn't understand, but from their reaction they start carrying out checks on the side of the boat checking to see if there might show signs of leaks He now assumed a commanding stance overseeing their progress as they approached the shoreline but his attention firmly focused on the boat's motion and balance. Then he sat Du Pont down in front of him and asked the others for some water to drink.

"My father and I built this! I remember working on this when I was just a child." I used to carry out measurements for my father and cut each section to his instructions. She moves well now in the sea, as good as any fish! He said running his hand along the woodwork. Water came, and they both gulped as much as the needed. As they drew closer to the shore the breeze off the water died down. There were cheers and shouting from a group that seemed like friends of the crew gathered on the sandy shoreline. Some waded out towards them to catch some ropes and assist bringing the vessel to a secure position. There were merriment and laughter. It seemed the catch was good and better than expected. The setting was one of joy and easy banter, the warm Sun made for a very welcoming and inviting location. Greetings amid some cheering and festive mood greeted their arrival. One woman waded out into the water a little and called out specifically to his companion, Yeshua. He jumped up and returned the welcome with a shout and warm smile. Du Pont surmised she was a family member. As they drew up and in one easy movement, Yeshua simply placed one hand on the edge of the vessel and vaulted over into the water. It was if he was doing this all his life. The change in the man was so different. He was like someone else. Then, with his obvious strength pushed the back of the boat inwards so that its bow lifted onto the sand and stopped. Wading towards the shore toward the women he strode over and embraced her, wrapping his powerful shoulders and arms around her. He turned to Du Pont with a beaming smile.

"Come, dear Traveller, you must greet my mother!"

She moved easily and as she did, Du Pont detected a lithe and full figure beneath her clothing. She came right up close to him and gave him a long searching inspection then a smile creased her tanned face and said something he didn't understand. Yeshua turned and translated.

"Welcome to Magdala! Friend of my son! He whispered.

She stood tall very elegant and straight. Her hair was loose and hung around her shoulders with strands of grey running through it. She exuded unspoken authority.

That evening, a campfire was set up and both fish and meat were served and they feasted and enjoyed what food and vegetables there were. Strange Hebrew music played well into the evening with seemingly no one questioning his presence. Du Pont looked to where Yeshua stood. He was within a circle of friends holding hands his face down listening to the lament from the small man, obviously the local rabbi. The entire setting enthralled him. This place, this stuff of biblical history, stories that would go out from here and survive the passing of time. Two thousand years of history would elapse and would pass through countless writings, stories that would be recanted and spoken of from churches down through the ages. The stuff of sermons the world over compiled, rewritten, re-interpreted, and lectured on, all emanating from this time, from these simple people. He closed his eyes and thought about his own story and his presence here. His personal convictions were abruptly recast and no longer accepted the supremacy of science as the source of all truths. Standing amidst these charming people, adrift from his own time, a purpose to all of this began to engulf him, he struggled to keep this pent up emotional energy from ripping him apart. He was experiencing a singularity of mystical proportions that was only beginning to take hold. Without any warning he began to tremble, tears start to well up inside, he wanted to scream for help.

An invisible hand touched his shoulder.

"Traveller be still for a moment my friend".

As it did, Du Pont experienced a strange calmness envelope him and the overwhelming sense of despair and loss faded replaced by feeling of wellbeing. No sooner did this happen, the festivities recommenced and prayers of gratitude ended and the music continued into the rest of the evening. Du Pont stood and absorbed everything that played out all about him. The sense of occasion, the aroma of cooked food mixed with music he'd never heard before, began to sooth his soul. As if reading his thoughts,

"They cannot see me, Traveller. It is just you and I."

Du Pont looked surprised with the appearance of, Etaanus in front of him.

'No doubt you have reflected on events from the mountaintop. These great events my dear friend, are shown to instruct you. To show and explain things that will enrich you, and uplift your soul.

"Why are we calling him, Yeshua? We both know what he will be known as for the rest of history...as.

"Now, I will show and explain matters of great importance. Do you recall Traveller when we first met? In the wilderness, you felt a power come over you, and again on the mountaintop?

"Yes, I do. It was unnerving and frightening".

No sooner had he answered a powerful cloud formed around the spirit-being standing next to him, and as it did that same power-drain sensation returned causing his knees to buckle forcing him to collapse onto the soft soil. They were in a garden filled with a wonderful perfume of wildflowers scented the air all around them. The music near the shoreline faded into the background.

Etaanus's presence exerted a powerful radiated energy through him.

"When powerful immortal beings come into contact with all living creatures, dear friend they emit a powerful force that causes the sensation you are currently experiencing. It will do you no harm. It is the consequence of their presence coming into contact with the material creation. You will find it will infuse you and lift your native life force with more power and health. Higher spirit beings possess unlimited access to God's power, and due to its purity and nature, it will impact with mortals in the manner you feel, because as mortals, your life force is not as pure and possess limited energy".

Du Pont suddenly felt a life-force race through him. A band of light curves outwards from Etaanus like a string and touched him around his shoulders. He began to feel energy course through him like a wave that was intense as it was pleasant.

'Your spirit Traveller has its own energy, but of inferior purity, as with all mortals, but it is this force and its nature that you seek to understand my friend, you seek it in your learning and numbers. There are different and varied spirit beings in the other realms, all with varying levels of purity and power.

With that Etaanus extended his hand and the entire surrounding darkness exploded into light. A massive curved wall of colour moved from left and quickly encircled them. It contained varying degrees of coloured bands of light. From the dullness of dark shades to the most resplendent hues of gold to pure white effervescent light.

"Behold, my friend the power of our creator in all its forms. Each spirit in existence contains the spark of divine life. You see Traveller, matter in all its forms and manifestations is merely this energy condensed into a form associated with its level of existence within the creation.

Then, a series of images emerged from within the circle of light. Images of shapes. Starting with images that Traveller knew instantly by sight. The unmistaken designs of bacteria, slowly replaced with vivid structures of minerals possessing great variation. A magnificent sequence of images began to take form before his eyes.

"There is great order here Traveller, precision, and beauty working in great harmony within the creation. You will witness how all spirits in their varying level of existence, progress upwards in the levels of progression in perfection and form. This exists in the Great Seals of Creation and is beyond anything you mortals can conceive.

Now the band of colour changed and new images coalesce in front of him. Starting with large boulders and rocks, these appear and then dissolve into images of a whole range of plants and trees of great abundance, only to dissolve into a great vista of all living things, from birds of every hue of colour, to a progression wild beasts and animal life. Within the entire visage of images, Du Pont recognizes a shift in colour and purity of the surrounding light associated with each change. Then almost miraculously an image of human form appears midway through the band of the light spectrum.

"May I continue dear friend, perhaps this takes time for you...

"No! No. Please continue, Du Pont said.

...The entire material creation as you know it contains a spirit. It is in accordance with divine will and subject to laws beyond your comprehension that each alteration and transformation of a spirit progresses up through the material creation as an act of divine will. All matter in the material creation harbours a spirit. As a man of learning and science, you pursue a quest to understand the nature and structure of matter.

Du Pont stood transfixed as he grasped the enormity of what he was witnessing in this vision. He looked at Etaanus, who was standing close to him. A new power energy now took hold. Du Pont was in commune with this angelic creature by a telepathic process. Thoughts passed between them.

"All Spirit is condensed into matter; much like on earth water can undergo changes with a liquid, to solid, as with ice, or be condensed as vapour. Within the spirit realm as throughout all creation both material and ethereal sacred laws are at work. Our creator is love, and all things progress from that to order and beauty. Little things grow and become larger. Single events become multiple things, and simple things become complex, all in precise obedience to God's immutable laws. All creation is precise and orderly. There is nothing capricious in the workings of the creator or his love and thinking for his creatures"

Du Pont instantly had a flashback to dialogue back in his own time... "God not only creates, but he also sustains"

Du Pont stared at the imagery of unfolding truths beyond anything he could foresee or imagine. Then as he tried to assess deeper meanings, the light shifted towards to purer form of light. Then emerging from these light images both male and female spirits appeared, shaped into a form of perfection itself. Beings possessing great purity and grace. Their physical appearance transcended anything any mortal could envisage. Spirits from the highest realm of existence that was most proximate to where the Creator exists. Beings of great presence and which life force and energy sweep over the man of science? Only for the presence of Etaanus next to him, Du Pont would have experienced the full force of their power.

"Once each spirit ends its progression up through the material creation, it now, depending on its sojourn on earth, enters a sphere within the ascending steps in the ethereal realm, Etaanus continued.

"It is the purpose of all mortals to attain this upward progression. This, dearest Traveller is where Heaven exist. The highest of all the ethereal spheres in existence. Before he assumed a mortal existence, Yeshua was the most perfect Spirit Being ever called into existence by our creator.

Suddenly, an intense flash of golden light washed over them dissolving the entire circle of light and causing the whole fabric of the surrounding landscape part wide open. An iridescent light of great power exploded for a few seconds almost blinding Du Pont, his hand instantly shot up to shield him from its intensity. Etaanus reached out and touched his friend, causing his vision to change. He now possessed insight and visual acuity to look upon a realm that defied human imagination. A vast kingdom opened up revealing a place of utter beauty and colours of the most vibrant kind. Colours that made all earthbound colours in comparison only a mere reflection of the awesome cascade of images before him. As his vision attunes to the sight, he saw a figure in the distance move towards them. Within moments the figure drew closer, and as it did, Du Pont gasped at the realization of what he saw.

A magnificent being of great stature and power stands mid-distance. It's a face he barely recognised aglow with radiance, wearing a long white robe, and golden sandals. As the apparition becomes clearer the figure reveals wings of gold extended outwards. The face looks towards the mortal and instantly Etaanus, voice enters his thought.

"Behold, Traveller you may bow to your creator. This is the first Son of God the Almighty, a perfect creature conceived by him. All other spirits are his inferiors, in power, perfection, and beauty. It is he, and he alone created all existence. In him, God bestowed all the power to create the entire realms of existence, including all the angels, dominions, and principalities. He is in every way as near to perfection as God himself, and it was he, and he alone, planned the entire process of redemption, which of necessity, called for the creation of the material universe to come into existence. It was he that the great revolt in heaven was aimed against, not God, but against his first born. It was a rebellion against this first born, and so it followed, redemption was to follow a path of the most utmost risk ever undertaken by a celestial being.

"...To assume a mortal existence, to forgo all its power and might, and to render all his knowledge in the celestial sphere to naught. As I have already spoken to you in this

matter, all recall, all recollection, and memory as the most perfect creature in existence, are expunged. That you now know Traveller, in this very special time here is Yeshua. Yeshua Ben Joseph, as he is known in these times is a mortal. He has walked the earth without recourse or knowledge of his identity in heaven, and is now in his thirtieth earth year. You should know his time in the Judean wilderness was the beginning of his instruction and tasks that are required of him. As he overcame each difficulty his powers grow. Likewise, with all mortals on earth, as you overcome the weaknesses of your base nature; Gods gifts and blessings come to you. Slowly, over time his native powers will increase. His intellect even as a child was of a high order and beyond his earth years. It follows because his spirit is of the purest possible in a mortal form. He possessed gifts of immense mediumistic ability and clairvoyance.

Etaanus paused for a brief moment allowing his companion to take in and absorb the truths presented.

Du Pont's brain raced trying to process what was unfolding. The impact of such potent truths pushed his mind to unknown depths of uncertainty. His entire human will turned to turmoil trying to assemble and contemplate such mystical processes and power. A power almost beyond human reasoning. Finally, he started to piece together some understanding of what was unveiled.

"Is Yeshua aware of all of this and his task ahead? He whispered.

No sooner had he spoken a rumble roared across the scene and the entire image dissolves and splits in two, followed by immediate darkness, and silence. Du Pont slumps down next to a large boulder. His world of physics lamentably is rendered useless. Matter harbouring "spirits!

"Is there more of this to come?

"Indeed Traveller. But have strength and without fear. This will enrich your knowledge and wisdom of matters of great importance. As a mortal, Yeshua cannot have any recall, of his own identity or place in his former abode. In his heart, he adheres and loves God's laws here on earth. He is already aware of his great task, as instructed by some of God's spirit-beings, and through his intellect. He possesses gifts of a high order due to his purity of spirit. As an incarnated spirit of the highest order, his mediumistic gifts will continue to grow in strength and power".

"And his place in human history Etaanus. What of that? This redemption you speak of. What purpose is served in all of this?

Etaanus raised his hands, and his entire radiance diminishes. In a matter of seconds, his colouring and build quickly remoulds itself into a mortal appearance. A complete stranger stands before Du Pont. The man before him appeared different. His appearance was that of a Sheppard or Fisherman. Ordinary in every way that befits the times they found themselves. Du Pont just stared

"Don't be alarmed Traveller. When we spirits attune our presence to a mortal state, we take a less perfect form as humans, then our place in the higher realms. It allows us to walk the earth unnoticed by others. In the Higher realms, our spirits undergo greater

purity towards perfection and cause the shaping of our bodies. All spirits shape the nature and embodiment of our physical forms. So, on earth, as befits our spiritual purity and development our physical forms are less perfect.

You look very normal. Du Pont said quietly with genuine surprise.

Then, from nowhere there was a loud noise. It seemed to come from the camp side amid the festivities, only it didn't sound festive. There appeared to be some disturbance, commotion, followed by women's screams and children. They both turn and hear agitated raised voices followed by a destruction of tables and that of objects being flung about. As they both turned and head towards the noise, an anguished scream breaks the calmness followed by a stream of high-pitched voices arguing. As they draw near they see a large circle has formed amid tears and calamity. Broken jars lay scattered around the fire. In the circle, four of the more energetic men are on the ground struggling to hold down one of the younger boys in the camp.

He is no older than seventeen. Despite the four men fighting to restrain him and pin him down, the youth seems more than able to fend them off. Shocking still is the violent contortions he is putting his body through. Blow after blow he lashed out at those struggling to contain him. Despite their apparent superior physical power, each of them is reeling from the unusual fight and strength of the boy. Worse still is his violent and disturbing verbal abuse that flowed from his mouth. Obscenities in whatever tongue was spoken, shocked even traumatize all those onlookers. His eyes are almost protruding from his head, his mouth misshapen and foaming a discoloured vomit. Two more men join the efforts of two of the taller fishermen while the others try and tie both his hands and feet. More fists' flare as the struggle is taking its toll on all of the males attempting to subdue him. Then with one violent jerk, all six men are cast off and tossed aside like rag dolls. Two of them were thrown nearly ten feet such is the strength.

A shocked and paralytic fear now enveloped the campsite. The youth stood up, panting, his body showing all the signs of violence, but his face is distorted with raw hatred. He ran and grabbed one of the women and violently threw her on the ground. He instantly sets upon her and commenced to become sexually aroused and started to lift her clothing. He pins her down and forced himself between her legs. The young woman screamed as she realized what was about to happen. Du Pont was about to launch himself towards the youth when an arm gripped him.

"Stay! Traveller. Don't move! But watch.

No sooner had he, when from the gathering, Yeshua broke from the crowd and on one effortless stride reached out and grabbed the top of the youth's head. The youth turned and instantly his body began to convulse. His arms go limp and fall lifeless to his side. Then Yeshua with both arms grips the boy's shoulders and locks around them like a vice-like grip. In one single effort and using his obvious upper body strength, lifted the boy clean off the girl and tossed him to the ground. No sooner has the youth hit the ground, the Nazarene was on him and with just one hand placed a death-like grip down on the youth's forehead. With his other, he placed his free hand over his chest and pressed hard. Now despite the flaying of arms and legs, the boy seemed fixed into the ground unable to exert any further struggle or aggression. It was as if an invisible anvil stopped all physical exertions. Yeshua then let out a roar and uttered a series of words in the local dialect. Everyone around dropped to their knees; much of the sobbing and agitation began to subside. The boy's body jerked spasmodically. It convulsed and sounded like he was began to choke. Both arms and legs became lifeless almost disconnected from the rest of his body. Then Yeshua released him and pulled the upper part of the body into a sitting position.

Gently he draped his powerful arms around him tightly, until he was staring into the lifeless eyes of the child. He looked straight into his face and in a raised and commanding voice said a word. A few seconds elapsed followed by a piercing scream of an animal erupted causing the boy's body to tremble and gave one last gasp, and then collapsed into the arms of Yeshua. A woman and man ran immediately over and threw themselves on both man and child kneeling on the ground. Yeshua leaned forward and gently kissed the boy's head. With that, the child's eyes opened and looked around at the carnage. A look of complete confusion and bewilderment filled his face with no recollection whatsoever. Yeshua still kneeling embraced both the mother and father of the young boy. The small man, the rabbi, cried out a lament and came and took Yeshua's hands.

An act of respect and relief. The tall graceful elderly women Du Pont met earlier from the shoreline stepped forward and said a few words over her son. He reached up and took her hand and gently held it to his face. Both went and sat with the young women who had managed to recover her ordeal. Yeshua reached out and placed his hands on her head, and held it briefly. Her demeanour took on a more peaceful and calming aspect. A few seconds pass. After a few minutes, the mood and the festivities of the evening were coming to an end, and tents were been erected to retire for the night. Others would return to the local village of Magdala itself.

Du Pont was led to a small tent and shown where he would be spending the night. He was in no mood to sleep. He needed to talk with someone. Anyone.

"Do you understand what's happened here tonight?" Etaanus asked gently.

Du Pont while shaken by the experience quietly drank some wine.

"Demonic possession. Something I didn't believe in, up to now."

Etaanus stood.

"Wait here for a moment, I will return here shortly."

With that, he turned and moved away towards the shoreline. Du Pont let out a sigh of relieve. He looked on in utter amazement as the figure of his spirit companion commenced to dissolve into the darkness of the evening. For all of his abilities as a man of science, the last few hours simply defied everything he accepted as natural phenomena. Another world existed outside his reign of imagination. Things beyond his world of pure science and his notion of reality were being re-drawn. His field of human knowledge in particle physics didn't come close to acknowledging that which transpired before him in the last number of days. Deities, of mystical origins both powerful and graceful, had entered his world of human experience. Now, in this place, this desolate and ancient part of history, his very basic concept of existence was being reshaped. He gazed around and was about to enter his makeshift tent when the soft sound of sandals caught his attention.

A figure of a young boy approached He was almost close when Du Pont saw it was the same boy involved in the struggle and fighting earlier. He tensed, unsure what was going to follow. The boy was carrying a small wooden bowl. Reaching out, he handed the scientist the bowel. It contained fresh dates and some fruit. He studied the young boy for a few seconds, then took the bowl and smiled gratefully. Instantly the boy's face broke into a broad grin in complete contrast to what took place earlier. He had a wholesome and handsome face, devoid of any markings or scratches from his ordeal.

Even at seventeen, he possessed the attributes of the strong and healthy physique that suggested he would mature into an attractive older male. There was also great humility in his bearing and seemed completely none the worst from the events at the campfire. He spoke in a native tongue. Du Pont assumed Aramaic or some other. Showing his appreciation by raising the bowl he smiled and bowed slightly. The boy pointed to the dates and gestured with his hands towards his mouth. Du Pont sampled them finding they were sweet with a delightful flavour. He offered some to the boy, who eagerly accepted with a wide smile. While there was little by way of dialogue, they both enjoyed the moment. For several minutes, little was said while they shared the remaining contents of the bowl. From the camp, rising into the night air evening prayers filled the mood of the setting. As a fitting end to the day a slow harmonious chanting broke out across the camp, nothing very loud, but enough to add a sense of thanksgiving to a hidden God. A tranquillity settled on the shoreline and Du Pont sat and soaked it all in. Magdala, a place and moment in time, which would burn into his soul and his memory.

Then, without any warning, the boy leaned over in a peculiar position as if he was about to topple over. He dropped the bowl in a reflex action to catch the boy from falling. As he did the boy gasped and let out a muted sound. Disturbingly, it appeared the youth was suspended held upright by some unusual force. Du Pont jerked back instantly, sensing he was confronted with some ominous event. The youth appeared to have fallen into an immediate deep and restful sleep. Both his arms hang down by his side in a most unsettling posture. Slowly the man of science stood and retreated staring at what looked like a young boy was about to go into another frightening demented episode. Du Pont was about to shout out and call the others. The boy spoke.

"Traveller, please be seated. Du Pont froze. A man's voice spoke

"What is this? What the devil is this?

Traveller, even as you see before you this young boy, it is I, Etaanus that speaks to you.

Du Pont was stunned. "What's going on? How can you be?

"In the name of God in the highest, I am truly Etaanus your faithful companion. Now be at peace my friend, be seated and I will explain much. Have no fear."

Du Pont moved back and sat. He stared at the boy.

"You see before you, Traveller something old as the mountains and hills all about you. Earlier you witnessed this boy's body falling under the possession of a demonic spirit. Its base and less pure spirit can make itself readily capable of taking possession of any mortal. Evil spirits have the power to take over a human body and do its will and other vile acts. You witnessed this earlier. Moreover, they can do this easily, as the baser nature of mortals lends itself to be amenable to the influence of evil spirits. The least capable of these demons from the abyss, and ultra-mundane levels of existence can rule with impunity over mortals.

My God! Why is this possible? Du Pont asked.

"The boy before you possess highly mediumistic abilities. Innate abilities to surrender their energy through deep prayer and meditation. The submersion of one's spirit is as close as mortals can come to reaching consciousness with higher realms of existence. Equally, my dear friend, we spirits of the higher realms, can enter a mortal's physical body and bring great blessing to them. This boy, while in this trance-like state, experiences great peace and ecstasy. When we return him to normality, we will replace his energy we used in performing this rite. He will be fully refreshed and nourished and will have no recollection what so ever of what has occurred here.

"You spirits can do this!!

"This is done in accordance with the Almighty's wishes, and only carried out for the glory of God's name. Down through the ages of time, and through the chronicles of human history, God's spirits have related teachings and blessings to humans in this way. Carried out with great decorum and within precise conditions.

"And evil? What of evil, does it have this same power? Du Pont pressed

Yes, but constraint to limit's. Mortals who become possessed by evil spirits suffer greatly with their health and physical wellbeing. Their energy is usurped and never replaced, so over time their physical condition deteriorates. The material creation as you know it on earth presses down harshly on your mortal souls' Evil has a significant hold and influence on all earthbound creatures and exercises great control.

Then, with little effort or warning, the boy's body was raised slightly, seemingly by an invisible force and then laid gently on the ground.

"You should know Traveller, all living mortals possess this ability to meditate and surrender part of their life force. As long it is conducted in honour of God, we spirits are ever willing to accommodate these processes you see before you.

Du Pont was troubled. He had seen the way the demonic creature had usurped and manipulated the boy's body and mind. The image of a raving demented youth still fresh in his mind...

"Where is good in all of this Etaanus. Surely you high spirits can stop this demonic possession?

"Hence my friend, the task of Redemption! The spirit replied.

Slowly Du Pont knelt over the still sleeping figure on the ground, gathering his thoughts, and where this was leading.

"By Redemption! You mean, Yeshua's death. His martyrdom on a cross. And what precedes it, Etaanus.! The psychopathic brutality and wanton sadistic depravity that he will have to endure before his end. Bloodthirsty mobs wailing for his humiliation to be laid bear, half-naked and beaten to an inch of his life. This you call the Redemption!' His anger barely concealed.

"I never got it! Never accepted it. Never believed in any... His voice faltered,

"Never understood how this so-called Redemption was worth the savagery and manner of his death. Even, why his death was worth it. What's that all about Etaanus? I've read enough of New Testimony mythology to remember how all this ends. These people will turn barbarous on him, and nothing short of his near mutilation of his body will satisfy them". He hissed.

Then, the young boy groaned slightly and began to stretch, and then woke. There was no further dialogue. The conversation had ended suddenly. He looked up, a slightly bemused expression on his face and looked around. He jumped up and dusted himself off, and smiled completely oblivious to what just occurred, still smiling and with a nod, turned headed back towards his parent's camp. The physicist suspected this wasn't the end. He had questions and wondered if he might find some way to head-off, how Yeshua's end might happen. Inwardly, he knew that wasn't going to be permitted.

Your anger is well understood my friend, a voice said breaking into his thoughts.

Etaanus was standing off to his right seemingly appearing from nowhere. His expression was one of reflection and compassion. The entity displayed warmth toward the scientist and gently beckoned him to draw closer and sit on an old log lying close to a small fire.

"*My teachings here traveller, are to try to bring you to an understanding of mighty things. Matters of great importance, and value to human knowledge. Great truths that will enlighten your age of men, to cast a beacon of light into the dim and darkness of human intellect. Truths that break the bonds of ignorance that has distorted great teachings and writings down the ages.*"

Why has Yeshua to die? Du Pont shot.

"*I will so enlighten you if, you will allow me.* Etaanus replied gently

Then bowing his head and raised his arms outwards

"*If it is your wish almighty Father, let it be*".

Then without any sense of movement or orientation deep darkness enveloped them like a cloud. Within a matter of seconds, it slowly cleared. Instead of sitting at their camp side, both of them are sitting in a small fishing vessel that swayed gently in the middle of what seemed to be a lake. It is late and now without campfire light, they are surrounded by darkness. Du Pont gripped the edges.

"What's happening? He asked anxiously.

We are still in Galilee, my friend. Don't be afraid. We are in the Sea of Galilee. Now traveller, behold the great canvas of the Eternal. His companion then stood.

Across the entire surface of the water in a complete circle, a great blue light of colour unfolded and rippled across the water surface all around them. It seemed to reach high up into the heavens completely encircling them, and placing their tiny vessel at the epicentre of this magnificent vista. Du Pont was speechless. Etaanus's stance and posture changed and like a command extended his hand outwards. He turned to the scientist.

"In the realms of the beyond, there is Heaven and the great spheres of enlightenment. Spheres, where spirits of the departed afterlife on earth, has run its course. There are many, and depending on how each being has lived its life and attitude to its creator, may enter any one of these levels.

A massive eruption of colour mixed with the purest of white light appeared and dominated half the entire spectrum that surrounded them. A vista of great beauty unfolded. A vision of unseen beauty ever witnessed by a living mortal. Then a great rumble filled the very air around them, and from the very opposing part of the vision, a darker and menacing dominion opened up and spread outwards occupying most of the great encirclement they now sat. This is the domain of evil, and hell itself. Terrifying images begin to form within the abyss with all its varying shades and hues of darkness devoid of colour, and in the extreme parts utter darkness where no light entered. The pit of utter desolation. Within, there was a vast ocean of spirits of the departed, in numbers so great it was beyond counting.

"You see before you traveller, the enormous great gulf between the realm of the dead, and eternal light. All fallen spirits are destined to remain here in the depths of utter despair. These are the spiritually dead. They know nothing. They have no knowledge or appreciation of their lot or misery. "This realm of the ultra-mundane is reserved for spirits who waged open revolt in the great kingdom of Heaven, and when they occupied mortal existence on earth. Their attitude was one of utter hostility towards the will of God. This is their wretched inheritance. A sphere of existence without tone, colour, and devoid of any light. They are chained to this place without hope".

Then in the gulf between two spheres, a blinding flash of light cascaded outwards and as it does, Du Pont stood and gazed at something that mesmerized him. Galaxies of every size and shape began to materialize into existence. The appearance of the cosmos as he knew it, star groups appeared, large orbs of planets materialized and shimmered briefly then fading into the background. Slowly, the unmistakable image of iridescent blue of the Earth itself appeared and seemed to straddle the gulf between the two realms of light and darkness.

'Behold the great chasm between the forces of light and those from the abyss. All spirits trapped in the abyss are prisoners of the great evil one, and this is how it has been down through the ages and chronicles of time. You asked to what purpose redemption is set.

Du Pont just stared at what is transforming before him. Images of sublime beauty and colour populated with creatures of great presence and joy occupy the place of great light. In sheer contrast beyond measure, he stared fearfully at sights of utmost horror and debasement causing him to gasp at the vista of Hell. Creatures that once held high places in the dominions of the higher spheres now possess hideous shapes and appearances occupy these lower depths.

Before redemption was possible, a great bridge had to be created to span the huge gulf between the kingdom of Heaven, and the depths of the Abyss, my friend." Etaanus whispered.

"The material creation had to be brought into existence. It was essential and part of the divine plan. This great plan necessitated a bridge that permitted souls that wished to cross over this gulf and return to the kingdom of God. The material creation was brought into existence so that these wretched spirits could progress upwards in the material sphere, and attain the highest levels, of the human form. Their pathway if you recall, would conform to the steps you were shown previously."

Du Pont stared at his guide in disbelief consumed with everything he was shown, bringing a profound sense of humility. Nothing in human history or his life on earth came close to identifying truths unfolding before him. This was utterly new. Everything was beginning to overwhelm any beliefs he held.

"However, my friend, for these forsaken spirits to shake off the bondage of hell, terms of their freedom would need to be enforced on the powers of hell. Evil and its princess of the abyss must be forced to yield their supremacy, over these unfortunate spirit beings"

Du Pont turned

"A sacrifice, Yeshua!! He blurted.

Etaanus nodded solemnly

"Yes, Traveller. A sacrifice!

With that, he waved his right arm, and the entire vision melted into the night sky. A stillness and unearthly silence settled over the small vessel. Neither spoke. Then with both the scientist and his companion moved to the back of the boat. Du Pont was exhausted and completely drained and yet, for all of that and his mind raced to absorb the context of these mystical things. Surprisingly, he also feels a paradoxical sense of joy. These revelations of the day were evocative and yet unsettling. Without thinking too deeply, the man of science felt a sense of trust toward his companion. A supernatural entity, yet capable of great human feelings and tenderness. Then, with almost effortless movements Etaanus repositioned himself and stood over the scientist. There was pity in his eyes.

"There is so much I could relate to you, traveller. This mortal existence on earth takes a great toll on you, and your spirit. It bears down on all you mortals without reprieve. The sacrifice, we spoke of, is part of Redemption. So, it follows that redemption requires a Redeemer. The material realm of earth and all the material creation is the boundary where the two domains of good and evil collide. It is here on Earth my friend that a Redeemer must wage war against the powers of the Abyss. He said quietly.

The scientist tried to imagine the significance of everything.

"And so, a spirit of the most high must wage this battle on earth, as a mortal in human form. In so doing it enters this domain where the powers of evil have great sway and hold over all earthbound creatures. A task of great importance...and great risk. A risk that, whichever spirit undertakes this work, will fall under the powerful and pervasive influence of evil, of which all earthbound spirits experience in a great manner of ways. Satan and

his legions exert great power on earth. A redeemer could easily succumb to its power, and fail of apostasy." He said.

Etaanus paused, to allow these truths impact on his friend, then continued

"This high spirit became human and assumed a mortal existence, and commenced to wage a battle against evil, and all its perversity and deception, for that is how it binds mankind in its grip. Empty promises, great deceptions, with a mixture of untruths that lead mankind to great despair and hopelessness. Only after enduring all that the forces of evil hurl at this Redeemer, will he earn the right to impose God's terms in the abyss. He must wage a defensive battle only, while on earth as a mortal. He must endure all that evil musters at him to break his mission and purpose. To deprive him of his will and beliefs in his task. Again, as with all incarnations into human form, all previous knowledge of their place in Heaven is removed. Here free will and purpose guide this pilgrim on earth. He experienced life and a mortal existence as with all of the earth's creatures. Often full of doubt and uncertainty with life and its entire vicissitudes."

Yet Yeshua, has no knowledge of former his existence in Heaven?

"As a mortal, none whatsoever, my friend. He does possess great gifts and is aware that these are blessings sent by God. He lived his life on earth in obedience to the laws of God handed down to Moses and Abraham. I might add in passing that these two biblical characters were also very highly place spirits in God's kingdom that were also incarnated as mortals on earth. But Yeshua's awareness of his previous existence in the dominion of God is completely expunged. His spirit and purity are altered and attuned to accommodate an earthly existence. His intellect is dimmed as a consequence of his materialization as a mortal. Hence the supreme risk of this undertaking. Do you follow me?

Etaanus reached out and took his companion's hand.

"These are great truths contained in the Book of Seals Traveller, truths you must relate to men of your age. This is what he meant when he asked you to be strong and to tell his story."

Du Pont felt a chill pass through him. A task of Revelation imbued with truths that would shake human beliefs.

"Is there more"? He asked "

"Yes, indeed dear Traveller, there is more.

"...To complete the task of redemption in every detail, this most perfect of spirits took an active part in every detail for the task at hand. Including the very process of his incarnation. As you know, nowhere is God's creative process more evident than in the creation of all life itself. He doesn't call into existence all the creatures of the earth, in an instant. No, instead he endows both male and female species with the ability to produce offspring. The union of the two in the great act of collaboration of creation and in

accordance with divine laws. Male and female join in union to bring forth life. So, it is also with human procreation, the joining of the male seed and female reproduction brings into being, children. With this great act of redemption, this highly favoured spirit undertook the task in every detail from the moment of conception to his passion and earthly death by crucifixion.

Du Pont studied his companion with renewed intensity taking in everything he was hearing.

"*How do you suppose that was accomplished, my friend?* Etaanus asked

"Well I can tell you what we're supposed to believe, but I'll suspend that "

"*You may well indeed. Your creed and beliefs refer to the 'Immaculate Conception! Yes. God's laws of creation and procreation are divine and immutable, of which there are no exceptions. That applies to laws in both Heaven and Earth. There is no such thing as a virgin birth my friend. Conception would take place between man and woman. However, you witnessed first-hand tonight how spirit beings can employ human agents to carry out deeds for the good or evil. Earlier you saw the young boy's physical body being used as an instrument to communicate with mortals. Spirit beings take possession to carry out certain tasks. Human's with innate abilities to surrender their energy life force, ones with mediumistic gifts can facilitate the spirit world participation in these rites.*"

Du Pont looked incredulously at his companion for a few seconds. '

My God, Joseph! Mary's husband was capable of...

"*Acting as a human agent. Yes, Traveller. He also had these abilities. And so, in his deep trance state, the highest of the high's spirit came upon him and consummated the union. In every manner, a most remarkable union of spirit and mortal impregnated Mary and conceived the child of Yeshua. Of course, as mortals, you would find such a marvellous story impossible to consider, but only because you have no knowledge of such matters dealing with the spirit realm and its contacts with the material world*". He paused and bowed his head for a few seconds.

"*Such is the thinking and planning nature of our divine creator that all-natural things that exist in all of the creation, conform to divine precepts. The conception of a special child was truly immaculate, but not for the reasons you have accepted in your teachings. But for the most powerful spirit in existence choose to partake in the creation, with human parents of his mortal conception. This act of conception is a great gift to all mortals to partake in collaboration with God's planning in the ascent of spirits into the material world.*

Then standing, without warning his image undergoes a transformation of light and brilliance and with a few moments Etaanus, the man, was transfigured back into the former magnificent creature he first appeared.

"*It is time for you to rest Traveller to have some peace and sleep.*"

And then he was gone, dissolved into the night. Suddenly the boat jerked and Du Pont fell backward losing his balance. It was late well into the small hours he managed to look about to get his bearing when surprisingly the boat was silently propelled towards the shore. Then in the clearing light from the campfire, a figure was pulling a rope that was still attached to the bow of the vessel. As he drew nearer the figure waded into the water up to his knees, carefully guided the vessel to safety.

It's was, Yeshua Ben Yosef.

Expertly he drew the vessel through the water into position. With great ease, he reached up and took Du Pont's arm and helped him jump down into the water then steered the boat into a secure mooring.

"It's time you slept, my friend. You must have many questions? He said with a smile.

λ

CHAPTER SIXTEEN

Sal Madere.

From one of the bedroom windows of the master bedroom suite, Claudine Du Pont stood and watched.

In the garden, her two daughters sat together. The house itself felt lifeless, almost soulless. All of them put their own lives on hold throughout the upheaval in the last few weeks, but she was deeply grateful her eldest and youngest retained great friendship between them. This place was their anchor to sanity and a sanctuary, but a ghost of desperation haunted its spaces. Now emptiness echoed throughout its rooms, where there was once life, stillness filled the house. She watched them sitting in the shelter of the great oak tree towards the furthest point in their garden. She couldn't remember the last time both her daughters spent time alone sharing their secrets.

While it was sweet to watch she sensed there was something a little odd in the way they sat. Heads were dipped with not too-much talking taking place. Both sat under a large canopy almost impervious to the torrential downpour washing the grounds around them. They looked insular and abandoned. Their father was absent, and no guarantees he would ever share their moments of solitude or laughter again in this place. A hand reached out and took the others in a gesture of comfort and solidarity. As a mother, she knew her offspring well yet despite their moments and differences in outlooks and widely divergent views of life, there was friendship and an inseparable bond. Yet, something was amiss.

"How long? Michelle asked.

"At the most, three months sis. Well, it's not possible to be greater than three."

She took Michelle's hand and carefully placed it on her tummy.

"My God! I can feel a bump. Michelle said.

"That's right you can. Denise replied

"But ...that's? Michelle left unsaid.

"But that's not supposed to be for another few weeks!

"Yes, I know".

"You mean you might be pregnant for nearly, what twenty weeks!

Denise fixed her sibling a stern look,

"And I know that's not possible. We didn't... Well you know".

She smiled nervously at her younger sister. Michelle knew well her older sister didn't take chances in her relationships, forever sure-footed, Denise always knew the kind of men to avoid and yet, she had fallen totally for Paul. Their relationship just mushroomed over the last number of months, and now it seemed they were both about to become parents. She guessed something wasn't going to plan- one of which, was informing her family. That she understood, but sensed there was more.

"Have you shown yourself to Paul? I mean you seem to about twenty weeks?"

"Stop it! It can't be twenty weeks. Ok! It's simply not possible. I've told you that already. Denise snapped. Michelle was taken aback but pressed further.

"If ye were taking precautions up to now, well they're not entirely reliable. You know that!

Denise shot her younger sister a look of reprove. "I can still count the number of times, we were together Michelle, and when we were intimate. She said softly.

"And, when we first made love. This is very, very weird. All right.!

Michelle saw straight away the worry. And, it wasn't to do with telling the family. There was more.

Did you call Stephanie? Michelle asked. "Yes, she knows.

Upstairs, Claudine looked on. Having focused all her attention on her besieged husband, she had overlooked her children's needs and fears to the extent that certain things went unnoticed, until now. Her distractions of late were to do with the survival of her husband. Her thoughts began shifting away from the medical concerns to matters of science. What exactly was her husband doing that triggered this entire crisis? What part of physics crept into their lives and almost crippled his home life, and those at CERN. While these dominated her thoughts, something was afoot much closer to home. She continued to study both girls in their private moments, their mannerisms and body language, and then she raised her hand to her mouth as a thought dawned on her. It was, Michelle who was doing the counselling and-not the other way around. Then, a further thought crystallized in her head along with more attentive focus on her eldest daughter.

A little after 9.30 pm a taxi carrying her brother Francois pulled into the driveway and came to a halt. He quickly paid the taxi and made his way inside. A warm and welcoming embrace greeted him from his sister. The time on the journey was a turning point for him. As a deeply devout committed servant he was drawn to the mystical aspects of his vocation and the teaching of the gospels. Central to those teachings was the miracle of continuity and enduring nature of Christ's teachings. He sat back into the sofa letting his thoughts percolate.

Over two thousand years, these truths and tenants of faith survived and somehow spread down the ages of Christianity retaining the essence of Christ's words. A miracle despite the absence of print media, television, and the Internet and more. The workings of great events often occur when least expected, and to his mind, something extraordinary was taking place here. He would need to bring those around him, loved ones on a journey of faith to reach the same place he now found himself. After they had eaten, Francois Burgoyne changed out of his robes into more casual attire, as was his custom when staying in Sal Madere. A large pot of coffee was made and then set down between them.

"I have something that I wish to discuss with everyone and I pray, you will listen to what I have to say, with your heart."

Claudine avoided staring at her eldest daughter. Denise fixed her uncle a steady gaze wondering what's on his mind. Michelle gave her elder sister a furtive glance.

For the next two hours well into the early morning, Francois summoned all his strength and depth of faith to reveal what he believed was unfolding before them. All the features and facts, as he understood them, he laid out and their significance. He held nothing back. Layer by layer he explained how the convergence of disconnected events fell into a pattern. He was initially convinced that some of these were some kind of warning, but now in his heart what they were involved in, was infinitely more significant. He saw them as a bell-ringer, a set of signs intrinsically linked to Fletcher's work, and his role in peeling back deep secrets that ordain how our world works.

He touched briefly on the mysteries of a belief that humans cling to, and the presence of the "face" of the Shroud. Such convergence of matters of physics and metaphysics were innately beyond the realm of mathematical odds. A matter of great mystical forces must be at work. The choice of place, the choice of a person, and then the markings, ancient parchments, the recitals of texts of great historical and spiritual value, can only suggest that they were witnessing, a calling.

"We are, or Fletcher himself is, being summoned to something. Or place where time is no longer meaningful, as we simple human beings understand. If it's Fletcher, and I now believe that everything we have seen, that has caused us great distraught has a purpose. I now believe he is no great harm"

Claudine and her daughters sat speechless. Denise awkwardly repositioned herself on the settee, alive to every word. She gently and discreetly rested her hand on her midriff.

"What purpose Francois? Claudine asked

"I cannot be sure dear sister. My belief is Fletcher's spirit, his soul, will provide some answers.' The room became still.

"Do you really believe that Francois, Michelle prompted? He reached and laid his hand on hers.

"With my entire heart ma Cherie. Your father is a seeker and a good man. I believe divine forces are at work here, and he is part of some purpose or plan that will reveal itself in due course. Have faith, all of you. I've prayed to Almighty God to protect us all, and Fletcher. I only ask you to keep faith also. Some great mystery, some greater wisdom was at work here and we are part of it.'

Building Two- CERN

Felix Deveraux sat with Paul Melrose in Du Pont's office on the first floor of building two. Its a little after 8.30 am. There were outstanding issues that both men needed to consider. Deveraux had taken to wearing suits of late. Today he chooses a silver-grey pinstripe, which tended to formalize his mood and his status. Problem was, he wasn't feeling that way.

"Let's suspend the science for a moment young man and focus on the religious aspect." He said

"Are you sure you wouldn't prefer talking to Doctor Ambrosiana? Melrose asked.

"You have a more balanced perspective. Deveraux said

"Carina is not entirely dispassionate. Her faith is very strong, and I know her thinking about this already. What I had in mind is how we link science and these very mysterious circumstances. Starting with the markings over near the CMS tunnel section 16a. These intricate Riemannian calculi of yours. I think there's a connection I think both are linked in some higher field equations. Then there is the Shroud Image in Fletcher's screen".

It was obvious Deveraux was troubled. Reputations and legacies of great theoretical groundbreaking work could come undone. Worse, the possible terminal demise of a senior research fellow during a highly publicized experiment would bring massive public scrutiny and possibly ruin for some.

"There's something else that's troubling, my friend.

"Such as? Asked Melrose.

The Director stayed quiet for a few seconds. He didn't like secrets, but what he was about to show the younger scientist would be just another burden shared. Issues continue to pile up, none with plausible explanations. He reached over and pushed a small disc into its slot on his terminal. He turned the screen around so that Paul can see.

The screen opened showing the command centre at the launch of the Euclid 4 beta 8 beams run on that fateful day. It flickered on, as a video feed from one of the many cameras installed within the centre itself came to life. It showed all the Euclid project teams immersed around their large semi-circular screen banks. They recognized themselves in some of the shots, as a series of multilevel shots were condensed into selected views some showing the moment the initial excitement of the trial unfolded. Then the camera angle showed the tall image of Du Pont moving away from his group and moving towards the large glass wall partition that looked out onto the main gallery where the massive CMS structure stood floors below him.

The image suddenly showed the time sequence, only slowed down to half the frames per second of normal speed. Both men stared at the scene that opened up before them. From a range of camera angles, it seemed no one was remotely aware of what followed at that precise time. Du Pont's rather blurred figure is seen standing amidst the excitement all around him. Then in a single simple gesture, he appeared to reach out with one and touch the surface of the glass. In that moment of moments, it seemed the most natural of gestures to want to touch the enormous forces that were unleashed below him. To be in commune with the most fundamental forces of nature. What happened next caused Melrose to gasp in astonishment?

Almost within the blink of an eye, the area around Du Pont's outstretched hand glowed an intense white light for less than a second. Brief, and hardly captured on the camera's lens but unmistakable contact of energy emanated outwards from his hand. Then in just as brief as the eye could discern, the glow ran along his arm and enveloped his entire frame. What happened next stunned Melrose.

The figure of the American was lifted upwards, no more than a matter of inches and then the light, which engulfed him, disappeared. He was seen gripping his hand and fell backward and collapsed to the command centre floor. Deveraux tapped a button and the screen went blank.

Paul Melrose sat for a few seconds, speechless, stunned. He returned the older man's studied and troubled gaze.

What! In all that's...Holy fuck! This was no ordinary medical episode! He gasped.

"It would appear not. Deveraux whispered A few seconds pass.

The moment of silence allowed both men to consider how this played out both internally within the organization, the outside world particularly, and to the family. Melrose became agitated.

"He lit up! Like a *light bulb*. What could possibly do that?

Deveraux sat forward and interlocks both his hands. He had a decision to make. "I am assembling all the directors tomorrow, and I am then going to show all of them what you've just seen. Then I am recommending that all further experimentation involving Euclid to be suspended here in Geneva till we come to terms with what exactly we're dealing with here. What I need you to do for me now Paul, is to set up both the time and place to meet with the family"

Melrose nodded unsure if this was the right thing to do. He was too stunned to grapple with an explanation of what he just witnessed. "When that is done, we're going to assemble the best minds we have at our disposal here on campus, and we go through all the profile decay patterns. Where these exotic particles or receptor mass-less particles first made their appearance." Deveraux said.

"What are we looking for DG? That's a lot of computing resource, it could take...

"We're looking for an Aberration! Any goddamn anomaly that's off the charts to anything we know or understand about fundamental physics!

He stood up from behind his desk and fixed his young associate physicist a steely look.

"I want to know is this physics as we know it, or is they're lurking out there an alternative to this kind of science. For all our sakes, and that of Fletcher's!

It was a little after seven am in Sal Madere. Both daughters were still asleep. Claudine and her brother stayed up most of the night and had adjourned to her husband's study, in part to try and reinforce his presence, and somehow he might have left something for them to find.

"I know you and Fletcher have nothing in common Francois, but he deeply admires you. 'You mean our beliefs. We're polar opposites remember."

"He is not completely agnostic you know. He portrays that to shield some doubts."

"I didn't think he had any. Francois added pouring her water.

"Do you know Francois there is something we need to understand a little more? He shot her a look as he settled into his chair.

"I haven't seen any clinical information that suggests what happened to Fletcher. Have you?

'How do you mean? He asked

"My husband was in pretty good shape. No medical problems. Yet, he is supposed to have experienced a cardiac attack of some kind. It doesn't make sense? These beliefs you spoke of earlier Francois, the metaphysical aspects, did you mention any of this with your Father Provincial. I know you're both close?

He flashed her a smile. "Indeed dear sister and at length. He is a man of great wisdom and spiritual depth. Given what I've have told you all earlier if there is a divine dimension to all this, it matters not how it happened. He said quietly.

"Francois, there is something else I need to talk about. She hesitated. She needed to choose her words. Her brother was very attached to both her daughters, and if anything drew his ire or darker side of his persona more, it is someone causing his beloved nieces some upset.

"I need to talk about…Denise!

He stopped mid-air with his glass, gave her a quizzical look, and returned the glass to the desk. Leaning forward he looked her straight in the eye.

"What about Denise?

Tears quickly fill her eyes, pent up stress over the last weeks gripped her as she fought to control all her feelings from erupting in the privacy of her husband's office. Her voice quivered unable to express the depth of despair that was starting to consume her. The fight in her was slipping; her outward shield of strength was crumbling inside. The nightmare she was living through seemed to have no end, it kept her and her family imprisoned inside a cocoon of utter hopelessness, and now there was more. The images that rose up in her mind from her brother's revelations earlier touch a part of her being with raw fear. Now perhaps, another part of her family was about to be embroiled in something she simply wasn't sure she was ready to deal with.

"Claudine, what is it? What about Denise?

Tears welled up in his eyes, as he held her, allowing all the terror and fear stored up in her to simply unfold as she cried out and sobbed uncontrollably. She cried out as if begging someone to rescue her from falling apart. Finally, the sobbing eased as she felt the comfort of her brother.

"Tell me, Francois, has God abandoned us? Is this a punishment for something we've done? He drew back and saw empty despair. So different from the resilient women he knew and loved.

"God never abandons any of us. It is we who sometimes abandon him! Look at me, dear sister, I believe with all my heart that this will soon end with great joy"

He took out a small handkerchief and dried her eyes. "And no, this is not a punishment." It's an invitation, Chère sœur. We're all part of something involving Fletcher. An invitation to reach out and summon God's help. That's all Claudine, reach out. You'll find he always answers."

He moved and sat her down, and poured her a fresh drink. Then he pulled up a chair opposite her. Smiling he reached and took her hand.

"Now! Tell me. Denise?

In the small hours of the morning standing just inside the main gate seeking shelter from the driving rain, a figure of a man stood in the shadows looking towards the house. All the lights were off, only for one from a small window on the ground floor. He stood and imagined the turmoil raging inside those walls. He had some answers. All that was needed was to be asked, and he would answer. Benjamin Mochti turned the collar of his coat up to ease the wet and piercing rain soaking through him. He had to act soon before it was too late.

Office of Director-General.

After the morning coffee was finished, everyone was directed to the private study of Director General's, which was a little unusual, but at precisely 8.00 am and all the key directors of CERN top team assembled with a mixture of intrigue and anticipation. Among the first to arrive, was Monika Reinhardt then Miles Kingsley followed by others including Carina Ambrosiana, Jim Kennedy, Amber Jenkins, last to arrive was Manfred Gruess. There were at least fifteen in number that filed into the room that morning. No one knew what the meeting entailed, other than a brief note from Professor Deveraux that it would take no more than an hour. The excitement throughout this entire group was still palpable from the results from Euclid 4 beta 8, muted only by the news of their colleague Prof. Du Pont's slow but steady recovery in hospital. As soon as everyone was present all took a seat at a large circular table.

Deveraux waited for a few seconds then stood and asked all come to order. His tone was unusually formal and business-like. It became apparent that something was afoot. Of the group, only four of them knew the real story as to Du Pont's true status in the hospital.

'What I am about to show you, is highly confidential, Deveraux said without any preliminaries.

"It's still very raw with me. It has only come to my attention in the last day or so".

Everyone listened, some casting a few glances around the room. Then Deveraux leaned over and switched on the player and a large wall-mounted screen come to life. The disc ran no more than two minutes. At the end of the first showing there were silent gasps around the room. Then, Deveraux replayed the section again only at key parts, did he pause for all to study, then continued. Twice he ran the disc, during which there were, mixed reactions all around the room. It's apparent this was more serious and disturbing then at first. When the disc was finished and the screen went blank there was complete silence.

No one said a word. Even Carina Ambrosiana, and Manfred Gruess, who were privy to all the event details up to now, was stunned.

"For those of you here let me explain, why this is troubling."

He paused, noting the look on all the faces around him. Men of great honour, of immense capabilities and integrity.

"Fletcher's... Prof Du Pont's, life hangs by a thread. He has not regained consciousness, and lies in a coma.' There were stunned looks around the room.

"He's on a life support machine, and there appears to be little or no brain activity. It's been that way since that event you have just seen, during the Euclid beam run. His doctors are currently making a determination as to when this life support machine is... switched off.'

Murmurs of disbelief filled the room. Some of his associates sat in utter shock, most of them assessing the consequences in their own minds. The silence felt like a wake, the passing of a colleague and a friend. Deveraux knew this would affect each and everyone in the room. All had close ties with Du Pont.

"Colleagues, Friends. Can any of you here in this room suggest an explanation, as to (a) what was the source of the light, it's brilliance and its origin and (b) What energy field, or cause lifted Fletcher's entire body like that...because quite frankly, I'm out of answers"

No one immediately responded. It wasn't often Felix Deveraux spoke like this.

"DG. May I?

It was Miles Kingsley the tall English Professor and Head of Detector Technologies.

"As I see it, we have not established causation here. We know for certain Fletcher did not display any markings or burns on his body whatsoever on his admission to hospital. We were there. I saw nothing on his body. Whatever that was DG, it left no physical evidence...Now, I know what we all saw here, and it's disturbing to watch! But ...there was no physiological damage that I am aware of...other what happened subsequently."

He stopped suddenly. More glances around the group. An awkward moment followed for a brief few seconds.

"What do you mean?...*Happened subsequently*? Asked the American, Jim Kennedy quietly.

"There is more! Deveraux said sharply.

'If, I may continue DG, please'. Kingsley pressed on.

"Bear with me Jim. Theoretically, this disc proved very little. Yes we saw something very visually but it was perhaps an optical effect".

"I'm sorry Miles that's absurd. We all saw Fletcher being lifted. That wasn't optical. Said Carina Ambrosiana.

"I think what Miles is referring to Carina, is our legal status here. Are we culpable or negligent in some way? Deveraux said sharply.

"Am I right, Miles?

"Precisely- DG. This disc exists only here. Medical records so far I am aware suggest Fletcher's condition as well, some acute condition. We must think very carefully on how this could be construed".

Again, the room went silent. Unease crept into the meeting, as each of them felt slightly uncomfortable with the issues of legal liability, possible negligence, and any suggestion to cover up the disc's existence. Following on from the Paul Melrose episode, then the apparent vandalism in the tunnel itself, and those markings, CERN might not come out of this too well. The unease changed to tension. The mood turned to annoyance and impatience.

"May I ask again, the American insisted.

"What happened subsequently...to Fletcher. Did something happen after he was airlifted from here to Geneva?

A murmur went around the room. All eyes turned toward Deveraux who sat stoically at the centre of the round table. Nothing was said for a few seconds as the team sensed there was more. A few seconds passed. The room fell silent.

"DG, maybe its... time. Whispered Manfred Gruess

Deveraux sat motionless and then nodded imperceptibly. He reached over to a small table and lifted a large cream-colored envelope marked "HIGHLY PRIVILEGE INFORMATION" and placed it down on the table. He paused and considered his decision.

"I agree, DG. It's time. Carina Ambrosiana said quietly.

Deveraux slid his hand into the folder and removed six large black and white photographs of the stricken scientist, taken at different intervals over the last few weeks. Carefully he selected them into chronological order and placed in the centre of the table, and slowly sat back. Hands from round the table reached across and turned them to study. An eerie silence gripped the entire group as the images burn into the consciousness of those present.

"Oh dear God!! Dear Jesus...What is this?

The room dynamics stalled as the pictures of Du Pont's altered appearance sunk in. For nearly a full thirty seconds, no one spook as hands passed different shots across the table to others. One or two of the scientists stood up and moved away to the window lost in some inner conflict. Others just stared, unable to quite comprehend what's confronting them. Deveraux made eye contact with Ambrosiana, Kinsley's, Gruess, and Monika Reinhardt. Each of them knew from the beginning but seeing their colleague's reaction still unsettled them. Finally, when the shock of the pictures passed, a sombre mood settled in the room.

'You can see how all this might look in the wrong hands. Deveraux said quietly.

'How is the family coping with all of this Felix? Asked one of the group.

"Not well, my friends. They're just about hanging in. He replied.

At that moment Felix Deveraux made an executive decision. The pixilated image of the Shroud Image was going to stay locked in his desk. This group needed to know just enough so he allowed the conversations to run for a few minutes and in the process help share some of his burdens and demons. Each of them, men, and women were at the frontier of particle physics, confident, assured, and competent, yet for all of that, the images he shared had shaken each of them. Some more than others- all nursing troubling thoughts and some involved fear. He tapped his spoon on the edge of the cup and conversations came to a halt.

"As you are all aware, we've put Euclid on hold till we understand all the physics and good work so far. So, ladies and gentlemen, we must consider if these matters are the product of science, or something else"

He let his remark sit, and gauges what comes next.

"Something else!! What do you mean DG? Asked someone.

While the session with the Directors was in progress Paul Melrose wanted time to think about more personal things closer to his heart. A new part of life was going to open to him, and while he was happy, overjoyed in fact, he needed to think how ready he was. He was deeply in love, and that wasn't going to change. He was, however, nervous about becoming a father. He knew Denise was ready, surprised, but also overjoyed. He headed underground to the main accelerator beam tunnel. Within ten minutes he descended to the lower tunnel ring of the LHC and donned a safety helmet and a high visibility jacket.

The tunnel itself being over several miles in circumference, on foot wasn't an option. Still, he indulged in walking along some of its sections sometimes to think. The occasional flash memory of his own bizarre experience was now a distant image. A further 200 meters and he came to the section of the tunnel where the markings occurred. Not surprisingly, a team of technicians was working on routine splicing work going on nearby. Standing, he looked around the curved tunnel wall taking in how surreal the entire setting had become.

Within seconds he noticed something different. The arrangement of markings over the tunnel curvature looked changed. Altered in some way that wasn't noticeable before. It was odd, yet something seemed off. He stood for a few seconds not wanting to rush, but something was amiss. Concentrating for a few seconds he moved closer. Looking carefully, his attention was drawn to a detail. Standing back to check both sides, he whistled to himself not sure if he was mistaken. The curve of the lines as he originally saw them were shorter on one side of the tunnel. When first seen, the opposite ends of the curved ended on the opposing walls directly in perfect alignment with each other. Now it was skewed, the left-hand side was noticeably two feet higher. Any sign of the remaining lower portion mysteriously erased. Leaning closer, nothing, not even the heat marks remained. His face became tense. He traced his fingertips along the wall. There was no mistake; the curved line had become shorter. There was still symmetry but the entire episode became more sinister and deeply unsettling. Melrose slowly stood back and studied the bizarre circumstances fighting to preserve some composure. If felt as if some menacing presence was at work. Personal issues in his life simply vanished from his thoughts.

CHAPTER SEVENTEEN

Magdela

First light entered the tent brought a warm and welcoming breeze. It's followed by the rich smell of food, that of freshly cooked fish. From nowhere a figure of a man, a complete stranger entered his small abode and beckoned him to rise and bided him with gestures to follow. To his immediate contemporaries, he was known simply as Traveller. Now, however, the scientist, the physicist, and man of the 21st century with his conscious mind fully rejuvenated decided to take matters into his own hands. He eat sparingly but finished the food. During his sleep, something inside him rekindled a need to confront lingering doubts as to why he had been summoned to glimpse into other realms of existence and chosen for some higher purpose to visit a place unknown to mortals. His mortal agnostic beliefs lay in ruins, and yet there were questions. Questions from his time, his personal convictions, his own private morality, and judgments upon which humanity cried out for truth. The world he left behind suffered greatly and avoidably at the hands of religious beliefs and creeds and abstract mythologies. Conflicting deities with inhuman doctrines caused and inflicted great hardships and injustice throughout human history. This was going to be a day where truth imposed its own requirements. And so it would be.

Emerging from the tent, he was confronted with something very different from the previous evening. Rather than the rich texture of browns and ochre-coloured terrain and lush green vegetation coupled with the mixture of sounds of people that existed hours earlier, it was now was completely deserted, just the sound of the sea lapping on a shore.

He was completely alone. Except it wasn't as he remembered it. The ground and the entire surface as far as he can see turned black, the sand, and stones and the small hills were completely devoid of colour. The beautiful tranquil village of Magdala was gone. The sky of azure blue of the previous day was replaced with a darker tone deepest blue, almost menacing, as it was unnatural. His view looked out over a flat body of water that slowly began to shed its colour replaced by a stain that came from the distant horizon and began to consume the entire sea in an ink-black stain moving across the surface like a shadow, rendering his entire vista into a scene of utter desolation emptied of colour, tone and life. From nowhere an earthshaking rumble rolled across the entire terrain, a sound with a deep resonance of power that shook and reverberated through everything around him. A surge of tectonic energy rippled through the surface under his feet causing him to stumble as the force began terrain-altering transformation in every direction around him. Everything started to shift. Stones began to bounce on and across the ground and large boulders start to roll, amid the intensity of vibration. Just as he crawled to a small tree stump near him, a scene opened up on the surface of the sea.

Du Pont almost stopped breathing. Out of the sea, the surface of the water opened outwards as if is being unzipped by some invisible hand and rising upwards in dark silhouette, a shape. The unmistakable shape of a cross. After a few seconds does the man of science recognize the image as that of a Crucifixion? A body lay impaled with outstretched arms, a broken and battered figure with the distinctive sharpness of twisted thorns embedded on the head. An image and vision of utter barbarity as the cross itself tilted out of silhouette-revealing a figure in stark contrast conveyed all the markings of savagery and grotesque cruelty etched into his body and consummated in a single drop of blood falling to the water's surface.

Slowly the sea around the cross began to flow a crimson red, as the last drops fell. The apparition was stunning in its simplicity; its imagery and the message of the unmistakable things to come.

"It's the fulfilment of his great task of Redemption". A solitary voice called out.

Etaanus was standing next to him dressed in simple Sheppard's clothing.

"*Now watch my friend, and behold!*"

The vision remained suspended, emblematic of a broken mortal hanging as a limp and lifeless form. Now as the rolling rumble deepens rock and huge sections of the hills are rent-free from the earth and seem to collapse and disintegrate into molten chunks of ash. Du Pont stands transfixed at the unfolding vision. Looking upwards the awesome sight the earth around him seems to elevate upwards. From the impaled crucified form at the centre of the sight, a radiated gold light erupted outwards in all directions. It's gold light further illuminating the extent of crimson red had spread across the surface of the sea. A figure of pure white began to materialize above the crucified form, a figure of a man.

"Etaanus! What is this"?

"As a mortal, he did not fall into apostasy. He endured all the forces of evil that could muster to break him. Now he will impose his task of redemption on the apostates of Hell. He will wage an offensive battle in the abyss, as a spirit of undiminished power. Behold, the cause and the source of all existence".

He bowed forward in a manner of great respect towards the light.

It is his spirit you see departing his mortal being." He said.

Du Pont started to feel his skin to glisten and glow ever so slightly. An immense strength took hold of him; faltering he turned to witness his shepherd companion commence to reform into his original angelic transformation. His eyes become dazzled to the explosion of light that surrounded Etaanus towering figure holding a lance of Gold.

Within a few seconds, four other spirit creatures appear each as resplendent as Etaanus himself, although attired completely different. These were warrior spirits, their large extended wings were silver armour, their eyes glow pure blue and each carrying long swords of gold and sapphire.

"Have no fear! Traveller. They are your guardians."

The boundary between substance and matter merged into an alternative realm of time itself causing the man of science to fall inwards into a vortex, a place where three-dimensional space became elastic and without form. There was neither a sense of up nor down and, where normal sensations of gravity and direction appear suspended. Mysteriously invisible energy enveloped him permitting him to experience a gift of super-sight, an ability to peer into forbidden places. Places no mortal while living can ever witness. At first, it seemed that everything about him is rising upwards until he realizes the illusion, they were descending. The symbol of the crucified form and the emergent light rekindled a fear as he remembered Etaanus prophetic words to wage a battle in the abyss. Instantly Du Pont knew they were descending into the depths of the Abyss, into Hell itself.

Within an infinitesimal moment, he saw the figure of Yeshua appear. The scientist gasped at his appearance, his face, his whole physique was altered and bathed in light as pure as he had ever witnessed. All four of the surrounding creatures bowed before him. Suddenly, the image and vision of the crucifix and the seascape dissolved. Etaanus moved out in front of where they are standing.

"Traveller, the final act of Redemption is at hand. Yeshua the man and mortal, now as the Christ, will impose his will, against his brother Lucifer, the evil one, and prince of the abyss. Lucifer had utilized and harnessed his most potent powers over his dominion of men, to bring this Nazarene carpenter to his knees, and to Apostasy, and failed. Now he must reap the consequences. Cast your eyes upon the depths Traveller, and witness the final act of redemption.

For as far as the eye could see, and to the limits of human calculation, an army of countless legions from the heavens opened up above them. Elements of some of the potent legions of archangels descend upon them arriving in waves upon waves in numbers beyond counting and stretching almost to infinity. Their luminous powerful light shun down into the depths to reveal a realm of utter doom and darkness. Leading the assault into the Abyss stood a figure of intense light and radiance, the mortal, which had walked the earth, and endured the insufferable agony of both mental and physical pain, now vanquished all before him. Creatures of every conceivable sort, hostage and chained to the bonds Hell, screamed in revolt as the light consumed the Abyss. Sounds of utter despair as the fruits of retribution rained down on them.

For, what appeared an endless time the boundaries of hell were redrawn and set to such an extent causing prince of hell to scream a piercing howl of submission. Large misshapen life forms appear shaking violently as the lights from the swords of Archangels drove these deformed and grotesque spirit beings lower into the depths without exception. A war without equal raged on of which no mortal had ever witnessed. Etaanus extended his arm out and touched Du Pont gently, bringing an end to his physical shaking

"Our creator is one of infinite love and justice, Traveller. The powers of hell from henceforth will be curtailed by boundaries set by divine and immutable laws.' Before this great task of redemption was accomplished all who dwelt in the depths were enslaved here, and all on earth were subjects or inured to the Prince of Hell. That was their lot, and in many instances, evil possession was allowed free rein to usurp mortals and use them as agents of great evil. No more! The great task of Redemption is at hand. A bridge was now open to all fallen spirits who so choose of their own volition, and change of heart may return to the realm of light. No longer was there a barrier, and so Traveller, it was time, for the entire material creation to be brought into existence and permit all forsaken spirits, to shake off the bonds of evil, and turn their minds to their lost and separated God. Do you follow and understand these great things, my friend? He asked gently.

"Hence the Creation itself became the spheres of progress where all spirits progress upwards from the depths, through the material creation itself, and the Earth.

The scene before them was one of the great contrasts as the legions of the heavens returned from the depths of the pit triumphant, led by a single powerful entity. Time itself its concept lost meaning. The imagery of the most vivid kind had taken history and time itself and unfurled into a canvas of spellbinding visions before the scientist's eyes. Past and present notions of time were rendered void, as great events ever before the birth of human history meant anything, now played out with majestic clarity. Revelations of a remarkable kind, of happenings within another realm opened up to be witnessed by a single mortal.

As a man who never believed in deities or God, Du Pont simply nodded. Absorbing the details of such a cataclysmic clash of the realms of good and evil left him speechless. The breath of wisdom unfolded before him played out in such imagery mesmerised him.

"Evil still exists Etaanus! How does this alter Mankind's Redemption?

The spirit entity moved closer, this time holding in his arms the great Book of Seals.

"Evil and the prince of the abyss can still rule over those, who willingly give their allegiance to him. Spirits who've turned from God, and converted their utter hostility to his divine will to wage open warfare for that's is what spirit rebellion is, and sided with Lucifer. He was permitted to retain dominion over those who have abandoned all that is good and wish to enslave humanity. Ever since the forces of evil introduced money into mankind, it has given it unlimited dominion and complete power over them. Evil may not, however, under force or coercion rule mankind. Such vile possession of humans such as you have witnessed rule over mortals with impunity, is over. I might add my friend: spirits of the depths have no recall or understanding of their former glory in Heaven. None. They know nothing of their wretched circumstances or former state.

"Why not show them how much they have fallen. Du Pont said.

"The gift of freewill Traveller. Each of us all possessed this great gift, to accept or reject the divine will of the creator. All life on Earth is a test. To show by an act of will, that we accept God's law, and our journey through life as mortal existence is to surrender our beliefs to him and his laws, or chose to follow our more base instincts and become drawn to evil and all its false promises".

He paused and put his hand on the scientist's shoulder.

"*What use is free will my friend if all who have fallen could see and recall their former existence in the abode. Their glory and perfection as it was, and now, in contrast, their pitiful lot. They would without hesitation give up and return to God's house, but for the wrong reasons or purpose. There would be no merit or justice in their ascent to the higher realms of Heaven. Do you understand Traveller, God is infinite love and just. He tries his creatures and allows them great freedom of action, the result of free will? Such as it is, free will permits mortals to choose their beliefs and actions. Now, as a result of the redemption, those who chose to cross that great gulf and return to God's kingdom, may do so as an expression of the gift of free will.* He answered gently.

The man of science recoiled as truths of great wisdom were revealed in a manner of untold power and imagery along with explicit natures of good and evil. Both narrative and illumination of ideas, the presence of uncharted realms of existence came about with great spellbinding beauty and power. He felt nothing but utter and complete humiliation in his surroundings. Du Pont had witnessed something that no other human being had ever been shown. At that moment he crumpled and dropped to his knees and cried.

"These great events my dear Traveller, have been lost or obscured by the written hand of deception and falsehood down through the ages and chronicles of time. Meanings of sacred truths and texts imparted and transcribed by God's spirits to mankind have become corrupted by man's weakness for power. One word here altered in places can, and did change the entire passages, leading to error. Human minds adding their own truths, giving different accounts of Christ's teachings and meanings were utterly distorted, leaving in their wake a patchwork of untruths and error, and like all human thinking, ephemeral."

Etaanus lifted his right arm, and the entire vision slowly dissolved before him. A mist of cloud formed momentarily, before clearing revealing a beautiful meadow, of long flowing grass and wildflowers. The vision of these previous events dissolved from sight. Time itself seemed to shift to the physical space of another age, and then seamlessly transitioning to a place of a more worldly and familiar setting. A beautiful tranquil scene of great peace washed with vibrant colours surrounding them. A gentle breeze tossed the long grass and the Sun's warmth and light washed over them lifting the scientist's spirit in the welcoming sun on his face. Then the unmistakable sound of water nearby a stream of rushing water running over stones. The angelic figure pointed and led him to the edge to where the stream ran.

Its sound of babbling water eased Du Pont's troubled mind. A Little to their right, the sound was more pronounced splashing coming from slightly elevated ground as the water springs to the surface into a small pool. It trickled over the edge and ran into the stream itself. Etaanus gently bade him scoop up and drink from the pool. Responding Du Pont leaned over and cupped both hands and drank. The water was cool and welcoming as it's refreshing. The scene enveloped both of them, and for the very first time since their meeting in the Judean desert, Du Pont looked to Etaanus with great affection. A bond had developed.

He reflected how was it possible that a mere mortal could feel such deep friendship towards an entity of great power, and nobility. He had taken him to witness things that were deeply humbling and sometimes haunting. Yet, for all of that, this magnificent creature from another sphere of existence had become a Sheppard, a comforter, and friend. Then in a surprising gesture, he came and smiled.

"May I call you, Fletcher? He asked.

This brought a smile to the scientist.

"Yes, I would like that very much.

"Truths travel long distances in time Fletcher down through all the ages. And like this beautiful stream, we drink it, and it infuses us, refreshes us, particularly if we drink its

revitalizing freshness from its source. It's at its most purity, at its source. Further, from its spring, the stream picks up impurities, becomes less nourishing!

He studied the scientist for a tentative few seconds letting the import settle. Du Pont returned his stare, and then like a small light bulb switching on in his mind, he stepped back.

My God!! This whole thing! This Time inversion...is about getting to the source of...Truths! Etaanus nodded and smiled

"Go on, my man of science".

Du Pont took another scoop from the stream and splashed it over his face. Without warning, he burst into laughter.

"Yes, Yes! I think I understand Etaanus. The further I drink this water from its source, much further downstream, the less pure it becomes... less refreshing."

"Less invigorating! Etaanus added quietly.

Du Pont allowed the significance of the moment to settle. This simple benign metaphor rang true, Etaanus reached out and place his hand on the scientist's shoulder.

"So, it has been with Christ's teachings, his words his intellect, and his wisdom. Little of the purity of his teachings retains any of their purity over humanity due to great misdeeds of falsehoods in writings. Within the chronicles of time untruths, false interpretations, and deceptions were perpetrated into holy scripts and so-called sacred texts. Is it any wonder that a great portion of mankind no longer finds great comfort in their religions? It no longer nourishes their souls. Beliefs, no longer hold people as it once was. Faiths are diminished. Human souls are bereft of the strength of conviction. Truths and teachings have lost its freshness much like this stream further down its path from this spring. All earthbound spirits, mortals like you Fletcher have a deep thirst for truth. A truth that would fill your spirits with fullness, an enrichment of truths that comes from Heaven. A wisdom that confirms that life on earth is but a short time before we all return to the realm of God's Kingdom."

Etaanus looked to his companion with great caring.

"It's a message that, Yeshua, would like you to carry.

"Can you carry water that far?

"Is that what he meant, when he asked me, to be strong, and tell his story?

"Yes, indeed my friend. There is divine purpose to all this and where there is a purpose, there is great order. If you choose to accept this offering, as a pilgrim of truth, God will bless you.

Etaanus stood and turned away and slightly raised his face to the heavens. His eyes closed, and then he bowed as if he was in commune with another realm.

"May I show you something that relates to you, my Friend?

The scientist glanced towards his friend with a wry smile.

"Will I like it?

It will be... instructive!

Du Pont was about to respond when out of the corner of his eye, figures approached in the distance. At first, they look like a mirage of shimmering shapes heading in his direction. Then, in a matter of a few seconds, there were in all six of them. Men and women. They approached in pairs. He sensed they were couples, and dressed most elegantly, almost of another age and time. The men wore black and purple robes to their waists and brown leggings with black leather boots. The women wore a range of blues and cream-colored long full-length robes. They came right up and stood on the opposite bank of the stream and stopped. All of them smiling and bowed towards the scientist and his companion stood. Etaanus bowed towards them.

"They can see you Fletcher, but cannot communicate with you, nor you with them".

Du Pont looked in admiration, for no other reason than their appearance. They were extraordinarily beautiful couples with a radiance that shone from their complexion and almost ivory and olive skin. The scientist smiled and waved across at them. They were young couples and as best he could tell in human terms their early thirties. Then he turned to Etaanus slightly mystified but smiled,

"Lovely people. Very striking. Who are they? He whispered to his friend.

Etaanus gave him a mischievous smile.

"They are your departed parents, dear friend.

Du Pont stood rooted to the ground.

"What!

Then one of the couples raised their hands and waved eagerly in his direction.

"They are your parents, Fletcher. You are their progeny. They reside in Heaven now and restored to their most vibrant state. Much of their appearance reflects their great purity of spirit. Their physical forms have reached such perfection, that it mirrors their spiritual state. Hence the reason, that you do not immediately recognize them. It is with all who return to God's place in the higher realms, their mortal appearance; their spiritual bodies undergo great changes such that if they returned to earth, many would not be recognized.

Then with a mere gesture, one couple extended their arms and slowly their appearance altered briefly back to how he knew them on earth, and as he always would remember them aged, graceful and stooped. Du Pont stood and trembled with joy as tears trickled down his face. He just looked across a stream that spanned an eternity as a great emotional wave gripped him. Then with a simple gesture, blew them a kiss. The female stopped waving, and then to Du Pont sense of joy, she returned the gesture. His father held up his hand and opened his palm, in a gesture that the scientist knew from his childhood, that sign of approval a simple gesture his father always gave to show his immense pride in his son.

"Etaanus! How can I thank you for this? He whispered.

Before his eyes, their slow reincarnation was restored to their new glory and youthful radiance. He stared in awe for a few moments and found the two other couples also beam with great love and affection towards him. He looked and smiled a little unsure as to their presence.

"And these people, Etaanus? He asked gently.

Etaanus smiled and moved closer to his side.

"They are your parents also! My dearest friend, you have lived on earth, many times, incarnated as a mortal. In each life, you had parents that nurtured and loved you as much. So it is with the other couple, your parents of a former existence. You have, as with all mortals, only recollection of this life the one you are experiencing now. Previous life's on earth merited their own experiences and spiritually grew and harboured different attitudes to God in that lifetime. For some, only one life on earth is sufficient, for countless others, they must return to earth many times, on their upward sojourn in spiritual development and love of God, and his fellow men.

Etaanus reached out and placed his hand on his companion's shoulder.

"As pilgrims on earth, you and each of your fellow mortals must take responsibility for their own salvation, and take up the path that Redemption has opened up for you. It is a time of probation, and the freedom to choose. The choice to reject evil, and embrace all that is good".

Instantly, all the images and forms on the other side of the stream dissolved into shimmering white lights and fade into the brightness of the warm sunshine of the afternoon. To see his beloved parents again, to touch that special moment in time, to look into their faces, to connect and briefly relive their presence left him with a profound sense of loneliness. He stopped fidgeting with his hands. His nerves and emotions became mixed. All of his science and deep connections with physics come to a halt. His mind and entire thinking were challenged to peer beyond everything he knew or accepted. This serene and beautiful setting, and what it represented would last for eternity.

"Am I Dead, Etaanus? Is this place, where we're standing real? He finally asked.

"Why do you ask? Does it not feel and look real".

"I'm very lost. Am I alive? Am I having a dream or complete breakdown? His voice quivered

"You are very much alive Fletcher. You are a spirit. It's your spirit that is having this wonderful experience, unencumbered by either space or, time. It is the purest form and expression of your being. As a disembodied spirit, you can visit parts of God's creation, and witness great things. As one of God's messenger's I am trusted to impart these mighty

teachings in ways that you can witness, and understand. By showing you some aspects of different parts of creation, you will gather, as a non-believer that human error is fine with God. You are all his beloved creatures and, as mortals can only grasp a glimpse of his magnificent creation.

The scientist and man of the 21st century got down and sat on the soft grass and stared into the trickling crystal water. A fresh breeze caressed the long grass. He felt its presence almost blow away other things within him. New thoughts and beliefs ignite within. The existence of a power that marshals forces and wields events with such impeccable order and beauty transcended anything he knew. Here, like the evening by the campfire under those vivid stars, he reflected on the underlying purpose of what was happening to him. To be cast into the realms of the supernatural, mystical places, dominions of super beings. The domains of demons and the existence of places beyond the material universe or cosmos, reshaping how time and reality are experienced, such extraordinary events consumed him. It was all, quite overwhelming

If, I'm not dead, then ...Where is here?

His spirit guide came and sat next to him.

"Here! Is simply a place in God's kingdom Fletcher? It's a mirror of your mind, a place that mirrors what peace, and happiness means to you and in your soul. In dwells deep inside all mortals on Earth. All you need to do is access it in your heart, and believe. And it will be given to you. It is your inheritance. Then without warning

"Do you still question my friend, the existence of a being of unfathomable creative power? A creator of unimaginable love, which wants you to inherit the governance of the universe because that is your destiny, my friend. It is your inheritance —as part of God's plan to oversee and comply with his divine plan. It is God's plan. That is what redemption means, when every last spirit, shakes off the chains of bondage in the depths of the abyss. Then, and only then, when every last spirit leaves the pit of darkness, will the prince of hell, and Lucifer is accepted back into God's kingdom.

Du Pont nodded. A vale of darkness lifted, as new wisdoms and truths took hold. Bowing his head he wept briefly, as an emotional tide welled up inside him, choking his words trying to keep feelings in check.

"No! No, my friend. I no longer have doubts".

For some minutes, there was little said. Both mortal and entity allowed the moment to pass in silence and some reflection. Du Pont quietly recalled a phrase from his time "disruptive 'technologies'" inwardly amused at the notion of what he now knew and witnessed. His exposure to certain truths would constitute a whole new meaning to that very term in ways that were simply unimaginable.

"I am truly humbled by all of this Etaanus." What is it you want me to do?

Rome. Vatican City

The taxi bringing Brother Alphonse Sienna had no difficulty in finding its way deep inside the lush grounds of Vatican City. At a spot rounding the curved driveway, the passenger halted the taxi. He preferred to make the rest of the short journey on foot. The air was unusually humid and warm even for that early in the year. The gardens were immaculately laid out and populated with large great oak trees that stood like sentinels to a special building. It was a little after 9 pm and he was no stranger to this place. He spent several evenings in prayer in the past, and held the occasional confession when its occupant deemed fit. After walking a brief three minutes the trees gave way to a broad opening to the centrepiece of the entire setting the Holy Father's residence. A magnificent 3-story off-cream coloured building split into three segments with the centre section recessed back nestled between the other two sections. This evening his host was someone he greatly admired.

Cardinal Giuseppe Bonaire an Italian, a seasoned Curia veteran and an accomplished linguist. He spoke several languages fluently, including Hebrew. He was also a Jesuit Cardinal one of only ten within the College of Cardinals. The other, the head of his order, Superior General, and leader of the largest and most powerful religious order in the world, Father Dominic Beitel.

When Brother Sienna reached the top of the steps a plainclothes well-attired security guard stood waiting. A man whose job it often befell to lead many a distinguished guest to meet the Holy Father in private away from prying eyes. He took the Jesuit's small travel case from him bowed slightly and immediately led him indoors. Inside a large lobby of oak-panelled walls greeted him, which in turn was partitioned by a large imposing wooden staircase leading up the landing on the first floor where two solitary robed clerics stood waiting. His call, a few days earlier had determined where they would meet. Absolute privacy was assured. This would be a long evening, and while neither of the three had any clear ideas on how their discussion would progress or end, each felt inwardly, the matter had all the potential to be brought to the occupant of this residence, the Holy Father himself. All three knew each other, after warm embraces and pleasantries completed, the Cardinal led them down an ornate hallway, and then into a beautiful booked-lined study. A desk sat under to a large stained coloured glass window, while a modest circular dining table covered with a white linen cloth was set for three occupied the far end of the room.

An elderly man appeared from an adjoining room carrying plates and immediately began to set down plates of food. A bottle of sherry was added to the table and two small candles were lit. When they were certain they had complete privacy and alone their faces turned more businesslike. Without much preamble, the senior Jesuit poured water for the others.

"Troubling and strange events in Geneva, Alphonse? He said

"Indeed my brothers" Sienna replied. With that, he extended both his arms.

"Let us pray. Merciful father our thanks for all our blessings we enjoy. We beg your divine guidance in all matters of both spiritual and temporal. Please guide us this night. Amen, amen".

"So Alphonse, I have read the documents. There is much that haunts me". The Cardinal said. Sienna barely touched any of the food during the meal. He sat quite intense as he finally chose his words carefully.

"Our fellow brother Fr Burgoyne, your eminence is connected personally to this family. My reading of the man is that of a devoted apostle of Christ and not prone to any hysterical conclusions and yet this litany of facts and events are extremely evocative". He said.

Cardinal Bonaire merely nodded. He had his own notes of Father Francois Burgoyne.

"He is a man of impeccable credentials your Eminence, has seen much of this world, but I've never before seen him so moved or convinced that something…miraculous, even mystical was at work." The other men looked at each other for a moment.

"You brought some material with you, Alphonse, yes?

Sienna reached into his briefcase and removed all the copy material that he and Father Burgoyne had assembled and gone over in great detail.

"The one that caused great unease with both the scientist and our brother Jesuit in Geneva is this!

The face of the Holy Shroud and the screen image are both handed across the table. Then he selected some slightly blurred photographs of the American Scientist from CERN publications, and then shots from his hospital bed. Both Cardinal and fellow Jesuit gasp at the contrasting images. Quietly both men make the sign of the cross as the mood around the table became sombre and subdued.

"This one spoke Aramaic…while in some form of catatonic state. He had no recollection and does not speak either Hebrew or Aramaic. Sienna added.

"They're all physicists you're Eminence, preeminent in their field. The scientist in question doesn't belong to any faith. He is completely atheist".

Cardinal Giuseppe Bonaire glanced up and studied the other men, noting the context of the notes translating the Hebrew text, and its meaning with inward disquiet. As Head of Congregation for the Doctrine of the Faith, one of the most powerful departments of the Catholic Church he had seen many instances come before him. Most cases intrigued him and allowed a certain dispassionate view to be taken. This, however struck him with unease. The men sitting at the table were distinguished scholars in theology and their fellow Jesuit in Geneva was a Scriptural Scholar with a command of Hebrew and biblical studies. This was no gathering called on a whim.

"Such unbelievable coincidences, defy any chances of being pure chance my brothers. It is *my* sincere belief, and those of, Brother Burgoyne that we may be dealing with some divine event here. No one can be absolutely certain of course. The man's physical transformation is most disturbing as you can see. He is barely alive, yet there was no rational explanation for his abrupt appearance change" Said Sienna.

They continued, the conversation went on well into the small hours. Each detail of the happenings was rehashed over and over and looked at in the light of scientific reasoning, and theological doctrine. Across the table, each of three great minds of the Catholic

Faith wrestled with the circumstances of an American scientist and those of his immediate families.

"Are we perhaps guilty of not recognizing signs my Brothers? Asked the head Jesuit finally.

"What, if the teachings of Christ found new ways to express themselves. Move beyond the historical legacy of Christianity into something that is of our times. Science finds a way to permit us to understand deep truths about who we are".

The Cardinal studied the faces of the men around him, all passionate in their love of their church, no doubts as to their authentic devotion to its future.

"There is always a mystery in understanding the workings of Almighty God, my friends, He said, standing for a moment trying to improve the circulation in his legs.

"However, I think it's premature to take this further. Superior General I think we should offer some support, but in a very discreet manner. Meet with Father Francois Burgoyne and the family. See what follows next with this poor man, his medical prognosis, and let's meet again soon. Then the senior cardinal hesitated for a moment.

"My heart tells me, this may… truly be something mysterious. We must be prepared to offer guidance if there are mighty things at work for good or evil. We the Church must be ready. Let's us pray over the coming days for this man's life."

"Agreed, your Eminence", said the Jesuit leader. It was just after 3.30 am.

"I need to be kept informed, Brother Alphonse. The cardinal said

"Of course, you're Eminence. I trust you will keep all of this. He said, gesturing to the notes and folder on the table. The group eventually stood bringing their intimate gathering to an end. All three were tired and pensive as they moved out of the study and strolled down the hall towards the main landing. Cardinal Bonaire walked with both hands grasped behind his back. His head slightly lowered. He nurtured some thoughts that he kept to himself. At 73 years, he knew how to keep secrets, dark ones at that. Most unsettling was how this whole affair was coming to light, not from divine revelation of sorts, but more to do with its origin. Geneva, and what it housed in the bowels of the earth, a Particle Beam Accelerator. Science and what it's capable of doing with knowledge, both old and new was always a source of intense interest for the elder cleric. When they reached the top of the ornate staircase, just a few wall lamps lit the scene, he turned to the others.

"My brothers, this night we must pray for this man and his family and may Almighty God bring him to no harm and his beloved church. Buona Notte".

All three shook hands and embraced each other, then the two Jesuits turned and descended the stairs, and were shown out into the night to a waiting car. The Superior General looked at his fellow Jesuit and saw the worry and fatigue etched in his expression

"You need a good night's sleep, Alphonse. Are you planning to stay with us here in Rome for a few days? The other man cast him a glance.

"Afraid not, Brother Dominic. Tomorrow I go to Milan. I am going to the Convent of Santa Maria Dele Grazie, He said staring out at the loneliness of papal gardens. Both Jesuits exchanged glances

"There is an issue there also". Alphonse Sienna said.

β

CHAPTER EIGHTEEN

He arrived first and parked up one of the narrow streets to the side of the building. Quickly locking the Morgan he walked the short distance to a small café where they agreed to meet. Just as he was shown to his table, Denise arrived at the small entrance and joined him. Both quickly discussed her father's condition.

"The doctors tried to be more upbeat, but still baffled by his general appearance. She said. Then she quickly changed the subject.

"Well, everyone is very happy for us, and our news" She said

"I need to meet with them soon, today if possible. How did they respond? He asked. She smiled and took his hand leaned over and kissed him "I didn't have to".

"How do you mean? He asked.

"My mother! She just knew and, besides I am starting to show somewhat. How are you feeling about Fatherhood? You OK with this? She asked

He broke into a broad grin took her hand and kissed it. "At first, a little scary. Now, my love I'm overjoyed at the prospect of being a dad. What more could I ask for? I love you, Denise Du Pont.

With that, he pulled her to him and kissed her deeply on the lips. As he did, she took his hand and slid it gently over her tummy. He paused his mouth open with surprise.

"My God, I can feel you already. Is that normal? You're how far? She held his boyish gaze for some seconds.

"At least twenty weeks, my love. She whispered. A few moments passed, she could see in his eyes. That awesome math's brain working.

"Is that ...correct. *Twenty weeks*!

He broke into a broad smile and chuckled as if enjoying a very private intimate moment. "Didn't realize we were... He left unfinished.

She looked at him with tenderness. "Me too my love. It felt a bit strange. Because I remember well when we first made love." Don't you?

"Yes, I do. It was a little rushed if I recall but wonderful. It felt so right. He chuckled.

"It was the night, we got that call from Stephanie in the middle of... Don't you remember? She whispered and immediately blushed with embarrassment at how inconvenient the timing of her friend's call was. Then she stopped. They both looked at each other as their smiles faded.

"That's *not twenty weeks ago*! Both of them said in unison.

Despite impending motherhood, her uncle's revelations some nights earlier went beyond belief. She had trouble coming to terms with his views on all that was taking place that she hardly gave any thought to her pregnancy's timeline. She remained impassive and said little keeping in check the inner alarm rising inside her. She reached across the table taking his hands once more and clasping them tightly in hers.

"Come! And stay with us tonight in Sal Madere! Uncle Francois is staying also".

She sensed Paul needed some male company and if nothing else, her uncle might be the only one around that might help ease his worries. He pulled her to him and kissed her gently brushing her hair aside.

"I love you. We will come through all of this intact. He said

"We're going to need you too, my sweet" She replied.

Meanwhile, in the city of Geneva, a man with different persuasions and perspectives was preoccupied.

Benjamin Mochti quietly and discreetly made it his business to keep himself informed on the progress or otherwise of the American physicist. Rumours he heard circulating suggested the medical team was struggling to determine both his physical and neurological progress. He sat alone that Saturday in his small office after finishing his shift on nights.

It was nearly sixteen straight hours, and Friday night was unusually hectic for Bartus San Jovanne hospital. As a student of the more obscure Gnostic collections, he thrived on the readings of mystics. Forgotten words. Words born out of old wisdom from mysterious ascetics who wrote down and scripted meanings that transcended mere human wisdom. Some contained insights garnered from other worlds, some suggested from Angels themselves, to guide and direct human history. It was that theme, scripts of warnings and trepidation kept, Benjamin Mochti vigilant to the plight of the senior physicist. There was a purpose to all of it, he sensed it. Question was, how does he help these unfortunate people. Abruptly, as if reading his thoughts, his phone rings.

"Mochti! He answered.

Listening intently to the voice on the other end of the call.

"Yes. Of course! It would give me great pleasure, Father Burgoyne".

Putting down the phone he slumped back into his chair and pursed his lips. Perhaps it was time to confront aspects of this whole episode with something he knew quite a bit about.

Elsewhere both Denise and Melrose spent the best part of two hours by her father's bedside. The wing where he was kept was quiet and peaceful. It's ambiance occasionally punctuated by nurses looking in to check his status. Lighting was kept low around the bed creating a sense of isolation. Medical equipment clicked and hissed to a rhythmic and steady cadence. Melrose sat on a small chair studying the altered state of the man he admired. Stricken and laid out like a corpse, and yet, life was present and breathing was steady. He cast his mind back to those screen images some days earlier. The light flare that erupted from him. That unseen energy lifted his full six-foot frame upwards before his collapse. Neither of the family knew of these things and perhaps it was just as well. Mingling amid all of this, intruded other thoughts. His work with Euclid.

He studied the figure lying next to him pondering over and over what lurked in the background to all these dark events. What sinister intelligence was at work that ordained such a response? Did they unwittingly disturb a force of malice? He thought.

"His appearance does seem to have changed, Denise says quietly. "He seems quite tanned. It's a little strange. He looks a little less haggard.

Some hair re-growth was evident. His appearance took on the look of a prison inmate almost menacing and threatening. They stayed for another hour and used the privacy of the room to return to their earlier conversation, that of impending parenthood. Reaching out and took her hand he squeezed it gently.

"You're quite confident aren't you? You seem to be more certain than any of us that he's going to make it. He said

"Yes, I am. I just feel it, Paul. My father will know his first grandchild"

"Want some water? He asked. "Sure, it's warm in here. I'm parched".

Both of them stepped outside into the hallway and moved towards the nurse's station a few feet away. In a small alcove next to a coffee vending machine they found a fresh water dispenser.

"Yes, thank nurse, just a little thirsty. May I ask if you might turn down the temperature setting in my father's ward? It feels a little sticky."

Melrose filled two plastic cups with chilled water and handed one to Denise.

"I'm tired, or maybe it's just hospital air, but I think we're done here. She said

"Could do with some fresh air. How about you? "Yep, fresh air works for me fine. Melrose replied.

"Let's check with Dad one last time then we'll leave. She said.

She was deeply in love, and now this motherhood would bring a new dimension to her life, amid the trials they were going through. There was a new chapter of her life beckoning, regardless of the upheavals.

"Denise! Pardon me... Mademoiselle Du Pont! An urgent voice called to her.

It was a young nurse. She approached slightly breathless.

Yes, what it is? Denise asked noticing the nurse's manner. "I wonder if you might come with me. It's your father! There is...! He is fine, just there is something that perhaps you need to see. If you please! She said

They reached the door and push straight in and moved to the centre of the room.

The sight that greeted them was completely unexpected. Her father's figure remained as they left him moments earlier with one difference. His right arm at the elbow was raised upwards at near 90 degrees. More intriguing still, as they drew closer was his fingers.

They had nearly curled into a peculiar form. It took both his daughter and Melrose a few seconds to collect themselves. Denise just stared. Melrose moved closer viewed this new development with deep unease. The young nurse was anxious. Nothing like this came within her normal experience with trauma patients. The scene remained calm-the steady and strong breaths of the prone figure filling the calmness was reassuring, and no major clinical issue seemed to be unfolding. The arm did look incongruous, even surreal in this altered position. Either muscular or reflex action had caused it to assume its posture. Melrose looked dumbfounded for a few moments, and then his eyes are drawn to the fingers and their form.

It looked familiar. Something looked normal, just he hadn't figured why.

"My God! What does this mean? Denise whispered.

I don't think it's bad, Denise. I don't think it's bad at all. He says squeezing her hand.

He focused on his fingers. They appear to cup around if holding something very slender that would fit into space between their tips. The door pushed open and two young doctors rush in and were all over the dials checking vital signs neither of them paused to see, what triggered the alert. Once all was normal, did both of them stand back and take in the scene. Then catching everyone off guard the older of the two reached out and place his fingers around the raised arm, and took its pulse. There was silence for a few seconds then he smiled.

"His pulse is very strong, quite good in fact. He said. Then the doctor drew back and studied the patient with some level of detachment. "It could be a reflex action, but it's hard to say. It's as if he wants to hold a pen. To write something. Melrose shot him a look.

"That was it! He spent more time than any with Fletcher Du Pont in their offices at blackboards, or his desk working on theories. Always when they were stumped, Fletcher would hold his markers while they worked on solutions.

"My God his right! It's what Fletcher does" He whispered.

Turning to the nurse and the two doctors "Quickly, can you fetch some markers? Anything that writes! And a pad of some description!

The young nurse rushed out of the room. Both doctors emptied their pockets removing some markers in their possession. Denise stood in silence trying hard to control her emotions.

Sal Madere.

Father Francois Burgoyne sat in the garden in private meditation in the mid-afternoon glow of a sunlight garden. In keeping with the habits of a lifetime, in times of turmoil, he sought to find solitude where he could pray and find solace. He found strength reciting selected Psalms in the tongue of some of their origins, Hebrew. Sitting upright with both hands placed on his knees, head slightly bowed, he prayed and tried to imagine the workings of the divine mind. . "Thy will be done on earth, as it is in heaven."

And for all of that, an ungodly fear stirred within. His spiritual compass offered nothing. An empty mind fatigued and weary from the avalanche of crippling questions that assaulted his faith left him feeling helpless but not weakened. There was also defiance. An intersection of mystical forces between the world of science and more potent aspects of the metaphysical has reached out and touched those he loved and his own limitations as a simple priest. The sound of his sister's steps broke into his thoughts as she came and sat beside him.

"I think it's time Francois. She said He cast her a look.

"You mean...?

"We meet with the Felix Deveraux, Francois' Her face showed resilience.

"Not only is he Director-General, he is a friend. We invite him here, with Paul, and perhaps some of the others, and tell them you're thoughts. Maybe, we should also include this Doctor Mochti. He was a little aloof and...

"No, its fine Claudine. I agree, perhaps he should join us as well".

Claudine's determination was starting to emerge. "I think together we can summon some explanation and meaning to what is behind all of this." She added.

From inside the house in the background, the sound of the house phone ringing intruded. Claudine quickly stood and moved across the garden and promptly inside. In less than a minute she came to the doorway.

"Francois! There's been a development in the hospital".

ε

After 6.15 pm they entered the hospital and led to the ward by Paul Melrose. They entered and joined Denise, Michelle, and a few medical staff.

Doctor Schultz was sitting in a chair making some personal notes. He stood and came and joined them. Claudine stared at the somewhat bizarre scene instantly noticing her husband's somewhat improved colouring. He no longer looked as aged and skin pallor looked decidedly healthy. A small metal table was moved into position directly beneath the scientist's elevated hand. A large writing pad lay on the table with a black felt marker. Nobody was too sure what was to happen next. Her eldest daughter joined her and took her hand. Melrose stood back and kept to himself. Francois Burgoyne stayed back from the gathering and surveyed the entire scene. Armed with his own convictions, he took in this new development with a renewed sense of reverence. There was meaning here, some purpose was at work.

Doctor Schultz asked the remaining medical staff to leave. Then casually he moved over to a small couch that was brought in recent days and asked the others to join him. "Claudine, this could be a most positive development. He said

"Your husband's, neurological condition is unchanged. His recent scans show slight motor functions, but there is also heightened wave activity in his frontal lobe and temporal lobe region where certain brain executive functions occur. That's what we do know. His vital physical functions, heart, respiratory, and circulation is, quite frankly, puzzling. They appear to be in excellent condition, including red blood cell count, despite how he looks".

"And this arm movement. Is that normal? Michele asked.

Schultz looked down almost studying his shoes. "No, I can't say this is normal, Mademoiselle. But then, there is nothing normal about any of this'.

They stayed for an hour and had some private moments alone with the scientist. Nothing further developed. Each took turns to have a little time by the bed and then left.

By 8 pm that evening they all had returned to Sal Madere. Of all of them, Denise was the most upbeat. Sensing how the visit affected the family, she decided to use the occasion as something to celebrate. She more than any, sensed her father was not going to die. Her uncle reinforced that belief, but not in the manner she expected or fully accepted. Uncle Francois was a deeply spiritual man and saw some divine providence in all of this. She was borderline- but took comfort in it anyway. With that in mind she and her sibling took it upon themselves to cook dinner and use the evening to gather and comfort and support for what lay ahead.

Claudine, her brother, and Paul Melrose retired to the living room and rested. It would also permit everyone to think about the impending new arrival to the family. A moment to cherish, full with the hope that the child's grandfather would be around to enjoy that event when it happened. Claudine approached Paul and hugged him.

"I am so happy for you and Denise Paul. You have all my love and blessing. She said smiling. He reached and embraced her. "Thank you, Claudine, I'm so happy if only we could share this with Fletcher". He said She held him close.

"Fletcher thinks the world of you! You know that. He sees you almost as a son".

"Yes, I do. He is like a father to me". Tears welled up in his eyes. "I would give up everything, just to have him come back to us. Everything!

"We all know that Paul. Now your job is my daughter, and my grandchild she beamed and hugged him one more time. You will always be welcome here in our home my love. Now, be gentlemen and fix us some drinks"

"That goes for me also, my son, Francois said, getting up and embracing him. "You are my Denise's guardian now. Love her well, and may our almighty God bless both of you! He said with a smile.

"That means so much to me, Francois, Denise is my soul mate'.

He shot his sister a glance even a slight nod seeking her approval to bring up something.

"Maybe it's time to share my thoughts with Paul. Tell him what we think is happening with Fletcher" He said. A slight awkwardness filled the moment as they considered how the younger man, and father to be, would respond. Melrose looked at both of them mildly puzzled.

"Tell me what?

"Sit down darling, and take some time, there is something that we need to share with you. It's something that Francois believes, and it might go some way towards making sense of what was happening here. She said.

In the kitchen, Denise and Michelle prepared some duck and were about to complete blending a sauce, when Denise felt a jolt. She stopped and placed her hand on her tummy.

"My God, I felt that! She gushed. Michelle gave her a quizzical look.

"What is it, Sis? Denise paused and gave a nervous chuckle, unsure of what she felt.

"I think the baby moved, almost kicked!

"You got to be kidding me. Michelle replied. Neither spoke for a few seconds, each amused at the suggestion. "Come-on Sis! You OK? Want me to take over here. You go and rest up'.

"No I'm fine Michele, we're almost ready to serve. It was just weird. Thought, I felt movement that's all. Denise said, almost embarrassed.

Michelle resumed finishing but gave her older sister a discreet glance. At second glance she noticed her sister was more advanced than they realized. Someone's timing is a little off! She thought to herself but made no more of it.

While events out at Sal Madere were settling in for dinner, elsewhere in the heart of Geneva Dr. Peter Schultz returned to the ward on the second floor, to make his last check on patient 421 for the day? He stood over the figure of the stricken scientist bathed in a low subdued bluish light. His studied and concentrated gaze concealed deep feelings of uncertainty surrounding this medical case. It was clinically ambiguous to say the least. For now, whatever his personal feelings he would be clinical when the time came to consider the need for the support mechanisms in front of him. This could not continue indefinitely, and having completed his notes and checked some vital indicators, he turned to leave. No sooner had he reached the door, he paused and looked back at the incongruous sight of a comatose patient with an extended arm. A thought crossed his mind. He paused as an idea came to him. It was quiet. The hospital was settling down for the night. Already night staff was on duty and would be starting their rounds shortly. Crossing the room to the bed shrouded in low soft light. His patient was breathing very slow but at a steady pace. Cautiously he looked at the set-up, with the markers and pad placed on the small table. Reaching down he picked up one of the felt markers and held it for a second. As if having second thoughts he hesitated for a moment. But some strong impulse urged him to continue, and without any great effort or fuss, he positioned the marker into the nearly closed fingers of the prone figure. With great ease and delicate movement, he presented the marker just in the right position into the hand of the scientist. Its placement was consistent with those of someone wishing to write. Surprisingly there was no rigidity or stiffness, the fingers, while cold was flexible enough to allow him to exert just enough pressure to hold and grip the marker. The specialist stood back. It made the scene that bit more surreal than before. Still, he was drawn to doing it without reason.

Then he just nodded and muttered to himself. "Goodnight my good patient. Rest well".

Just after 4 am, two nurses entered the ward to check on patient 421. It took them just under thirty seconds to notice the patient's posture had returned to his normal posture and seemed stable and peaceful. Except for his arm now lay lying by his side. As they approach one of them stepped on a black felt marker lying on the ground near the bed. It broke and snapped under her foot. Quickly it was picked up and disposed of. They were about to complete their checklist and record readings when they first noticed the writing pad was turned and seemed to have been disturbed. One of them reached over to tidy the patient's bedclothes when she froze. She stared down almost disbelievingly at what appeared on the pad. She called out to the other to catch her attention. Both carefully assumed a measured and cautious approach. Checking the patient's status, his vital signs, and that everything that should be in order, was in order. Adjusting their eyes both of them leaned over and tilted their head to try read a scrawl of lettering of some sort was printed.

נקקמ ישד דקגעק'למם קסארשםמגןמשרט

Once over the initial shock, the more experienced and senior nurse went and intuitively lifted patient 421 right hand. His fingers of his right hand were covered and marked with black marker stains. Both looked at each other, knowing what each was thinking. Both spoke French

"You were at Nurse's station all evening. Right! One asked

"Yes of course! The other replied. "And no one has entered this ward, without me knowing.

The hand stains on the patient's right hand caused both young women to step back from the bed, almost as a reflex but tinged with fearfulness. "Let's establish some details. Get your patients logbook and record the time, and circumstances when we discovered this'.

The Meadow of Revelations.

The sky had turned a pink sunset into the most radiance of muted colours casting an almost mystical spell over the meadow. Du Pont became deeply introspective. His mind was overflowing with images that spoke directly to his heart. He had spent his entire adult life, chasing mysteries, a seeker of truths. Dr. Fletcher Du Pont sought them in realms of equations, complex models while building some of the most groundbreaking technologies to attain that goal. His intellect peered into and dissected the primeval forces of nature, and fashioned new ideas that rewrote an understanding of the physics of life, and everything within it.

The sun was beginning to set, and evening breeze brushed him and gently tossed the surrounding grass in the meadow. It also ushered an awakening that he had never experienced before. Then there was a presence he felt that followed him. An omnificence force seemed to be lurking about. Some new level of awareness filled him so different from anything that he could explain. A more metaphysical aspect upended his life's work concerning *matter* and its very nature and structure. An entirely surreal aspect shown to him by his angelic companion spoke of spirits entombed within matter. All substances harbour spirits. Laws laid down by man simply dissolved, laid aside to be replaced by more mystical truths. Truths of a higher realm. Immersed with inner struggles, new ideas came calling. The mere physics of time as he understood them surrendered to more profound truths regarding the tenuous nature of time itself. These gifts bestowed to him an ability to experience another realm, which heralded the existence of more profound laws, which confronted all scientific notions he clung to including his beliefs. He was faced with another equally unsettling idea. There was no such thing as *Death*, just transition.

Du Pont stopped as another truth took root. An idea stirred. He was to be a Messenger. A Messenger bearing truths. Truths that he was witness to.

The majesty of creation revealed in a manner that held him spellbound, diminishing all his human certainties. His human eagerness and futility to even attempt to decode the workings of creation in all its splendour slammed into his consciousness. Every notion of physics he held dear became dismantled. Leaning over he cupped a handful of water and drank. He drank some more and washed his face letting its coolness drench his skin. Repositioning himself on one of the flat stones he sat and let his feet mingle in the passing stream. No sooner had he done so, the water flow changed beneath him. At first, he was oblivious, lost in questions that haunted him. How little he knew or understood the nature of things. Little did he appreciate how the simple stream trickling beneath his feet would bring further revelations? His dangling feet felt a change but hardly registered with his brain. The stream continued to flow, but not quite as expected. His attention was drawn when he noticed his feet are on longer immersed in the stream.

He glanced down and saw something slightly ominous. The continuous flow of the stream separated and partitioned into three separate flows of water. Space opened up causing three streams to run as separate and distinct flows with the bed of the small stream becoming exposed where they parted and separated. The scientist rose slowly to his feet, sensing the abnormality of it. Something unusual seemed to be at work. The physics was unnatural as he watched now three streams progressed on downstream all divided by two parallel dry bed patches. Positioned between him and the setting sunset a tall outline of a man in silhouette gazed down the slope to where he stood. Then, moving in slow deliberate steps it advanced towards him. Within a few seconds the scientist he recognised his observer, Yeshua Ben Yosef.

He moved towards him and as he did Du Pont noticed a difference. The face, the expression had changed. His companion possessed a countenance of an older man, instead of the man he had gotten to know, the figure before him had aged years beyond his time. The eyes were ones of an altered soul, that knew more than perhaps he should. There was maturity and intensity that had shifted the vibrant personality of man back at the shoreline of Magdala, to something else. The eyes burned with intensity armed with an intellect that looked out at the world and saw much more. An intellect beyond anything the physicist ever encountered powered by force of presence. Du Pont could feel it as Nazarene drew closer. The manner of his bearing also seemed changed; his strides were more assured, full of authority. There were etched lines in his face, that weren't there before. Du Pont remained quiet for a moment.

"Yeshua! Has... this Redemption begun? He asked quietly

"Yes, it has begun, dear friend". But *your* task is also ready to be declared, my friend. He added.

The Nazarene moved around him and then beckoned the scientist to follow him until they stood on the stones over the stream. He repeated something the scientist did earlier and immersed his hands in one of the three streams. He then slowly drank the water cupped in his hands.

"You are also a great seeker of truths? He said "Do you understand what *belief* is my friend. The Nazarene reached out again and took his arm. "Now my Traveller friend, take my hand and step into the stream.

He held the scientist's hand as Du Pont slipped into the water and positioned his stance so that both feet stand in water. Then without warning, Yeshua crossed both his hands and placed them over his chest.

"Look at me." He said, *"Belief is everything*! Traveller. Belief! To have an unshakable indestructible belief in my promises. My words! Lean on, my words my friend. Not on your own reasoning, not on your feelings or emotions of despair or things that come about of their own accord. Have faith in *my* words"

Glancing down the three strands of water changed course and does something quite extraordinary. Each individual streams began to intermingle. One stream changed its path and crossed over intersecting the one next to it, as it did something similar to the next. The water in obedience to some force began to weave all three strands. All crisscrossing in an unnatural pattern intertwining as it flowed. The scientist looked on sensing a hidden significance. The Nazarene stood over him on the small pile of flat stones.

"It has been your life's work, Fletcher. The streams of time have confounded mankind, dear friend. You are consumed with questions. You seek to understand all things, and amid those questions, that great question of Time itself. How and why you are here? To you on Earth, *Time* is but one aspect of your existence. You cannot conceive time beyond the three realms of Past, Present, and the Future. You see time as one single passage from youth to the end, with aging and old age to a mortal death".

Immediately the water flow gathered energy in all tree stands with increased power governing its flow and interchanging paths.

"Notice this stream, it contains three separate paths, notice how it exchanges each path and stream"

The physicist studied the surreal pattern of water run around him. Observing, trying to fathom the essence of the *Time* reference. Yeshua came closer and placed a hand on his shoulder.

"Like the threads of a chord, that is woven together for strength. The fabric of time has other aspects. Here, in this stream, you can but take one step of you're choosing, and stand only in one strand at a time in this stream. Now think, my dear friend.'

Like a thunderbolt from nowhere, the scientist suddenly saw the significance of the scene unfolding and the awesome message contained within its sheer simplicity. He was experiencing everything through imagery. This enigmatic Nazarene, renowned for his parables all steeped in imagery and powerful parables was showing him something strange. Suddenly a spark within the physicist saw a parallel.

"Look at me, Fletcher! All Time is a woven fabric that is intertwined. You can step from one to another in these realms of existence. Did you ever conceive the possibility that all time had strands that occur at the same time? There is no past, or present, or future, in the sense you mortals experience it. They occur simultaneously. Within God's creation all things follow great laws. A great many are unknown to you. You have my friend moved across one fabric of existence to another to this place here with me. As if you moved across the ribbon of one strand of this stream to another'

No sooner had the words been spoken, the significance and context erupted inside the scientist. An alternative experience of time began to unfold, simply by revising the notion of time itself. All existences occurred simultaneously. Rather than seeing time as a sequential flow, it is merely experienced in an instant. The *Now*. The mystical Yeshua turned to him. There's a change in his countenance, a sadness and sorrow full of pity. A face that saw and possessed with an ability to reflect all that he observed in human nature.

"Let me show you something my friend. Hold my hand"

One further step to the left and they both stand amid the smallest of strands of the stream. As they did, the gentle breeze began to shift around them. In seconds both were engulfed in the ferocity of gusting winds that caused trees about them to bend convulsed in a whirlwind of near storm proportions. Du Pont stumbled almost losing balance when the Nazarene's hand gripped him. The same powerful arm that hauled him into that darkened cave when they first met. In seconds he could see little the surrounding pasture and meadow dissolved into the whirlwind of dust both blanketed in a swirling cocoon of noise and leaves. Without warning the winds abated as quickly as it came. The turbulence faded and slowly the air cleared allowing Du Pont to merge into a different scene. The contrast was completely stark to where they stood only seconds earlier.

A large expansive plain of desolation opened before them. Rolling for hundreds of miles in all directions a flat landscape of rock and scrubland stretched in all directions. An eerie tranquillity filled across the empty landscape. They appeared to be standing on an outcrop. A few seconds passed. The dawn early light is just beginning to creep over the far horizon. The scientist turned to the Nazarene standing next to him. His profile defined his features with a strong well-defined bone structure. Staring into the distance, his face filled with sadness. Just as the scientist is about to say sometimes, the whole facial profile of the mystic illuminated- his face reflected an enormous burst of light erupted from the surface in the far distance. Turning instantly the scientist looked as a massive dome of radiant light rose up from the far distant horizon in a gigantic flash and formed into an ascending orb of pure energy.

It rose upwards its luminosity enveloping the entire landscape for miles in its ungodly purple and orange glow. Darkness instantly became day. Du Pont stared and quickly knew what he was witnessing. It is the year he would never forget. 1945 AD July, "Trinity" the infamous name given to the very first atomic detonation. The blast released a visible shock wave in all directions levelling everything in its path. Then, after several seconds, the fireball began to expand and ascend high like a majestic mushroom up into the skies over Alamogordo, New Mexico.

"Behold the Trinity of man" Yeshua, said with sadness etched in his features.

In that single instant, the meaning of time was vanquished. It was beyond the understandings of mere mortals from standing in someplace he was shifted from one strand of time to another.

"You, and many similar to you, my dear friend has been blessed and gifted with great intellect. What you choose to do with it, Fletcher is the outcome of your own free will, alas. Another gift that my father has bestowed on you. You must open your heart my friend. Open them to the voice of my father who speaks to all of you through your hearts. Your inner self will find whatever you seek if you will only ask. When you do, do it without any doubt. Belief, and when what you seek comes to you, gratitude. Let your intellect be creative, and you will find wisdom in your hearts. That is the source of all power, and where all my father's love dwells within you".

The whole sky above them glowed as the physics of nature was given expression of its awesome destructive power. The face of the Nazarene simply gazed at the workings of mortals.

"Where will your quest lead you, Fletcher? This is not for the glory of God, is it? He asked gently. For Du Pont, yet another moment of unknown truths. Laws of immeasurable and unfathomable power. Human events and human history were transcended by a higher governing wisdom. All human constructs and notions of time were altered before him. He tried to grapple with the idea of past, present, and future concepts that were intertwined like strands of a rope. Each of them deeply interlinked and woven into some higher fabric of reality.

"Would it possible to see my family in their time, Yeshua? He whispered.

There was the briefest of smiles. Almost in the blink of an eye, the scrublands of the southern parts of New Mexico disappeared. Within that moment all fabric of time shifted and the mist that had wrapped itself around them altered. Without any sense of movement, the scene was replaced by a beautiful garden manicured and graced with immaculate shrubbery enclosed with a surrounding wall and tall trees. Du Pont inhaled and held his breath.

His home, his beloved Sal Madere appeared before them.

A wave of emotion almost overwhelmed the scientist as they stood in the garden itself. It was as he remembered. It's lushness in sharp contrast to what went before. The house and its open windows draw near, and then he saw them. He moved with urgency towards them and then stopped. It was so real and close he could almost feel their presence, only there was the gulf of eternity between him and those he loved. He reached out and tried to touch. He drifted inside and saw his wife, his beautiful wife sitting with two others both were men he knew so well. Both he held with great affection then moved to another part to see his two daughters.

He could see them, but not hear them. They were engaged and preparing a meal.

"Thank you for this Yeshua" He whispered. Tears ran down his cheeks.

"You are truly blessed, dear friend. His companion replied wrapping his arm around Du Pont's shoulders "There is more my brother".

The Nazarene moved past him, and even though they were separated by a timeless gulf of existence, he reached out to the eldest daughter and placed the palm of his hand on her midriff. Du Pont looked in amazement. Then, even more, stunning was what followed. His eldest daughter gave a slight flinch and placed her hand on her tummy, and seemed to say something and smiled to her sibling. She was incapable of knowing or being aware of anything. The significance of this majestic moment gripped the scientist and the imagery of what he just witnessed. He looked to his mystical companion.

"More! Is my daughter somehow involved in all of this, Yeshua?"

The Nazarene stood, never taking his eyes off the scene before them. His eyes shone with intensity toward the eldest daughter and her precious condition. Nowhere did mortals come as close to the creator as in the intimate act of collaboration. The creation of life, the heralding of an impending spirit up through those spheres of progress to assume human form, and experience the creation in all its glory and it's vicissitudes. Then, Du Pont looked at his daughter closely, and instantly recognised her condition. To tell them he was standing close to them, and with whom he was standing with, overwhelmed him. To scream so that his voice would carry across the boundaries of eternity and let them know just how close he was to them.

"Fletcher, my dearest friend. It will be time soon for you to return. It will be a good time to return to them".

Sal Madere.

Around the table, the mood was strangely calm along with an unexplained sense of contentment. Despite ever-presence of crisis, there was serenity.

It was one of those days that left Claudine drained; still, she was relieved to have her brother return. His presence helped to contain the innermost fears that stalked her. Paul Melrose sat opposite her. It sounded all very mysterious. Just then both Denise and Michelle entered loaded with an assortment of dishes. Two bottles of wine were placed in the centre.

"Well, maybe I could ask when the big arrival day is? Francois asked.

Claudine managed to smile and then stood and brought back small-sized candelabra from a shelf and placed in the centre of the table. She then placed four candles and lit them.

"Before we eat perhaps we might say grace. Asked Francois

"Of Course, Francois. Why don't you do the honours?" Claudine said

Our most gracious and heavenly father, we offer our thanks and deep gratitude for all... No sooner had he started, the garden window blew open and a gentle rush of air filled the room startling everyone. It gave Claudine a slight chill catching her completely off guard. She pushed back her chair. The Jesuit stopped mid-sentence. She moved across to the window and paused. Looking out into the garden and straight at the small garden table where the chessboard is sitting. For several seconds she stared almost hypnotised at something that caught her off guard.

In the middle of the board, a single candle burned brightly casting a gentle glow into the dusk of the evening.

She stared at something that shouldn't be. She turned to call the others to come and look only to see something even more unsettling faced her. All were sitting around the table. No one spoke, no one stirred. A muted silence descended around the table. In the centre of the table, the central candle in the candelabra burned a single flame.

" Dear God! She barely whispered.

ε

CHAPTER NINETEEN.

Second Floor —Bartus San Jovanne Hospital

"I don't bloody care who is the duty matron, get me the log details for all of yesterday! Merde! Gunter Sylvester said.

Then slammed down the phone. He knew, Doctor Peter Schultz when he got there would ask the same questions.

How does a comatose patient get to write something down? As Registrar, he knew also this might not end well if this were a breach of hospital security and conduct. He'd face the full brunt of what would follow. The next thing he ordered strict visitation rules to the patient 241. Then, the last thing on his list was to inform the senior attending clinical director which, in this case, was Peter Schultz who was due to arrive shortly.

After nearly two days the call was made, and the families of Professor Fletcher Du Pont were summoned. Within the senior clinical circles of the hospital a growing sense that case 241 was spiralling into a morass of unknown dimensions without any clinical or medical protocols to guide them. That day when the call went out, the family insisted on knowing in advance what was in store for them. When the detail of the writing was conveyed, little further action was taken other than to monitor the patient. Then pressure was brought to bear by the US Embassy and through the power of the Director General's office of CERN. Professor Du Pont was a Senior Fellow and an eminent light in the scientific world. Nothing should be done to jeopardize his clinical care. Nothing. Professor Felix Deveraux took the call from the family as soon as the news reached them, both agreed it was something that should remain private and confidential.

A more interesting call is made later that afternoon. It was between two men drawn into this from two opposing positions in matters of faiths. Father Francois Burgoyne, a member of the Society of Jesus, and Doctor Benjamin Mochti, as devout in his rich Jewish faith as anyone. The spoke briefly and exchanged opinions that connected both men in ways one would not have expected. Just before 4 pm a few days later, the family visited the patient in his room and spent some time alone with him.

Benjamin Mochti joined them a little after 5 pm also provided them with his insights and his experience with trauma victims. They moved to a small meeting room where staff often met. It was tidy and functional with some loose chairs. They gathered with Doctor Peter Schultz, who had collected all the notes on his patient's status. The incredible suggestion the Jesuit had posed to the family the previous few hours was still reeling in their heads, along with the unsettling event at the residence. Quickly Schultz placed the pad down on the table allowing all to look at it.

Claudine and the two girls sat on each side of the doctor. Paul Melrose remained standing leaning against the door jam. Francois sat opposite the women next to Dr. Mochti. After the initial pleasantries were exchanged they sat forward and pondered the hand-scrawled note. Dr. Schultz was the first to speak.

"Madam Du Pont, would you know if this is your husband's handwriting? He asked.

She looked and studied the scrawled writing finding it hard to answer. It's writing in a style, or language she knows nothing of. She studied it further then cautiously pushed it across the table and turned it around.

"Does anyone in your overseas staff know what this it? She asked.

"Very few of our staff has seen this. He replied. Paul wandered over behind the two men and looked over their shoulders.

Its Arabic or looks like Arabic. Maybe Mideast? He said. The Jesuit studied the scribbled text, then muttered to the man next to him; "Unmistakably Hebrew! Mochti nodded

"Yes, it's Hebrew. He said finally as if something else bothered him.

He gave Paul a look. Not for the first time this disquieting language aspect is turning up on his doorstep. The Jesuit, however ignored everyone ran his fingers across the body of the script trying to remember his Hebrew. Mochti leaned over to offer some assistance to the Jesuit.

"Francois, if I may, He said. Then read to be sure he followed its structure its grammar.

"It's what we refer to as Leshon HaKodesh. *The Holy Language!*

"Holy Language! Is that Hebrew, or something else? Denise asked.

"Oh, it's Hebrew all right Denise. To be precise it's...! Mochti paused and looked at the Jesuit.

"Francois, would you like to...

"Yes, of course, Benjamin! He took off his glasses almost as if he was about to lecture some errant student.

"There is Modern Hebrew, spoken in Israel. It's the official language. Then, there is the more ancient Biblical Hebrew it's a Semitic language of which this is. The text we're looking at here is of the more pure form of Hebrew.'

All gave each other a look. Melrose shifted uncomfortably. Doctor Schultz just sat back and rubbed his eyes to allow his mind to absorb one more aspect of intrigue and clinical ambiguities around this patient.

"Now let me try and interpret what this says." The room went quiet while the Jesuit concentrated on the hand-written pad.

"As best as I can read the transliteration, it speaks of wisdom'. He whispered to himself.

Melrose felt startled. The mere mention of the word had unsettling connotations. . . Mochti stirred in his chair. Claudine sat forward keeping her thoughts to herself. She looked over at her brother as he grappled with a text written by the hand of her near-dead husband. Looking for some glimmer of confirmation of proof, evidence a rational mind behind the writing in front of them. Something that offered further comfort or some new shred of hope.

"Please bear with me! The Jesuit said. "Some special wisdom is to be discovered, and...

There's an aspect of the text that's confusing. Where does the key emphasis lay?

Mochti looked on taking in every line. His face absorbed in both the text and its context. He saw an alternative emphasis. He looked up and glanced around and stared up at the ceiling. This was chilling, as it was remarkable. To him, it made complete sense. It confirmed everything his instincts were screaming at him from the beginning, and here was proof.

"No good father, if I may. That's not quite what it says". He said respectfully

Eyes around the table stared at him. "It is very revealing. What it actually states, in very simple terms is...

..רקהקןשדקג נקקמ ישד דקגעק׳למם קסארשםגןמשרט

Extraordinary Wisdom has been found and revealed' He said softly.

Like a death sentence being passed in a courtroom, no one spoke. Each of them closed their eyes and paused to find the strength. A message from the hand of a loved one had seemingly spoken. Claudine stood and folded her arms, and paced around the small room. If ever she needed a cigarette, it was now. Then she locked eyes with the young Jewish doctor.

"You're sure that's what written here, Benjamin. Certain of its origin?

"Yes. Claudine. Absolutely certain. He replied. She glanced at her brother. There seemed to be little doubt. "Can I ask, how the marker or pen got into Fletcher's grasp? Asked Paul

"Ah, am! It was my...idea. Replied Schultz. "It was an instinctive thing. It felt right. I'm not sure why I did it! I agreed with Mister Melrose's assessment last time you were here. It was if our patient was trying in some way to send us, or write!"

Claudine leaned and gently touched his shoulder in a gesture of appreciation. She felt deeply grateful.

"Thank you. It was very... insightful of you. I'm glad you did".

"It was really sweet of you". Michelle said

The Jesuit remained silent. It was yet another sign of some significance that spoke volumes to him and his beliefs. *Extraordinary wisdom.... Revealed.*

Just a few simple words containing enormous meaning. Pieces were converging and morphing into something of great underlying purpose. He knew of such things. As a man of unquestionable faith he was coming to the belief that each inexplicable event that haunted all of them was underpinned by a guiding mind. A mind of great wisdom was at work, and without question was nothing to be feared. His thoughts turned to readiness. He needed to prepare and to prepare those loved ones close to him. He retreated into a silent prayer to seek some inner strength. To see this through to the end whatever that might be.

Denise stood and made eye contact with Doctor Mochti, and then to Paul. With a single gesture, she nodded towards the exit.

"I need to be excused for a moment. She said and moved towards the door.

Melrose caught her signal and followed. Slowly Doctor Mochti stood.

"If I can be of any further assistance to the family, Francois, Madam Du Pont, please call me. Now if you will also, excuse me. He said.

Once out into the hallway he finds both of them waiting.

"Did you want to see me?

"Well yes, Benni. We both do." It's then he noticed.

"As you can see, I'm pregnant. Very pregnant! Denise gushed awkwardly.

Yes! Yes, I can see. Congratulations. You look good Denise. Paul, I'm delighted for you both. This is wonderful. How far has it?

"That's, what we want to talk to you about. We're not really sure Benni. Melrose said quietly.

Mochti studied them for a second.

"Ok! What can I do? Is it my professional or something more?

"Ah! Professional. We're not sure just how far it's...? Denise left unfinished.

"I'd like you to examine. Check out, if everything is OK. A further few awkward seconds followed. Mochti nodded. He sensed this was still a delicate matter. Professionalism aside he felt a great deal of empathy towards both of them. He particularly liked Denise there was much of her father in her.

"When would you like me to..?

"As soon as possible Benni. As soon as possible! She answered sharply.

'May I ask how do you feel? He asked gently placing his stethoscope in his pocket

"Great, I feel very good. It's just that, well I'm a little worried. No, confused. Her voice trailed off

"Tomorrow morning. In my office, 8.30 am. He said.

He turned to Melrose and shook his hand.

"Congratulations, again. My office. You know where it is of course. He smiled and headed down the corridor.

The following morning, Paul Melrose made a quick call to the office to say he would be late and left it at that. When they arrived in the hospital on the other side of Geneva, they were shown to the section when Dr. Mochti was waiting in a small clinic room.

"Good morning Denise, Paul. How are you feeling this morning?

"Kinda Big! Denise smiled awkwardly.

Mochti gave her a quick cursory look.

"I'd say at least twenty weeks. This you're first prenatal? He asked.

"Ah, Yes, as a matter of fact"

"OK, let's get started. Paul, do mind waiting outside. There's a coffee shop down at the end of this floor. Give us about thirty minutes would you? Melrose leaned and kissed her, and left. Mochti guided Denise to an elevated chair.

"Seeing this is your first let me give you a quick overview. We'll do a complete pelvic examination, then a breast examination, and check your urine. Then we'll take a blood sample, and carry out a Pap smear then if it's OK with you, I'd like to do an ultrasound. She smiled. He had a comforting and reassuring way about him that was welcome. Nearly an hour later, when he was finished, Mochti sat down to a small desk and completed his notes. He said little, letting Denise come and join him next to the desk.

"Can I look at your hands Denise, and then your feet?

One look at him told her enough. His expression was pensive as if he is rechecking some of his notes. He looked up from his notes and glanced again at her size. After looking at her hands there was slight swelling. Similarly, when he examined her feet, he found swelling. He paused for a few seconds.

"How long do you think you're pregnant? He asked gently removing his glasses.

We, think it's about 20 weeks, but my size, Benjamin. It's odd.

"Indeed well, that's only because you believe you're twenty weeks. He smiled to try and reassure her. He sensed her growing anxiety.

"Denise, do mind if I ask a colleague to join us. I need to consult...and'

"What's wrong Benin? She blurted.

"Nothing! Denise, absolutely nothing. But, you're *not* twenty weeks.

Her heart quickened. Just then, a knock on the door and Paul stuck his head in.

"Everything all right! He asked. "Impeccable timing Paul! Come on in. Mochti said.

How's that Benni?

"Well, pregnancy is going quite well. Denise's in very good health, her blood pressure is excellent. But you're beyond twenty weeks, given your physical symptoms I'd say more like thirty to thirty-two weeks"!

No one said anything for a few seconds.

"That's impossible! Denise said sharply.

"I'm sorry Benni, that's simply impossible!

Mochti said little, allowing the moment of disbelief to pass.

"Why do you say that?

Before Denise could answer and say what she knew.

"Because we weren't intimate until more recent times. Conception couldn't have taken place until... Paul left unfinished.

"Benni are you absolutely certain? Denise pressed.

That was the second time in the last twenty-four hours that he was asked if he was certain about anything. Given the surreal circumstances around this family, his thoughts were immediately distracted and driven in directions that he dared not consider.

"Can you say its sex, Benni?

"Not yet! But do you want to or need to know?

'I'm not sure? Denise said finally looking over at Paul

"Why not leave that for the moment. Mochti said "Look! You both have much on your plate at present. I can see this has been a little taxing for you this morning let's talk again next week. I'd like to schedule another check-up. In the meantime may I discuss this with one of our Obstetricians here in the hospital? He's a good friend, and tops in his field."

Of course Benni! And thank you. You've been very kind. Denise said

Melrose came and shook Mochti's hand.

"For everything Benni. Thank you".

Then both of them left. After the couple left, Benjamin Mochti gathered his notes. He picked up the ultrasound image and looked at it ever so carefully, then back to his notes. He pondered much of what he heard, the disbelief on both their faces. His prognosis had completely blind-sided both of them, and yet her pregnancy was progressing well. They would be parents sooner than they realised.

It didn't take long to drive from the hospital through the Old Town centre of the city in the Morgan. Neither said little both absorbed in the details with Mochti's examination. Paul made a quick call to the campus and made his excuses. She did likewise to her office. Things sitting on her desk could wait. Once they cleared the centre of the city they headed to one of their favourite spots overlooking the shoreline of Lake Geneva close by to one of the jetties. The last remnants of snow in the distance mountains were giving way to the bright warmth of the midday sun. Once there, both walked hand in hand to a small part of the shore where large boulders nestled against the main road frontage. They found empty seating and sat. Denise seemed more relaxed.

Finally, she turned to Paul

'Something's not right darling! She said quietly.

He just nodded and gently squeezed her hand. "He has to be mistaken. You can't be pregnant that long. I mean... You just can't be! Unless of course there was..."

As soon as he suggested it, he regretted it. She shot him a look.

What!

"Sorry, Darling I know shouldn't have thought uh... there has never been anyone...

"No, there hasn't. No one! She said wrapping her scarf into a tight ball. He turned and pulled close and held her tight. Then he took her face and kissed her deeply.

"Whatever the time is, we'll be ready. I love you more than anyone I've ever known Denise." He saw the worry and anxiety in her eyes. Something was amiss.

"There hasn't been anyone in my life for a long time, you know that don't you, She said.

For the next hour, they sat and let the warmth of the sunshine wash over them. She rested her head on his lap, her bump apparent

"Is my math's right? I know that I can't be this far advanced!

"Yes, I did the numbers as well. Benni must have got it wrong somewhere. Paul said.

Sal Madere

Back at the residence, Claudine sat in their dining room, holding her third cup of coffee with some of her husband's papers and an assorted selection of photographs. Next to her, she had a copy of an internal report from CERN on the circumstances of her husband's mishap. It made for uninteresting reading. Nothing was certain or clear. Very strange for a place that was so precise about everything it did. Her brother remained in her husband's study in prayer and keeping to himself. Then there was something else she felt. Neither of the family spoke of it much, but it was there. She had felt it that evening. A presence yes. But there was more. Something different. Notwithstanding the candles, there was a calmness and stillness over dinner. The apprehension that hung over them in recent weeks was missing, replaced by an air of hope and yet without any obvious reason.

Her daughter's pregnancy which would normally have created a bit of a storm seemed to have moulded itself into their lives as if was the most natural or expected thing taking place. Even odder was the sudden change in Denise herself. Apart from her size and progress, her daughter seemed to be becoming rather motherly in ways she never expected in her eldest daughter. Oddly it seemed to be the most natural thing to be happening them right now. Even her brother. The staunch advocate of absolute Christian values and the sanctity of marriage and parenthood seem to have fallen under some spell. No outburst of rebuke. No recanting or moralizing of lapsed virtuousness. None, only acceptance of some unspoken truth.

Not so accepting some days later and, somewhat more circumspect was Doctor Benjamin Mochti. He came to see things from a different perspective. He wondered if he was the only one who thought certain aspects of this impending pregnancy was not going to be routine. He thought that firstly because of what he knew. Recent history aside, he was also unsettled with Denise Du Pont. Her complete shock and misjudgment of her first pregnancy caught him off guard. Secondly, and perhaps more surprising lay in front of him. His recent examination had been thorough, along with his usual meticulous attention to detail, he was happy with his assessment. Her physical condition was excellent and in keeping with her stage in her trimester, she was carrying a female, her daughter. By all accounts, she would deliver a girl, in a few weeks. However, his colleague Professor Michael Kells, the attending Obstetrician had taken a closer look at the ultrasound results, agreed with the good doctor on the essential details of the patient, except in one aspect. Denise Du Pont would deliver in the time expected, a baby *son*. That was odd in itself, but given with whom he was dealing with, this was a little ominous and not to his liking. He fidgeted over his phone. He considered calling Melrose and then thought the better of it.

ε

A Jetty, near Capernaum – Galilee.

The effect of seeing his loved ones had shaken him and took a while to deal with its after-effects. His home, its place in time, and his loved ones. So close, and yet so disconnected. The unseen mysteries of temporal time and all its surreal properties were daunting and incomprehensible. He cast his mind to the simple images of intermingling streams woven and fashioned like strands of a rope. Was it possible that our notion of past, present, and future were really one and the same? In this alternative reality could such distinctions be meaningless or meaningful. With such sublime ease, he was experiencing a transition from one place to another almost without travelling anywhere. These places came to him creating an instant reality that enveloped all around him rather than experiencing a transition from one to another. He also felt drained and began to experience a massive sense of distance. A separation of dimensions he found impossible to grasp. Being physically close, while being utterly displaced.

New thoughts invade his mind. Death must be like this he thought. Having an existence, being able to see loved ones, and yet so out of touch. Visibly close yet, with the gulf of infinity in between. Was this how it is for the departed? The duality of existence and the ability to be in many places? The celestial equivalence of the uncertainty principle, that piece of quantum physics that consumed him back in his own time. Isolated and separated yet able to experience an alternative existence. An existence where emotions, senses, and feelings we had on earth were retained even amplified and more intense, continued within us into other realms. He, a mere mortal never accepted the possibility of the afterlife, another place we went beyond the vicissitudes of mortal existence. He never believed or accepted any such idea, until now. Not only did this possibility manifest itself, it completely consumed him within its reality. Struggling with these notions Du Pont tried to stop thinking like a physicist.

Thinking involved reason and logic. To preserve his sanity he marshalled every ounce of reasoning to fathom the lessons he was experiencing. In his own personal history and life, he theorized in-depth about the existence of higher dimensions, parallel realities within his world of physics. Now, nothing in his framework of understanding prepared him for this duality of existence. As abstract as those theories were, they paled into insignificance to what he has witnessed. All doubts were dispelled. Time and dimensional space, location, all we call living, our concept of reality was only a tiny aspect of a more mysterious world. Other levels of existence continued all around us. The afterlife, this notional idea of living on after death, was even more real and powerful than he ever imagined or dismissed. From this biblical land to the plains of New Mexico, to his garden in Switzerland, time and space dissolved from one to another. Looking around he found himself facing a small wooden jetty that extended a few feet out into a lake.

Standing nearby was Yeshua. He was draped in a long dark brown robe with a cord tied at the waist. Over his head and shoulder, he wore a shawl giving his face a shadowed appearance. He had a dark well-defined beard. He noticed a group standing back from them like sentinels. His first consideration was his followers. Perhaps some of the historical apostles he read and remembered. The Nazarene advanced towards Du Pont until they were face to face, then embraced the physicist tightly and held him a few seconds. All sense of loss and sadness simply left him. It's a moment where the personal chemistry of two mortals fused into a close bond. The Nazarene slowly pulled back and gazed into the eyes of the scientist.

"Do you still have it? He asked. Du Pont returned his gaze. Confusion etched across his face.

"Do I have what? Yeshua

"The key! The key my friend. Do you still possess it?

Du Pont looked blankly unsure what he asked.

"You used to keep it close my brother"

Deep within the recesses of his mind, a spark of recollection. A moment of personal arrogance and defiance came back to him. A single moment from his time summoned him to remember the origins of how all of this began. Slowly, without reason, his right-hand reached into a small satchel until his fingers felt something. Something that shouldn't be there, his fingers gripped the small object and slowly withdrew it. His old key, the keepsake from his father. He stared down at it, then back to the Nazarene whose gaze looked through him.

"You will use it henceforth to unlock my truths, Fletcher.

Reaching out he closed the scientist's grasp around the simple object

"Do you understand my purpose? My task here on this Earth? Do you recall what my brother Etaanus asked of you? ...*Can you carry water that far?*

Yes!! I do. Du Pont whispered. "I also understand, how little we know. How little humanity understands? We're lost in oceans of doubt, uncertainties, and plagued with ambiguities. I know I must take all this and... Try and find a way" His hands shook.

"I never believed in anything. He said almost choking on his words. "Forgive me Yeshua. I knew nothing. I'm so humbled. This...Creation and its foundation are unlike anything we mortals could ever appreciate."

The Nazarene reached and pulled him close and embraced him again.

"Do you remember when we met encountered each other in my cave? He whispered

"I asked you to be strong. To have faith and belief! Do you recall?

Du Pont shook his head recalling that moment finding the cave hidden into the side of the hill... a hand reached out and plucked him to safety. It was happening all over again only this time the darkness of night was replaced with human blindness, rescued from ignorance by all he'd witnessed.

"I have something for you my friend to bring to your times". The Nazarene said.

Du Pont drew back and returned the gaze of the intense hazel almond eyes. There was no pity this time. This time there was purpose with intent and determination. He noticed all the tall figures have moved to form a circle. These were no Apostles these were Celestial Beings. Materialized into a human form they stood tall, with nobility, graced with great wisdom and power. The scientist straightened himself unsure what to expect.

"It's a gift I give you Fletcher. From my father. It is yours- if you will accept?

The only sound around them was the gentle lapping of water on the jetty. The air was calm, hardly any wind present, complete stillness. With that, the Nazarene closed his eyes for a brief moment then held both his hands in front of Du Pont.

"It will bring you some turmoil, but you will overcome everything. I will send you an aid.'

From nowhere a glow of pure white light spawned into view and slowly grew into a beautiful orb of iridescent light. Slowly in a matter of seconds, the air chills noticeably while an image began to take form. A distinctive and familiar shape began to manifest inside the orb of light. The atomic structure formed revealing the intricate pattern of revolving subatomic elements whirling round and contained within majestic elliptical orbits. Du Pont gazed in awe to look directly at its absolute structure. Abstracted in theory, but never witnessed by human eyes in all its glory. The atomic structure of matter. It pulsed. Its image radiated and subsumed with both strong and weak nuclear forces that bound the primeval forces of matter and energy. Then from within the structure itself, a complex set of values and symbols began to appear and encircled the glowing orb. Du Pont instantly recognised what he was looking at. The nucleus and fine structure of matter.

As the symbols and numbers converged, a transformation began to unfold. Complex equations materialize from within the atomic image. He studied and followed the sequence as it revealed its sublime beauty. The image began to release and convert into pure energy into a mild pulse of heat. Followed by a slow disintegration of the nucleus, splitting it into two, symbolic of a fission event that precedes a triggering of a nuclear detonation. His quest to understanding nature's hidden secrets was unveiled but never in the manner he remotely considered. A shock wave instantly expanded from the centre. To dispel all doubt a mushroom cloud emerged within the orb, replacing the entire atomic structure. It lasts just seconds, and then a series of even more intricate symbols materialized, with a rapid sequencing of atomic numbers.

"Dear God! Can this be possible...? Du Pont whispered

Despite the unmistakable portent of nuclear physics, his attention was drawn to something new. Something he'd never seen before. Before his eyes, some of the numerical values glowed brighter the others, signifying a shift in the fine structure. Hydrogen atoms appeared and mingled into chemical transitions to nitrogen-oxygen structures. Then a 4-dimensional image of equations of more complex physics followed. The mind of the physicist becomes transfixed barely struggling to keep up, with the implicit and rapid change and alteration of values that seemed to slow down almost freeze-framing the awesome sequence the precedes nuclear detonation. His mind raced to absorb to entire sequence and meaning. He gazed into the heart of *matter*, its very essence, and its inner workings. The entire coalescing of fundamental forces of nature that ordain how all life on earth works. Abruptly the image glowed in intensity, and then a mystical finger appeared and inserted itself into the heart of the image. Du Pont's formidable powers of focus and intellect became hypnotic and began to follow what he was being shown.

He watched with deep intent taking in everything now, working with great pace to maintain the intricacies of the magic that was unfolding right before him.

"Is this, what I think this is? Du Pont whispered.

As if teaching a young student, the finger movements slow down and pause to allow his mind to grasp the nature and substance of what he was witnessing. Finally, the finger moved to a set of symbols and altered them into reverse order and paused. It held its position within the orb and stayed motionless for some seconds. The physicist kept working through all the phase-transitions his brain could muster, racing through all the iterations while mentally considering each consequence. Then the finger continued in one final step and inserted a new symbol, a symbol of a neutrino particle. Instantly the entire image of the atomic structure dissolved, replaced by the image of a mushroom cloud. Then it does something startling. It reversed the detonation sequence. Du Pont leaned back for a second, as the realization of what everything meant slammed into him. He took a sharp intake of breath.

"My God! This awesome power hangs over all humanity Yeshua.

"Yes, it does Fletcher. Mankind's thirst for knowledge is not matched by his wisdom to harness it wisely"

The physicist ran his hands through his hair.

"This vision! It's a gift. It reveals something we never dared contemplate. To disrupt a process that's so lethal. Dear God, now we can prevent...*Nuclear Holocaust*. This is priceless! He gasped.

The Nazarene raised his head his eyes became intense. The sharpness of thought and wisdom flashed across his face. Captured for a brief few seconds the scientist knew he was staring into the source of infinite wisdom. A haunted look came over him as the Nazerene raised his hand.

"I know dear Friend. It is a great power of divine origin. Mortals must have respect for its use. It does not come within man's preview to use it to enslave others and all of humanity".

Du Pont looked into the distance.

"Will my mind recall all that I have seen here, Yeshua? He asked nervously

"Yes, your intellect will be empowered to understand all. Have no fears. Remember my friend. Belief, and unshakable faith in all I represent, He said.

Du Pont stepped back and momentarily broke the circle. A window of knowledge that rendered all destructive elements of catastrophic nuclear detonations came from a source beyond comprehension. Physics from a higher realm could ordain how all nuclear weapons cease to function or exist. If he accepted, then it was his to share and to champion. Turning around, all that remained before him was the Nazarene. The daylight resumed its normal state. They were alone on the jetty, only this time a boat was moored at the end of it. Standing facing them he saw, Etaanus.

"There is more for you to see and understand, Fletcher. It's almost the moment for you to return to your own time. But first, join Etaanus. Further truths await."

Milan, Italy

The evening was drawing in and his arrangement was precise. His appointment to meet with the curator was a little after 6.45 pm. The air that time of the evening in Milan was warm and without any fresh breeze, gave the city a clammy feeling. The streets were filled with commuters on scooters fighting they're through the narrow alleyways to get to their homes. Father Provincial of the Jesuit Order held his briefcase in one hand and his android in the other. The map on his device indicated it was another block around to his right, and he would be there. It was nearly 6.45 pm, his timing was perfect. He crossed over the tram tracks and walked into the Piazza di Santa Maria Delle Grazie. After a brisk walk he emerged into the sunset and was confronted immediately with an imposing red-stoned cathedral-like building, Santa Maria Delle Graze. To the side of the main façade, he found the door unlocked. His appearance in a black suit did little to attract any attention other than a silver chain with a simple crucifix was just visible inside his jacket.

Once inside the impressive structure a vista of immaculate gothic arches ran the length of the entire central aisle. Its lighting cast deep shadows upwards giving its high cathedral architecture an austere spectre of hidden stories and histories. He stood for a moment to admire the magnificence of its design. A blend of Renaissance and Gothic. Standing for a moment he took in the magnificence of its imperial design and its effect on all who entered. Stillness filled the entire structure allowing him some moments to recall his purpose of the visit.

"Brother Alphonse? A voice finally called out.

A middle-aged diminutive nun was standing waiting. She approached from the shadows with great reserve and bowed slightly. Then without any preliminaries, she took his hand and genuflected.

"It's an honour to receive you, at such short notice Brother Superior." He smiled and with his free hand made a gesture of the sign of the cross towards her.

"May God bless you sister? I am very grateful to you. Are we alone? He asked

"Yes, your message did ask for complete privacy and…"

"Wonderful. Yes indeed. It is of great importance. May I ask your name?

"Sister Francesca' She replied with a slight smile.

"Is this your first time to visit to see the master's magnificent work?

He looked at her carefully in the dim lighting, trying to gauge or discern anything that might cause alarm or further anxiety. He noted her turn of phrase the *master's work*. "Right sister Francesca, you are aware why my visit is necessary. May we proceed? Would you lead on?

She nodded then without any further conversation led him amid the darkened shadows down one of the side aisles. Neither of them spoke till they came to a small dining hall in the monastery. A small rectangular section no more than 20 meters wide of plain off-white walls. The first thing that struck him was the presence of a large canvas screen dominating the entire width acting as a huge blanket obscuring what lay behind. They stopped. He said little, imagining what lay waiting on the other side.

"How long has this been here Sister? He asked.

"Just two weeks now, Brother Superior. We declared work was to carry out necessary repairs. Once we noticed the.... manifestation we took steps".

The senior Jesuit tried gauging her response to the occurrence.

"This way, if you please, and mind your steps. She said.

Discreetly and with minimum disturbance they stepped around the large canvas and found themselves standing in a dark space facing a wall. Sister Francesca pulled the canvas closed behind them ensuring complete privacy. Slightly elevated on the facing wall, and spanning the entire width, he could just about make out the outline of the 15th-century mural. Sister Francesca moved to nearby temporary equipment and flicked a switch. Immediately three small powerful lamps illuminated the enclosed space filling it with a strong white light. Like a bolt, the entire magnificence of Leonardo's legendary depiction of the Last Supper dominated the entire back wall.

"Novissima Cena"! He whispered.

In all its glory the famous mural looked down on him, and while he saw it many times in books, nothing prepared him to see the masterpiece like this. Leonardo's great work and all it suggested. His eyes were drawn to a series of steps made into makeshift stairs positioned to a spot just under the piece itself.

"Do you need to me stay with you Father? Sister Francesca asked.

He looked carefully at where he needed to focus. He knew what he was looking for.

"Thank you, sister, perhaps if you give me a few minutes. This won't take long".

When left alone, Brother Superior Alphonse Sienna opened his briefcase and removed a folder. With precision and easy movements, he selected photographs from his folder and laid them down on a small timber bench. Then he removed the newspaper clipping and laid them beside the pictures. He straightened himself and looked up at the mural itself, and moved along until he saw what he was here for. He stared at the image. Moving carefully he mounted the steps until he was almost at eye level with the mural images. It's doubtful if anyone in recent times was as close to the masterpiece as he was now. In an instant he stared incredulously at a face he came to know. Disbelief and shock fade as he made certain his fears were as expected. He got back down the stairs and picked up the pictures and the paper clipping. Once again he ascended the steps and stood in his spot. He glanced carefully at both pictures. His hands start to shake slightly, then slowly shifted his gaze along the image of each apostle, till he came to it. It took a few seconds to be certain. There was no mistake.

An additional image stared back at him, an image of someone that should not be there. His breathing increased trying at best to grasp what faced him. It's identical in every way, even right down to its location at the table, and similar to the pictures from Spain. A complete replica of the physicist, Fletcher Du Pont looked back at him. Unconsciously he made the sign of the cross. Then as efficiently as he can he took out his phone and steadied himself. He took measured breaths to calm himself and then focused and shot a series of photographs. Five minutes later Sister Francesca returned, entered the closed space to find the reverend Alfonse Sienna kneeling at the small table in prayer. He seemed momentarily oblivious to her return immersed in private thoughts. He finally looked up and held her stare. He smiled and rose.

"You have extended a great service to me, Sister Francesca. May our heavenly father bless you, and keep you well. I am deeply grateful sister."

Again she bowed and gave him a nervous smile. Averting her eyes upwards towards the masterpiece.

"Beautiful isn't it? She whispered. "I wonder how Leonardo would respond to his work been altered like this?

The Jesuit gave the masterpiece a final look. Indeed what would the great artist think? The scene had many dimensions to it. Deception, Denial, and Betrayal. How ironic he thought to himself that it should become a backdrop to something both troubling and mysterious, both physical and meta-physical. He turned to the young sister.

"I will see myself out, Sister Francesca. Thank you most kindly for allowing me to visit".

"You are most welcome, Brother Superior. Anytime."

He smiled and then, as quietly as his arrival, he picked up his briefcase and left.

By the time Alphonse Sienna boarded the train later that evening, his conversation with the head of his Order in Rome was brief. There was no mistake and no doubt as to the authenticity as to what he saw and verified. Nothing appeared to be what it seemed.

Earlier that day and 100 meters down, Paul Melrose needed to do something. It took him just under five minutes to get to his intended location. At that time of the day, some of the routine maintenance on the beam pipe was completed, so he had the place to himself. The wall markings still troubled him and since their first appearance some weeks earlier they remained deeply mystifying. The only issue was a legacy one, an eerie feeling hung over that part of the tunnel structure. When he arrived there was a large partition erected to screen off that part of the tunnel. He quickly stepped inside the partition and moved to where the markings were and once more attempted to extract some further insight into what it all meant. Inwardly he was convinced such markings had significance. More so now considering the conversation back in Sal Madere with the family and the startling ideas proposed by Father Francois. Between his impending parenthood and recent events, his mind became restless. Whatever about the science, mystical notions, and thoughts the Jesuit brought to light, everything was unnerving?

Pouring over his notes his eyes are drawn to details of the markings the last time he studied them, except now some of the arrangements had mysteriously altered, again. His heart started to pound. While preserving their previous layout and form, the scorch marks on the right side of the tunnel were no longer visible. Stepping back he rummaged through his battered canvas bag and pulled out a fistful of crinkled notes. Hand sketches he made of the original marks. Standing he moved back to his spot and glanced down at his notes, then upwards. In an instant, his mind realised what he was looking at. The markings represented *a timeline*.

A timeline encompassing a message, which involved curved space-time. Only it's suggestive of time going backward.

"What would Fletcher think of this? He muttered

"Fuck! Could this be...a signal!

His eyes fixed on the remaining visible portion of the curved symbols then glancing down at his notes his eyes tightened. It's essentially Riemann space-time geometry worked out on the tunnel surface, which in itself, was curved. How ironic and yet how more symbiotic could this get. His hands began to sweat, and his mouth became parched.

"Why didn't I see it before? This is a time clock...in reverse. I know what this is?

"Jesus! This is a... *countdown!*

Shaking, he moved to the end of the curve looking to see if it was still there. It was so faint the first time he saw it it's a wonder the symbol was noticed at all. He leaned in much closer trying to control his rapid breathing only to find the elongated eight-infinity symbol was missing. Instead, in its place, a newer symbol was scorched into the solid concrete wall. He raised his hand to his lips and held his breath.

"What the hell is going on? He gasped

The infinity symbol was replaced with Ω omega. The very *last character* in the Greek alphabet. In eschatology terms, the *End of Everything?* In physics, the Omega Meson particle.

"Jesus! He whispered.

He stared at the symbol allowing his mind to come to terms with what was being played out. Alone one hundred meters beneath French soil, he blessed himself making the sign of the cross.

$$\Omega$$

CHAPTER TWENTY.

When matters of great scientific or medical significance don't make sense or lead to dark places it often-triggered responses to find answers from unexpected sources. Sources from which, even deeper puzzling aspects arise. Such were the circumstances confronting four separate groups in high places when it came to one singular topic. That of an eminent physicist hanging to life by a thread.

One such group sat in private, on the second floor within the huge CERN complex. Another gathered inside the Vatican, deep in the most secretive enclaves of the Roman Catholic curia. Equally absorbed, were a team of doctors seated around a table reviewing and dissecting all known medical details that were leading them towards the unpleasant and unpalatable decision. Finally elsewhere in a hospital with a different setting two doctors sat in a small-darkened cubicle studying scans of a pregnancy that is to all intense purposes appeared normal? Only it wasn't, it was anything but.

Director-General's Study

Felix Deveraux sat patiently glanced at his watch waiting for his special visitor. It was his study. It was also a Thursday and his bridge night, but that wasn't going to happen this evening. Sitting in one of his chairs opposite him was Paul Melrose. Standing by the window an anxious, Manfred Gruss, his Deputy Director, and Professor Carina Ambrosiana. After listening to Melrose the previous day and his brief analysis, the DG felt he had little choice. He called an informal group in on short notice, keeping the circle to a small close gathering. Each of them had exhausted every avenue to understanding the nature and fall-out with the Euclid program. Sitting on Deveraux's desk laid three thick reports. One is technical, preliminary document all to do with pure physics. The initial results of some of Euclid Beta 8 compelling and absorbing data on the appearance of particles of unknown origin. Two, a separate, and more troubling report-contained images of his friend. Disturbing images that led to some truly shocking evidence as to what might have caused his accident. It also contained a series of pictures of its effects and appearance. Third, a further report, on the heat-generated markings within the large Hadrons' beam tunnel equally sinister and ominous in everything it suggested.

Neither report left CERN's Director-General feeling good, the opposite in fact.

On each count, despite some of the best minds at his disposal, no one could unveil anything that came close to providing a meaningful or authentic explanation. That was about to change he hoped with his expected guest. While waiting, they all listened with barely concealed dismay to Melrose's thoughts regarding the significance behind the heat markings. The reaction was muted and deeply unsettling.

The Vatican. Rome

Cardinal Giuseppe Bonaire knelt before a small altar slightly to the left of his Holiness Leo IV. It was 5.45 am, and the private mass was coming to an end. After this privileged and intimate ceremony, the Pontiff stood and blessed the small group gathered. Then as his custom, he spoke briefly on a personal level to each of them. He moved to Cardinal Bonaire his head of the Congregation for the Doctrine of Faith and had a few well-chosen words. That was followed by the two men of the church walking down a silent hallway in private dialogue that lasted no more two minutes. Then in keeping with tradition over the centuries, the Cardinal knelt and took the ring of Peter and kissed it. Standing, he held the Pontiff's stare for a second then bowed and silently withdrew, taking his leave and retired to his study down a short hallway. Already seated waiting for him, was the Superior General of the Jesuit order, and his brother Jesuit, Alphonse Sienna.

'Ipse meus et frater in Christo' He said taking his seat behind his desk.

"You're Eminence! The Head of the Jesuit Order said. A large ornate silver Coffee pot was placed on a small table and cups were placed in front of each of them. A few seconds passed before the Cardinal ventured a comment. He studied brother Sienna in particular.

"I assume dear brother, it's as we feared He finally asked.

"Yes, you're Eminence it's all of that. There is no doubt, any kind of forgery is out of the question. Alphonse Sienna replied. Quickly, he took his photographs and passed his android around to the two other men.

'And from Geneva, Alphonse, what are the latest developments?

"It's as before, you're Eminence, but our Brother Francois's thesis is even more startling now. I might add he has been asked to meet informally of course, with CERN's leadership. This is a crisis for them."

'I see! A key question arises my brothers. Are we looking at evidence for proclaiming the existence of undeniable fact?

The other two men knew only too well this was looming and gave each other an uncertain look. When issues of a miraculous nature are raised, the Catholic Church traditionally operated a hermeneutic of suspicion. Any claim of the extraordinary or miraculous event must be proven, not presumed. For something to be worthy of belief, it came before a process of ecclesiastic authority. A commission of experts in both scientific-theological matters handled claims. This required that moral certitude ought to exist and that normal human explanations fail. The person or persons must be mentally fit, moral, and obedient to ecclesiastical authority. And, above any suspicion of financial gain. The process was often lengthy and rigorous while being able to point to good fruit resulting from such claims and deeper commitment to prayer. Proving undeniable fact was sitting squarely in front of them. All three men over the next hour began to meticulously comb through every facet of detail of events in Geneva.

Small conference room –Neurological unit.

Doctor Peter Schultz, not for the first time in the last few days rubbed his eyes and looked up from the reports and Brain images placed in order around the circular desk. Opposite him, Doctor Joseph Heinz played with his glasses as he studied the same images of the brain of patient 421. Two neurosurgeons, the best in their fields poured over every aspect of their patient brain motor functions or lack of. Other team members joined them.

CERN. Director General's Office.

The double-tap on the door was all it took. Paul Melrose jumped to his feet and opened it. Standing in full ecclesiastic black regalia Fr. Francois Burgoyne S.J appeared outside, his frame perfectly filling the door space. His demeanour added to his presence with a double-breasted cassock and a silver chain and cross around his neck. He wore a striking black biretta hat, and of course his full-length ferraiolo cape. In his right hand a small folder.

"Francois! You are most welcome. Deveraux said standing to greet him.

The Jesuit entered and nodded and smiled briefly to everyone.

"You know everyone here, Francois, yes?

"Indeed, Director-General. Good evening to you all."

When the brief handshakes were completed he saw the empty chair and sat. Everyone pulled their seats and sat in close to a small semi-circle.

'How are the family, Francois, Claudine and the girls? Asked Deveraux.

'Bearing up well, as you can imagine. Thank you for asking".

"They're in our prayers, Francois" Carina Ambrosiana said

There was a pause, and then Deveraux moved to a small table.

"Coffee Francois or perhaps something more?

Coffee! Thank you." Deveraux picked up his phone and ordered coffee.

"Paul, before we start, perhaps you might convey your news to our guest regarding section 24 in our Accelerator tunnel, our *heat markings*".

Melrose began and for the third time within a few days went over details much of which, the Jesuit knew already. Then with great care and reasoning he described recent alterations along with some details dealing with the symbols and their alteration. Opposite him, the Jesuit sat almost ramrod straight listening with great intent his face utterly impassive.

'...And to conclude, I believe, when this countdown reaches its finality, it will signal some event. I believe it will... in some way connected to Fletcher's recovery ...or?

"Or What? The Jesuit asked sharply.

Melrose didn't reply, content to leaving it to hang.

"Francois, your call and what Paul tells me- you have some insightful observations to make on all of this tragedy. Deveraux asked quietly.

The Jesuit leaned back into the chair and joined his hands. There was a haunted look about him.

"You all understand I'm not a scientist or a physicist. But I live a life, which brought me into proximity to matters of a spiritual dimension.

Coffee is brought in and left on Deveraux's desk.

"I believe that our mortal existence, our physical presence if you will, houses a greater potent force. Our spirit. That is the basis of everything I wish to share with you."

'Yes, of course, Francois. I think we all understand that. Deveraux replied.

Then without any preamble, the Jesuit stood and began to pace.

"I believe we're in the midst of some miraculous event. Something that transcends all scientific or human knowledge. I believe this because I know a several things that lie outside any known scientific framework. I know about the Shroud Image and its' appearance in your trial results. Its manifestation caused Fletcher a deal of anxiety. It had him deeply disturbed in part because he didn't understand it, and in part, because he didn't subscribe to its religious context."

Deveraux's face darkened. Each of them glanced at each other. All mildly taken aback with the Jesuit's directness.

"And, if that wasn't enough, it seems to have made its appearance, uniquely on Fletcher's computer only."

He looked at each of them, sensing he was on sensitive ground. He rotated his ring on his finger as if selecting his thoughts and choice of words. The conversation flowed back and forth over the next hour. There were no arguments even though some of the things the Jesuit outlined were alien and unsettling.

"May I ask, if any of you have heard of Theosophia? The Jesuit finally asked

"Perhaps you might enlighten us, Francois, Carina Ambrosiana whispered.

"It means Divine Wisdom. Written in another time, the Kingdom of Light a timeless piece of ancient writings. A complete and obscure body of work whose origins are rooted in Judean mysticism. It speaks of accessing this divine wisdom; its origins go back almost, precedes modern religious teachings. Accessing Divine Wisdom comes through submersion of the spirit. It comes from a consciousness where, in these times mystics moved beyond their own intellect to a super mind. Visiting realms where the conscious mind comes in direct contact with the divine. It's enlightenment it also speaks of experiencing an ecstasy to be able to interact with entities of higher mental capacities".

He paused allowing them to absorb what he was offering.

"I hold to the notion my friends that this world has its own mysteries. Mysteries that defy physics. The alteration to Fletcher's physical appearance so utterly changed suggests that most of his spiritual energy is *elsewhere*. Many of the ancient writings, some of the Gnostic origin talk and speak of the spirit embarking on a mystical journey to access divine wisdom without experiencing physical death. The physical mortal body succumbs to a near deathly state but does not expire, but the soul is free to wonder"

Deveraux stirred uneasily in his seat glanced at one of the folders on his desk. Paul Melrose then remembered something, which at the time seemed innocent in itself. His crazy equations in hospital contained an obscure *Souls Theorem*! Did he miss something?

'François is this what you think is happening to, Fletcher? Asked Manfred Gruess

"Yes, I do. But there is more. When, Paul was ill some time back he spoke in an ancient form of Hebrew during his illness. It wasn't just, his reciting an unknown tongue; it was what you spoke of."

In a single movement, the Jesuit took out a single sheet and looked at it.

"There will come a mystical time, a traveller of light will encounter a lord of another time...and extraordinary wisdom will be restored to man "Your words! Paul, spoken with near-perfect diction'

No one responded for a few seconds. Then as if anticipating their questions the Jesuit produced another page, this time; it's a scrawl on hospital stationary. He held it up the sheet and recited it's meaning.

רקהקשדקג נקקמ ישד דקגעק'למם קסארשםסגנמשרט

"Simply it means extraordinary wisdom has been found!

"Where did that come from? Asked Carina Ambrosiana, The Jesuit said nothing but looked at Melrose.

"From Fletcher's own hand" Melrose whispered.

What! Deveraux snapped.

"Why wasn't I informed he was conscious? This is unacceptable!

The Jesuit knew this was going to be difficult. He stood and walked to the window. The room became tense. Deveraux's agitation focussed on the Jesuit. Melrose felt uncomfortable having kept this from the others. The slow melodic ticking of the large antique clock was the only sound in the room.

'He's not. Is he? Said Carina breaking the tension.

The Jesuit looked at her and then at the Director-General.

'Indeed, Carina. Fletcher is still unconscious and remains so, and yet, this was written in his hand." The Jesuit added quietly.

Felix Deveraux was a man used to dealing with ambiguities, matters of a complex nature. This however stunned him. For a few brief seconds, there was silence in the study.

"How can that be? How can someone..? Manfred Gruess whispered

"There is a guiding intellect at work here dear friends. Fletcher is caught up in some mystical happening" Francois whispered

"What is this to do with Theosophia? Asked Carina.

Francois moved away from the window and returned to his seat.

"It's where a spirit is released from its captive imprisoned state as a mortal and is led to places. Places where they encounter wisdom. Mystics of ancient times believed Angels guided the mind and reshaped human intellect during these encounters. This recent event, the writing, in itself may mean nothing, but when placed in these circumstances, well...

The Jesuit stopped then selected and placed some photographs on the desk for them to see. Each of the two pictures had only one thing in common. The Last Supper

"Look very closely at them and, prepare yourselves."

It took each of them less than 5 seconds to see and react. Deveraux not believing his own eyes simply sunk back into his seat. The rest said nothing. Etched on their faces was utter dismay and disbelief. No one spoke. The head of CERN looked up at the priestly figure sitting opposite him. Finally, he summoned his composure and reached out and filled his cup with fresh coffee.

"Forgive me, Francois, but this is madness. How am I going to…?

"To What?

What do you think you can do? Francois snapped.

"Three! My friends. Three miraculous events…

"One, the image of Christ death mask or its representation, appears amidst the physics of particle decay, from nowhere! Two, Paul's almost mystical ability, not only to recite scriptural writings in an ancient tongue more than two thousand years old but in the language of Jesus Christ himself in a state of deep unexplained unconsciousness. Three, the passion of Christ commenced with that last evocative meal on the evening of his arrest the Last Supper. Two thousand years ago, yet two near-identical paintings, one from Spain, and the other in Milan capture its historical significance. And yet, you see before you the surreal alteration and additional depictions. I might remind you all, there was no such thing as a Thirteenth Apostle! Does anyone of you here think these are not mystifying in the extreme?

An uneasy silence lingered, no one had a rational response. All of them simply had to recall their colleague's whole physical appearance. His transformation that shocked them. Finally, it was the Carina who spoke.

"Why Fletcher, Francois? Isn't he Agnostic, Atheist? He doesn't believe in..?

The Jesuit looked down and fidgeted with the silver crucifix.

"I believe it is precisely that reason, good lady that this may have happened. And there's one other matter. This space-time-matter the markings in your tunnel. It suggests something relating to the bending of Time.

'*Warping* I think is the word you're looking for." Said Melrose

'Yes, thank you. The markings and other things are all hinting that there is a missing piece, to do with Time.

Deveraux raised an eyebrow and gave his fellow physicists a look.

"Francois, what you're suggesting it's, quite incredible. An intersection of sorts. The world of particle physics was somehow consumed within some metaphysical event. We have no basis in science to explain or describe that. Nothing" He said

"Mysteries often defy physics, Felix. Remember what was written in Fletcher's own hand" Extraordinary wisdom has been found.

"What do you think Francois? *This guiding intellect*.! What could that be? Asked Melrose.

The Jesuit turned and gave him a direct look.

"It's whatever took hold of your mind when you were in the hospital and set you to write these unfathomable equations. Some form of the calculus of numbers that defied all of us here. Has anyone in CERN managed to grasp what they actually mean?

Again, there was an uncomfortable shaking of heads. Their best minds couldn't extend any logic into the computational framework that Melrose transcribed all over his hospital ward.

"There was an existential aspect to them Francois and it was beyond us to understand." Carla Ambrosiana whispered.

Melrose was about to say something and then decided against it. The conversation and priestly revelations continued into the early evening, nobody was ready to leave. Despite the scientific mindset of those present, none of them dismissed what they were hearing. A whole new dimension to this problem began to unveil and yet, as strange as it was it there was a compelling aspect to all of it. For some inexplicable reason that no one could point to, it possessed authenticity.

Bartus San Jovanne Hospital

In contrast, as the evening was drawing in, after nearly two hours, the medical team in room 4H was almost reaching a consensus as to what was confronting them. A decision. Life support equipment was now functioning 24 hours around the clock each day since their eminent patient arrived some weeks earlier. While the biological process of the human body was supported by mechanical means, brain scans over the last number of days, barely registered executive functions. The analysis presented them with a quandary. No conclusive evidence that the brainstem had shut down, yet scans indicated cerebral activity was almost non-existent.

Irreversible coma was the prevailing opinion around the room. However, the recent reflex action on the patient's arm movement ruled out the possibility of a chronic vegetative state. The determination of clinical death was often a difficult issue where severe brain trauma was involved. Adding to this was his appearance. No known medical science explained the sheer scale of physical metamorphoses the patient had endured. All EEG tests, every 3 to 4 days registered consistent 'flat line' states. The key question hanging over Dr. Shultz and his team was trying to conclude the condition was now irreversible. A further complication was the most recent radionuclide scan showed minute intracranial blood flow patterns that spiked and ebbed, and these neurological bouts of activity preceded the patient's reflex arm movement. But since that event, there was nothing. Shutting down the life support process would be carried out within the strict protocols as applied in Switzerland, on both legal and clinical grounds.

"Do we know if there are any specific medical instructions regarding extraordinary medical interventions? Asks one of the team.

"No, there isn't to my knowledge! Replied another.

All of them struggled with what was confronting them. Terminating life-sustaining equipment took a simple action, a switch was thrown, and all the advanced mechanisms that support cardiovascular, respiratory, and key organ functions are shut down. Support for the body's ability to maintain itself is withdrawn, and faith and whatever else that may be in play brings its own finality.

Doctor Joseph Heinz, the leading brain trauma specialist, simply leaned across and placed his hand on his colleague's arm.

"Peter let's give it another 48 hours. If everything remains the same, we contact the family and then, then the decision"... He left unfinished.

Shultz nodded then looked around at the others on the team- no one needed to say anything. Each of them quietly nodded in agreement. Despite their professional dedication to preserving life, sadness and painful regret and resignation began to fill the room. It was never an easy decision.

After 7.15 pm Francois Burgoyne stopped talking and ambled to the window watched the last light of sunset disappear behind the distant Jura's. Felix Deveraux's study felt like a morgue, a room filled with uncertainty and doubt. For the three men and one woman, there was much to consider. The Jesuit had revealed his deepest thoughts to those he trusted. The very essence of his most cherished values in spirituality he'd laid bare to all. And while not offering anything new in scientific terms, he managed to convey an alternative perspective that neither of them dared to consider up to now.

A metaphysical aspect, an alternative explanation to matters that haunted each of them in different ways. Deveraux and Manfred Gruss attention became absorbed in the potential political and scientific consequences if this ever became public. How would they fashion any explanation?

Melrose shifted in his seat and reached for the coffee pot. He had other things on his mind now. New issues began to germinate and haunt him. Carina Ambrosiana stood and started pacing a little; she had her own questions along with certain directness to her approach. Never afraid to confront and meet issues head on, and after hearing everything from the Jesuit, her personal feelings she would keep to herself. She shot the cleric a look and then studied the others.

"Francois, what's the possible Church's or religious response to all of this? The Jesuit didn't respond immediately, he too had demons that inflicted themselves on the matter.

"It's a matter first, for the family, and perhaps we wait. He said quietly to no one in particular

"Wait, for what? Asked Deveraux.

"We wait until we hear ...what Fletcher himself has to say on the matter".

The remark was greeted by complete silence in the room, along with looks of disbelief on everyone's face. The casual manner of the response threw them all.

"That would be wonderful if it were true, Francois, but realistically, we must prepare ourselves as well." Manfred Gruss replied gently.

"Yes, we must. But not from Fletcher's demise. He will come back to us. We must be prepared, for the manner of his recovery. The Jesuit said.

His voice was strained, full of worry as to what that entailed. He wasn't sure if any of them would handle how his brother in law's recovery would transpire. But return he would, and if Paul Melrose's theory on the markings were true, they wouldn't have to wait long.

For Felix Deveraux, the strain over the last few weeks was getting to him. He presided over one of the most sophisticated machines on the planet, had gathered around him some of the finest minds in world science. Men with tremendous abilities to fashion and design mind-bending ideas in particle physics, and yet for all of that, his entire framework of knowledge was being catapulted into a mystery of unfathomable dimensions. What disturbed him further, was the tall slim priest, a man of formidable intellect in his own right had touched a nerve. He'd connected dots with things that he as a scientist found challenging to accept. Francois Burgoyne was beginning to unsettle him.

"To answer your question, Carina, the Roman Catholic has a process. It must establish *Undeniable Fact*, Burgoyne said, still staring out the window.

The Vatican

In Rome, that same evening, an oppressively humid day ended with an unseasonal torrential downpour that lasted for nearly 2 hours. Rain bounced off the glass windows of spacious wood-panelled study in the office of the Holy See. Cardinal Bonaire stood with his back to his desk, listening to the relentless outside downpour. He looked out over the pebbled courtyard three floors down, immersed in deep thoughts. Church dogma, ecclesiastical papers, and tradition occupied his mind. All-important issues that defined how the teachings of Christ were revealed to man. His, was where all manner of things, matters of heresy, miraculous cures, sexual abuse, and deviancy ended up on his desk. His mind, however, dwelt on a matter that caused him to reflect.

The Nicene Creed ends with the words... *we look for the resurrection of the dead, and the life of the world to come....*

Christian eschatology ordained three states in the Afterlife. Heaven, where souls see and are united with God. Purgatory, a temporary place of refuge for souls where purification and penance occurs, and while these souls are saved, they are not ready to enter the kingdom of God. Then there is Hell. No one is predestined to such a place, other than souls who openly defy and express hostility towards God's will and love. Dwelling in some other states of existence was not entirely open to interpretation by dogma. Church doctrine was suspiciously silent on such matters. And yet, sitting on his desk, was something that seemed truly authentic, somewhat provocative, but instilled great appeal. Deep inside his psychic Cardinal Giuseppe Bonaire still believed in the power of a living God and miracles. There was a knock on his study's door that broke into his thoughts. The door opened and Monsignor David Hume entered, carrying a large bundle of folders and research papers. A man in his mid-forties, a Scot has worked most of his clerical life in Rome in the Curia. Before he found his vocation and devotion to the Church, he studied Mathematics and Physics at Edinburgh University.

"Ah! David, you have something for me". The Cardinal smiled.

"Well, there are some things that your Eminence needs to read. He replied taking a seat and laying out the material on the Cardinal's desk.

"Before I look at this Monsignor, perhaps you might explain some of the more abstract nature of the physics of this to me, starting with the biography of this Professor Du Pont?

"Certainly, your Eminence!"

For the next ten minutes, every aspect of Fletcher Du Pont's professional career was covered. The folder was crammed with his achievements in theoretical breakthroughs, much of his published work, numerous scientific papers, and his work on superstring theory leading to his recognition for his Nobel Prize in Chaotic Systems in Particle Decay. Each note and attached literature described a man of outstanding intellectual abilities in his field.

"He's American, married to a French National, there are children and now resides in Geneva. And of course...there is ... The priest hesitated as he checked his notes. The Cardinal cast him a glance.

"Go on, is there more?

"His wife and children are practicing Catholics, and, as you are aware you're Eminence, Brother Francois Burgoyne, is her brother, a member of your Order if I'm not mistaken. He said with a slight cough, looking down and then continued.

"Professor Du Pont, however, is not Catholic. And from everything I've managed to read. He is assuredly atheistic in his personal beliefs".

Cardinal Bonaire listened with great interest, nodding to himself as his fellow priest paused.

"That's all there is to the man. Now, to the science"

Geneva. Later that evening.

Everyone stood and started to leave. All were tired while inwardly grateful for his sheer conviction of faith towards their colleague and friend.

"Francois you have given us a great deal to think over. Deveraux said

"Thank you most graciously, Felix It was something that needed to be spoken of. May God bless us and get us through this." The Jesuit replied.

"I wish I had that kind of belief, Francois. I hope you're right about Fletcher, his recovery but... He faltered choosing his words.

"We need to move quickly Francois. Very quickly indeed!

The Jesuit paused adjusting his chain and cross. Carina Ambrosiana moved closer.

"I've had a call from the hospital. The head of CERN's voice was strained

"I keep in touch, almost daily to see how Fletcher's condition is. Well, you know.?

"Of course DG! What's happening? The Carina pressed

"There's an imminent decision on Life Support. A clinical consensus within the medical team is, that perhaps the time has come to suspend further intervention. They are talking a matter of days.

'Jesus, No! Melrose whispered

"They wish to meet Claudine and the family, and family members in the States. Deveraux said. The Jesuit just stared back at the senior physicist, revealing little emotion or response. His face completely composed, fearless.

"Thank you, Felix". He said reaching out taking his notes and placing them inside his small case.

"Paul, you're taking us back to Sal Madere, yes? It was more a command than a request.

"Sure! Of course"

Francois Burgoyne turned and nodded to them all, then taking Deveraux's hand.

"We'll talk soon, thank you for your time and patience. May God bless you all. Paul, are we ready?' Let us be off!

Then strides out into the hallway. Two minutes later they were gone, leaving those behind feeling as if the very life force of the room left with them.

"What do you think Felix? His deputy director asked returning to his seat. Felix Deveraux settled back and stared up at the ceiling.

"Whatever we may think about religion, and some of its priests, by God you have to admire that man.

"I hope he's right Felix. Manfred Gruess said with deep worry lines across his face.

$$\Omega$$

Somewhere on their journey back, the Francois sensed his driving companion was preoccupied. Since leaving CERN's campus he had said very little. The suspension of life support alarmed them both. Each was emotional hostages, each their own jailers. The Morgan, despite its compact passenger compartment, purred along the autobahn hardly making any noticeable sound. Then as the approached their exit, Melrose, coughed slightly.

Francois! I think there is more to Denise's pregnancy.

Hospital Canteen

While those words were spoken, two doctors leaned against the long countertop in the small canteen on the ground floor of Clinique General Vallence Hospital. Doctor Benjamin Mochti cradled a steaming hot cup of Earl Grey tea. He was pensive and deeply introspective having listened to his colleague, Michael Kells, a Consulting Obstetrician for nearly an hour. Finally, he raised his hand.

"Michael! Listen to me very carefully. We need to be careful! You've overlooked something.

'You're kidding me Benni. You're saying I'm not thorough! He smiled

"No, I'm not saying any such thing. You know me better Michael. How does it happen? Both sets can't be right, He said with an edge frustration creeping into his voice.

"Faulty scanner! Some of the resolution software has a bug! Could be many reasons! Kells retorted.

"So, we both concur this pregnancy is, as we both determined well in advancement"

"Yes, of course, Benni. How many times do you need my opinion?

"Right so that leaves, how we interpret the last 4 ultrasound scans. Mochti replied.

"Yes, and for the last time Benjamin, this young Miss Du Pont will deliver a baby boy and I estimate its weight will be in the order of..."

"No, I'm really sorry Michael. I have a problem with your assessment. The sex is not in question. There's no doubt. The scans confirm the sex as female. The lady in question is going to give birth to a girl! Mochti smiled

Ok! Benni, I'll leave it at that for the moment. The Obstetrician retorted with a wry smile. Standing he moved towards the door.

"Gotta go! But mark my words. You're wrong. You're losing your touch, Benni. He joked and left.

Smirking to himself Mochti gathered the collection of scans and returned them to its folder.

Losing my touch! I don't think so.

Then, abruptly he thought better of it. Reaching for the phone he dialled a number and waited. After a matter of seconds, Denise Du Pont's voice...

"Denise! It's Benjamin Mochti. There was a brief banter, and then he checked his watch.

"Could you come to Surgery tomorrow? Yes, I know you're not due in till the end of the week, but I have some free slots that opened up, (he lied) and it might be good to do another routine check. He listened.

'Yes, that's fine. How are you feeling? Superb! Good. See you then"

Replacing the receiver then taking a little time to change out of his hospital clothing and in less than five minutes headed to the nearest small Italian coffee shop. It was just a little after 8.15 pm he sat alone savouring his coffee at an outside table.

The traffic was mainly pedestrian, mostly diplomats hunting along the avenue to find a place to dine. Sitting with his second Americano he had a flashback to when he was a reservist in the Israeli army during those long evening postings, waiting in the medical tent. Regular patrols arrived back late in the evenings. Fellow young solders such as himself, drained and worn out from long days. Sometimes an alert would come in signalling a chopper's imminent arrival with casualties from engagements either in the Golan or further south, in more dangerous places like the Bacquaa Valley. Bodies broken and battered limbs would descend on his team, young boys almost covered in shrapnel, some beyond repair.

Then, there were other nights he'd sit up in his tent, waiting. Waiting to hear the chopper's distinctive thumping sound in the distance hovering to prepare for more emergency trauma. They never came. Over time his commanding officer would come and give him some R&R time, to go somewhere to chill. One night he was told to stand down, all was quiet. Nothing of importance was happening. Still, the young Mochti had a feeling that perhaps he should stick around and stay focused and alert, checking supplies, blood bank supplies, supplies of morphine and the like. Three hours later, a rocket attack in one of the border villages south of the Golan Heights erupted with massive casualties and hundreds of civilians with horrific injuries flooded into their encampment that night. Luckily, they were ready. It was just a feeling then.

Well, he was having that same feeling again, only this time it was a lot closer to home.

Sal Madere- Residence.

When the Morgan pulled into Sal Madere, it was just after 9 pm. Lights around the house gave the residence an almost regal feel. From the outside, it appeared welcoming and inviting. Once inside, however, Melrose and Burgoyne were greeted with subdued warmth. Claudine was in the study writing a series of letters and updates to her husband's sisters in the US and Canada. Denise looked tired but got up and embraced both of them. Michelle just sat more preoccupied than usual.

"Doctor Benni called from the hospital. Wants me in tomorrow. It's just routine and his diary was good. "Did he say why? What does he want to do? Paul asked

'It's just routine. She said, trying to be convincing. 'How are you, Francois? How was it in Meyrin? She asked

'Well, it took them some time. It was difficult for them to understand Ma Cherie. They occupy a different world, different concerns" He said "It was somewhat of a shock for them, and frankly, why wouldn't they be."

Melrose also noticed the dining table was set for dinner. He knew the news from the hospital was going to be upsetting; both he and their uncle had planned how it would be handled. Over dinner was not an option. It could wait till later when everyone was more relaxed. He, on the other hand, was more drawn to the news of another visit to meet Doctor Mochti.

"Did he say I should attend? He asked suddenly

'No, sweetheart! Just me, and my bump" She joked.

After dinner, Francois nonchalantly looked around the table, and then surprised them asked if everyone would join hands, and then offered a short prayer, finishing with.

"Protegat nos Deus Omnia! Claudine smiled at her brother

'Don't tell me, let me get this... "May God watch over us? The Jesuit smiled.

"Almost dear sister. Michelle! Care to try? Remember your Latin? He teased

Yes! I believe it's, May God protect us all?

Excellent! Mon Ange

It brought a light banter around the table a moment of much needed light humour.

"Interesting toast Francois. Was it that kind of afternoon with Felix and company? Claudine's turn to tease her brother.

"Well, it's a crisis for them. Director Deveraux looked like he hadn't slept in weeks. He struggled to understand anything that had a metaphysical dimension to it. The others seem lost. This is having a heavy toll on them".

'He did very well. No one else could have done it better. Paul said

"Claudine, dinner was exquisite. Thank you, dear sister' He straightened his posture reached over and lifted his glass and raised it slightly.

"To our dear Fletcher. May he know Christ's blessings and love"?

The rest said nothing for a few seconds letting the moment linger.

"To my beloved husband, and father, Claudine said with her glass. The rest did likewise, then Francois moved around the dining table and placed his hands on Denise's shoulders. 'Girls, my beloved nieces, Claudine! I have a request to ask for permission."

Denise reached up and held his hand. Michelle gave him a quizzical look. "Go ahead, Francois! Since when did you need permission for anything in this house? Claudine said.

In that instant without any warning, she caught a glimpse of anguish. That tortured look she knew so well from the past when he carried his own crosses and secret burdens. His pained expression scarcely concealed something.

"I would like your permission to celebrate *the Mass*, here in Sal Madere, He whispered hoarsely.

He barely finished the sentence when the smile on his sister's face melted. The sudden oblique references of Latin at the table earlier, now a Mass! Instantly her blood ran cold, as the shock to what this all meant. The toast to her husband hit her like a bolt. Her glass crashed to floor shattering into tiny pieces, shocking the others.

"What is it? She whispered. Tell me!

Is it Fletcher! She screamed.

Denise sat frozen hardly noticing her hand being squeezed almost to numbness by Paul's vice-like grip.

"Oh God, please don't, don't say it! Michelle shouted at her uncle.

The Jesuit's face lost all colour. He came around and threw his arms around his sister.

"Fletcher is still with us! He is still with us...only the team felt it might be time to consider...

"Switching off his Life Support" Claudine whispered.

α

CHAPTER TWENTY-ONE

Final Voyage – Galilee

It felt as if they were sailing for some hours, the vessel moved effortlessly across the water's surface. The overhead sail was full, filled with a breeze that came in from the eastern hills. Hardly surprising, the vessel seemed to know where it was going without anyone steering or guiding its path, it simply glided with little disturbance or pitching. Both sat amidships, cross-legged, eating. In front of them was goats' milk, in two small wooden jugs, a modest size basket of figs, mixed with dates and a selection of dried fish portions. Du Pont never took his eyes off his companion.

He sat there, apparently enjoying each of the dishes.

"I find it very difficult to understand how normal you look. Look at you!

"What is it, my Friend? After all that you have seen, how we can accommodate our spirits into a mortal presence. You still find it incomprehensible" Etaanus smiled

The scientist didn't reply. He knew that this mystical journey of his was coming to an end but was still under the spell from the miraculous rendering of atomic and nuclear processes and its deep obedience to unknown mystical laws. He also knew his time in this existence was limited. There was uncertainty as to how that was going to happen. He merely reflected on everything. The magical way certain pieces of wisdom were shared with him. Every single truth he'd been exposed to came with exquisite detail in spellbinding imagery. Powerful majestic rhythms of colour of such radiance that his mind found easy to grasp. Wisdom, when presented regardless of complexity, flowed through him, filling every aspect of creation's most precious processes. Unimaginable things, which were beyond anything he could explain yet, contained unimaginable clarity.

"I am taking you to a place, of great instruction, my friend. A place where a great many struggle to leave and cannot". Etaanus said.

Du Pont studied the other for a second then saw they were no longer alone. Having appeared from nowhere eight of them, four at each side of the boat, tall sentinels stood watch looking outwards over the sparkling deep blue surface. He braced himself, as he felt his surroundings started to change. A dark mist in the distance began to descend towards them. A gust of piercing wind of hail started and erupted all around them, plunging the boat into a deluge of water. The entire vessel shuddered and daylight began to fade.

"Are these our guardians? Du Pont cried out above the torrent.

"They are from Prince Michael's Legions, Fletcher. They are Archangels."

"Why are they here?

"We are going into the Abyss, my friend. We visit the realm of the Lost, where mortals call Hell!

Now standing proud as their full angelic wings formed, one of them turned and bowed towards, Du Pont and in a single gesture extended its hand beckoning him to advance towards the front of the boat. Du Pont stood nervously.

"Don't be afraid Traveller. I am Raziel. Nothing you see and feel here can harm you".

The surroundings became ominously quiet and the rocking motion of the vessel ceased. The sound of the sea, wind and the creaking of the timbers give way to stillness. Du Pont moved towards the extended hand wondering *nothing you see or feel would harm you*. He positioned himself on an elevated plank of wood. He heard the unmistakable sound of sobbing, almost human weeping as everything darkened and all ambient natural light faded completely.

Plaintive cries echoed all around them. While not completely dark, he began to sense movements in the shadows accompanied by an acrid odour that filled his nostrils almost choking him. From nowhere images formed and emerged from the darkness, images of spirits with vacant expressions babbling in incoherent guttural sounds. Part speech of some kind, part animal. Du Pont shuddered. Without warning, something swept across him as if some evil essence had passed through him infecting every fibre of his being with its malevolence. Followed immediately by an invisible oppressive presence that induced a feeling of dread. Its effect caused his mind to panic and experienced an invasive sense of chaos. A mindless state of evil was feeding his brain with horrific and dreadful thoughts. He never considered such a state or place could exist. Then what little light was, images faded replaced by a darkness so deep it is beyond description. Ink black darkness made it almost impossible to see his own hands as he became immersed in infinite blackness. An oppressive and unyielding sense of presence started imposing its will, draining all feelings hope from his soul.

In quick succession, his mind started to desert him as a consequence of the sinister power that now stalked him. Something was aware he was here and had begun to assume mastery of his intellect. Now, an unnatural sensation filled him, a malevolence that drew nearer and nearer. His mind began to experience disturbing anguish with a crushing sense of despair. In seconds he succumbed to wave upon wave of trepidation and paralyzing fear. He lowered his head into his hands fighting to resist a force of overwhelming hopelessness. His body began to shake involuntarily as terror increased its hold. Etaanus moved towards him and touched him with the tips of his fingers. Instantly, all the on-rushing crushing fears begin to subside. Etaanus drew closer to him and infused a power to counteract the evil effects on the scientist's physique.

"We are in that part of the Abyss, where souls endure the complete absence of God's blessings. These pitiful spirits know nothing of their state here. Their chattering babbling sounds are the consequences of the servitude to Lucifer's power over them. His ablest of his legions are those who can inflict deep despair and despondency. That is what you experienced, their crushing power over all who dwell here. Those who dwell here in this Abyss have merited this due to their inhuman deeds on earth. Their treatment of their fellow humans caused great offense in Gods' eyes. Many of your fellow mortals fall easily under their influence on earth. As agents in this field, they exert great mental anguish. The best defence against these malevolent spirits is to ask God to send Heaven's mighty spirits of fortitude, spirits of courage. Many spirits are gifted in God's kingdom with great powers in peace, wisdom, and ability. You will see as we descend further, the gloom will

increase. All colour and light are obliterated leaving a realm of utter mental and physical anguish. This place you see before you require each of these wretched spirits to make atonement but are not everlasting...

...Prepare for what follows, my friend".

Du Pont started to recover but still shook with the reality of the ungodly place, eventually settling for a place nearer the back of the vessel. It progressively became darker, and as it did each of the Archangels standing begins to exhibit a radiance of light about their entire being. Incoherent sounds in the previous place were now replaced with groans and distant screams, and howls of distraught spirits. A deep soul-wrenching piercing noise filled the place. Without any rhythm and melodic substance, this sound reached a pitch that penetrated everything, reaching inside his head and began to disorientate innermost thoughts and his soul. His head screams, as if it would split such was the discordant nature of its sound. With little warning, each of the sentinels lowered their golden lances outwards pointing into the darkness. In so doing the immediate place is thrown into light, revealing a mass to creatures. Du Pont was struck speechless with the scene that opened before him. Spirits of unimaginable forms stared back at him. They appear half human half creature, their howls of utter anguish responding to the very presence of light. The physical shaping was incongruous to anything he knew. In some instances, many of the creatures possessed multiple bodies. A scene so grotesque, it was impossible to believe they were living spirits.

Some advanced towards the vessel with great menace and viciousness in their expressions. Most absorbing still, is the numbers. As far as they could see, countless creatures struggle to move about, such is their physical deformities. The sounds they emitted were screams as if their ability to voice or express their torments was removed and are reduced to primitive rasping grating screams. Their descent into this horrific place is accompanied by a remorseless excruciating noise.

"Their Spiritual rebellion towards Gods-will resulted in open hostility...hence their fall from grace. These were among the brightest and favoured in the God's Kingdom. Raziel said with anguish and sadness.

"These were once my brothers".

Then there was a transition and they were brought deeper into the depths to the layer of Lucifer himself. Du Pont braced himself. The instructive nature of everything he saw contained a power of indelible imagery. Impossible to forget the workings of imperial power. Hell, was like nothing he ever imagined. Its creatures once resplendent and noble, like his guardians lost everything. Then abruptly he felt a new sensation. A sensation possessed with a power that reached out and beckoned him to its captivating presence. It imposed itself on him similar to what he felt earlier, only this was non-threatening. A light opened up before them, revealing a large black stone pillar. Standing almost ten feet tall, a perfectly beautiful sculpted figure stood to gaze towards them. Even from this distance, Du Pont looked spellbound at the unexpected scene before them.

The Adonis-like figure had immaculate angelic wings as resplendent as those of his guardians around him. The view of him was a profile, that of a perfectly formed creature, and like nothing that went before. In utter contrast, the being looming before them was, in every sense a Light Bearer. Lucifer himself. Du Pont slowly rose captivated by the unexpected apparition beyond his imagination. A power of immense attraction flowed from the creature. It was almost hypnotic. It took hold and instantly Du Pont's thoughts turn. An unsettling turbulent set of emotions welled up inside him. A deep sense of hostility with little warning erupted towards those around him. In a short matter of seconds these emotions turned to open hostility, into a deep resentment to his predicament to everything that had happened. A pounding rage began to take hold along with an angry and vicious look to Etaanus.

"You're a sanctimonious bastard Etaanus! He rasped "You think you control me. You, and that misguided Nazarene playing with my life. Well, fuck you! It's not working!

From nowhere a soft voice filled the entire space.

"That's right Traveller you exercise your right to free will."

Du Pont glared at the figure, his fists clenched. His anger began to smoulder.

"Can you release me from these bastards clutches He roared back?

"Of Course! What is it you desire? Tell Me.? It replied.

The figure moved off his pedestal. It didn't so much move as it glided towards him accompanied by a pungent offensive odour that filled the air around the vessel. As the figure moved out from the shadows, its entire facial profile became illuminated. Du Pont felt drawn- compelled to leave the vessel and abandon the sanctity of his guardians. As he moved the figure's full facial became visible. At that same moment, Raziel's arm extended outwards and blocked his progress. He tried to push the past, but an invisible unmovable force kept him from advancing further. The image that emerged out of the shadows was hardly a face.

Instead of eyes, two dark holes were visible, giving the face no expression whatsoever. The nose itself to all intense purposes is a beak whose nostrils were tiny slits. The mouth possesses a sneering grimace that conveyed great cruelty. It was then he saw the holes in the face, two pinholes of light that pierced the darkness rendering a grotesque mask of contempt. Yielding readily, his ego fed off the power bearing down that sought to crush every instinct of joy and peace. An ocean of senses and emotions assailed him with feelings of possession within an unfathomable rage. Everything within him surrendered to a creature possessed with unlimited malice. Like a telepathic influence, he started experiencing an utter sense of depravity, hopelessness, and sheer crushing loneliness that pervaded the light bearer's universe. From all around them faces, in the billions appear from the gloom. Masks of expressions. Creatures that hardly resembled the human form such were their fall. Their entire spiritual natures had fallen under the spell of the evil one, causing their outward appearance to morph into misshapen deformities unseen on earth. Distressing in the extreme, these faces underwent further distortion as they began to hurl taunts at the sentinels themselves. The pungent odour began to choke Du Pont amid the relentless piercing sound the filled the Abyss.

The creature was about to advance closer when a shaft of light shot out from Raziel's golden lance causing the figure to scream and retreated quickly backward. In that movement, his entire face was transformed into an angelic radiant expression. Before them, the creature began to change and became transformed. Standing before them a manifestation unfolded revealing an entity possessed of a beauty and composure complete with striking features. The hair was long and curved onto his shoulders, a picture of stunning perfection. A figure of great nobility and poise stood before them. His face radiated like the sun, resplendent and illuminated. The transformation in appearance couldn't be more different than what went before. From behind him, Etaanus spoke.

"Behold, our light bearer, as he existed in Heaven, before his fall. As his title suggests, Traveller, Light Bearer possessed great intellect and perfection in form".

No sooner had the words been spoken, the image turned. Amid a great cry of anguish, Lucifer's form descended and convulsed back and forward until it was restored into the featureless creature that was his doom. Du Pont's thoughts became taunting screams of vile obscenities, images of inhuman evil poured into his thoughts. Acts of unspeakable horror assaulted his thoughts. He was without a doubt in Hell. From deep within the halls, countless legions buried in its depths came like an avalanche of whimpering sounds that no actor on earth could render. From every direction about them, a chorus of demented screams of torment and despair mingled with chanting that dissolved into the disembodied howling from the countless creatures. Du Pont with one final effort repulsed everything he saw.

"Please, I can't take any more of this pain. It's everywhere. It's inside my head. Enough! *Enough of this place!* He screamed.

Instantly he felt a change. The crushing oppressive grip on his mind lifted, along with his defiance and rage began to dissolve, and for the first time in his life, he knew the true meaning of peace. A soothing and comforting swell of calmness filled him. Gone was the hostility that wrestled his mind from him.

"Please! Etaanus!.. No more." He gasped.

As soon as he did the vessel turned, its motion becoming apparent and as it did a white tunnel of light opened directly above them. It stretched upwards as far as he could see. The vessel without appearing to change direction or momentum moved upwards, and as they did light came streaming through filling the vessel with rainbow colours. Du Pont lay on his back his body soaked in perspiration, his breathing hard, and parts of his mind started to heal. Within such traumatized experience he could never have imagined the magnitude of utter anguish that was possible. His head ached as if his skull was going to split such was sheer horror that consumed him. Just as he was on the edge of passing out Etaanus face filled his view.

A hand reached out and placed two fingers just about his temple. All lights faded and a great sleep brought him back to the meadow of long grass and perfumed flowers.

Wakening it was like recovering from a horrific nightmare. Sitting up, he saw Etaanus the man, sitting in a wooden box. A swaying movement revealed they were still adrift. They were alone, just two of them. Glancing around he saw their vessel was close to the shoreline with the lights of a small village glistening in the last of the evening light. The sky to the west had a spectacular hue of purple pink lighting as the sun was setting. Again, as on other occasions, the passage of time was vague. He had no idea how long he had been sleeping. Amidst, the sound of lapping water against the sides of their vessel he thought he heard the sound of music playing in the distance. Gathering himself he stood upright.

"That was ...horrific.! Did I really need to visit such a place, Etaanus? He asked.

"Such a place shouldn't exist. No one can remain the same, or live at peace knowing such a place awaits."

Etaanus moved closer to him and placed his hand on his arm.

"There is no such thing as Everlasting Damnation Fletcher. Those pitiful spirits will leave Hell in time, in accordance with God's divine laws, and whose attitude to God undergoes a change of heart. You felt at first hand, the power and supremacy of evil, and its pernicious nature. Do you remember how it's debased influenced reached out and touched your soul? Do you recall? All who dwell there are in servitude to the evil one. All have merited such treatment by their exercise of their free will, and how they choose. Some will dwell for a short time, others must atone for much longer since their offense was greater in God's kingdom.".

"I'm truly sorry Etaanus! Those words, things I spoke of were not of my mind. It controlled me. It was awful, the oppressive presence of..."

"Of Evil, my friend, Etaanus added gently.

My great task my friend is to instruct. Remember, dear friend you are mortal your soul is a divine spark that is housed within your mortal physical body is the source of all sensation, feeling, and emotions. It feels acutely the personification of evil in all of its aspects. You were spared others"

He leaned back and reached out and handed his shaken friend some water.

"Drink this. Soon, you will partake in some good friendships and food, with some wine. It will lift your spirits. He said smiling.

The scientist stood for a moment letting the horrific images of the dominion of Hell to pass. It took the soothing evening breeze and the tranquillity of the Sea of Galilee to restore his strength. Reeling from the trauma of near possession he was stunned how easily his persona succumbed to its influence. How readily his soul responded to its urgings, to assume a personality of intense perversion.

'I'll never recover from this! He whispered to himself.

His companion moved toward him. He looked at Du Pont with deep affection, as a spirit being he read his companion's thoughts. In one of those rare occasions, he permitted himself a wry smile as he studied the man he'd come to admire and cherish. Reaching over he and tapped Du Pont on the shoulder.

" Kneel my friend." He said gently *"I am one of Almighty God's, warrior spirits. I am a spirit of Fortitude.*

In a single act, he placed one hand on the top of the scientist's head. With the other, he extended upwards to the heavens and opened his hand outwards as if receiving something.

"Pour forth your power, great Celsior to your humble servant. He whispered.

In the evening dusk, a glimmer of heat began to glow as a bright orange light emanated in the palm of his extended hand. Etaanus face lit up and his entire complexion turned pure white. Instantly, the scientist's shoulders sagged for some seconds then, from his head to his heart an energy field passed through him instilling images of interlocking pictures. His loved ones and friends, beautiful animals striding with immaculate rhythms and finishing with images of oceans of majestic waves rolling over him, infusing his entire being with a joyful and uplifting fulfilment. He saw new views of interstellar cosmos in amazing detail and captivating pathways that connect distant stars into intriguing pathways and then to the Earth itself. Life, and the magnificence of the creation itself. It lasted only seconds, yet in that time all fearful and frightful images were dissolved followed by powerful surge of certainty in consumed him.

Etaanus lifted his hand and it was gone.

When Du Pont stood, his inner rebirth was completed. He felt a calmness wash over him He no longer felt fear. No sooner had the point of the vessel made contact with pebble shore Du Pont was able to pick out a single figure standing on the sand, Yeshua.

Even with some distance between them the physicist felt the same sensation as before. An aura, some invisible almost spellbinding magic that emanated from this most curious of men reached outwards over them. Advancing towards them, he was armed with a jug and a smile.

"A most welcome return my dear friend" He smiled drawing him close

"Tell me you are well. Let's not speak anymore of the torments you endured. Come, Welcome to Capernaum!

The Nazarene averts his glance towards the boat and beckoned Etaanus to join them.

"It's near the time for Etaanus's task in this place to come to an end. You should know he feels great love and bond for you, Fletcher. He will forever be your guardian, know this. But, it is also a time of joy. My brother has become a parent, and your arrival is perfect."

They move from the small beach and headed into the small village. Lamps burned brightly throughout the narrow laneways, young children despite the hour played and ran about, some being chased by small dogs. The music has a distinctive sound, quite melodic and rhythmic in keeping with several men and women were dancing in tune. As they entered a small opening, they found themselves amid groups of families laughing and engaged in animated conversations standing around a large table full of fruit, fresh meats, and dried fish. Various small wooden tables were arranged in a circle, giving the place a welcoming atmosphere. To the side, a large fire burned, a brier with chunks of meat slowing turning in its flames.

Du Pont sat and listened to the mixture of tongues all around him. This was what Aramaic sounded like, he thought to himself. Spoken with laughter and raucous joy. Friendships and families mingled, a gathering of neighbours seeking out the parents and then some spontaneously break into song. Hardly anyone gave him a second look. How little they knew. He thought. If they could have seen the things he'd seen, he wondered if they'd rest at night. All around them, all of us humans, stalked by demons of immense power and evil. How could they rest? How could they be happy? The Earth that boundary, the edge where Hell's limits are curtailed, but still fell under its enormous potency to corrupt and extinguish all that was good."

"And there is also good.

Etaanus's voice broke into his thoughts, as he came and sat next to him. The scientist smiled, giving him a mischievous look, held up his mug while his companion filled it with more wine. They both sat and watch the festivities unfold. More men with instruments joined the music. More melodic music followed, the fire burned brighter, and the aroma of cooked meats and fish added to the mood and atmosphere of the occasion. Du Pont turned to his companion.

'Yes, there is good. But will it withstand the things we witnessed earlier? He asked "Spirits of Fortitude! My friend. What is that?

Etaanus looked at him.

'*You are ready*. He chuckled with admiration Du Pont stared back.

"Yes. I am ready. He whispered.

Etaanus placed his arm around his shoulders.

"Many of the feelings you experience on Earth, be they good, or bad, can emanate from elsewhere. In God's Kingdom, all spirits take active roles in God's creation. Many guard and watch over every mortal who walks the earth. As I spoke to this matter previously, let me tell you, Fletcher, that surrounding each of you, are spirits for good, and those of evil. On earth, and because of man's base nature, evil has strong dominion over man. In all manner of things, particularly in matters of greed, envy, lust, anger, all of Hell's agents are equipped to instil these feelings. Utter despair and despondency, hopelessness all are tools in hell's legions. You experienced this yourself. You know of what I talk about, yes!

"So it follows, that there are more powerful spirits who can inject great resolute and courage in mortals. All you have to do is ask. Ask Almighty God, summon in your hour of great need, and ask to send us, his warrior spirits, who will instil courage, fortitude and strength into you, and it will happen". "Belief! Unshakeable in God's power, is all that's demanded. This is Yeshua Ben Yoseph's single message to you, my friend. You also experienced this tonight. I am one of God's Seraphim Beings, I am bestowed with God's power to bring you great inner power, and fortitude"

Du Pont was about to raise some other questions when suddenly the music got louder and the clapping began. Two women came out of the crowd and rushed towards them. They were in their twenties young and vibrant and while he couldn't understand their language, he knew what it meant. Dancing, there were being asked to join in the festive mood. They were four groups, all moving around a large fire, each with six to seven dancers all in a line, arms spread out over each other shoulders. In tune with the music, they moved a series of moves to the right each of their steps synchronized in harmony to music. Then, the entire movement was reversed and moved to the left.

Du Pont and Etaanus quickly join the two young women and two men making up the other group. From nowhere in the crowd, Yeshua appeared and gently intertwined himself between Du Pont and Etaanus, his arms flexed across their shoulders. Then in a moment of magic, the group began to shuffle a gentle melodic movement in keeping with the sound and rhythm of the piece. It's cadence and charming blend of drumbeat and strings and clapping had all five groups move in perfect movement flow. They circled both clockwise and anti-clockwise, occasionally the movement took on a more intricate set of steps, knees would rise and then the movement would reverse a number of paces, and then repeat. Du Pont was not a natural dancer with any sense of rhythm, but in that moment in time, he flowed with grace and fluidity he hardly could believe himself. As they danced the newborn child was brought into the circle by the couple, they were gently rocking the infant to the rhythm of sound. Then in a graceful movement they dance towards them, and remained in front of them, the women extended her arms with the child out to Yeshua.

Amid cheers, people started calling his name and urging him to accept. It seemed a gesture of great honour. Yeshua laughed, and moved out and took the child in his arms, and for the next few minutes danced with the child cradled in his arms to the loud cries of approval from the entire village. The dancing continued, Du Pont for a moment wished he could stay for eternity. Amidst these wonderful people, he was a stranger, yet he was part of everything. He felt safe, content; he clapped his hands to the music completely consumed in the moment. He was living in biblical times, surrounded by history. In a surprising unexpected act of tenderness, Yeshua danced his way over towards him and paused. Yeshua smiled at him. Then, the music ended and everyone began to clap and cheer. A clanging of a small bell suggested it was time to eat.

"Fletcher, meet my new niece, Isabel, He said beaming. Du Pont smiled and looked at the young infant.

"She is beautiful. She has your eyes Yeshua, He joked.

The Nazarene moved closer and smiled

"You also, my friend, will hold a child like this, and very soon. He whispered.

Du Pont was taken aback. Then looked into the Nazarene's eyes and remembered the garden.

"Yes, I know Yeshua". He replied.

In that moment the eminent physicist realised that things come down to an instance when everything becomes illuminated. A sharpness of clarity peeled away all uncertainty and truths make themselves known. This was such a moment. Some unseen almighty entities chose this time to bring him here to share an encounter with a mystical being. Its consequences defied every notion he knew of physical reality, human purpose, the meaning of existence. He had undergone an experience, and an encounter with an entity of unimaginable power, and also the man, Yeshua Ben Yosef. A figure of unfathomable compassion armed with an intellect beyond measure or description. In so doing, it revealed how incomplete human understanding of his task and his existence meant. Yeshua's mission of Redemption contained deeper and more profound consequences, yet here he was, cradling a child. From somewhere a notion crossed Du Pont's mind. This child represented a deeply existential event. Something taken for granted, continuance. A symbol of continuity and an act of great love but in compliance with more mystical laws, ones that ordain that all incarnated beings move through many spheres of existence. That upward progression which Etaanus spoke of. It was a concept of such mystical proportions that it took the physicist time to absorb and grasp its elegance. Then, from amidst the gathering a young man approached them and smiled, the father of the infant. He bowed to his older brother and then toward Du Pont. Gently he took the child and thanked them both, smiled with evident pride and left them.

Yeshua drew closer, a grave look crossed his face. He studied the scientist for a moment. The eyes looked with searching curiosity as if reading into the depth of his friend's soul. The man of science straightened himself and returned the gaze: - when it dawned on him he was staring at the face that haunted him from a screen from another age and time.

"Do you have any fear, Yeshua? Du Pont heard himself ask. The Nazarene hardly flinched the expression remained the same then, just a slight hint of a smile

"Being forgotten! ... He whispered back. "That's what's fearful to me".

A few seconds of silence. "I will not permit that! Du Pont said.

"Will you remember everything? The man standing before me doubted, I ever existed! Further seconds of silence. "That was then. I knew nothing. I was nothing! This changes everything. Everything! History has remembered you. Your martyrdom has seen to that Yeshua.

The other merely smiled

"Your own time and era have created many alternate truths, my friend. Many streams flow, many of them are without any value and offer nothing. Mortals drink from impure sources that spoil their thirst for truths. My truths have fallen under the hand of falsehoods, scribes have written with great errors, some from ignorance, and others with malice and a thirst for power over humanity. The stream that once flowed with sparkling purity that refreshed and imbued all who found it and drank, no longer retains its strength. Falsehoods have flourished in my name, great lies spawn like diseases that inflict great misery, and lead seekers of my teachings down wrong paths".

..."I hear the screams! of my lost brothers in the Abyss. I can feel their soulful sensations of utter despair. I hear all their depravities from those who dwell there. There is a time coming when the upward progress may not be so assured. He said gently extending his hand towards the scientist.

"Give me your hand"

He took Du Pont's hand then turned it, palm, upwards. As he did he felt an icy cold sensation grip the centre of his hand. From nowhere, a flame ignited from the centre of his palm. His reflex action is to pull back instantly, to avoid being burned. He can't. His hand was held fast by the Nazarene's strength, but there was no pain. No discomfort or burning sensation. He stared at the flame amazed at its iridescence. Its glittering had a purity and intensity while strangely giving off very little heat. Fire without heat struck him as unnatural. He watched it for seconds daring not to move his hand. He felt nothing physically and yet its luminosity hinted at something deeper. His very presence in this place was a paradox, why should this be any different.

What drew his curiosity more was it seemed to swing from being translucent to adopting a more opaque nature. Then he heard his Nazarene companion say something to himself as if summoning something to their presence. At first, he thought his eyes were struggling to deal with the glare, and then something quite extraordinary unfolded. Deep within the flame, its edging starts to trace a distinctive curving undulating form. As if the flame itself was assuming a substance. Then the curved edges danced and began to mingle, and in so doing, it started a manifestation inside the flame. This caused the flame to bulge outwards and tapering to a single point at each end. Then it began to change its colour, moving from its normal amber-red glow to a captivating purple hue.

Suddenly, with just the merest of changes to the flickering gaseous form, Du Pont started to discern something taking shape amidst the fire. While seeing it take form before his eyes, his brain took longer to accept what it represented. The intermingling of the curves morphed into a double helix chain. Du Pont inhaled sharply. Then, as if dancing in harmony, the twin strains began to mutate and build connections along the two lengths. At first, he seized to the notion he was witnessing a near-perfect rendering of how superstrings might behave. He was wrong. He was no geneticist, but he knew DNA structures when he saw them. Intricate complex lattice structures folded and moved in opposite directions in a symphony of harmony and choreographed magic, the very essence of life. All living entities were reduced and compressed into a beautiful ritual of geometry and composition. Within the image a different hue of colours resonated around selected strains in the chain itself. Quickly he guessed its significance, as Chromosomes mingled and locked into the two dominant strands. He's been shown how life worked. Within its pristine universe, it ordained how life unfolded, grew, and existed. Buried deep inside its myriad countless permutations, lay secrets of divine origin.

'Behold, dear Fletcher the living magnificence of Life! The Nazarene said softly.

The scientist gazed and became mesmerized at how elegantly the most mysterious processes of life could be rendered and wielded with such authority. He sensed there was a purpose to what he was seeing. As if reading his thoughts, Yeshua's face became pensive, his eyes darken. His youthful face and expression look diminished. He held the countenance of an older man, burdened with unseen tribulations.

"The spawns of the Evil One pervade all human thinking and deeds, He whispered. "Mankind live out their lives with the assurance of continuity of procreation. The gift to express God's plan, to bring forth children and grow in multitudes of great numbers. Males beget female and so it goes."

But as he spoke, the sublime intricacies of the DNA structure suddenly ruptured, causing a break in the chain separating certain chromosomes. Sequencing blocks of chemical proteins seem unable to re-bond along the labyrinth of the double helix form. The flame itself flickered almost faltering to retain its light. Slowly, it dawned on the scientist to what he was looking into. Human progeny, the continuance of an earthly existence was subject to new truths. The symbolism of the DNA sequence and its delicate equilibrium lay in the balance. He looked across over the flame and saw the brooding eyes of a wiser man. Yeshua Ben Josef stared back, his face deepened with sadness.

"You must help make choices, Man of the millennium. You must reawaken and reveal what is at stake in my task of Redemption. Evil consummates evil. The entire material existence will be fruitless to exist if mortals succumb and become apostates! Apostates to the reign of Evil. My Heavenly Father cleansed the earth once when evil had its way with a man. Complete and total submission to the powers of hell meant earth had to be purged. Next time it may cease the ability to create and produce offspring. All upward progression of souls through the material creation becomes pointless, without purpose, unless... 'The task of redemption is consummated." He moved closer.

"Mortal death on earth is but a path to my father's kingdom, the death I speak of is that of the Spirit. The spirit loses all awareness, cut off from all its former glory and plunged into the pit of utter darkness. Without redemption, the bridge that spans the great gulf between Heaven and Hell is broken, and the existence of the earth and the entire material creation loses all purpose".

Du Pont stared speechless:- stunned to what was being revealed. Disruption to the very building blocks of life deep inside the DNA structure would herald the end of human beings. Its magical creative process rendered fruitless. Humans would simply over time, cease to procreate, leaving a childless Earth. A Judgment passed.

The message inside a flame conveyed a truth about choices and the use of free will. Du Pont now stumbled to the startling truth as to what was been unveiled before him. Truths of divine origin have summoned him to a place where the arrow of time had been paused. He was given a mystical guide by the Keeper of the Book Of Seals and shown wondrous things, exposed to cataclysmic transformations shaped and harnessed by a power beyond the range of human reasoning.

'Will you do my will, dear friend, dear Fletcher of your time? The Nazarene asked gently. "It is a burden, but one that will bring empowerment. All great deeds will be accomplished with my Angels at your side. That is my promise to you"

Du Pont simply stared at his hands cradling the flame of truth shimmering before him.

'Yes, Yeshua! I only ask that you keep me safe. I don't know if I can accomplish all that you ask, but I am ready. Everything in my place in time is so lost. We know so little Yeshua. Where do I even begin...I have to explain all this to my family, to where...?

In a single gesture the Nazarene reached out and extinguished the flame and then clasped the scientist's hands in his.

'All in good time my friend. All in Divine Time. Now, look upon Etaanus Nuntius, my beloved brother. He takes his leave, and returns to my father's Kingdom"

Standing behind them, the Keeper of the Great Book of Seals stood poised, restored to his angelic form, his entire height glowed a powerful light only this time, its enormous radiated energy has little effect on the scientist. In one arm the great book itself, in the other a simple glass timepiece, with the last of the sand in the upper part almost empty. Time was almost at an end. He advanced one step and then lowered his body and bowed in a gesture of respect and farewell. Then the timepiece simply vanished, and in a final easy movement, Etaanus raised his hand to Du Pont turned upward and smiled. The man of science straightened himself in response and placed his hand on his chest for a brief few seconds at the creature he had shared so much with. Then its powerful light began to fade.

His entire form dematerialized until there was nothing. There's a moment of sadness, a sense of great loss. Du Pont was drawn and befriended to this high celestial creature in a profoundly personal way that deeply affected him. Now he was no longer present to Sheppard and guide him leaving him feeling desperately alone. He turned back to face his companion.

Confronting him was an appalling image of wanted brutality.

Staring back at him caused his heart to nearly fail. His entire spirit recoiled in shock at the image. A Crimsoned blood-red ghastly image faced him. It was of the slumped Nazarene; his entire upper body is exposed. All about the shoulders are ripped to pieces with exposed and open gashes with bleeding deep wounds. The face is bludgeoned, disfigured almost beyond recognition. The entire facial tissue is lacerated and covered in blood, both eyes closed from severe trauma, the nose distorted from and physical blows. Spasmodic and violent trembling caused him to try and cough which resulted in blood spurting from the side of his mouth. All his teeth are pulverized, causing his jaw-line to grimace with pain distorting his entire face into a grotesque mask of anguish. Most shocking of all, his entire upper part of his skull is clamped with twisted makeshift tore bush branches wrapped into a crude circular form, had been forced into the scalp, causing the deep wounds of the thorns to pierce the skin. Blood drained down over the Nazarene's face making it impossible to keep his eyes open. The entire image, only inches from him, caused by vicious depraved barbarity and cruelty. A scene of unimaginable brutality. Du Pont's entire physique went weak, both mental and physical functions go into shock. His last conscious feelings were of overwhelming shame, and anguish before everything goes dark.

Λ

Section 76 A. LHC Tunnel.

It was as he had expected. Each of them took turns to check and confirm for themselves. Melrose turned to the others.

"Look! Almost nothing is left. The entire ceiling is clear. Time is almost up.!

"Quite amazing, superb work Paul". Felix Deveraux said peering closer to where the curved markings appeared to end. Deveraux, Manfred Gruess, and Myles Kingsley stood back content to accept for now, that Melrose theory seemed authentic.

"If what you say is true Paul, this suggests the curved Time-Line has run its course. It's almost up. Kingsley said

"Begging the question, what comes after that? Melrose whispered

What became known informally as, the "Melrose Clock" kept them on tender hooks yet, it was precisely playing out that way. Deveraux tossed his head back and stared upwards at the tunnel ceiling his head beginning to spin. What else was there to all of this? Much more upsetting was news that none of them wanted to hear: their stricken colleague's life support system was reaching a critical phase, haunted them all.

A Cave.

Deep within the recesses of his mind, two immediate sensations enveloped him in a cocoon of warmth. The first was light. The dark place he occupied was infiltrated with a light coming from somewhere above him. A soft early morning light crept into the shaded space. There was also silence other than his steady breathing. Then, there was warmth. To be more precise, heat seemed to have enveloped him despite the hardness of the surface he was lying on. As he did his memory kicked in with a brutal sharpness the very last conscious image. The nightmare of the mutilated face caused his body to jerk disrupting his sleeping rhythm. Instantly he woke, his mind tried to recall his last movements, and where precisely was now. He shot up from his position and looked around. It seemed like the inside of a grotto. The walls were of cut stone hewed out of the rock, both walls and ceilings were rough and mottled. It's warm as if he were near an oven or some source of heat.

Turning around he froze. Sitting upright and looking down at his hands was a figure draped in long fine cream-colored robes. His long reddish-brown hair glistened in the trickling light that came from a split in the rock. The physicist got slowly to his feet and took some steps towards the other man. He was neither fearful nor nervous but filled with rage towards the brutality he'd seen towards a friend. Then in one single movement, the stranger lifted his head and straightened himself. His hair fell on his bare shoulders revealing his face.

Yeshua! Du Pont stopped dead and stared.

There was hardly a sound. Then, as if from deep inside the rock itself, a crushing and grating sound of rock on rock movement filled the cave stopped abruptly. The split where the light entered became wider allowing more early morning light to fill the place. It stopped remaining only partially opened but enough to illuminate the space. The Nazarene took a few seconds to respond. In complete contrast to the nightmare image witnessed before, his companion was flawless. He appeared serene. The skin was sallow and radiated vitality along with composure and peace that was missing in their previous encounter. Standing and letting the robes fall, his appearance took on a noticeable alteration in his bearing. Long clothing that wrapped around one of his shoulders and fitted his physique perfectly. Du Pont's first reaction was to advance towards him but as he does the Nazarene extended his hand.

"Allow the power currents to diminish from my body, my friend".

Slowly the radiated glow faded leaving his appearance return to some semblance of normal healing. His image of destruction earlier simply dissolved in the morning light. As Du Pont edged closer, he looked with dismay. Just below the hairline on Yeshua's forehead, he could make out the faint tiny marks. Scars formed a discernable circular path about his head.

"It is finished! Came the whispered reply.

Du Pont paused allowing his mind to absorb what he was allowed to witness. With a simple reflex, he reached out tentatively taking one of the hands and raised it. The robe fell back. Du Pont nearly reeled backward. He reached for the other hand, similarly identical.

"*Oh, No!* He gasped.

Just below each of the palms, and into the wrists are two elongated scars. The marks of nails. Extending his hand just below the rib cage and opened the cloth. Again a lateral scar mark of an entry wound. Du Pont began to shake consumed with shame with what he has missed or unable to prevent.

"Oh. Dear God! Then, his surroundings take on a new meaning. This was not a cave. They were in a Tomb.

Involuntary he cast his eyes around and then his eyes are drawn to the unmistakable residue of heat marks; some great release of heat registered in his mind. Du Pont stumbled from one notion after another as he grappled with something he last heard around a table. A biblical event was written into all passages of the New Testament of episodic proportions, the *Risen Redeemer*. He whipped around and glanced towards the split in the rock face, and noticed for the first time the curved radius of a large round stone. Finally looking down, he saw the feet. The scar marks of the nails

"The task is complete, my Traveller friend."

Then, in a moment that would burnish it into scientist's being, Yeshua reached out and wrapped his arms around the scientist's and held him.

"I return to my father's house soon my friend. Your time in this place is also complete. Do you recall, my telling, to have belief! The great task of Redemption is complete, and the gates of the Abyss are locked open for all who so choose to leave it. The material creation now has great purpose, my traveller friend. The bridge that spans the gulf of Heaven and Hell are full of obstacles, but not insurmountable one's Fletcher. Use this mystical experience and bring hope to all of your generations. It will be heard."

Trust in me and my promise before all other things" He said smiling.

Then reaching down he picked up a small towel like cloth and rubbed some of the perspiration from the scientist's face, and then handed it to him. Picking up a small battered canvas bag slung it around Du Pont's neck. Instantly a small key fell to the ground. The physicist looked down and saw his old key lying on the floor. Carefully he stooped and lifted it and looked intently questioning how it found its way here to this place.

"What is it, my Traveller friend? Do you have a question?

Du Pont slowly placed the key in the canvas bag and gazed at the tall figure.

"I... I have something to ask you, Yeshua?

History recalled that at one stage, so great was your fear, that you perspired blood. So, what was it, that brought you so...?

The Nazarene's expression betrayed something. Something that only he, and he alone knew of.

"It was that moment when all the powers of Heaven and its aids were withdrawn. The moment had arrived at a juncture where the task of Redemption was mine alone to carry and balanced on a knife-edge. Only Heaven's hand in sustaining me physically remained. Had that not being the case, my physical strength would have failed and I would not have left the garden of anguish alive" He said softly.

"You mean, you would not have survived. Du Pont asked.

"Yes! My Heavenly Father's sense of justice demanded that a Redeemer at the very end would defeat the powers of Hell wholly on its own. No more did Heaven's presence interfere with the final part. I was alone to wage and endure everything. It was my last obstacle, to experience all of Earth's vicissitudes. The fear was succumbing to it. To stumble and fall at the very end and I would become apostate and give up my task, and in so doing, Redemption would fail. I would become a legion in the depths of the Abyss. That's what struck terror in my heart"

Much of what followed was awful. Wanted depraved barbarity. Du Pont hissed

"History recites and described it all as you're Passion Yeshua. It went down through the ages of time right to my time into the twentieth century, as *the Passion*.

"It was never the physical torment my friend. It was what I saw. I have sight. As I child I could always see. See other things in creation that nobody could see, not even my family. Amidst the soldiers and the crowds. Hordes of demons roamed in their midst on that sunny day. They danced around invisibly mocking and taunting me, unseen by those deeply confused people. They usurped human passions with great ease, these hideous creatures used every human weakness at their disposal. Like plectrums flying over musical strings, they played on human passions unleashing unspeakable urgings to inflict all their anger and hatred. Those unfortunate soldiers were mere playthings in the hands of these demented creatures. They were utterly helpless unable to resist those primeval forces all about them. Invisible to all, they also mocked me and spat vile obscenities towards some of the legions. Some were taken by some of the demons and used their bodies inflict as much damage to my body, He paused

... "Other demons screamed to me, like the ones from the desert, pleaded with me to recant, and submit to Lucifer's authority, and all suffering would cease instantly.

That! was my greatest fear, my brother, in that hour when Heaven withdrew all its protective power to me, I would weaken and fall.

Du Pont felt an emotional surge. You're Creator! Yeshua! Where was he.? His voice became hard.

"He was there all the time because I possessed unshakable belief in my Father."

Yeshua reached and wiped a tear from his companion. Then Nazarene turned and dropped to his knees before the stone plinth. Raising his arms outwards he let out a cry that filled the tomb with power speaking in a language that was strange but there was enough to sound familiar.

"My Father, my Father! My earthly mission is fulfilled. Grant me your presence, and bring forth my transcendence. Send me my legions of the Heavens to anoint all the truths, and instil great joy in all who see and experience your grace".

The entire ground commenced to shake coupled with a low resonance of vibration that gathered in intensity, as it does, slowly the huge rock, began to move in tandem as golden light poured into the tomb. It lit up every crevice illuminating the plinth, and on it, a long blood-soaked shroud that lay discarded on the ground. At one end where his head lay, the outline defined stain of an image he recalled so well. The silhouette figure the Nazarene remained on his knees for a few moments and then rose to his feet.

"All you need to do my brother is ask and I will come to you. A rising spirit will soon join you. A spirit who will possess my gifts for you. It will become your *Sheppard*. Do you understand what it is I mean? He asked

'Yes, I believe I do. Du Pont replied

"The time is at hand, Fletcher, let me show you where it begins. The entire tomb interior mystically expands and began to transform into a beautiful ornate interior possessing a great ceiling decorated with stunning paintings of a great artist. A mirage began and then he saw them. Princes. Not princes of royalty or lords over kingdoms of another age, but princes graced in crimson and deep purple velvet and silk clothing. A Gathering a great many mingled under the ceiling of great art, Princes of the Church. The distinctive setting of Cardinals of his era.

'I had twelve!

The physicist slowly shook his head knowing what lay ahead.

"The number and place where you begin. Thirteen, my friend".

"Thirteen? Du Pont asked.

I had twelve until, you! "You are now *Thirteen*" A smile creased his face. Du Pont's eyes are still drawn to the scars. Buried in the recesses his memory he remembered the number of 166, the current membership of the College of Cardinals in the Roman Catholic Church. He was being pointed to his starting point. His task was clear.

"You have witnessed other realms of existence. You have passed through the chronicles of time to visit places within Creation itself, now it is for you to choose how you bear witness to all. Now, it is time for your journey to return to your time and place, he said with deliberate care.

"Remember me, Fletcher, You have my love, and my Kingdom dwells within you.

Tell them! Tell them all, you walked with Yeshua Ben Josef! It is within you. Never forget, my father's very Kingdom dwells in here. He said placing his hand over Du Pont's heart.

As soon as the hand touched his chest, the scientist began to feel an overwhelming wave pass through him. An invisible curtain closed around him as he faltered and slumped, only the powerful arms of a carpenter caught him and lifted him off his feet. With sleep creeping over him his last fading sight was looking up into the face that first stared back at him from a pixilated screen lost in another time.

Λ

CHAPTER TWENTY-TWO

The journey and the experience were like nothing he could have imagined. There was no "floating", there was no sense of movement or motion for that matter. His immediate sense was he was motionless while experiencing thoughts, that wasn't his. All notions of anxiety, fear, uncertainty, were vanquished out of existence replaced with sensations of sheer ecstasy and dwelling nowhere, and being everywhere at the same time. He was universal, all he needed to do, was to imagine, and those things became real. Emotions became amplified, particularly ones such as compassion, love, forgiveness, all exploded inside him crafting and moulding his entire being. He merely had to extend his thoughts or desires, and the world around him responded. His kingdom was based on the purity of thought. A spirit returned, fragile, but fashioned elsewhere in the depths of the refining pot of molten silver, finished and completed in the furnace of gold. Such was the spheres of progress his spirit passed through, that Fletcher Du Pont the mortal, found easy to remember. As the blanket of tranquillity began to fade, new sounds beckon. He heard voices. Then, he felt movement, his body experiences pressure, and awarenessof his own breathing. The sounds of voices increased, hands gently touched him. He felt the swaying lateral movement and knew he was being carried along somewhere.

Sal Madere

They were ready to leave at precisely at 7.30 am when Denise, broke her silence.

"I'm not going! She shouted.

Claudine was in no mood to argue, she hadn't the strength. It was going to be a traumatic day whoever went. Each of them had to find their individual ways to deal with what lay ahead, and what lay ahead was horrific. The hospital wanted them for 9 am if that were possible. Each knew this day might come. Life and its continuity brought certain challenges, and it seemed all were now exhausted. Decisions needed to be taken and nobody was entirely certain what would follow.

Ok, Ok! I'm coming. Oh, God!

Everyone that morning was a mere shell of themselves. Claudine knew her eldest daughter was struggling with her own fears along with her pregnancy. She had deep fears and now her beloved father's life support was the proverbial last straw. Claudine's brother, Francois kept very much to himself in the last few days, but now became a pillar of strength. Michelle hardly spoke and wasn't interested in any food or breakfast. Quietly that morning each of them, in their private moments, made personal deals with God. Within minutes later they rolled out of the driveway and left for Geneva. It would take them just over an hour to reach the outskirts. Claudine insisted on driving. Her brother sat up front, both daughters in the back.

Paul Melrose had decided to overnight and remain in one of the guest apartments on-site at the Meyrin complex. That morning, while it was dry, the air was crisp and sharp. He glanced to his right, and off in the distance the Jura's still had their winter snowcap. The grass had some lingering frost. Only those senior Directors closest to Du Pont were going to attend. A Six-Seater taxi waited in front of the main reception building to receive Felix Deveraux and his associates. Monika too felt deep unease as to what lay ahead; she cared deeply for Fletcher Du Pont and had insisted she wanted to be present if such a moment ever arose. This was such a moment. She stood and headed for the door, only to notice her coffee was still seating on her desk. She stopped and gave it a bemused look, the coffee was still piping hot. Quickly she picked it up and tossed it into her trash bin giving it no further thought. Five minutes later the entire team filed into the taxi waiting for them downstairs.

Paul Melrose followed them down to reception, as he did he saw through the windows of the building Otto Hugens his mechanic, park the Morgan it in his usual parking space. Melrose had hardly time to talk. Otto approached with his usual easygoing manner.

'She is all yours Paul, she purrs just like a pussycat". He joked, and handed Melrose the keys, and moved off.

Melrose smiled and gazed at his keys mildly confused then jumped into one of the seats next to Carina Ambrosiana. Within thirty minutes all of them arrived at Clinique Gerealle Vallence hospital. Felix Deveraux made it a point to get to Claudine and the girls and offer himself as their spokesman to whatever awaited inside. After pleasantries and some hugs, the group made their way inside. A muted sound of a helicopter air ambulance lifted off in the background and quickly faded into the morning air.

They stood for a few seconds in the reception, a little uncertain of what arrangements were in place. Then Claudine decided, if she were going to wait anywhere, it would be her husband's bed. With that, the entire group walked towards the stairwell and headed up to the second floor. Traffic and activity on the floor were normal, although a blue light flashed on the ceiling, which seemed an alert was in progress. As they walked, Claudine was a little taken aback that hardly any of the staff barely acknowledged her, or those of her family. Melrose felt everything looked very detached very indifferent towards them. Perhaps they know! He thought to himself.

When they turned into the smaller corridor, Claudine stopped short of the ward door. She needed to be strong.

"You OK! Mum", whispered Michelle nervously

Claudine, do you need to be…alone perhaps"? Asked Carina Ambrosiana. Claudine turned and managed a smile.

"No, I'm fine. Felix, we're very grateful to all of you for being here. Fletcher wouldn't have wanted it any other way, she said gently.

Reaching out she took her brother's hand.

"You ready, Francois?

"Yes, we're all ready. May God, bless us all. He whispered.

She gave him a fleeting smile for a second, turned and pushed through the doors into the room. Inside they were greeted with something none of them expected.

A deserted room with only two lights casting the room into a half shadow. A single unoccupied bed lay up against a wall completed the picture of an unused hospital ward.

There were no chairs and hardly any medical equipment. They moved to the centre of the room without speaking. An eerie silence filled the room as all eyes fixed on the unused bed. It took a few seconds to sink in.

"Are we in the right ward, asked Miles Kingsley?

"Oh, we're in the right ward alright, Melrose said nervously

"Maybe they've taken him to another ward. Perhaps... Claudine whispered

Before she could finish a crashing sound from elsewhere disrupted their thoughts. It came from outside somewhere in the corridor. Voices raised, many voices and getting closer. There was now shouting as if rapid instructions were being issued grew closer in the corridor. Something or someone in a hurry was heading towards them. Everyone turned, slightly caught off guard, their attention drawn towards the door. Suddenly the door burst open and a trolley with a man was pushed through. Various tubes were suspended above him and four green-robed medical teams flooded into the room. Amid rapid-fire questions in French, almost running them over, such was the frenzy. The lead medical, a women doctor, turned towards them,

Get out! Out! Please, this is an emergency unit. Please! Leave now. She shouted.

Claudine stepped back in complete shock. The team converged around the patient, trying to revive a male. Suddenly one of them moved aside, and instantly Claudine gasped in shock.

Fletcher, her husband fully dressed in his clothes was struggling to remove an oxygen facemask and trying to speak.

"I'm fine, I can breathe better now... a weakened voice was heard.

In that instant, they gaped at Fletcher Du Pont's figure stretched on the trolley push past them into the room. His appearance was that as they all remembered, restored and completely normal. For each of them, time stood still. As if caught in a cosmic spell, they became transfixed. In seconds their minds were held suspended between belief and disbelief at what unfolded around them. The group looked as if they are witnessing an event of paranormal proportions something that suspended all intellect and emotions. The essence of all rational thinking was ripped asunder. A ghostly paleness covered their faces ashen with disbelief. None of them seemed capable of rational thought, nor utter a single syllable. Their collective minds froze locked in some suspended state as their eyes survey something their minds refused to accept.

Claudine and her children stare, wanting desperately to believe they were not caught up in some hallucinogenic episode. Her mind screamed uncontrollable joy to what she was staring at. Both her daughters stood rooted to the floor engulfed in emotional trauma, speechless but overcome with tears of uncontrollable happiness. The moment deepened as one of the doctors turned towards them.

"This patient is in emergency trauma and has just arrived in from CERN, now please, you need to get out of here...or I will call...

The words pierced deep into their consciousness, the patient, *just arrived* from... Deveraux thought the ground beneath his feet had moved. Melrose felt a tram had hit him. In an only matter of seconds, all of them felt a spectre of something fearful grip them as this alternate reality, this wrinkle of time, washed over them upending their sense of normality. They were catapulted seamlessly into a past moment when their colleague was first rushed in. Claudine snapped out of the mind trap that held her and ran to the trolley and made physical contact with her husband. To feel his body, that he was real. She clamped her arms around him.

"My dear, dear husband! She sobbed

He sat up very slowly, uncertain of his surroundings and dazed. He reached and wrapped his arms around her. Instantly both girls rushed and wrapped their arms around their parents. For several seconds they remained locked in a moment of joy, and immense relief. The young doctor turned and barked to another.

"Get security in here...Now!

The Jesuit moved quickly and blocked the doctor's movements

"Back off! This is Professor Du Pont's wife and family! He growled.

After a few seconds, the calmness settled.

"OK, I'm truly sorry, but, if you'll let us check his condition!

A moment of solitude followed as the medical team worked in silence, professional and methodical. They nod to each other each carrying out a rapid series of checks. As they work the man they all know so well and missed began to sit up looking dazed and perplexed, but completely transformed. An eerie silence stalked the room, as each of his family and work colleagues simply stare at the man on the trolley, uncertain if they are experiencing this transformation. As if caught up in some fantasy of mass delusion, and yet so deeply joyful. No longer was the emaciated remnant of what was. Instead, a vibrantly composed figure looked at them making eye contact with each of them in a most personal way. His face possessed a peaceful demeanour, a searching look of someone getting used to his surroundings, making sure he understood the nature of his circumstances. His hair was thick, healthy with just a tinge of silver breaking through. It gave him a certain distinguished look and was remarkably tanned as if returning from a place of heat and sunshine. His face had an assured look, an expression that knew all there was to know of his surroundings or those around him. It lasted no more than a moment, and then there was a flicker in the eyes.

Then in a most reassuring mannerism, that was familiar to all, he nodded to himself for a second and broke into a smile. He coughed a little, almost choking as he tried to say something.

"Where is this place? He whispered

"Please Professor Du Pont. You've just experienced a mild cardiovascular episode, we need you to rest.! The young Doctor pleaded.

Claudine trembled while her two daughters just continued to gaze at the transition and appearance of the man before them, even more, baffling was his accent. It didn't sound American. Melrose stood the furthest back. He was caught in the midst of deep shock, as were the others. He reached out and caught one of the passing nurse's arms.

"*What day is this?* He hissed   She gave him an odd look.

"Friday... she retorted, jerking her arm free.

Date! what date is this, Please! He whispered insistently.

"April the 4th, she said and left.

Melrose nearly fell over as his whole body swayed. His mind almost convulsed with what he was hearing and experiencing. Anxiously he glanced around to see the faces of the others. All were in deep shock barely disguising the utter turmoil on their faces. A hand reached out and took hold of him. Monika Reinhardt moved closer to him. She'd seen and heard the last exchange. Fear etched into her face but there was something else. She moved awkwardly closer to him shaking.

What!.. What is happening to us? This isn't happening! She gasped almost as a whisper. He gripped her hand.

"I don't know. Stay calm, Monika. Keep it together! Then she inhaled, trying to control her reactions.

My coffee! My coffee shouldn't have been there. Not on my desk. She whispered to herself.

"Did she say April the 4th? under her breath. Melrose squeezed her hand.

The next five minutes lasted an eternity. The medical team went about their business going through an intensive battery of tests around the scientist. He sat there in his dark blue polo necked cardigan, wearing his favourite charcoal gray slacks, minus his shoes. Claudine sat up next to him consumed in the moment her hand clasped his. The girls sat ashen coloured but overcome with happiness. Nothing else impinged in their minds. Du Pont didn't say much he simply let the medical staff complete their final tests. There was nothing out of the ordinary. No unusual responses, nothing that suggested familiarity by the team. Their patient was a total stranger, one of many such emergencies they deal with regular basis, and except this one was lucky. There was no residual after effects, and the tests show remarkable levels in all his vital signs. If it started as an emergency, it certainly didn't end like one.

"Just one more test Professor, that's all, and we'll leave you some privacy with your family." The senior lady doctor said, leaning over him listening to his breathing.

Then satisfied her patient was out of any immediate danger, she nodded.

"How do you feel, no more chest pain? She asked.

Du Pont gazed around the room, searching and confronting his new reality. He fixed his gaze on the silent Jesuit standing in the shadow of the room.

"I feel no pain. Never, had any pain. He stammered slightly.

Melrose felt torn between sheer joy and the return of his chief and what they all just experienced. He fought off urgings to run towards the walls of the room and pound them to test their real. To reach out to any of them standing and shake them, convincing himself he wasn't suffering a hallucination of staggering proportions. Deveraux, with the others, regained some composure.

"Claudine! Thank God, Du Pont whispered.

245

He reached out to both his daughters

"Denise, Michelle!

They could see he was beginning to become more lucid each minute.

Francois Burgoyne, of all the people present, would recall everything that occurred and in what sequence. He remained bolted to the spot watching something he read about many times in his missionary past. The existence of Transcendent Power.

"Fletcher! My dear, dear friend, Deveraux said moving closer.

"It's so good to have you back with us. So good, my dear fellow! Everyone is here! Manfred, Miles, Paul, and of course Monika and Carina.

Du Pont took a deep breath and sighed, then without any warning.

"My deepest gratitude" He cried out, with his eyes closed. My thanks for guiding me. Nothing is forgotten! He whispered.

In that poignant moment everyone in the room experienced relief beyond description. The man they loved and knew had recovered, and all the dread and fear that consumed their lives were laid aside consigned to some deep part of their make-up. If any of the immediate family had noticed the seismic shift that swept over them, none of it registered at that moment. It was if the last number of weeks of utter trauma was erased, completely obliterated from their immediate recent past. An entire history ceased to have existed or taken place, and no one in the room was equipped to contemplate how such a seismic shift of time dilation occurred. As if all human experiences, personal histories, and memory were enshrined in a ribbon of time that dissolved as instantly as decaying quantum particles. And then as if ordained by some existential power, all-temporal time instantly corrected itself.

For nearly an hour, chairs were brought in and some time was made for the just family to sit around the bed and come to terms with everything. Du Pont's colleagues sat among themselves, relieved at one level, but deeply unsettled at another. Then, almost as if nothing ever happened, Du Pont raised himself and effortlessly placed his feet on the ground. He outstretched both his hands and moved his fingers then turned them over, and for one private moment he studied his hands, lost in some memory. He took a few steps and then stopped as if he was alone without anyone present. Claudine and her daughters looked on with immense relief and peace. She saw instantly her husband looked different. Different in a most charming and positive way. He seemed assured especially the way he was observing everything and most interestingly of all, his appearance; he seemed more youthful. The scale and contrast to his stricken state couldn't be more acute. There was vigour, a vibrancy that was intriguing given what preceded this and all they endured. He turned and went to his pregnant daughter and gently held her. Claudine detected something else, his gait was one who kept in shape, someone who worked out, and stayed in peak condition, and yet the idea seemed preposterous. Her husband seldom exercised to any great degree. There were other things, all of them good just, and she couldn't readily pinpoint what. His skin tone was healthy and radiant. Then he moved to his colleagues and slowly took and embraced each of them. There was energy or potency that filled the entire room. They all could feel it. A presence of someone possessed with unspoken charisma and a pervasive charm. There was a spark that was never there before. The more the hour progressed it became difficult for everyone to accept the utter transformation of his recovery. He moved towards Francois and embraced him and held him for a few seconds.

"We have so much to talk about Francois. So much." He said quietly.

After both daughters spent some time with their father, they reluctantly leave. Claudine insisted he returned to the bed and rest, while she sat next to him his hand clasped in hers. She had him to herself, alone.

'You've given us all, a shakeup, she finally said.

"How do you feel? Anything strange, sensations. Do you feel as well as you look!

Regardless of everything she was relieved beyond measure to see him so alive- so well. It was going to take time for her to accept things. Deep in the recesses of her mind, were things her brother spoke of, mysterious things. Only that I'm holding you, I'm not so sure this is real. She whispered to him gently.

Yes, this is real, my love. Everything we have, our family, we are real. It's something Claudine we should cling to with gratitude. Do you know why? He added."Because, my love, everything …Is not what it seems!

She studied him for a few seconds. Claudine Du Pont always took it upon herself to cocoon her husband and shelter him from unwanted attention or unbridled fame. That's how it always was between them. Now, that natural vulnerability was no longer. The last thing he appeared to be at this instant was vulnerable.

"It's just an overnight darling. I'll be fine". He said finally. He pulled her to him tightly and kissed her. She sat him down on the edge of the bed and ran her hand through his hair.

Are you hungry Fletcher? She asked then added without knowing why. "When was the last time you remember eating anything? She quizzed. He paused for a few seconds, and then smiling pulled her closer and whispered in her ear. She slowly withdrew and looked at her husband, her expression changed from a smile to a look of total disbelief.

After some hours alone with him, Claudine Du Pont began to leave, having managed to pull herself together. Aspects of what she heard caused her head to spin. Eventually, she made her way from the ward her thoughts reeling within. She found her brother quietly sitting in a corner reading his missal. The reception area was busy but not crowded. He smiled and stood. If ever there was a more grounded man, it is her beloved, Francois. He was the one that heralded the workings of a guiding mind. With absolute certainty and purpose, he'd placed his thoughts and views out there front and centre as to what was shaping her husband's circumstances. Now, on the surface there was stillness in him, a settled look, yet he was shaken by what took place. Some mystical event had for a brief moment in time dismantled normal experience, and in the process returned her husband to them.

'Francois, I prefer not to drive. She said

"Of course! Let me have the keys, He said.

They turned and walked out into the fresh air, a welcome relief from the closeness and heat of the hospital. Both said little as they head straight to the car. It was only when they reached it, did they noticed people standing in the car park at their cars. A quick sideways glance told them something was amiss. People were standing around, keys in hands staring upwards distracted by something. Following the general direction, they looked around casually scanning to see what the source of everyone's attention was. Then, in the second story of the building, they see the source.

Just outside one of the windows, there was a frenzy of activity. A flock of birds had perched themselves on the window ledge. Over twenty birds were jostling around one window seeking to perch there. All were snow white. Doves, all vying to find a space, just outside one window. It took a few seconds, and then Claudine raised her hand to her mouth.

'Dear God! It's Fletcher's ward. She whispered to herself.

Elsewhere, four men and two women retreated into their private domains. While they all shared in something beyond belief, all of the men and women close friends of Du Pont, each gifted with brilliant minds and intellects:- needed to find a place of privacy, a place of refuge and seclusion. Returning to the complex all of them retreated into their own private states to find sanctuary. To establish some constant into which to locate and anchor their sanity. Starting with establishing some basis, a reality check, that it was summer, the days date. Within their individual domains they retreated to ponder the imponderable. The circumstances were frightening even disturbing to grasp. Some shift of cosmic proportions once inside the hospital or somewhere along the way, Time seemed to have done something miraculous. It appeared to have folded back on itself recreating a memory of events compressed around April the 4th. Once they moved from that location, time quite remarkably restored its natural arrow of time.

Paul Melrose secluded himself in his tiny office sat at his desk, incapable of functioning. His entire notion of *present time*, the here, and the now was upended. His process of thinking was disturbed. Alone, he allowed himself to question what transpired a few hours earlier. He tried retracing how the day started. Then, from nowhere significant, an isolated simple event flashed through his mind, his Morgan. Earlier that morning he recalled, they were bundled into the taxi something strange came back to him. Leaving the building heading to the Hospital, Otto the mechanic.

"*Jesus that was some weeks back*," he whispered.

That was the day his Morgan was serviced. The same day April 4th, Euclid Beta 8 commenced. The day of the accident with, Fletcher. Something else rebounded in his head. He remembered Monika Reinhardt. Something about coffee on her desk. Recalling her terror and utter shock, he knew the event would change all of them profoundly.

As darkness drew in over Geneva, all of those present did something to ease the trauma of their ordeal; they sat in their own private domains, opened their diaries, and made entries. Each found safety in writing something down. Some narrative that defined their understanding of how they were suspended and witness to an astonishing event. It would be their chronicles of time, descriptive and life changing for each of them.

Alone, Du Pont sat in the only chair in the room staring out at the darkness of the early hours. He was aware of his breathing, steady and measured. He found the solace of the room's stillness comforting but needed to feel all was real, or imagined because what nobody knew, he was still connected to that other place. That *other time*.

Physically aware of his surroundings a part of his being felt left behind. Separated from a realm that mysteriously, he missed. A place that immersed his soul in wisdom containing a richness and completeness beyond human senses. He had become corrupted, infected by an existence outside human reach. Multitudes of images crowded into his conscious mind, images of immense beauty and complexity, creatures of extraordinary kindness came to him with gifts that were simply beyond his descriptive power. To absorb everything was one thing, to render it with justice and depth and expose these truths to others was daunting. Then, as if to reassure himself he stood and crossed to the wall and window and touched them. Running his hand along surfaces to touch solid things that were real.

Memory functions placed him in Geneva; his recall took him to his last actions as Euclid's process got underway. Then, there was that cave, the extended hand, the face, and the man. His mind began to work with great precision, recalling events that swept over him, swamping his notions of past and present. Then, in some magical way he compressed these thoughts with his presence in an alternate reality. This alternate realm existed outside the bounds of anything he could define, but he remembered all of it. All its magnificence and power. Even now in this hospital, sleep seemed unnecessary. There was no fatigue or any sense of needing to rest; his entire physical being seemed to have access to hidden reserves of mental and physical strength. As if it was the most natural thing to do, he moved to the door and emerged into the corridor to the calmness and quietness of the entire hospital floor. All was quiet only the distant muted voices of the night shift staff could be heard.

To his left a ward containing six beds each with a patient in different states of sleep, or sleeplessness. He could feel human frailty. Within seconds he stood in the darkened ward and listened. Amid the silence the sound of human struggles, the balance between living on the precipice of life or death. A young boy, his sleep punctuated with asthmatic problems turned and twisted. Next to him, a man lay almost lifeless his breathing regulated by a machine. In the corner, a younger middle-aged man, his heart had undergone repair. His mind absorbed his surroundings and the grasping tenacity all humans possess to cling to life itself. One by one he moved past each bed silently his steps hardly made a sound, extending his hand outwards and briefly touched each of them. The ward became still as if in obedience to his presence muted voices from down the corridor became more distant. Finally, in complete privacy, he paused in the centre of the ward briefly and called upon his images of another realm, the Meadow of tall grass, and the babbling streams. He could almost hear the breeze whispering through the grasses. Silently he turned and walked back to his ward.

It was a little after 4.14am. By dawn, the light filled his room and sounds of daily routines of a hospital began to assert themselves. Staff and patients spoke in whispers as the day's first light called all to work. In his ward, he paced back and forth without any urgency or concern. His mind piecing together aspects of his life. His lifelong passion for science, his family, and those deep-rooted feelings of belonging, and where he went from here. Purpose; living demanded purpose. He possessed the mind of a mere mortal filled with immortal thoughts. Truths of an alternative existence assaulted all his ideas and established wisdom. Looming deep within his soul Fletcher Du Pont knew decisions waited to be taken. How was he to continue with his life? To those close to him he was in recovery, getting over a medical condition...whereas he'd been on a journey, rich with unimaginable experiences and consequences? How does he convey all he knew, and share all he witnessed, and with whose company he was in? As a man with strong convictions, his entire set of values had been recast into a new order of importance. Intruding into these thoughts was also the issue of belief. A lifelong agnostic towards all things ethereal or spiritual, Du Pont was altered and recast beyond recognition. Not only did he believe now in other existences or realms of an afterlife, but he also became consumed with them. Science seemed utterly inadequate to fathom or make sense of things contained in other realms. The very concept of other realms used to be an anathema to him- an affront to all his beliefs. He couldn't fathom any equation or abstraction that depicted the mysterious workings of what he saw or became part of. Then, there was the enigmatic Nazarene that reached out and drew him into a landscape of immense beauty and horrific imagery. A creature of supernatural origins incarnated into a man with unlimited charm, grace, and boundless compassion. An encounter that he simply was so unprepared for. This man possessed a presence a persona of such power, that everything he came into contact with caused the elements of nature to surrender itself to his will. Seared into his consciousness were those plaintive eyes of Yeshua Ben Yoseph. Eyes that not only observed but spoke directly to his heart. His very presence had a mysterious aspect that drew people to him with great ease. Behind that mien of calmness was an intellect and wisdom beyond description. He was like no other mortal he had ever encountered. This was a call to arms.

Professor Fletcher Du Pont's own spirit spawned new beliefs into a tapestry of sacred convictions. He would need some time to craft and fashion a story that will shake many of those close to him, but that was another matter entirely.

Looking out at into a vibrant-coloured morning sky to the east, he remembered the tomb at that moment in the early morning light, when he found himself amid something miraculous, those intimate moments where he stared into the face of a dear friend, unbroken and triumphant. He would also remain profoundly grateful that he was spared the trauma to witness his brutal end on a cross.

"Tell them you walked with... Yeshua Ben Yoseph! were his last words before it all faded.

Then, intruding into his thoughts, the ward door opened, and two doctors entered. They were surprised. His bed remained unused- their patient didn't appear to have gotten any sleep.

"Good Morning Professor! How are you feeling? Asked one of them.

'Never better, young man. How do you feel?

For nearly thirty-minutes with the minimum conversation, the checkout went through a series of steps. Du Pont stripped down to his underpants. His physique was in remarkable shape, toned and tanned, and looked like a man who kept himself in condition. Both medics exchanged glances

"You're in good shape Professor!. One of them said.

"You get regular exercise, Sir!

"Not nearly enough. But I try." As they complete his examination, the door opened and Claudine appeared looking relaxed and considerably sharper than recent times. He moved took her in his arms, holding each other tight in a moment of tenderness.

"Take me home, my love. He said

"Where else darling. How about some fresh air first by the lake? She whispered.

With little time wasted he dressed into fresh clothes and started preparations to leave. Both doctors completed their notes and asked Du Pont to sign off his discharge.

Once formalities were completed they moved out into the hallway and were greeted with some commotion and noise from the adjoining ward. He reached and picked up his small canvas bag and slung it over his shoulder. Raised voices and expressions of laughter flowed from the corridor. Hospital staff from the floor moved towards the scene and started to assemble around the ward doorway.

Inside was a scene that amazed every one of the medical staff that morning in Clinique Gerealle Vallence. A number of the clinically ill patients, all with serious conditions, some life-threatening, were walking and joking with others, some of them enjoying a brief few moments with the youngest of them, the young boy. He was performing mini feats of gymnastics and splits to the joy of all. A scene that left most of the nurses and doctors speechless at the dramatic turn of events and the near-miraculous recoveries on display. Some of the doctors were all over two of the patients, who were near death hours earlier, and whose recovery was in doubt, were looking at a man in his seventies standing amidst of the other patients singing a verse.. Show me the way to go home..." There was clapping in time to his efforts.

The other, an elderly lady suffering from near renal failure, gently waltzed to the melodic singing. A scene of unrestrained joy filled the ward. Some of the more senior staff looked on smiling unable to understand what they were seeing. It was something each wouldn't forget in a hurry. Du Pont with his wife managed to squeeze by trying to avoid the commotion until the young boy saw the tall American move past the growing numbers of enthralled staff. Instantly, he raced and leaped onto an empty bed and shouted

"Merci Mon Bon monsieur! Merci.! Thank you, kind sir! He was no more than twelve years old. Looking straight at the American.

Then with ease of agility, he jumped off the bed and rushed towards the door pushing his way through the bewildered gathering of staff and his way out to the corridor towards Du Pont and his wife. Then in a simple gesture, reached out and took the scientist's hand. "Thank you, monsieur! He repeated this time in a low voice with a tender smile.

Then turning he walked to his ward, to join the others. Staff stood back and gave the tall American and his wife curious inspection and close scrutiny inspection. No one said a word. Du Pont just smiled at the youngster, nodded to no one in particular.

Out of curiosity, he peered into the ward to a scene of amazing faces. Furtively he glanced down at his hands and hesitated for a second. It was time for him to leave. One of the two doctors who checked him over earlier moved away from the group and gave them a searching and inquisitive look. Uncertain of anything, he stood gazing at his former patient for a few seconds. Looking perplexed he stared with incredulity at the most intriguing happenings going on inside their intensive care unit. Claudine stood and stared bemused and slowly turned on her husband. He looked a little distant, yet was the picture of health and vitality. She moved away and saw for herself the drama of the unit, and the moment a young child singled out her husband and graced him with a gesture of great tenderness. Quietly moving towards one of the doctors.

'Doctor! May I ask if my husband's is well enough? How was his medical check-up?

He gave her an equally searching look still maintaining a smile, uncertain he fully understood everything.

"Your husband, Madam, for a man of his years, and age. He hesitated.

Remarkable! He is in better health and condition than I am. In fact better than some athletes I know, he added. Then turned. She walked back and took her husband's arm, and led him away out and down the long corridor towards the exit and badly needed fresh air. Her heart pounding in her chest.

Two hours later, they sat in a small café on the lakeshore and let the open vista cleanse them of all things medical and hospital air. Her relief and feelings towards her husband's health were beyond measure. He reminded her of how he was many years ago, lean, rested, and sharp. Despite those years, and the workload in CERN and one of their leading physicists in his field, he looked younger. He held her hand and gently caressed it.

How bad was it, my love? I mean, while I was ...ill. You, the girls?

A few seconds passed between them. "Terrifying! Absolutely terrifying my love.

"No one knew or could explain what was happening with you. Medical staff was baffled and what made it all so frightening were the changes. Your appearance, it was like nothing anyone had experienced. It was shocking" "My appearance! What are you talking about?

'Fletcher my love, you're the whole body changed, you aged beyond belief in a matter of hours, and you're entire...It wasn't you darling. It was someone else. It was if, some older more decrepit person replaced you. A total physical stranger."

Tears welled up as she allowed the angst and trauma of those images to return. He pulled her close and kissed her on the cheek. "I'm decrepit, am I? He teased with a reassuring smirk.

Then looking at her he turned serious

"I wasn't ill." In fact, I was well looked after".

Studying him for a few seconds, she wondered what that meant remembering a small detail he whispered in the hospital. "What was that about a boat and eating dates and figs". She finally asked.

"I will tell you something my love that will,...might, even shock you but it is all true. But, that can wait". He smiled.

Let's head home, I need some time to reflect, meditate, and rest. He said.

Meditate! She asked, taken aback. He didn't respond but smiled at how crazy that sounded.

"Our eldest daughter, tell me all about that? He asked diverting her response.

It took less than hour to take the scenic route and leave the outskirts of Geneva and headed west. It was a beautiful morning and already the temperature was climbing. Claudine drove, letting her husband sit and enjoy the trip back. She let him soak the views and spectacular scenery, almost rediscovering its splendour that appealed so much to them when they first thought about moving there. Once off the autobahn, she took a route back to Sal Madere with considerably less traffic. It was easy driving and allowed her time to ease her husband back into events in their lives. Intuitively she tried to evade questions regarding duration, the issue *of elapsed time*.

His illness had run into weeks, and she needed to handle the issue with great care and delicacy. Uncertain how he might react and discussing Denise's pregnancy might be awkward. But at the appropriate juncture in the journey back, she filled him in on all the details. She also brought up some other aspects relating to her brother and his more unusual insights on her husband's illness. Du Pont merely listened with great interest, preferring not to respond, but took in every aspect, and the kind of reactions it provoked.

"Francois went public with his views and conclusions. He became so passionate and stubborn about God's will. Talked at length, about a guiding mind, or something like that with Felix and some of the others. She added.

Paul was impressed with Francois. The word miraculous was mentioned a few times'

He leaned back and pushed his sunglasses back and closed his eyes for a few seconds.

If they only knew. If they realised what awaits us all

"How is Paul coping with all of this? He asked finally

"Very well in fact. It took some time, but now he seems happy with the prospect. They're deeply in love you know. He adores our daughter." She laughed.

Du Pont just nodded. Inwardly, he was over the moon preferring to keep his thoughts to himself for the time being. "He's a very good guy, our daughter is very lucky and blessed".

Claudine shot her husband a side-glance, not quite used to hearing her husband use such phrases. She smiled inwardly still soaking up the reality of his presence and recovery, filled with immense relief that all of this was real. Looking over at him he looked more attractive to her now, as if it was that moment when they first laid eyes on each other. Her love for him was as certain now as it was then, enriched ironically by the experience of nearly losing him altogether. His expression on his face reflected someone at complete peace with himself, caught amid the speckled flickers of sunlight on his face. Reaching over with her free hand, she squeezed his hand for a moment.

"Darling, what was all that about? ...the young child in the hospital? Why was he thanking you like that? She quizzed.

He glanced at her and smiled.

"He was seriously ill I'm told, and seemed to have made a complete recovery, probably happy and thankful to be better. You know kids. He said dismissively.

"And, all the others? She asked casually.

Geneva. Barthus-Sant-Jovanne

Doctor. Benjamin Mochti sat with some of his team reviewing patient records and trying to dispense with them as quickly as possible. One patient, however, was starting to worry him and yet his source of worry was not medical. Denise Du Pont was due the next day and he was determined to clear up certain matters on her condition and her pregnancy. Through exhaustive tests and clinical examination of his notes, he was more than certain of the outcome. Always thorough and left nothing to chance, and apart from having some ties to the family, he was innately drawn to the circumstances surrounding them.

Equally preoccupied, but much more absorbed was Paul Melrose.

Earlier he had spoken by phone with Denise. She was beyond happiness, her father had recovered just as she knew he would. She sounded like her pregnancy was all the more fulfilling now, things are finally beginning to fall into the place and she could focus on the changes that brought. For that he was grateful, but he was born with a curious mind and with it brought profound questions that caused him to withdraw into himself. As a theorist in all matters dealing with abstract issues, mathematical frameworks, spatial dimensions, he knew that something unique in the chronicles of the time had occurred with seamless execution and hardly anyone noticed or cared. Time simply inverted itself just as he was leaving CERN earlier the previous day. Twenty-four hours later he was still caught up in its occurrence. A brief notification on his laptop screen abruptly appeared. It was a summons. It came from the Director-General himself, calling all of those listed to meet with him and the Deputy DG at 4 pm. Nothing else only a cryptic note, no agenda, but he could guess what it entailed. If he were right, he would be centre stage in explaining what they witnessed the previous day.

Getting up he left his small cubicle-like study and walked downstairs, and headed to the Advanced Computing Centre to speak with the only other person he felt he could talk to, Monika Reinhardt. When he got there the centre was busy, over 15 over CERN's top computing specialists were immersed in an array of activities, all dealing with the global GRID. Quietly he navigated his way to a glass-walled office in the far corner of the floor. Venetian blinds gave the occupant complete privacy and seclusion. Knocking twice, he entered.

He found her sitting on a small settee, shoes off, both feet resting on a small cabinet. Clutched in her hands a large latte. "May I come in? He asked

Oh!! Please do. She responded sharply.

Thought you'd given those up, He asked with an edge in his voice

"You may well ask! She spat nervously. Standing she put down the coffee and came closer.

"Tell me, you're as troubled by what happened yesterday as I am. For my sanity Sake! Tell me you saw and experienced what I did! That it's not a dream!

"Yes. Yes, Monika. It wasn't any dream. Something truly amazing transpired beyond anything I can explain, and we were part of it. .

"It was real, and it started here. It began here in Meyrin, Monika as we were leaving".

She gave him a disbelieving glare and then slumped down at her desk.

For the next twenty minutes, they both went through events that previous morning, covering every detail. The grass that morning on his way to the office was frosty when it shouldn't have been. His episode with his Morgan, simple and innocuous as it was, became the trigger. She went into detail on her movements and singled out the appearance of coffee on her desk that morning at a time when she supposedly had given it up many weeks earlier. It seemed at that moment, time itself flipped and its arrow of progression folded backward like a flat surface folding back on itself.

"It was so poignant Paul. I never gave it another thought. She said.

"None of us did, Monika. Neither of us did and, I think, that's what's on the table later on with the DG."

Du Pont's Residence.

The garden looked immaculate. It caught the light just right for that part of the day bathed in a warm glow of sun and light, its shrubbery around its edge in full bloom finished off with a table set for dinner under a blue canopy. Both women ordered their uncle around like he was a manservant. Francois did what he was told, as preparations for a long-awaited homecoming was almost complete. With places set, Denise sat on an adjoining garden seat, issuing instructions to her younger sister while her uncle took it upon himself to have soft cushions arranged on seats. A small glass of malt sat on the table.

Inwardly, Fr. Francois Burgoyne was emotionally drained, while overjoyed that his almighty God heard his prayers and lamentations throughout the last few days. He'd gotten very little sleep, his faith and beliefs tested like never before. He was a Sheppard to his family and a lightning rod for others. Last few hours he secluded himself in his room in private and prayed prostrate on the floor in complete submission and gratitude to an invisible lord and master. The demons of doubt had flooded his soul planting seeds of despair and mistrust in his own relevance. To matters placing his vocation and devotion on trial. Now, he was gifted with an answer that was deeply personal and spiritual. *"We wait and hear what Fletcher has to say on the matter when he returns"*...remembering his own words only some days earlier.

Then with a little warning, they all stop and turn as the noise of a car rolled into the driveway and pulled up next to the house. Claudine was the first to get out, and then her husband gingerly stepped from and car and stood and looked straight at them.

Amid screams of sheer joy Michelle took off and charged towards him. He moved and caught her in his arms and practically lifted her with ease off her feet in a tight embrace. She held him tightly and broke down in tears of joy.

"You're never going to leave this place, on your own again Dad" She bellowed.

Denise came and hugged him tightly and, for a few seconds, time stood still. A reunion that nearly wasn't, was completed ending where all their silent prayers dreamt of.

"It's so, so good to have you back Pops, Denise whispered gripping him tightly as tears rolled down her cheeks.

Claudine stood reflective at the scene before her. Her family restored and bonded. Then the girls stood back and admired the tall man that was their father, and saw a figure of someone they love beyond measure and so proud of. His presence exuded charm and grace that made them both look at each other. Their father cut a dashing image of a man of youthful vigour caused both women to gush and hug each other with their admiration and joy. Finally, each took his arm and led him to the garden, where standing waiting was Francois. Unlike normal times, he was in his full regalia of a Jesuit. Du Pont paused for a moment and smiled

"Is there malt somewhere for me.? Both men moved and embraced each other. It was a special moment as the Jesuit held him close.

"Almighty Father in Heaven, our deep gratitude and heartfelt thanks for bringing our loved one home!

"Amen. Du Pont replied. Then turning towards his wife

"Claudine! Girls! Come over here" They all come and gather around him, each wrapping their arms around each other forming an intimate bond of togetherness with their uncle. Then after a few seconds.

'Yeshua! "For everything. Send us your blessings. You have my undying devotion. Amen"

"Amen! They all replied.

Francois Burgoyne nodded and smiled at his brother-in-law.

"Words fail me, Fletcher! I've prayed for this moment for your return".

Then moving that bit closer to him, he noticed the small canvas bag.

"Extraordinary Wisdom! Yeshua? "Is *that* who I think you spoke of? His face now an expression of incredulity

The physicist gave him a knowing look for a second.

'Francois! Be prepared *for what comes next*!

CHAPTER TWENTY-THREE

Some days passed and Sal Madere became a place of solace.

Immersed within an atmosphere of great relief and much thanksgiving, the anguish that consumed it over the last number of weeks was dispelled replaced with sheer joy and expectant return to normal life. Du Pont himself took to reading as much as he can. Preoccupying himself reading every newspaper there was, sitting alone studying all manner of events, particularly international news, and anything dealing with strife in war-torn parts of the world. Claudine and the girls were kept busy just keeping up with this newfound appetite to read. He read and consumed everything, often well into the night.

When he wasn't reading, he was found glued to the TV flicking through channels scanning everything that hinted of upheaval. The family became bemused, he was never such an avid follower of news that often left him depressed until now. It seemed he couldn't get enough of it. Yet behind it all, they all knew something was different, a noticeable shift the way he responded to things he hardly ever showed interest in the past. The intensity of interest moved from matters scientific, and towards more issues of human nature. Over dinner these last few evenings his banter and chitchat took on a more humanitarian aspect, hardly ever referring to his love of his work or experimental physics. Yet his humour and wit were in abundance much to the delight of the family. He began to spar more openly with his brother in law, only more so, baiting him, teasing him as if behind it all he was calibrating something in his mind or, as his wife suspected, he was re-establishing a connection with life itself.

Claudine noticed a small piece in the press, telling a story of a few patients experiencing a complete reversal of fortunes, much to the joy of family and medical staff combined. Even more intriguing, was not one mention or reference to the passage of time. Newspaper dates suggested that time had passed by, and yet he seemed to have taken that in his stride as if knowing this was the consequence of the experience he had gone through. Some days later the weather had turned balmy and much of the surrounding countryside took on a distinctive summer feel. The evening air remained warm, making it inviting to stay outdoors and enjoy the calmness that living in the countryside had to offer. Dinner was going to be a garden affair with most of the preparation well underway. Both daughters spent much of their time ensuring their father rested, not even allowing him to meddle in culinary affairs. Denise watched her sibling put her personal touches on their father's favourite dish, lamb. Francois switched from clerical garb also into to more casual attire. Du Pont changed into denim, a blue open-necked shirt to match his slacks, and cream-colored loafers.

In the privacy of their bedroom, he put down some papers, then catching her momentarily off guard he gently took his wife in his arms holding her close cherishing the women he adored. As if by instinct she responded and draped her arms around his neck and clung to him.

"Let me just hold you, Claudine. Just this moment let me just feel your presence. I so missed this. To hold you. There was a moment when I thought I'd never do this again.'

Her scent, her hair, that closeness they shared was always special, both physically and emotionally. Her closeness brought something else. The trauma they both endured triggered a more spiritual connection, a pairing of souls that brought new things to them. Now he felt something different. An Intimacy of thoughts, a togetherness bound by some thread that linked mind and soul into something new. She held him tight, just to have him to herself for that moment.

Also, decisions were taken. There will be no rush to return to his work instead they would use the period to spend more time together. More time and space to do just this, to hold each other and cherish life and living as a pairing.

'You OK? She whispered

"Yes, I'm so OK my love. It's hard to find words to say how I'm feeling. Alive. I've never felt more alive. He smiled

He took to staying indoors over the last few days, now he felt recharged. Fully relaxed they head down and move out into the garden and to the smell of freshly cut grass. Something that Francois discovered he enjoyed doing. Du Pont found his favourite spot and sat reaching for a glass of his malt, with mobile in his other hand. For nearly twenty minutes he caught up with his friend Felix Deveraux back at CERN. There was much to discuss, most of the conversation was light. In the kitchen, Denise was using her cell phone issuing instructions to Paul Melrose, to get there on time for dinner. Michelle tasted some new additions to a sauce while simultaneously matching her uncle in chess-moves out on the small table in the garden. Du Pont wandered over and sat next to his brother in law pondering his next chess move. Du Pont studied the board.

"I think she has you on the run, Francois! He joked

"That's only because it seems that way, my friend.

Within a half an hour the distinctive purr of a Morgan pulled into the house, and Melrose made his way into the garden. Denise went and took his hand, and kissed him then led him over to where both her uncle and her father were sitting. Du Pont jumped up and grabbed his young assistant embracing him.

"Paul! So good to see you. We didn't have time in the hospital. I am delighted for you and Denise becoming parents. I couldn't be more pleased. Now sit my man, let me fix you a drink".

'Not so fast Pops he has some things to do with me first. Denise said dragging him away.

"Take your time son, we'll talk later! Du Pont grinned.

"How are you doing, Francois, getting your ass kicked again. Melrose goaded the Jesuit.

"Not so, young man, this game is still mine to lose." Burgoyne said still studying the board.

When dinner was eventually served, everyone settled into a relaxed mood. The banter was light. Inwardly, Du Pont sat letting the conversations flow. He was still dealing with aspects with his return. Gradually he was beginning to experience something new to him, Impatience. Small talk, the rituals of everyday life were starting to test his normally laid-back manner. It wasn't until dessert was finished that Francois brought the conversation around the table to a pause.

"Loved ones! Can we raise our glasses, first to my niece's wonderful meal, and this beautiful table, and then to Fletcher? Glasses touched.

"We are truly blessed. We thank our almighty God for his presence here this evening. "To you Chief! Melrose said quietly.

Du Pont raised his glass. "To be here is to be in Heaven. He said

Dad! It was Michelle's turn.

"When you were... Unconscious! What was that like? Did you have any of those out of body experiences that people often talk about?

Everyone smiled. It was so typical of Michelle, forever the more inquisitive of the siblings. Du Pont leaned back and took a sip of his wine. He cast a glance around the table at smiling faces.

"Yes! As a matter of fact. The entire experience was full of things. Interesting things.

"Such as? Asked Claudine.

Well! Some very serious things. Aspects that at one level were...frightening! Other times beyond belief". "Kind of an Afterlife? Denise asked casually

'Your father doesn't subscribe to such things.! Stop trying to tease him. Claudine laughed.

"It was very real. Real enough as this garden. He said looking at his drink.

Everyone stopped laughing for a moment and gave him a mischievous look.

"Are you serious Chief? An Afterlife"! Melrose jibed.

Glancing round the table there was nothing but faces of great affection and love. He considered the moment carefully; none of his loved ones had glimpsed upon the things he experienced. Other existences. Without any of them seeing what he saw, how was he ever to impart all he knew.

His thoughts receded to another place reflecting on how his task might come about. Who, if not his intimate close loved ones could he share his most profound messages and truths that he carried. One such reaction could well be, he was suffering more than they realized. Some deep trauma had gripped him in a delusional state, one that altered his psychological makeup, rendering him hopelessly out of touch with reality. They would seek to cocoon him from the outside scientific community fearing a great loss of reputation; a once-great formidable mind had succumbed to simple notions. An intellectual cripple, he could just imagine that impact on their lives. Then he remembered words from a former place. *And, like all human thinking and handiwork. Ephemeral. Be strong...have belief in me...*

He stared around his beloved garden, its setting, his home in the foothills of Switzerland and thought back, of vast spaces of desolation amid the Judean wilderness, the utter loneliness, and yet a birthplace of momentous ideas that shaped human history. Single ideas imbued with the power to move nations. Here armed with the potency of truths sitting amid his family it would be his place and time to share. It was poetic how a question came around to the afterlife. Simple and innocent and yet deeply poignant.

Where could he start, and most importantly how could he describe whom he encountered?

Standing he wondered around the table and refilled their glasses, bending and kissing his wife. She reached, took his free hand, and kissed it. Replacing the bottle, he moved to the small chessboard and stared at is pieces. Whispering as if addressing an invisible gathering.

"It was here we stood. It was just after Alamogordo". The flash was still fresh in my mind. We moved towards this window and I saw you both. You were both preparing a meal. You both laughed, Francois and Claudine were sitting at the table inside. Paul, you had just arrived...

Yeshua...moved and reached out and touched you, Denise here. You felt a mild jump a kick from your child". He moved nimbly around the garden almost reliving the moment, while everyone at the table put down their drinks. No one was smiling now.

"The was a candle here! He said pointing at the chessboard, he touched it gently and it ignited. I wanted to send you a message, a message of my love."

The garden fell silent. Then, Melrose slowly rose first. No one spoke.

"Fletcher, Chief... Please come and sit down. Please.' He whispered

Du Pont turned and looked at them, Denise nodded, and tears flooded her eyes.

"Yes. Pops. I knew! I knew.

She got up and went to him and hugged him. All of them rose and came to him put theirs around him. Gently Claudine led him back to his seat. Glances around the table finally fixed on Francois. He sat nearest his brother in law. He nodded to all of them and all pulled their chairs closer.

"Fletcher! Do you want to talk to us? Do you wish to tell us everything?

Everything"

'Excusez moi s'il vous plait'   A voice suddenly called out from the darkness.
Startled, they turn to where the voice came from. There was silence. A voice called out again. Melrose jumped to his feet. From the shadows of the overhanging beech tree, a figure emerged from the darkness. A young boy looking at them. Everyone froze. Claudine then slowly stood.

"Puis-Je vous aide"? May I help you?

With some hesitancy, the boy advanced enough into the lighting. The appearance of the child stunned them. It was late in the evening.

"My God, it's the young boy from the hospital! Claudine said finally recognizing him. Then moving towards him sensed his nervousness, she smiled reassuringly

"Parlez –vous Anglais? She asked gently.

"Yes. I speak English." He said.

Then bowing slightly he moved past her and headed to the table to the others. He showed a certain grace and politeness seemingly aware his sudden presence was completely unexpected. Du Pont looked bemused. The others just looked at the child's appearance, well-dressed smart style. Yet at best guess he was no more the twelve or thirteen.

"What is your name, young man? Francois asked

"Emile! I am thirteen years old. My parents are in the car, near the house." Each gave each other a quizzical look.

Parents! Car.! "What are you doing here so late in the evening? Denise asked moving over to him.

Before they moved closer, the boy gave a large exhale of breath, and then to everyone's shock almost fell over abruptly stopping in the most abnormal posture. Leaning almost at an impossible sixty degrees the boy looked suspended like a puppet without strings. Almost on reflex Denise and Claudine reached to stop him falling over. The child appeared to fall into a sudden sleep with both eyes closed accompanied by deep breaths. All stared at the extraordinary sight before them.

Du Pont in a flash moved with speed and got to the young boy.

'Claudine, Denise! Get behind me and return to the table. He said.

Francois moved equally fast and joined him. Then there was a deep intake of breath, and the child's body took an upright form and posture. And then...

"*Blessings from the Almighty most high, on all of you!* A commanding voice spoke. A voice that only one person in the garden knew.

Etaanus! Du Pont whispered

"Indeed, my friend. God's blessings on you and your beloved family".

All of them felt an invisible power reach out and touch each of them. Claudine moved and joined her husband, shocked and not sure what was unfolding. Tried as she could, her speech stalled, her voice unable to utter a sound. Melrose went cold reached and took Denise in his arms. Francois reached into his shirt and began to unclasp a silver crucifix hanging around his neck.

"Have no fear. I am one of God's servants. What is happening before you is in keeping with all that is good and pure? Be at peace, and I will explain".

The Jesuit blessed himself his colour drained from his face moved forward to confront the entity. Whipping out the crucifix and extending it towards the boy.

"It's OK, Francois! It's fine, please. There is no evil here only good. Du Pont whispered. "Etaanus has been my guide, my companion, my Shepherd".

The boy's head was bowed and then in slow succession began to recite in an unknown tongue. Finally, the Jesuit looked up and closed his eyes as he too listened and recognised certain words in *Aramaic*, the sacred language.

"Hallowed be thy name thy Kingdom comes...thy will be done on earth...

When finished, the Jesuit sank to his knees and silently prayed for a few seconds.

"As a man of the God, your devotion and prayers are heard always in the highest, Brother Burgoyne'. The boy spoke.

"Please rise my brother and be seated, for there is little time, and I wish to relate to you, the divine purpose to your loved one' recent trials'.

Slowly, still gripped in a state of shock, they all sat back at the table. As they did, the air around then became disturbed, and from nowhere a beautiful and graceful snow-white barn owl flapped his wings came from the darkness and descended amidst them and perched on the small chessboard table. In so doing everyone collectively felt a powerful calmness descend over the entire garden and the tensions that attended the boy's transformation eased. Still, each of them found it difficult to speak.

"You're beloved one, has been taken to places, beyond your wildest dreams, and has endured much, and seen much, that has caused him a great burden to rest on his shoulders. What you see before you is in keeping with God Almighty's creative being, and no harm comes to this young boy. In fact, God's power flows through him, and with your touch, he has been restored to good health.

Du Pont looked over at Claudine.

"We, in God's kingdom, have protected this man these last days as he was brought to new truths and his brief encounter with our beloved Redeemer. He has choices to make, in the manner of how he brings truths to humanity. He has seen and witnessed a great deal and been given gifts to help him if he so chooses. We ask and pray, that you all love each other, and express God's love in what manner suits you each. Now all is arranged, this boy's parents are asleep, and will have no recall to this evening's great happening. He finished.

Suddenly, falling like snow petals in a snowstorm and appearing from the darkness above the entire garden, snow-white doves began to arrive and descend sporadically landing on branches throughout the garden. The family sat speechless uncertain how to respond to the magic of the moment. Francois walked towards in the middle of the garden and looked upwards and closed his eyes trying to stop the tears flowing down his face. The moment and the import of what he had heard filled him with awe. None of his previous thoughts dared to comprehend the mighty workings that he now sensed were at work. Du Pont moved towards the young boy. Then, out of keeping with the boy's normal movements, his arms open and made a gesture of a cross.

"May God's love have no limits to you all, and your future family, the voice said softly?

Then the boy's entire body gently was laid on the ground. Within a second the young boy bounced to his feet completely unaware of anything.

"Thank you, Monsieur, again for making me better! He said with a wide grin then turned and ran towards the waiting car.

Both Du Pont and Claudine followed him, but within seconds the car quickly drove out of the driveway and into the night. When they walked back to the table, all four of the others sit and look at Du Pont with a mixture of unsettled awe, and a new sense of respect. The night air was still warm as each of the family stared at what was all around them. The barn owl stood almost motionless its' glowing round eyes stared almost knowingly. No one at the table stirred, none had anything to say each reeling from the episode. Du Pont came and saw the distraught looks. His wife was still shaking. He put his arm around and held her close. Michelle was pale but remained composed.

"What was that Pop? Her voice barely audible

"I have to tell you all of this from the beginning." He said softly. What I'm about to tell you is ...wonderful, majestic and miraculous".

"Fletcher, Is all of this connected with everything that has been happening at work? Melrose asked.

"I will try and explain, but first, let me show you something very special. Du Pont said.

He reached down and lifted a rough and battered canvas bag from the ground behind his seat. He placed it on the table and carefully began to untie a ribbon of leather string holding the flap closed. Claudine noticed it first when they were leaving the hospital but choose to say little. Reaching in he felt something that seemed to surprise him. Something that wasn't supposed to be. Slowly he withdrew an object made from wood. Pulling it clear, a beautiful hand-carved the shape of human hands. It's fine detail showed all the finger joint details, some with exquisite details of palm lines were visible. Even in the candlelight from the table it was cut and polished with great attention to detail. A darkened piece of wood of unknown type or origin. Carved with sublime skill, polished by a hand of a master craftsman, a carpenter. He stared at it then held it for a moment.

"That's beautiful!" Denise said gently taking it from him.

Then reaching back into the canvas bag, he very carefully extracted an off cream-colored cloth folded into a square. With great care, he laid it the table and began to unfold it in front of all of them to see. Denise anxiously moved closer, still uncertain of things. Du Pont looked around the table desperately wanting them to grasp and appreciate the extent of his experience.

"There are things around us that are truly beyond anything we could imagine, so I'm going to start at the beginning. Starting with this! He whispered.

He opened out the cloth. On it was the clearly defined etching of the face of a man. The candlelight caught the image of a young man in his thirties. His eyes are wide open. Each of them stared letting the image sear its presence and outline deep into their consciousness. They stared allowing their minds time to grasp what they were looking at. It was almost hypnotic in its impact.

"Dear God, Fletcher, it's the face of.... the Shroud! Melrose whispered. Claudine crossed herself.

"Mon Cher Jésus! She said bringing her hands to her face.

For the following hours well into the early morning, Fletcher Du Pont began to describe how he became part of a fabric of time that shifted to a cave. Taking his time starting with his transition from his earth-time to his arrival into the blistering heat of the desert landscape, undulating, hidden crevices outlining how it became a stage, where some of the most guarded secrets of all existence unfolded before him. They settled around that table none of them realised, things would ever be quite the same again.

As if to signal something special, a handful of the doves fluttered off their perches and quickly circled the garden creating a spectacle of white flurries, then others joined them, followed by a larger group until nearly fifty beautiful white doves encircled them swooped down and moved in circles, filling the entire garden with feathers that cascaded down smothering the ground in a carpet of whiteness. For a few moments of spellbinding magic, their garden became a sea of white feathers.

Paris. Jesuit Aumonerie, Rue De Planage.

Two days later, events began to move with stealth. Just after 11 am that morning over Paris, a low-pressure system brought a wet and breezy morning; the phone rang in the offertory Aumonerie residence. Quickly the call from Geneva was put through to the Father Provincial's study.

Alphonse Sienna reached the phone. "Francois! My brother, how are you. Tell me the news of the family. He said in a raised voice. He listened intently for some minutes while fingering the crucifix around his chest. "Francois, that is wonderful, our prayers have been heard. Is your brother-in-law at home?

Already! It seems most remarkable for him to recover."

He listened and then slowly sat up and gripped the phone. The voice at the other end relayed a story that lasted nearly forty minutes. At one stage the senior Jesuit lowered his head taking in all he heard. He knew the back-story, but nothing prepared him for the revelations coming down the phone. Details were kept vague but knew he was listening to something of a profound nature. The quiver in the voice at the other end told him all he needed to know. Quietly he blessed himself.

"Yes, of course, I'll come. We have a house in Geneva, as you know".

"Oh! Mon Dieu Francois! What must we do? He asked

"Yes, of course! We will pray. I will arrive in Geneva no later than 4.pm ".

Father Alphonse Sienna replaced the receiver paused to digest the tone of the call. He knew he had another call to make, this time to Rome. How was he going to relate what he heard? For over twenty years he knew, Francois Burgoyne. Never, in all that time had he known him to be unsettled. The voice on that call was that of a man shaken. Events of a supernatural character had begun to manifest itself, including the manner and nature of the recovered physicist. He began arrangements to get to Geneva later that day. He sat for a few moments and then decided it was time to inform his Head of their Order.

Sal Madere became almost monastic. Her husband's body had finally succumbed to all that took place and slept late the last few mornings. Claudine felt a great peace finally settle around the house. Both her daughters seemed to come to terms with how things might be. Denise, of all of them, showed remarkable resilience. She possessed an air of assurance much like her father and pregnancy seem to suit her. Impending motherhood felt right. Those difficult weeks leading up to her husband's return seemed over each of them taking some time off from their normal activities spending most of their time at the residence. There was much to take in. Their entire spiritual and human compass began to coalesce into private and personal reflection. Her brother had taken to rising early and taking off for long walks in the surrounding countryside. He spent quite some time in the gardens, reading and thinking about his own issues. He was still a pillar of strength to all of them, and now when he needed it most, to her husband also. This evening would be interesting. A friend of his would be arriving, a fellow Jesuit. She cleared and prepared the dining room to allow a measure of privacy where she suspected her husband would undergo some degree of ecclesiastic scrutiny and probing questions. She had no idea of how long it would take but made certain that a peaceful and private setting was created.

Her thoughts could now turn to her eldest, and her physical wellbeing. At lunchtime, that day, Paul Melrose made arrangements to meet with the DG, Felix Deveraux at first, in private.

Diaries were cleared and every precaution to preserve as much discretion was put in place. Since his friend's recovery, Deveraux was anxious to have some face-to-face time with him. More for personal reasons, the head of CERN needed someone to discuss the entire surreal nature of his colleague's return and its impact on their whole understandings of matters that simply confounded all current thinking. After parking the Morgan, he went through the main doors of the Science Administration block and headed to the top floor. Then down a long corridor and left and found Felix Deveraux pacing around his office,

"Good of you to see me DG! Melrose said, with a crisp handshake.

Without preamble or formalities, the top scientist in CERN went and sat behind his desk. He had thousands of questions. "Well! How is he?

'He's remarkable. In better shape than me! Melrose said taking a seat.

"Claudine, the girls, Denise! How are they doing? Deveraux asked,

"We're all just about racing to keep up. It's been very demanding if I'm being honest".

"I can only imagine."

"Not certain if any of us could imagine, what's to follow. Melrose said.

Deveraux sat back. "I see. Has there been, any further developments?

Yes! There has Felix"

"Do we need the others for this? Deveraux asked "Perhaps. It might save some repetition". Melrose said.

Deveraux picked up his phone and asked that certain members would join him.

Rome. The Vatican.

Others were equally faced with perplexing questions. Less the 700 kilometres to the South East, inside the Vatican City, Cardinal Giuseppe Bonaire sat straight-laced facing the head of the Jesuit Order. Their meeting was called at unusually short notice, but news from Paris and Geneva suggested something may be unfolding in the foothills above

Geneva. The room reeked in Renaissance styling and antiquity with a polished long oak table and walls dominated with beautiful tapestries in silk and fine purple rich hessian cloths.

"A remarkable recovery you say, Brother!" the Cardinal asked mildly

"Yes, you're Eminence. The man was almost reincarnated from his illness. Fr. Beitel replied. Both men took time to assess and consider these developments, things were beginning to shape and mould themselves into something approaching a doctrinal dilemma.

"There is also reports that he wasn't the only one...that experienced a complete reversal of health, your Eminence"

The Cardinal, lost in his private thoughts, stopped and gave the other man a steely look. "What do you mean?

'We have a report, from an unimpeachable source, that six patients left the same hospital, only two days later, completely against medical odds. Some were unlikely to survive. All staging a remarkable, almost miraculous turn of fortunes." The Jesuit said in a low voice "From the same hospital as this Scientist? The Cardinal asked with dismay.

"Indeed, you're Eminence, not only the same hospital but from an adjoining ward. The Head Jesuit hesitated for a moment. 'There is more... The hospital's closed circuit had this Dr. Du Pont standing inside the unit in the very early hours of the morning. His presence was very brief, but there was a strong suggestion that whatever occurred was not coincidental!

Cardinal Bonaire moved to his widow, both hands joined behind his back.

"Our brother Sienna is visiting Geneva as we speak, yes! He asked looking out into evening sky. 'Yes, you're Eminence, as we speak".

"I see. I have a feeling about this. We may have to intervene much earlier, Dominic. Bonaire whispered 'I completely agree! The head of the Jesuits replied

"We await what my Provincial, Sienna finds and then we follow our hearts.

When Miles Kingsley wandered into the Director General's lavish office he wasn't entirely surprised to find Manfred Gruess, Carina Ambrosiana, and Monika Reinhardt all seated around Paul Melrose. In that instant, he knew this wasn't going to be about physics.

"Welcome everyone thank you for coming." Deveraux smiled. Before you arrived, Paul was giving me news of Fletcher and the family. It goes without saying how relieved and overjoyed we are at his spectacular recovery."

After brief preliminaries and inquiries as to his recovery, Melrose stood and moved towards the large spacious window as if seeking some comfort from the distant mountain peaks.

'Look everyone! This is a little difficult to explain, but let me..! I'm not very sure when the Chief, I mean, Professor Du Pont is going to be back here, and when he does be prepared. Be ready that's all I'm saying for someone that's... changed."

"How can you be sure of that Paul? Miles Kingsley asked "I just know Miles. He's gone through something very profound, and deeply spiritual experience."

"Yes. Its called post-dramatic-stress Disorder. *Come on Paul*!

This is Fletcher! Spiritual? You're kidding me, yea! Give him a couple of weeks to get back on his feet, he'll be right back in the thick of things. Kingsley said dismissively

Carina Ambrosiana studied her younger colleague, her intuition suggested Melrose was affected by things no more than the rest of them, but hidden behind those pale blue eyes there was unease. She cast a cold calculating look at him.

"What's happened out there at the residence? Is Fletcher OK?

No one spoke for a few seconds. "He wants to take physics in a new direction. He spoke of changes to...certain subatomic processes, and he needs to speak with you all".

No one responded for a few seconds. Finally, Deveraux stood and joined Melrose at the window. "New direction! Aren't we already pushing boundaries?"

"Look, everyone. Listen! Melrose said raising his voice slightly.

"Remember a few days ago, Fr. Burgoyne gave us his views. Do you recall? Deveraux nodded.

"Yes, we do Paul. All of us understood what he was trying to suggest, but we're..."

"Well forget what he was suggesting. We're way beyond anything he discussed. Fletcher was never ill...Not in the way we understand. He wasn't ill."

Everyone gave him more than a passing glance. 'I'm not sure of a few things myself to be very honest with you. Not very sure of anything. I've witnessed first-hand, things that are beyond any known laws of science or nature. And I know Fletcher has more to tell. Much more to speak of. So prepare yourselves when you meet with him. Fletcher is changed!

Paul? Should we be, worried? Monika Reinhardt asked

'What do you mean he was never ill? Explain! Asked Carina.

Melrose thought for a few seconds wondering how best he might put it. While he had a Christian background, he was challenged by everything he heard and saw in Sal Madere. He also privately had an entirely new disposition towards Denise's pregnancy as well.

"It looked to us, like he was ill, his near coma, but that's just because, it seemed that way. Fletcher was...caught up in some kind of intersection between our version of reality, and something else."

They all slowly got up and moved around the room, allowing a few seconds to take in what was being suggested. Carina Ambrosiana focused her attention on Monika Reinhardt for a second, then back to Melrose.

'Let me rephrase Monika's question, and please, take your time before answering. Will these matters with Fletcher, disturb us? She asked

'Without a shadow of a doubt, Carina" He said.

δ

After 4.30 pm that same day a silver gray taxi came through the gates of Sal Madere and glided up the curved driveway to the house. A slightly built man in dark clerical garb exited the cab and stood to take in his surroundings. A setting that was appealing, reclusive, and private. The door of the residence opened and, Father Alphonse Sienna saw Francois Burgoyne emerge into the afternoon sunshine.

They both quickly embraced.

"You are most welcome dear friend, Burgoyne said with a smile of relief.

"Come inside and meet the family'

"Thank you, Francois. How are you feeling? He enquired.

"Not entirely sure Alphonse"

When they entered the hallway, the senior Jesuit stood for a moment and made the sign of the cross. There was stillness- a settled ambiance about the house. In the background, soft classical music played from somewhere.

'May God bless all who reside here? He whispered to himself. Leading his friend into the main living area, Francois turned and paused. Du Pont and Claudine stood in front of the fireplace looking quite relaxed, along with both girls.

"My loved ones. Allow me to introduce a dear friend and fellow Jesuit, Father Provincial, Alphonse Sienna.'

Claudine came over and took his hands and gently bowed.

"You're most truly welcome Father Provincial. She said smiling.

"Likewise, you're very welcome Father. Added Du Pont.

The senior cleric took Du Pont's hand and held it. Then he looked down at the hand he held then returned his gaze to the eyes of the tall American.

'I believe the honour is all mine, Professor. He said with deliberate annunciation. Turning, Du Pont smiled and introduced both their daughters. The senior cleric gave both girls a firm handshake and smiled.

'First, let's dispense with the formalities dear friends, please call me Alphonse"

They moved and sat, but not without both girls taking Sienna's jacket and taking his bag. They settle into the comfortable soft armchairs and let the moment of the introductions pass. There was light chat and some humorous exchanges between both clerics. As they chatted, the senior cleric noticed a series of photographs laid out on some of the coffee tables. Most were family shots featuring both daughters, and some more recent and informal settings. One in particular, caught the Jesuits eye.

It was Du Pont himself standing at a podium delivering some presentation to a scientific gathering. A most recent one at that. Looking across the coffee table now at the man in the flesh, Sienna was struck at the difference in the scientist's appearance. He saw only too clearly for himself the enormous change in the man's youthfulness and vigour. More so when in contrast with the shocking images of his recent illness. Sienna began to understand they are dealing with something special.

'Father, you're staying for dinner but first, some refreshments Tea, Coffee, or something stronger. Claudine teased with a disarming smile.

"We'll both go with Tea! Dear sister.". Then the senior cleric looked at Du Pont for a few seconds and turning slightly serious.

"How are you, my friend? You have been through much. He said delicately. Adding, "Perhaps, too much for a mere mortal to understand"

Du Pont remained impassive his face betraying little gauging the senior Jesuit. Leaning forward, he gave his brother-in-law a side-glance then locking eyes with the other man

'I've seen enough Brother Sienna"...

...Enough to rewrite all that was ever written in science, or all of the sacred scripts etched into stone." He whispered.

The Jesuit just stared back for a few seconds and saw only radiance in the eyes of the other. Here was a man who, by all accounts had given up any notion of divinity or existence of a supreme being, now stared back at him with utter conviction. A conviction brought about through some internal personal crises of enormous proportions despite the outward calmness, the Jesuit likened the physicist to someone who had undergone some deep experience and was still in the midst of coming to terms with its reality. There was something else he detected, but couldn't pin down. He hunted for an answer in the expression facing him across the small coffee table. Tea came, and Claudine quietly played host for a few moments. The Jesuit sensed her inner strength also and knew enough of her brother's character to see this strength ran through his sister also.

"Did you study science or physics also, like your husband, Claudine? He asked, sipping his tea.

"No! That was all too boring, Alphonse. I did Political Science for my sins. She laughed. "And enjoyed it! Thought about going into Journalism, but Fletcher got in the way!" She smirked.

That set the tone into a lighter vain and the conversation flowed easily for a few minutes. On first impressions, Claudine took to the senior Jesuit and liked what she saw. She felt great dedication and devotion. Her intuition spoke of a man of great conscience of spiritual depth, and also great warmth. She readily understood the closeness with her brother, both fellow travellers, both warriors to an ancient cause and yet, she knew enough to know when it was time, so she stood.

"Well if you gentlemen would like some privacy, would you like to…

"Yes, of course, Claudine!

"Father's, this way. Du Pont said standing.

Deveraux's Study.

If he could imagine himself standing in the corner listening to himself as some detached party he could see how incredulous his position looked to those of his immediate peers.

Paul Melrose was only concerned with two people in the room whose opinions would sway the others, Felix Deveraux himself, and Carina Ambrosiana. He also knew something else. Despite some ambivalence towards religious issues amongst most of them they had one thing in common, rational minds and logical thinkers. The mysterious unsettling events following Euclid lead each of them into scientific cul-de-sacs. Nothing made sense. None could unravel a string of absurd inconsistencies that followed one after the other. Occurrences that fell outside any remit they possessed, or along any plausible scientific dictum.

Like random pieces of an unknown puzzle, each event left them bereft from forming any coherent explanation, until now.

"Remember people, Fletcher was convinced that lurking in the depths of some of our collisions was what he called receptor particles. Exotic entities that possessed a unique hidden quality ...a frequency to detect human thoughts..." He stopped for a moment to let them absorb the very concept.

"We all recall how convinced he was it could show up in Beta 8 in fact, he almost willed it to make an appearance. Our detectors were specifically primed along with new super sensitive algorithms to detect and mark its presence."

Each of them gave Melrose a look of distain.

'He was intensely driven at this stage, and as you all know by now, troubled with this Shroud image as well"

Lowering his voice he made eye contact with each of them.

"Well, what if, this exotic receptor particle detects intense human thought, and somehow, through some yet unknown process, responded! We were all shocked with the Shroud image and its sudden appearance, I know you were Carina, but my friends, brace yourselves. Brace yourselves for what's to come. Fletcher, when you meet with him carries insights that make sense, right down to the markings in the beam tunnel, even some of my strange calculations.

"Are you certain Paul, that there is nothing here, which hints or suggests... Deveraux paused for a second.

"Delusion! Fletcher has fallen into some..."

"Certainly not DG! He's in peak almost unnatural physical condition, and intellectually he's as sharp, if not sharper than I've ever seen him".

Everyone seemed relieved although the thought of some emotional issue did cross some of their minds the more they heard. This took getting used to and no one was prepared to argue against Melrose's logic. It even brought some comfort when they relived through the astounding experience of time dilation recently.

"What's this New Direction? Asked a worried Manfred Gruess.

This proved difficult for Melrose. He was torn between the pure conviction of his boss and his human weakness of uncertainty and doubt. Du Pont had suggested he only go so far and leave the rest to him when he joined them at a later stage. He continued.

"Somewhere within this intersection where pure physics and metaphysics coalesce, certain truths, certain facets of atomic structures and physics were exposed in a manner that renders nuclear processes to be...halted. Some more primeval law, more fundamental beyond anything we're aware of ...is harnessed.

He paused for a further few seconds, already startled expressions became apparent. The air in the room almost suffocates. Carina Ambrosiana expression was one of dismay.

"To what end? Gasped Manfred Gruess, not sure what he was hearing.

"To disrupt the fission process chain-reaction, Manfred. To stop it in its tracks. In effect to render all Nuclear Detonations useless. Impossible! No more functioning Nuclear Weapons! That's what he means".

Sal Madere

Du Pont sat opposite both Jesuits at the dining room table. The room was such that the sunset cast long shafts of elongated light through the large garden windows. At different locations about the room arrays of flowers gave the room a tranquil perfumed scented ambiance. Alphonse Sienna sat directly opposite Du Pont placing a leather-bound notepad in front of him. Then meticulously he positioned some sharpened pencils to one side. The next act surprised the scientist. The senior Jesuit placed a small recorder on the table halfway between him and the physicist.
"Do you mind Professor? It's the only piece of formality that happens here. He said

'Not at all Alphonse. I would deem it essential".

The Jesuit leaned back hoping this to be as informal and relaxed as possible. Francois sat slightly to the left. He brought his cup of tea with him.

"Where would you like to begin, Professor? Sienna asked gently. Du Pont sat forward and clasped his hands together as if he had given this moment an inordinate amount of time to think how he would describe and explain the most surreal experience any human being could endure.

He glanced down the table at his brother in law. As he did the Senior Jesuit leaned quietly pressed the recorder button.

"Father Sienna, Francois... I never accepted the existence, the supremacy, or need for a Supreme Being or God. It was to my mind, pure mythology, utter fantasy, and a means to control and dominate human intellect. A subjugation of minds and spirit to subvert simple people and rule over and determine what they believed in. Landlordism of the mind if you will".

The tape ran silently.

"I am, to the very depths of my soul never been so wrong…so completely flawed in my thinking and my shame. There were profound reasons why I say this. It's imperative that I must extend this gift. A gift from someone I encountered, that quite simply mesmerized me and dazzled my mind and my soul'. He hesitated.

Both Jesuits listened and watched with rapt attention. For the next few hours into the early evening, Du Pont used all in his power to describe moving into a realm of paradise, a place in some other realms he never knew existed, or populated by forms of mystical creatures that defied normal descriptions. Places of infinite beauty and entities of great nobility, and love of all living things.

"Entities? The Jesuit probed replacing tapes.

"Could you ascertain if these manifestations represented good or evil?

The physicist started to sway slightly back and forth, recalling images that were vivid and real. Some leaped out from his imagination.

"I was shown, both aspects. I was brought to see and understand how different both realms were. I was shown Kingdoms, Dominions of existence of unimaginable indescribable beauty. Creatures of power, great love with endearing concern for all mankind, and then…. The horror of hell, the Abyss, populated by numbers beyond counting, amidst creatures of great horror and deformation."

His voice became agitated

"Then, there was…the carpenter. My friend, I only knew him as, Yeshua. Yeshua Ben Yoseph!

Sienna's expression froze and looked hard across the table at the scientist.

"What charm and generosity, and they turned on him, tortured him, brutalized him, beat him until I could hardly recognize his face. His voice trembled.

"I could do nothing. Nothing, helpless to stop the psychopathic cruelty they visited on him. Debased demons reigning free over the mob and the soldiers using them to inflict…"

Du Pont fought to control his voice, his body started trembling. Francois moved swiftly to his feet and came around the table. He fought to stop Du Pont's body from shaking. The senior Jesuit looked across, his face drained of colour while his fellow priest held his sobbing brother in law in his arms. The dining room burst open and Claudine came through followed by both daughters. All stand back as Francois cradled his brother-in-law holding him and allowing the trembling scientist a moment to regain his composure

"It's Ok. It's so Ok, Fletcher! He whispered. He nodded to Claudine.

"He is very real to us also Fletcher, Yeshua is real to all of us."

Du Pont looked up, tears streaming down his face

"Yes, I understand that now. But you didn't meet him, to listen to his voice, the manner of his speech. He became my friend, and they mutilated him, Francois. They beat him until…Oh, God!

His body shook uncontrollably as he tried to contain feelings completely consumed with guilt. Everyone stood helpless not knowing how best to respond despite hearing enough that sent a chill through each of them. At once, Alphonse Sienna instantly knew what it was that he missed earlier... dislocation. The man across the table was experiencing a profound sense of separation, he belonged elsewhere and had yet to detach himself from something or persona, that was responsible for a seismic shift taking place inside. The physicist final gathered himself and took some handkerchiefs from Claudine.

"Do you wish to leave this Fletcher, for another time perhaps? Father Sienna asked

"No, I'm sorry everyone, everything is still so real, so vivid. I'll be fine. Remembering then, a voice deep inside his soul, *be strong have belief!*

"I'll be fine. Let's keep going!

CHAPTER TWENTY-FOUR

Over the following days, most of Switzerland basked in temperature in the high twenties as a high-pressure system settled over central Europe bringing record temperatures. Geneva sweltered in heat as warm air currents swept down from the Jura's bringing unusually dry winds that delivered long sunshine days. Tourists swamped the capital many eventually finding relief from the dry heat by gravitating to the shores of Lac Lamon with onshore cooler air. Out in the surrounding countryside and on higher ground cyclists and hill walkers crisscrossed the Swiss landscape in their thousands, finding and discovering vantage points to enjoy all that the country had to offer.

The residence of Sal Madere nestled high on the slopes evolved into a kind of sanctuary, a refuge from the outside world. While most of the family went about what might be termed normal activity with an impending birth on the horizon, the physicist himself shunned all outside activity instead hunkered down in their dining room with two members of the Jesuit order. For over two days, and breaking only at night with some sparse moments to eat, they ploughed on. Over five notepads were filled with descriptions that were truly monumental in all aspects of religious thought, matters of doctrine, and most profoundly the teachings from a source that impacted on Christian and other faiths.

"You describe, Fletcher the manifestation of spirits ...incarnated in all substances, including matter. How did that occur? Francois Burgoyne continued.

Both Jesuits very sensitively took it in turns to probe certain aspects of the revelations that were starting to emerge even at the risk of breaking the Scientist staggering descriptions and concentration. Du Pont remained prodigious and relentless with details in his explanations, leaving nothing out.

"The physical nature of creation fulfilled a divine plan. It exists as a pathway for upward perfection by all souls from the depths... It accommodates laws in accordance with divine will which ordains all matter was a dwelling place for souls incorporated and manifested as matter."

And so it went on. Step-by-step Du Pont spoke, sometimes almost reliving each moment. The first encounter with demons, their taunting demented cackles, the arrival of Archangels, their form, and the ability to communicate in thought. They're rendering and use of supernatural power. As he spoke, miniature tapes that rolled silently soaking in every aspect and its astounding truths captured every word. When Du Pont came to how time itself progressed or halted, he painted a picture of seamless transitions from the birth of creation itself, to standing in his own garden. How the concept of Time morphed into something more sublime beyond human reasoning. How he saw the nature of his reality change and his visions of heavenly realms. Both Jesuits occasionally looked towards each other becoming more convinced that no actor or impressionist could construct the images conveyed. The richness of the descriptions made each of them make the sign-of-the cross while they listened. Du Pont pushed on, his telling was eloquent, his depictions riveting and yet disturbing as he painted his first encounter of a desperate and desolate Nazarene in the Judean wilderness. The cave, and that of a hand that reached out of the darkness. A suffering nomad, alone with immense mental anguish.

In gripping detail, he detailed how his experiences were orchestrated by the arrival by a creature know to him as Etaanus and then...the Nazarene himself. What began to impress both clerics was the manner Du Pont a man without any religious conviction spoke in measured terms with his descriptions. He seemed changed and became the embodiment of a profoundly spiritual nature. The more it progressed the senior Jesuit felt he was witnessing the very essence of 'undeniable fact'.

He raised his hand gently.

"Fletcher, this next part of your whole spiritual experience is of extreme importance. Can you tell us, how you encountered, and how you knew you were dealing with Jesus of Nazareth himself?"

The scientist considered several ways he might answer such a question. He looked about his mind recalling the nature and personality of the carpenter from Nazareth.

"An overwhelming certainty of being in the presence of authority. His face, the gaze that saw right through you. When the Archangels appeared, every one of them paused in his presence, subservient, obedient and with great reference towards him... "

"Etaanus! The Seraphim, known as the keeper of the Book of Seals.

He explained things to me that were extremely metaphysical in nature. Laws ordained in Heaven, laws steeped in wisdom that suggested that all incarnated spirits lose their identity and recollection of their previous existence once they cross that boundary of incarnation. Such was the risk of Redemption, and the enormity of risk confronting the redeemer and his task"

The process was beginning to drain him. Not only did he recall all he knew, but he also relived them as well. His voice sometimes changing as his account of things went swiftly for one vivid set of experiences to another, no pauses, but rapid as if in his mind he slipped back in time and began to relive each encounter.

"The Entire fabric of Time with Space was remoulded like a canvas as if infinity became interwoven all around me. After the period in the wilderness, he became rejuvenated, and began to manifest new powers, these grew in stature each time he overcame personal demons, temptations, battles of human weaknesses. His demons grew vicious, once causing his speech to fail and struck him with a stammer to halt his dialogue with me. His human nature was tested and only as he overcame each of them, his gifts and power grew. He commanded things, by sheer will. My moments with him had no time aspect he merely wielded an immense control over the very elements of nature and brought me to places that came to us...He rendered these truths, through powerful imagery, extensions of his intellect.

"Time was presented to me like a stream, which split into more elemental fabrics of reality that only a Being of unlimited power could have done. I was in no doubt ...I was in the presence of an omniscient creature And for all of that, he befriended me, took me in, and shared with me his secrets". His voice faltered and softened.

"Francois, there was one horrific image that haunts me...The carnage of his injuries brought about by depraved mindless actions. Actions whipped up by demons, legions of them took possession of everything in sight, turning crowds of simple people, into blood-thirsty mobs, driving the Roman legions into depraved animals unleashing unspeakable acts of humiliation and cruelty on this single human. These creatures of the dark harnessed everything at their disposal to break this messiah in half. It was only in those final hours did the powers of hell realize what was at stake. Every human agent was usurped to crush this lone Nazarene. If Redemption was to be successful, only then could this lone warrior from Heaven after his mortal death, descend into hell and forced its compliance to God's terms. He spoke of these things to me he described things, no one, only Yeshua Ben Yoseph, Jesus of Nazareth could have seen… There was a moment…when I saw… his bloodied crushed face in vivid detail. His voice faltered.

"I believe now it's why his face called out to me from my screen. It all makes sense now. Lost in its retelling he glanced across at both men. The senior Jesuit stopped writing his face filled with pain and mounting reverence towards the man across the table.

Standing at the door Claudine had silently entered and had heard everything. Her face was full of compassion, unsure what to say. Francois sat his face in both hands imagining and following every word. Then Du Pont took a folder next to him, reaching he removed the photographs of the image of the Holy Shroud, the image that originally caused him so much grief and slid it across the table.

"This bears no resemblance, to what they inflicted on him". He whispered.

For a few moments, no one had much to add. The room fell silent, each absorbed in all they heard and staring at what was in front of them. It was 7 pm.

'Perhaps, that's enough Fletcher? Alphonse Sienna finally said.

"I agree, Alphonse, it's enough for both of us, all of us, Francois said.

Du Pont gently sighed feeling tired and needed to rest and time to himself. Reliving his moments brought back painful thoughts along with empty feelings of separation. Feelings belonging somewhere else, and not entirely part of his present surroundings. Claudine came and took his hand and held him. Both Jesuits came slowly around the table and took it in turns to embrace the scientist, none of them saying anything. It was in the gesture, expressing what each of them was unable to convey. Each deeply affected and as scriptural scholars in their own right, both men found the experience riveting and yet so touching. Neither had any further doubts.

After retiring from the dining room Du Pont climbed the curved staircase and went to the bedroom. Once inside, he immediately slumped onto his bed.

Inside in the dining room, both men of the church sat alone each wrapped in their most private thoughts. It was getting late and the evening was drawing in. The skies to the west were a vibrant pinkly crimson colour with hardly any breeze. The heat of the day lingered giving the evening air a laden feel to it as if the very elements of nature kept a hushed and tranquil vigil over the residence. Inside the room, its own atmosphere was filled with hushed reverence. To Father Sienna's right, a stack of personal notations, transcripts piled high of much of what was spoken. Four small cassette tapes sat on a neat pile and sitting taking centre stage of the table, a square piece of clothe canvas of timeless and unimaginable value. In the presence of such an object and all it represented in Christianity, both men recited in unison the Lord's prayer, one of them in English, the other to himself in Aramaic.

Some minutes passed allowing each man to recover while keeping personal emotions intact. Both in the grip of utter shock as they gazed at the face that stared back at them, with the hint of residue scars across the top of the forehead. The haunting facial image of a resurrected enigmatic Nazarene gazed at them across the epochs of time, almost taunting them with questioning eyes. *Where are my truths, I bequeath to you.?*

There was some further private prayer as both men of faith reflected on everything they've heard and witnessed. Finally, the senior cleric rose and moved to his friend. "It's time Francois and it's late in the evening." Sienna said

"I will say my farewells to your family. We have weighty matters to consider too" The other man looked at him.

"Tell me, Alphonse! Tell me as a friend and fellow priest. Do you no longer have doubts?

The Father Provincial hesitated. "No, my old friend. None. I believe it all. God help me"!

Then the Father Provincial went and thanked Claudine for their kindness. 'You and your family enjoy God's blessings. He said taking her hand.

'Thank you, Alphonse. Safe journey to you." Claudine smiled.

Both Jesuits walked to the awaiting car.

"You must prepare him for what's to come my brother". Sienna said

"Yes, I know. But he is ready, you know that! Francois replied.

"I go to Rome in the next few days my friend, if there are any other matters call me! Sienna turned and got into the taxi, and within seconds was out and through the gates heading into night and uncertainty.

Ω

Two days later.

'What do you mean, they can't be sure! Claudine Du Pont asked with disbelief.

Both her Daughters had returned from Geneva late in the evening, having spent much of the afternoon with Doctor Mochti and Denise's Obstetrician. She was drained more from lack of fresh air and the heat of the afternoon, and her size was making it hard for her to settle.

"They just don't know, or are not certain Mum!" She says throwing her hands in the air. Michelle moved next to her sister, with a coffee, equally confused.

Seriously, Mum they really seemed a bit confused despite having the scans and all manner of tests. She blurted.

"Everything is going OK, though? Claudine asked

"Yes, things are fine. They also confirmed a date. Claudine smiled.

'Go on! When are we going to have our first grandchild?

"Six weeks, the 20th, give or take! Denise said

"I see. How is Paul? Is he ready for this? Claudine asked reaching for her coffee?

"Yep! Has been busy changing the apartment, buying all sorts of trinkets to give the place a cosy baby-friendly look. Then turning serious she looked at her mother.

"How is Dad? Did things go well here the other day?

"Look, girls, over the coming weeks there are going to be things that will impact on our lives that we need to be prepared for. Good things, and potentially life-changing. I want us to be...ready. We are going to have a new addition to the family, and your father may make certain decisions that might be.... a little different than what we might expect. She said.

"Like what Mum? Michelle asked

"Outside attention, Mon Cheri, a voice broke in from behind them. It was Francois. He moved away from the doorway.

"Like your mother said, my children, let's just be prepared.

She gave her uncle a fixed stare.

"Francois is Dad going to be OK, Is he going to be normal?

They couldn't miss noticing how aged their uncle looked, and how recent revelations had gripped him taking him hostage. He'd taken to keeping to himself in the last few days, fighting with the inner struggle that seems to have gripped him deeply. He looked like someone locked in a titanic battle between long-held beliefs and the emergence of something different. He gave his youngest niece a quizzical look because her simple question went straight to the heart of his inner turmoil. How did revealed truths impose themselves on mere mortals? How would one respond once the power of conviction had asserted itself as it had now with his beloved brother-in-law?

Where does one begin? Truths bring burdens, and if history was anything to go by, those that brought new light or wisdom to fellow humans suffered greatly at the hands of those that felt threatened by such truths. He had only to look deep into his church's history. Heralds bringing Christ teachings to darkened minds found themselves persecuted and subjected to remorseless suffering at the hands of their fellow man. In this different age, the tools employed would be different, but no less brutal. How would certain groups respond to what his brother-in-law now knew? Truly tectonic forces would be unleashed when confronted with some of the secrets he and his fellow Jesuit had heard and understood in the last number of days. Teachings of the true Christ revealed in a manner of blinding clarity, confronted articles of faith, and posed new dictums on science. Our puny human intellects would convulse in the face of these revelations. Could he continue to live and devote his life as a priest, when theologies of his church were at odds with theologies of truth? He studied his young niece.

"Your father will always be the man you hold dearly and love. He is a good man he is the best of us. He is also a special man. Who for reasons that we're not privileged to know have been exposed, or subjected to miraculous events of unimaginable significance. This brings with it, blessings, the nature I'm not sure of, but I believe he is under Gods protective hand and has been gifted with a vision of things that defy our comprehensions...so we must expect that he will express what he has seen in a manner of his choosing. He said soulfully.

Claudine looked at her daughters knowing that whatever transpired in the coming weeks ahead, they'd handle it. After all, it couldn't get much worse than the last number of weeks.

"Right now, we focus on our new family arrival, and make things as comfortable and organized for Mum to be. She smiled, standing and stretching her arms.

" Now if it's OK with you all, I'm heading to my bed".

Later, that night a little after midnight, a phone call ended between two senior men of the Jesuit order. Father Alphonse Sienna SJ relayed a shortened version of events to his Father Superior, Dominic Beitel in Rome.

As a result, both men knew neither of them would get much sleep that night. The Father Superior simply stared at the receiver in his hand after the call ended. Slowly rising he went to his small desk in his bedroom and picked up one of two folders and opened the one with father Francois Burgoyne's name on it. After nearly twenty minutes of intense scrutiny, going over every aspect of his fellow brother Jesuit, he closed it. One of God's warriors devoted to the purity of Christian dogma, and a scholar, along with being a student of Judean Mysticism. How so apt he thought.

He reclined back in his chair and stared at the large picture hanging on the opposite wall of his bedroom, that of his Holiness Pope Leo IV.

4.20 am

She tossed and turned trying to find a position that helped her ease the ache at the small of her back. Twice when she woke, she felt the kick. The sign of life, the beginnings and stirrings of her child only this time she felt something else, a presence. Denise struggled in her bed and was about to sit up when she looked over towards the corner of the darkened room. Sitting in her favourite chair, her father sat silently keeping a vigil. She sat up.

'Pops! Are you OK? She whispered. What are you doing? Can't sleep?

He came and sat on the side of the bed.

"Seems I can get by on very little sleep. Just wanted to spend some time making sure you're coping with all of this.

Having trouble sleeping? He asked. She repositioned her pillow and then took his hand.

"So glad you're back with us Pops. So happy. Now all I want is to have your grandchild and get back to being able to lie down properly! She joked

He reached out and placed his hand gently on her forehead.

"Any wishes for a boy or girl?" He smiled,

"As a matter of fact, Paul and I asked that same question. You know what? Pops, it's something even our hos...pit."

Within a few seconds, she slipped effortlessly into a deep and peaceful sleep. The room's silence punctuated only by her steady breathing. Reaching over he pulled the covers over her shoulders then bent over and kissed her gently on her head and left the room.

The following morning the sleek silver Mercedes rolled in the gates of the residence drove and halted at the front of the house. The occupant in the back seat knew the setting well and guessed that not calling ahead wasn't a problem. He came visiting his old friend and wanted to see for himself how his colleague was recovering. Felix Deveraux, stepped out and walked casually to the front porch and pressed the bell push. Within seconds Michelle opened the door and greeted him and gave him a quick hug.

"He's in his study Professor. Has been there since a little after 6 am, I know because I saw him before I went for my run." She said.

'Coffee Felix? She asked leading him to the study. "Yes thank you, Michelle I'd love some. Merci."

She pushed in the study door.

"Dad! You have a visitor, Professor Deveraux". Du Pont looked up surprised and dropped what he was reading. Both men embraced each other. Deveraux held his friend and gave him studied look over.

'My God, Fletcher it's true! You look remarkable, you're looking wonderful!"

"Thanks, Felix, I feel good, very good to be here.

Deveraux found a chair and sat. He looked at his friend finding it hard to accept the complete transformation. "How are you my friend, how have you been keeping?

The American looked at his fellow scientist for a few seconds guessing this wasn't entirely a social visit. He guessed the encounter with, Paul Melrose some days earlier may have caused some concerns:- so, the visit wasn't entirely unexpected.

As the head of CERN settled, he noticed his colleague's desk was littered with notes and most of them of a technical nature. All of them handwritten, and in the unmistakable hand of his fellow physicist. Handwriting he knew well.

"You're meant to be in recovery. What's all this? He joked, reaching down and picking up some of the notes and placing them on an adjacent chair.

One glance at a single page caught his attention and drew him into the detail. Deveraux's nonchalant expression turned to deliberate focus, his brain quickly absorb just enough to cause him to shift his gaze back to the American. Then Deveraux noticed copies of American publication Foreign Affairs sitting on the desk. Few of them are opened with sections full of coloured highlights on leading articles dealing with the proliferation of weapons of mass destruction. Du Pont matched his gaze except the friendly eyes had turned cold with intent and purpose.

"Fletcher, talk to me. Where are you going with this? Deveraux asked quietly.

"Is this the new direction this Nuclear... Paul spoke of? The door opened and coffee for two was left on a table. Michelle smiled

"Enjoy! And left them to themselves.

For the next three hours, both men lent over pages and pages of notes. At one stage, both of them were on all fours looking and dealing with equations that nearly peeled off the pages implanting themselves inside their minds.

Fission chain-reactions, composed of complex phase changes in nuclear processes had both men locked in mental combat, not with each other, but with more fundamental and deeper laws governing physics. Equally, Du Pont's handwritten notes contained other laws that transcended any known features of atomic physics. Notations of unknown origins, that were sublime yet laced with new surrogate values outside the boundaries of known physics. Deveraux's eyes slowly turned towards his colleague. At one stage Claudine stuck her head in to check, to find both men sitting silently pondering the implications of what lay scattered around them. Spread over a small table a series of scribbles written on parchment from another time, written down, and scribed while swaying in a boat in the Sea of Galilee. It was there:- those mystical symbols conveyed and replicated in the vision and expressed into known critical components. Deveraux stood and began to pace, trying to think who within CERN had worked on Nuclear Programme's before joining his organization. Someone better equipped to understand how these new elements could be harnessed.

It was obvious to him there were aspects of weapons design that was beyond them. They would need others. Yet, the prize was so compelling, too awesome to ignore or to dismiss. An ability to render all nuclear weapons incapable of inflicting their massive destruction force on mankind was spellbinding as it was imperative. Both atomic forces, the strong and weak forces ordained how all matter behaved permitting the conversion of these fundamental forces into weapons. To his way of thinking this was a subversion of nature itself. Yet, everything was bound up in the most seductive of all equations in modern science, $E=MC_2$ the complete inter-changeability between mass and energy, the twin sisters. That violent release within the detonation process imposed by instantly causing the mass of plutonium to surrender its entire mass into a pulse of energy expressed with such destructive consequences. Some would argue that such items were morally neutral. Such weapons could save the planet from Earth-crossing devastating asteroids, on the other hand, be used offensively to attack nations. Good and bad outcomes from the same source. Du Pont still poring over the parchment glanced at his colleague,

"Do you see how this plays out in U235? It prevents absorbing neutrons, no cascade of energy" He whispered.

The other physicist finally raised his hand. He needed to think for a moment to consider the full impact of what was contained in the symbols and notations scattered around them. There was the science, and science had its own theology but there were other dimensions. Human morality for one, as well as political dynamics and the equilibrium of power itself. Nuclear power. Many argued its presence guaranteed an unholy peace across the planet. Its menace lay in its utter destructive nature if unleashed on mankind.

'Fletcher! What do you think we can do with this? This is momentous!

"We share it! Du Pont shot back. "We sear it deep into the minds of the Superpowers. We create a shield! We employ physics, our kind of physics to neutralize the process going critical. A Shroud, Felix! We design the means, a Shroud that encircles our precious planet. A simple, but potent message.

'No power on Earth holds humanity hostage to this dreadful legacy. We roll back that dice that started in 1945 in New Mexico! He whispered.

CERN's Computing Centre

Her office sat on the third floor of a tall glass concrete building, an imposing structure within the Meyrin complex of CERN. It was late on a Saturday afternoon. Monika Reinhardt slaved over the finishing pieces of an algorithm that worked like a sieve; only its purpose was refined and honed like a razor. A hunter algorithm. The culmination of work over the last few weeks ever since Euclid beta 8 spewed its vast volumes of collision data.

In computing speed terms, one single Tera flop represented 1trillion floating-point operations each second. She was overseeing speeds over 24 Teraflops of data output. Bringing her formidable computing skill to dissect and harvest billions of ghost's particle decays, she was hunting for something that appeared like a shadowy ghost some weeks ago. An unknown. Something she had primed her algorithms to detect and pinpoint within a billionth of a second, and with two large Cray machines at her disposal, she finally believed she had narrowed down her search. Like a stalker, she had corned her quarry down to a mere five million collision events. It was a little after 4.30 pm the thirty-year computer wizard had forgotten all notion of time, except she was hungry. Over twenty-two hours had elapsed since she started into her computer domain determined that this would the day she would isolate and identify this unknown exotic atomic particle. A notional idea of a particle that existed up to now only in one place, in the imagination of Professor Du Pont.

An interesting, if not highly problematic notion. The existence, almost existential in its concept, suggested a receptor particle a particle of unimaginable power imbued with an energy frequency that responded or detected human thought. Somewhere buried within the colossal maelstrom of particle annihilations it traced its magical presence, for just one billionth a second and her algorithms had noticed. Marshalling all of her powers of concentration she initiated a series of complex filters search engines to seek and direct the two powerful Cray's to yield all they knew. In some of the routines, a matter of seconds was all it took to process. Others, a matter of hours, and in this case, Monika Reinhardt thought it would be the latter.

With a single touch on her keyboard, she issued her command, then stood and headed to the canteen for some much-needed nourishment. She was gone no more than an hour before returning to her office. Instantly upon entering her study, she saw her screens were in pause mode. On one large screen, suspended and captured in the most infinitesimal moment in time, is a curved path of nuclear decay except this was different to anything she had seen before, this is no ordinary particle if it *were a particle at all*. At the deepest most fundamental level of quantum physics, particles ruled the domain until the concept of super-strings took root.

Another level of matter beyond mere particles. *Strings*. Entities that existed only in theory, a concept beyond conventional physics formulated by some of the finest minds and advanced thinkers in the world. One such thinker was Professor Fletcher Du Pont. This idea was extended to consider if these infinitesimally small units vibrated. In so doing, these strings vibrated across a whole range of frequencies of which certain frequency bands determine particle behaviour and type. Now, an even more intriguing possibility opened up. If within its frequency range it became sensitive to frequencies that emanated from humans. A Receptor, a matching of frequencies, frequencies triggered by human thought. Monika Reinhardt drummed her fingers on her keyboard. Thinking to what she and *one* other person knew. It might emerge for reasons that defied and broke all the known laws of experimental physics; it behaved like no particle ought to do. It regenerated, for the briefest of milliseconds, and then disappeared. It so doing, it bestowed something exotic into other surrounding particles, a seemingly bizarre vibration frequency. She rushed to her seat and stared at the image for a few seconds. As if in autopilot mode her fingers danced at speed across her keyboard bringing up the supporting data, beam luminosity profiles, magnetic flux levels, collision energy levels, her fingers raced across the keyboard, trapping and freezing all key event triggers that correspond to this particular event. Then in quick succession, she turned to other terminals arrayed around her desk and started bringing up new material. Something she nursed in the recesses of her mind was now been given the impetus to push and test her theory. If she were correct, it would add a definitive piece to the puzzle surrounding her colleague, Professor Du Pont. Her heart began to race as the other screens responded to her demands and new data appeared. It became a question of alignment. When he was stricken, Euclid 4 beta 8 was one hour into the beam run. If her theory was true the emergence of this most special of special particles made its mysterious appearance roughly at the same moment Du Pont experienced his attack. Was there a connection? More to the point did one trigger or cause the other.

Just after 6.30 pm, a restless Paul Melrose was disturbed by his phone ringing on his desk. He grabbed it with some frustration.

"Melrose! He listened for a few seconds.

"Anything for you Monika! How can I help? He asked placing his feet on the edge of his desk. Listening further he slowly brought his feet down off his desk and stood with mounting excitement. A further few seconds passed.

"Jesus! Monika, are you certain? Give me a few minutes and I'll be right over! Replacing the phone he checked the time on the wall clock pausing to think, trying to remember where he last left some note he wrote to himself. He gave it no further thought and headed down towards the Computing Centre a floor below him.

Later that evening a weary but relaxed Felix Deveraux left Sal Madere, easing himself into the back of his Mercedes. A single wave of his hand to his tall American friend standing by the driveway, and he was gone. Feeling satisfied Du Pont picked up a newspaper quietly considered the forces he was about to unleash across the political landscape of the entire planet, starting with his personal reputation and scientific capital, including those of his fellow physicists. His new physics would soon become a storm in its own right.

"Paul wants a word Pops, Michelle said handing him the phone.

Du Pont leaned back and listened. The conversation is a mixture of excitement tinged with exhilaration on the other end. News of a new previously unknown particle had made its appearance. Du Pont listened to the news for a brief few seconds.

"Have you shared this news with anyone yet Paul? He asked.

"Excellent! Then let's sleep on it. Give my best to Monika. Tell her well done! I'll see to it she gets the accreditation". Then he handed the phone to Denise.

Later after the call was finished, Paul Melrose and, Monika Reinhardt remained muted for a few seconds. Both struggled to reign-in their excitement.

"You didn't tell him! She teased.

"No, we need to be certain, Monika." He said.

Turning he studied again the frozen set of data, matching the split millisecond of the particle trace on the screen to the seconds captured on the video-cam shot of his chief. That moment when he was almost lifted off his feet, the timer had it to the nearest milli-second on the video.

There was no more doubt. The perfect synchronicity of two events. Monika Reinhardt just sat there her feet curled up under her in her chair looking utterly drained. Already half her staff had left for the day, and she was about to drag herself off to her apartment.

"You fit to drive? Need a lift? He asked.

'No need Paul. Thank you! She said, getting up and rearranging some of the cushions on the small slightly battered settee. In seconds she lay down and kicked off her books and pulled a rug over her shoulders.

"Do you mind switching off the lights, on your way out? She said yawning.

"You were great Monika. This was your day," He said.

Five minutes later, Melrose wandered out of the computing centre and headed out into the warm night air. It was just after midnight. Strolling to his Morgan the young scientist quietly opened its door and slid into the driver seat. That moment he knew nothing was going to be the same again in CERN.

Lac Laman.

Late in the afternoon a few days later he and Denise were resting. Taking a few hours off relaxed on a bench along the Rue de Grosse overlooking the lake when the first niggling pain was felt. It lasted a fleeting few seconds.

"Ouch! I felt that" She said suddenly sitting upright. Melrose jumped to feet place almost dropping his lunch all over the bench.

"What's happening? Is it? She laughed and took his hand.

"It's ok darling. It's just the beginning. Time is approaching that's all. Now finish your lunch! Nothing is going to happen today." She teased.

He quietly fished out his cell and found a number. In seconds Benjamin Mochti's answered. They spoke briefly and then thanked him and put away his phone. Sitting closer she leaned her head on his shoulders. He finally told her his news. It was a change from all the talk of babies.

"It appeared from nowhere, Denise. He said.

"You're Father and I theorized that within particle behaviour at the most fundamental element lay a type of superstring. Not really a particle at all. A string! He smiled

She gave him a quizzical look. *A String!* You're excited over a…String.

"What do you think a String does darling? It vibrates! He was almost whispering trying to contain himself.

"At the quantum level it vibrates, and like a stringed instrument it produces a note, only it's not a musical note. It gets more interesting my love. You can tease me and laugh all you like! What if its frequency was so delicate so sensitive, it became receptive? Denise became less amused as the notion took hold.

"Go on. It's receptive, meaning it can detect, what?

His excitement almost choked him. "Its frequency resonates in a manner that detects human thought, my love. Can you imagine! Deep in the heart of physics lies a sub-atomic entity that connects with human intelligence, our very thought processes. It connects with our brain the physics of thought, which takes place in our minds, and transmits!

"You mean like… *Telepathy?*

"Yes! Only now, we have evidence. We have the proof that elements of our physical world, our reality, can be tied in some amazing way with human thinking and imagination. It could be the start of a whole new breakthrough in neurological science! He hesitated for a few seconds and then gazed at her bump.

"Who knows my love; our next generation might witness things beyond our wildest imaginations". No sooner had he spoken, Denise's face registered shock as a bolt of pain shot through her almost choking off her words.

"Oh, God! Paul that one hurt. She blurted.

"You can't be experiencing labour!

"Oh yes, I can! She replied taking deep breaths.

"Come on, we're getting to a hospital. Now! He said sharply.

They both gingerly walked the short distance to his sports car. Once inside they waited if there was going to be further pain.

"How long was the last one, before that one? He asked

"Not very long maybe half an hour," Denise said trying to position the seat upright into a slightly reclining position. He gunned the car out onto the road and headed north.

Back at Sal Madere both Claudine and her husband finished the call from their daughter. While there was some urgency, there was no need to panic. Their daughter was much nearer hospitals if this turned into an emergency. However her instincts suggested that it might be something significant, but not urgent, but one look at her husband's face made her mind up.

By the time they left the residence, Denise and Paul were winding the Morgan round the outskirts of the city towards the hospital. It would take no more than 15 minutes to get there. Denise turned and looked over at Paul

"Receptor particles, Vibrations! Maybe our child heard you? She chuckled sarcastically.

Doctor Michael Kells was well accustomed to panic, especially those of first-time parents to be. The call was cryptic, but he could tell from Melrose's voice over the phone that things were coming along at a pace. He was happy in his conclusion as to its sex. He now had to consider his patient's condition although mildly surprised that she might deliver early. He's convinced birth was still some weeks away, but wanted to be certain, hence his advice to come straight into the hospital.

Sal Madere the scene was less frantic.

Francois sat alone in the dining room and at his request; all the blinds on the windows were closed. On the dining table, two large candles sat one at each end both of them alight. It brought an intimacy of silence and reverence to the room. He spent the night there without sleep in effect, he kept a private vigil. Sitting in the centre a simple canvas cloth lay open etched with the face of someone he devoted his entire adult life in servitude. The Jesuit had passed the time in deep prayer, sometimes in meditation and then sat opposite it and looked down on the face recalling all he had heard and seen in recent days. It would be only a matter of days, and this most sacred of objects needed to be taken to Rome where it's very existence and significance would be exploded onto the leaders of his church. Then, there was the witness himself. The one plucked innocuously from the cradle of physics, an unbeliever up to recent times in anything other the laws he unlocked either on blackboards or huge Particle Accelerators.

How could he explain any of these truths? Then there was the chilling manifestation in the garden only some nights ago, the presence of a supernatural force that almost unhinged each of them. Rising in the stillness of the room, he moved around the table constructing in his mind what lay ahead, how certain matters of Cannon law, Scriptural teachings were going to play out. While he moved he noticed some articles new to the Du Pont household. Baby things, tiny carrycot, and soft toys lay in one corner. He stooped and picked up a small soft blanket, and thought what it meant. An impending new life would soon arrive. A powerful symbolic image the birth of a newborn, bringing with it changes around its arrival akin to the birth of new truths. He wondered for a moment if it wasn't entirely coincidental. Yet remarkably he had only to recall and witness the profound changes in his brother in law, along with his personal conversion. Fletcher was in every sense a man recast and reborn. His recent experiences altered him beyond anything anyone could have imagined. Transformations like this only occurred when human beings undergo some profound and deeply moving experience. Now with only flickering candlelight filling the room, his eyes fell on the centre of the table at this canvas relic. It cast a spell over him, like a moth to a single flame and drew him in almost compelling him to look into the face etched onto the fabric of the canvas and respond to his message.

'What do you ask of me?" He whispered.

When Benjamin Mochti took the call, he made some quick alternations in his schedule and agreed to attend the clinical session, if that were agreeable with the couple in question. Ten minutes later he made his way over to the maternity wing of the hospital to where Dr. Michael Kells was meeting with Denise. When he arrived he when he heard her raised voice on the other side of the door. He pushed through and found Denise sitting upright in a surgical seat gasping in pain while the Obstetrician holding her hand taking her pulse.

'They're coming more frequently! Melrose said

'And the pain is getting more intense! Denise gasped. A midwife just arrived and was preparing to carry out an internal inspection.

"Can I help Michael? Mochti asked

Claudine pressed down on the accelerator. At this stage she knew all the short-cuts off the autobahn pushing the Saab through the country roads with ease and confidence. She memorised many of the tricky bits and knew which stretches of the road she could make up time. Her husband liked to let her drive preferring to study many of the features of the rolling countryside oblivious to her driving prowess. Geneva's outskirts began to loom in front of them, the majestic Jet d'Eau towering mist appeared in the distance. They were making decent enough time, a little uncertain if the alarm from Paul was just jittery nerves or perhaps things were happening much sooner then expected. A little after 3.15 pm they reached the hospital car park and a parking spot. Another piece of real estate in Switzerland that she was overly familiar with.

CERN- Niels Bohr Block

While events and little dramas around the Du Pont household moved towards their own inevitable outcome, circumstances elsewhere took a more calculated more measured approach for entirely different reasons. The governing Council of CERN's board convened in an emergency session in the Niels Bohr building to discuss some new proposals dealing with their recent experimental programs. Interestingly, Euclid was not listed on the agenda. Dr. Felix Deveraux and Professor Manfred Guess would preside over the session. The Council itself represented member states, twenty-five in all, who contributed to CERN's annual budget for ongoing research into high-energy physics. Today's session would be in private, a closed-door two-day event. Since 2 pm that afternoon Felix Deveraux had stood onto the podium and called the Council into session. Sealed glossy dossiers were distributed around the large conference table each marked "Sensitive and confidential".

Most if not all had some hand in seeing that Felix Deveraux was elected to the post of Director-General of the Organisation. He was in one sense beholding to them for supporting his ascent to his current role. Intuitively, he gambled on how they would respond to his proposal, to the explosive content to what lay in front of them. Smiling inwardly he reflected at the irony of both the enormous political and scientific pun with the use of the term "explosive" because that was precisely the implications before them. His gamble lay in the mix of personalities sitting around the table. Most of them were pacifists and devoted to "pure science" to fostering scientific endeavour to serve humanity. But first, Deveraux took it upon himself to set the stage to outline a new proposition. With the preliminaries out of the way, and the opening remarks completed, Deveraux flicked a small switch and a large screen dropped into position at the far end of the chamber. It dominated the entire wall.

In seconds the video fired into life, and a large image of Professor Fletcher Du Pont filled the entire screen. Recorded earlier, it showed him sitting in an immaculate navy blue suit, white shirt and sporting a silver gray tie sitting in his garden in an armchair. He looked tanned, rested, and composed. His appearance caught a few of the delegates off guard; there were vigour and energy that was new. Deveraux returned to his seat.

Du Pont's voice resonated strength and power filling the room and instantly held everyone's attention...

'Gentlemen, fellow scientists, seldom in one's lifetime does the opportunity come along that bestows greatness on people to be part of something special. Sometimes it occurs once only in a single lifetime, sometimes never. Opportunities by their very nature come to pass, not to pause, so we must grasp these special moments when they arise, and apply ourselves to whatever course or pathway opens up to us. Before you all, is a folder that deals with the physics that governs both the strong and the weak nuclear forces that ordain much that occurs in nature. It also governs how we apply these physics to the procurement of nuclear weapons.... He paused. Everyone glanced around the chamber.

'Within other disciplines, some issues confronting humanity, are not easily overcome. Issues such as Cancer that stubbornly defies our best efforts, our best minds. It's the presence of complexity over the presence and application of will. The will exists.... sadly, so is the problem. We on the other hand as physicists possess within our hands the ability, and the science to do something that rids our people of this earth, of the appalling threat of Nuclear weapons. Not, my friend's Nuclear power, but the perverse use of our physics to inflict massive destruction on populations. Within these folders we have before us, the means to disrupt how the spontaneous chain reaction in neutrons within Uranium 235.'

Everyone in the chamber sat up, intrigued what they were hearing. The source of the words on the video came from someone they all know well and held in the highest regard. This merely added to the unease that began to permeate the setting. Deveraux studied each of them as the video progressed looking to detect either alarm or dismay. The chamber began to fill with both.

"*This challenge confronting us is.... not a disease, which defies us. It's no longer, the presence of complexity that taunts us here my friends...more the absence of will. Now, if you would all open the folders, I will take you through how we can begin to change the landscape of this phase of human history...*"

Over the next two hours, Du Pont's voice filled the chamber with complete mastery of the substance dealing with the subatomic processes. Delivering with the force of his convictions he took his audience through a complex process of retracing the fission conditions of nuclear chain reactions. As he spoke his image is replaced with intricate schema, filled with detailed equations, and some new unknown variables that were new and outside the purview of some members of his audience. Each member of the council worked through the narrative, some taking notes and scribbling sidebar formulae on the side of certain pages. As they progressed through the process, some leaned back in the chairs slowly realizing what lay before them. Others remained focused, their arms folded giving little away.

When the video finished, Deveraux rose and handed the next part of the discussion over to one of his colleagues seated to his right, Dmitri Suslov. A theoretical physicist with a deep understanding of some of the newer designs in weapons technology, a passionate pacifist in his own right and one of the few present who was assigned the task of developing and engineering a frequency inhibitor. This stepped up the discussion to another level. It dealt with the means to transform the theory into a practically viable means to disrupt the magnitude of fluctuations in neutron density, a key factor within the detonation process in nuclear weapons.

A further two hours followed while the group began to give their own views and reactions to everything before them. The debate that followed became forthright. As one set of answers is offered, more probing questions erupted each with differing objectives along with some reservations. Titanic political consequences were involved, including formidable Industrial-Military forces that would shudder at the implications of what has been contemplated. Each of them recalling *"It's not the presence of complexity...it's the Absence of Will.*

As the questions flew and the debate raged well into the evening, Deveraux's thoughts receded into some of the broader challenges that lay ahead for him and CERN. From nowhere in particular, a note was passed around the chamber and finally Manfred Gruess passed him the folded sheet. He discreetly opened it, looked at the scribbled handwriting. It merely said.

"Where is Fletcher? He needs to be here!

CHAPTER TWENTY-FIVE

Hospital

For a couple about to become grandparents, they remained remarkably composed. There was no angst or worry, just impatience. They waited to see their daughter and their grandchild arrive into the world safely. Claudine and her family had seen enough of the inside of hospitals to last a lifetime. If there was one single thing she could point to that defined her husband now, was his calmness. As if reading her mind he took her hand and held it. Denise and Paul put their trust in Doctor Kells who decided to keep them in the hospital, things were moving faster than any of them expected. Baby was going to make an appearance soon.

The arrival of his first grandchild brought back a memory, the imminent assurance that life continues. His face suddenly darkened remembering a place where secrets were born. A place where certainties of human existence were scrutinized by deeper minds. An image began to intrude. DNA structures, with chromosomes spiralling into the evening light, and saw all it contained and all it represented. He recalled the face of the Nazarene and how creation functioned. This upward ladder he witnessed. A progression of spirits through the material creation was subject to truths. Truths not fully understood on earth... yet. A voice called out to him disrupting his thoughts, a voice he knew.

Standing in full gown, was Doctor Mochti.

"Professor Du Pont, it's truly so good to see you. He beamed extending his hand. "God has answered all our prayers.'

Mochti was a man who understood contradictions well. Both his training as a doctor and upbringing equipped him well to accept things as normal where others would question. He sensed the man before he had become an enigma in his own right, a man of contradictions and someone who was altered in some way.

"Fletcher this is a wonderful occasion. I'm deeply happy for you and your family". He looked to Claudine and took her hand. Madame Du Pont, a pleasure as always!

"Is there news yet, Benni Du Pont asked?

"It won't be long now! How are you, Fletcher? You seem well." He probed.

"I'm very good Benni, and truly grateful to you. For everything! He said taking the other man's hand firmly. Mochti smiled and knew this was not the time for further questions. Now, it was all about Denise, and her baby. He turned to Claudine.

"I'm also so glad for you, Claudine. This night will be very special. Goodnight to you both.' He said, then turned and quietly faded into a maelstrom of hospital life.

Nearly twenty kilometres to the west of the hospital, the lights of the Niels Bohr building shone brightly into the evening. The Governing Council was winding down its day. A day taut with mixed emotions, standing ovations as the realism of new truths were brought to light, as well as moments when deep anxieties nearly ran riot. As detailed exchanges over the ability to reign in the physics of nuclear detonations took place there were counter-arguments to the effectiveness of this new model. Many took the view that possessing the means to "disrupt" the fission process was truly spectacular, converting this new knowledge into effect carried great risks to political paradigms. Mutually Assured Destruction, while troubling in its own right, had preserved a nervous standoff of superpowers and ensured peace. During the closing part of the evening, the source and origins of the *Du Pont Conjecture* as it became known as, was raised by some members. Deveraux summoned some of his senior Directors to the chamber.

It was time! He reminded himself. The moment had arrived and this was where things were going to escalate beyond the politics of science.

It was time to share all he knew and most importantly, with what he now believed in. He governed and presided at the pleasure of these great minds sitting around him. Nervously checking those present Carina Ambrosiana, Myles Kingsley, and others of his senior council filed into the chamber. It was going to test every fibre of his being to share all that had happened in recent months leaving nothing out. It would also prepare them for the following day when they would all be reunited with Fletcher Du Pont himself. As he did, three large screens lowered from the ceiling into place so that all the council members could have unobstructed views.

"Ladies, and Gentlemen! For the next hour, I wish to show you something truly amazing as to events that have shaped and altered much of what we believe in."

A large image of the shroud of Turin flickered to life filling one of the screens. A second screen came to life within seconds it contained a large set of complex equations completed in a hospital ward sometime in the near past. The third screen took a few seconds, and then the familiar Large Hadrons Collider tunnel came into view and then zoomed to a segment showing a set of scorched heat markings. The entire chamber studied the surreal images for several seconds the entire gathering fell silent.

Sal Madere 23.10 pm

Francois Burgoyne had just finished the last of his notes and reflections.

Sitting at a long wooden garden table with a small garden lamp and single candlelight providing just the right amount to finish entering his most private thoughts. Aspects of what he heard in recent days caused him to reflect in his faith and beliefs in the true teaching of Scripture. A mystical event had reached out and touched their lives dispelling any doubts that humanity was entering a new phase of enlightenment. The presence in this garden of a spirit of great nobility from Heaven had come calling with a startling revelation. Abruptly, the house phone rang out breaking his thoughts. On reflex he broke the spell of his inner thoughts and was on his feet and got to the phone.

It was Michelle.

Listening for a moment the voice on the other end was full of joy and great relief. He closed his eyes for a moment relishing and savouring the news. His eyes moistened with tears and relief.

"God has smiled on us tonight Michelle. Give thanks to him my dear niece. It is important to express gratitude for all things. Give my love to Denise and Paul. They're in my prayers tonight. Thank you for sharing this great joy"

He said as tears filled his eyes. Replacing the phone, he turned and walked back to the garden and sat at the table. Reaching over he turned off the garden lamp leaving the burning candle his only light. He picked up his glass of water and gazed upwards.

"For everything, dear Father, a baby girl. My new young grandniece"

Day-2 Niels Bohr building

At precisely 11.0am the chamber filled with entire the council well in advance of the start of the second and final day. Each of the delegates sat in their seats the mood had shifted. Men and women devoted to knowledge, pure science, and the source of un-distilled truths were rocked by what they now knew. A good many didn't or couldn't sleep well. A respectful, almost reverential atmosphere quickly took hold as they anticipated the presence later in the day from one of their own. Today, the focus would be on intent. How would CERN as an organization with its pioneering pedigree in high-energy physics extend its reputation?

To throw down the intellectual gauntlet and confront the menace of nuclear weaponry. Felix Deveraux kept to himself that morning shunning all contact with Council members. He preferred to stay in his office until the council was about to sit. In the chair by agreement and selection were the delegate from the United Kingdom, Professor Jonathan Spencer-Jones, a visiting professor from Harwell, the former UK's atomic research establishment. Deveraux would take a back seat role in the day's proceedings particularly in how the politics would be handled and how it would be promoted internationally. Professor Jones stood and adjusted his microphone, called the session to order.

"My friends, colleagues, and Fellow scientists...we have some significant decisions to make here today. Yesterday was an extraordinary day for all of us."

For the next two hours, the Englishman confronted all the issues with a blend of directness and delicacy the occasion demanded. Scientific imperatives, political expediency, or for some, divine guidance, for many, the evidence was enough. The Du Pont Conjecture is immensely persuasive. Vision and leadership would determine much what was to follow. Little did any in the chamber know, that the scientific pearl of wisdom was only the beginning? Theirs was just one part of a tapestry of things to come.

'Knowledge has been thrust upon us, my friends. Knowledge not of our choosing ...but verifiable and viable means to end the madness of such terrible weapons. As a scientist, and as a human being the absence of a will, is not an option for us," Jones continued.

On one of the screens a new technical schema slowly appeared, it was the first of one large diagram, broken into three large sections each part showing up in the other individual screens around the chamber. As they did, the lights dimmed plunging the entire chamber into a muted semi-darkened setting.

"...Before you are the blueprints the theoretical framework, and a configuration matrix that underwrites the design of a powerful frequency inhibitor. The first of its kind, and like nothing we've ever imagined could be constructed. It will resonate at frequencies we didn't know exist and can alter atomic structures. It will take over four years to develop, and cost just over €20.0 billion to create a functioning prototype version. To deploy! ...Well, my friends, we're talking in terms of a platform with truly international dimensions. Blanket coverage of the entire planet, we talking in term in excess of $300billion over a further three to ten-year horizon. Satellite-based primarily, complimented by land-based systems, positioned globally and located throughout all the main continents. Strategically in high altitude locations. Alpine peaks, Himalayan's, McKinley, in North America, Vinson Massif, in Antarctica. A Frequency Shroud enveloping our entire plant disrupting all nuclear fission processes on earth. The silence in the chamber was deathly.

Everyone studied the three images of a device, whose design and construct was almost biblical. At that moment an intimate sense of destiny descended on the chamber and those present felt they are summoned to become the tipping point. Evangelists empowered to neuter a lethal and destructive process. Named after the brilliant Danish physicist who first formalized the abstract equations between the electron and radioactivity, now became a staging point behind a radical idea.

Before he made plans to leave for the conference. Fletcher Du Pont beamed from ear to ear as he cradled his first granddaughter in his arms. Glancing towards his tired and drained daughter, he paced back and forth in the maternity ward proud and completely overjoyed. Claudine sat by the bed teasing her husband to take great care with the fragile new bundle.

"She has your eyes, Claudine! He joked. Sitting equally elated and overcome with emotion was Paul Melrose. He was short for words and simply beyond joy.

"Well done to you both. You have a beautiful daughter. We're so proud of you. Du Pont said admiringly to both mother and father. Michelle moved in and anxiously took their newest family and cradled her.

'Come on Pops she has your ears" Du Pont came to the bed, leaned over, and kissed his eldest. Then, turning he took Paul in his arms.

"Now the fun begins! Speaking from experience, young man your life only gets better from here". He smiled.

Wearing an immaculate silver gray 3-piece suit, he prepared for what was about to begin. He reached his cell and punched a number.

In the hushed garden of Sal Madere his brother-in-law picked up and answered. "Francois, will you stay for a few more days with us. It's important to the family you're present. You've been a pillar to this family and I need you now and for what's to come. You understand what I'm saying?

He replaced the cell in his pocket.

How does it feel, Pops? You're officially a Grandfather! Denise teased.

"Beyond words sweetheart. She is just a marvellous gift".

"Angelina! We're naming her, Angelina Claudine.

Melrose added with a smile. Claudine took the baby carefully from her husband and kissed Angelina on the head.

"Hello, young Angelina! I'm Grandma, She said in a hushed tone.

"Isn't time you were somewhere else? She said kissing her husband on the cheek

'Yes, of course! It's time" He replied.

He moved towards the door. Turning, he found them all looking at him with unspoken admiration. He winked at them. They noticed yet again that aura, a charisma that's now part of him.

"Knock 'em dead Dad! Michelle smiled

"Angelina Claudine! What happens next, is for you! He grinned.

CERN.

Inside the Council chamber, the time for a decision is approaching. It would be a vote each member allowed one vote, no abstentions was permitted, but there would three rounds of voting. If there were dissenting opinions, a second and third round would follow. Felix Deveraux was beginning to fret looking around searching for signs from his team if his colleague was near. Time was just after 16.00 hours and the vote was scheduled to take place at 17.00 hours. His cell buzzed in front of him. It was a brief text' *Outside, and Ready.*

Deveraux caught Spencer Jones's eye, and then nodded. The Englishman tapped his microphone and got everyone's attention.

"Council members!" Would you so kindly and stand and welcome back, our esteemed friend and colleague Professor Du Pont. The chamber doors opened and Du Pont entered the chamber and ambled toward the podium, as he does he was met with spontaneous rapturous applause amid a standing ovation as all the delegates rose and clapped his return. Some leave their seats and go to him. In seconds, formalities were ignored as fellow scientists surround the tall American. Some took his hand and rather shaking it, held it with both hands and bowed slightly as if greeting a member of royalty. They gathered around him, sharing and displaying more than scientific admiration, but also expressing long-standing genuine affection towards one of their distinguished brethren. It took nearly ten minutes to restore some semblance of order as each council member made it their business to exchange some personal greetings with the scientist.

'You ready for this, my friend? Deveraux asked quietly

"Yes, my friend. More than ready."

Finally, when all had returned to their seats, Professor Spencer Jones rose and commenced making a summarized presentation of everything, including the now called Du Pont Conjecture that took place to date. Rapidly and with great efficiency he covered how the council handled the pure physics and made certain recommendations. Then he quickly moved on to the deployment challenges facing them, as well as the enormous political forces that would be marshalled against them. Throughout it all, Du Pont sat motionless barely nodding to everything he heard. More than a few meters from each council member some of them stare at him completely taken at his appearance. Then a single voice cried out from the group.

"Let's hear what Fletcher has to say.!

Eventually, Du Pont got to his feet and cast his eyes around the chamber finally fixing his gaze to the far corner to where Felix Deveraux sat. He selected his opening remarks carefully aware of the enormity of the subject matter itself, controlling his pitch and tone his delivery became more clinical and measured. The words flowed easy, words filled with authority and his audience responded. The chamber turned electric as they started to feel the energy of his voice, its timbre held them listening to each word. For over an hour without notes, he summarized how the fission and neutron phases could be restructured during certain transitions. Then with evangelical precision, he explored the creation and instant pulse of instability within the chain reaction process. This became the mass of plutonium going super-critical induced scattering of neutrons disrupting the conditions at the atomic level for the detonation to go Nuclear. As he did, he failed to notice his recollection of the new physics revealed to him in his former abode went over many of the heads in the room. As he proceeded he touched on physics of a more obscure nature, physics that went beyond the understandings of most in the room. Physics of a higher order, abstract concepts dealing with fields of energy and power, unknown to this generation of physicists sitting around him.

One by one, they started to glance at each other, while following his delivery including his references and logic to higher-energy physics took many of them into spellbinding almost magical realms of science. Finally, and nervously, one of them slowly stood up from his seat and looked at the American. It was the council member from Israel. He raised his hand to catch Du Pont's eye.

"Fletcher! Fletcher. What is this? Then another delegate stood. Du Pont halted.

An awkward almost embarrassing silence creped into the proceedings. Du Pont turned and faced both of them, knowing what is coming next.

'Fletcher! This is profound! Breathtaking". "Where did all of this new material come from? The Israeli whispered

'This is beyond me too, Professor! This is staggering. How did you reach? "How did you fathom these new constructs? He asked.

More of them started to stand, all of them studying their colleague in the centre of the chamber with renewed intensity. Each of the groups accepted everything as a piece of inspired thinking. All the previous models were considered brilliant and inspiring, but when they listened and absorbed how this body of knowledge came about, and the intricate detail that Du Pont covered, stunned most of them. Much of the content was simply unknown to them. Du Pont raised his hands and regained everyone's attention.

"Truly remarkable my friends, more remarkable again, as to its significance. This will be our Shroud! A protective shield against anyone mad enough to try and hold humanity hostage and our grandchildren's futures. Time's up, on Nuclear Weapons!

At just a little after 6.30 pm the joint press conference assembled and settled in one of the large public auditoriums on the first floor of the main administration building.

Members of CERN governing council gathered around the central podium where Director-General Felix Deveraux stood, facing an international press gathering of over one hundred journalists. It was scheduled to begin earlier, but certain issues dictated otherwise. Deveraux tapped the microphone and called the conference to order.

"Ladies and Gentlemen, thank you for your patience. As you are aware, our business here in CERN is High Energy physics. Always has been, and will continue to do so. But today is a momentous day. A day when our work in pure physics can report a substantial breakthrough in how we understand laws that govern our world, our physical reality and provides us with a deeper and meaningful respect for mother nature herself...It gives me great joy, as a physicist, to work with some of the finest minds in particle physics here in Geneva, but also our worldwide fraternity of fellow scientists, who pursue excellence in research...and cherish life itself. This press conference is about to express how we here in CERN pursue goals, our ideals to shape our understanding of the workings of laws that define how our reality functions. This process has extended our knowledge to the use of nuclear power and energy'. He paused.

"It also grants us the power, and the obligation to harness that power properly...in the service of humanity. I would like to invite my esteemed colleague Nobel Laureate, Professor Fletcher Du Pont to address you all.

The more seasoned Journalist's sensed something big was going down and immediately got their IPADS ready. Du Pont moved easily towards the podium, members of the council reached out and patted him on the shoulders. Du Pont smiled and then gently placed both hands on the edge of the stand. He took a few seconds to take in his audience.

"Where were *you* when that crazy guy in CERN announced: No More Nuclear weapons!." That's what they will all ask in the future? He smiled with animated arms open wide.

Everyone giggled and broke out into laughter instantly took a liking to the humour by the American. Du Pont let the lightness of the moment wash over his audience for a few seconds. Then, the laughter subsided as the words *Nuclear Weapons* suddenly registered. He let the moment linger allowing everyone in the centre to settle. One of the reporters looked up from his pad.

"Isn't that the guy that had an accident here some time ago? Heart attack or something. She remarked to a colleague.

"Think so! Nothing wrong with him now! Uttered the other.

"Getting the genie back in the bottle ...is not always as easy as it sounds. Particularly when that genie, is the physics of Nuclear Weapons." Du Pont pronounced turning deadly serious. The gathering got attentive as the tall scientist began to address them. With the richness of conviction and delivery, Du Pont brought the entire media gathering, and ultimately a much larger audience on a journey. A voyage of reasoning, starting inside the nucleus of the atom, all the way through the forces contained in matter. The science blended with logic, moved flawlessly without breaks or interruptions as he took his fellow human beings over a landscape of weapons paranoia throughout the developed world. An engineering program behind a simple concept followed this. A Shroud.

An invisible blanket that surrounded all of humanity, ensuring that nuclear weapons could not function. A shroud of peace. Camera's rolls, tape recorders recorded, pens filled pads with notes. Keeping up, catching the details, some hardly believing what they are hearing. It went on, for over twenty minutes no one spoke or attempted to interrupt with questions.

Sitting in her ward, cradling her baby, Denise Du Pont watched TV with rapt attention. Next to her, Paul Melrose looked on at the explosive news breaking across the networks, with close-up shots of the face of a loved one, filled screens across multiple channels. Tears of joy and pride ran down her cheeks.

Even as his daughter, she marvelled at his skill in presentation. His very appearance, his whole personality exuded a powerful presence that lit up the TV screen. Within an hour every major global network replayed segments of the conference either in edited parts, or the entire piece. Newscasters were falling over themselves with captivating headline tag lines. Print media went into near meltdown as print runs were rescheduled to be the first to hit the streets.

END GAME for Nuclear Weapons.

Explosive Message: for Mass Destruction Arms.

MAD turns to MAS Mutually Assured Safety.

Physicists Pull Plug on WMD"

CERN Scientists uncork Super-Beam. GAME ON!

On the CERN campus itself, most of the staff gathered in the large canteen hall. The entire senior leadership of CERN along with its governing Council mingled all with either cups of coffee or various beverages. Momentum was gathering as the news cycle filtered across the globe spreading like a contagion of euphoria. Du Pont sitting on a stool surrounded by some of his team and former Director Generals of the organization. All of them watched in awe as the speed and coverage swept out from Geneva enveloping most of the major capitals of the northern hemisphere. Within twenty-four hours it would be worldwide.

Rome. The Papal Apartments.

As the excitement mounted and began to percolate across Europe, deep inside the Holy See within the Vatican City, four men in purple robes sat in front of their own TV set. Of the four, one man concentrated at the face staring out at him from the Television screen with close scrutiny. Cardinal Giuseppe Bonaire fixed on the face of a man he felt he knew too much about. Much of it troubled him deeply. Sitting next to him, the Dean Of the College of Cardinals, beside him, Secretary of State of the Roman Catholic Church, and the Prefect Emeritus of Barcelona, Cardinal Joseph Mendoza On an adjoining table sat a recorder, along with a dossier prepared for each of them by the Father Superior of the Jesuit Order of which all four present were, Cardinal Bishops and members of the Order.

With entirely different thoughts and sitting next to his sister, cradling a glass of his favourite malt, Father Francois Burgoyne watched TV as events unfold. Looking sideways at his sister he saw her attentive study to the manner the news was handled, and the banner headlines. Her mind raced. Message content and banner headlines often collide with truth. She watched as the various news agencies distilled the breaking news and altered them into something else.

"My husband has become an Evangelist. Dear God! She whispered.

Over the following twenty-four hours, the promise of Shroud-Technology gripped every capital on the planet, with a mixture of ecstatic joy, deep scepticism, and downright opposition. As the news grew, so too did the imaginations of pacifists worldwide. Religious fervour climbed to new heights as many Church leaders heralding the breakthrough as a sign from God himself. Others took refuge in reciting biblical quotes and inciting people to rise against weapons development. Over and over with hundreds of networks across the globe:- one face dominated screens, Fletcher Du Pont. Re-runs of his presentation cropped up on nearly every channel, his highly articulate charismatic persona dismantled the necessity to possess Nuclear Armoury with understated authority. Behind the image of the man, and the message itself, lay another aspect that was there for all to see if they choose to do so. A presumption. A certitude that only came when someone believed they are holding all the cards. While the events from Geneva rippled outwards like a tidal wave around the world, there were places, World Capitals, and Institutions watched with alarm and deep disquiet. From Washington, Moscow, Jerusalem, New Delhi, and others, top-level teams from scientific and military groups went into overdrive. So-called Shroud Technology left senior advisors gobsmacked at the potential implications.

Washington: "Mr. President, We have no immediate response to this one. This, if it got off the ground would almost neuter our Nuclear Capability! His Secretary of Defence gasped in exasperation.

In London: "I'm sorry Prime Minister, we didn't see this coming. This threat, or problem, is credible and authentic!

In Tel Aviv: "How serious is this for us, Jonas? The aging Prime Minister asked finally. "Catastrophic Sir. We need to take steps to acquire this new...Shroud Technology and do it soon!

While in **Kremlin,** Moscow..."Are you telling us, Comrade, here in the Politburo, that this can.? Yes, General Secretary, the capability is only a matter of time. Our entire nuclear deterrent would be rendered useless, as well as others of course.! Marshall Oleg Kunodov replied.

Within two days, a considerable number of people from around the globe got little sleep. In thousands of offices around the planet, only one name dominated screens and highly classified briefing documents. All asking the same question. *Shroud Technology. How?*

A week after going public, CERN's entire technical and publicity apparatus swung into gear, publishing its blueprint on the technology roadmap of its Shroud Blanket program along with a comprehensive invitation list to all major political power blocks to attend a global conference. Two major networks had proposed a face-to-face live interview with both Deveraux and his American Director Fletcher Du Pont. Both invitations were accepted without any restrictions on the content of the questions asked. Within days, World opinion unleashed an avalanche of questions creating an unprecedented level of public response around the globe. In its wake, political leaders found themselves confronting a new kind of paradigm shift towards nuclear arsenals globally. The Council of the United Nations responded, inviting all the major nuclear powers to a conference to discuss the proposed development of this new Shroud Shield.

Sal Madere

While the wave of publicity rippled across the networks from east to west, within the confines of Sal Madere, Du Pont used the occasion of his granddaughter's homecoming to step back from the affairs in CERN. Finding refuge and peace in the confines of Sal Madere and its garden, he was happy to leave all of the external turmoil he had unleashed to his brethren in CERN itself.

Before moving into their apartment Denise and Paul decide to spend the initial days in Sal Madere. Also, Melrose was also keen to spend time with Du Pont himself. There was a matter of significance that needed his attention.

"Fletcher, can we talk for a moment?

"Sure! You have my ears'

"We have some strong compelling evidence that detects an exotic particle event appearing within the CMS and your accident, to the nearest one billionth of a second". Could this, lay behind your mysterious experience of late?

Melrose had all theoretical skills to prove that a receptor particle existed and was a real possibility. All it might take was a high level of intensity and concentration to create the conditions to connect. Sipping his drink, Du Pont's mind read through the detail in front of him. While he did, Melrose sifted through the notes the work Monika Reinhardt completed. "It's here where theory and reality converged! He said

"So, chief...I have to ask you something?

Du Pont slowly looked up from the notes at his young assistant.

"Go on. Ask?

"Our video feed showed us what happened. We saw it all on the monitors. It was frightening Fletcher! It was very unreal and disturbing.! Was your thought-process somehow triggering the event that caused you to...?

Du Pont raised his hand.

A momentary image filled his mind. In that other place within a cave, terrified and frightened. In vivid detail,he recalled the small circle of stones with Etaanus! With a sheer act of will, a single flame ignited and burned. A power to command such things came about not in some absurd act of magic, but by the expression of will. An existential moment where physics intersects with human faith? The challenge of belief, an act of faith that mysteriously summons a connection between thought, and a physical outcome.

"I'm sorry Paul I'm not ready to discuss or talk about that"

'You sure?...I thought this was very important to you.?

'Yes, it is! But for now, it needs to stay in the box it came in. Du Pont said gently. There are things here that need to be handled with...profound caution!

"I'm not ready to move this on! Not just now". With that, he smiled at his young assistant closing the folder in front of him. Then taking the rest of the notes gathered them into a tidy pile. With great care, he reached opened a small briefcase, and placed the entire bundle inside and locked the clasp. Fixing Melrose a friendly look.

"There are other things that need to happen first, Paul. Trust me! There is a time coming quite soon, and this material will be next. The world right now is turning itself inside out with our recent revelations. Let's give the politicians some breathing space. Let them come to terms with what's confronting them right now. Our next step has nothing to do with CERN, and arguably much more daunting".

Melrose shot Du Pont a puzzled look. "What could be more daunting than what we've just?

'Here! Du Pont cut in. "Right here. This is what's next.

Placing his forefinger down on an old newspaper on his chair. Melrose picked up a slightly worn and battered newspaper. It was over four years old, but its headlines were unmistakable. *Habemus Papem! Leo 4th Election.*

Melrose stared at the pictures containing the gathering of the conclave and the election of a new Pope. He returned his gaze to his chief.

"The Vatican! Rome? He whispered.

"Yes! This was the last promise I made.

"I have to go there, Paul!

CHAPTER TWENTY-SIX

The Vatican.

The inner sanctums of the Holy See and the workings of the Roman Catholic Curia was always a place with secrets and historical intrigue. Upon a labyrinth of ancient histories and subterfuge was built an edifice of splendour and grand design. St. Peters, and the Vatican Dome dominated Rome's skyline for over 300 years casting its shadow over a once deeply pagan city.

It's early on a Wednesday morning; just after 8.15 am when the first knock on the door was heard. Cardinal Giuseppe Bonaire stood and welcomed his expected guests.

The large teak door opened, in the doorway his esteemed fellow Cardinal, Secretary of State Paulo Estazzi, smiled, and entered, followed by Cardinal Dean of The Sacred College of Cardinal Jerome Misner, and Cardinal Emeritus Prefect, Mendoza. All greet Bonaire warmly. The study itself was immaculate in taste but sparse to the trappings of the Office. A light stand in the corner was the only extravagance, along with a well-stocked bookshelf, mainly the complete works of the gospels written in over twenty languages. Tea and coffee are brought and set down on a small silver tray on a table. The Secretary of State of the Roman Catholic Church was relatively old for his position; he was 86 years old and suffered over the years with diabetes. His silver-gray eye's surveyed the world around him, like a Sheppard minding his flock, wary of anything that resembles the sound or presence of wolves.

If Francois Burgoyne, was a warrior in God's army, Cardinal Paulo Estazzi, was its Gladiator. He carried himself like an ascetic chieftain noble, with an almost uncanny ability to read people's character instantly. Seldom did his holiness, Leo the 4th meet or greet any head of state, without his Secretary Of State present. Cardinal Jerome Misner was German and in his early seventies, lean and lanky with a doctorate in Medieval History and a deeply spiritual man. As Dean of the Sacred College of Cardinals, and to many, the intellectual right hand of the current pontiff. Last, was the Prefect Emeritus Cardinal Mendoza, a Spaniard? He was born into wealth, and subsequently walked away from it when he was in his twenties. He shocked his family by leaving the family business, and fortune, to join the Jesuit order. A man who had subsequently cheated death twice in his life, leaving him the conviction that God had spared him for something greater.

"You've all listened, my brothers, and heard the tapes". The Secretary Of State said without preamble. All nodded. The senior cardinal opened the folder in front of him and took out all its contents. Pages of transcripts were opened revealing extensive colour markers and personal notations. Then there were external notes collated and chronicled from events surrounding the entire scientific environment. Hospital reports in detail, describing a series of unexplained factors. Then in a series of photographic images, were those of the scientist's condition, and his present appearance.

Finally, there is the "alleged relic" a simple cloth, canvas, which held an image. Puzzling and deeply unsettling was how an image could have been transferred onto the cloth itself. As far as matters of doctrine, this had all the hallmarks of full-blown crises. All four Cardinals had nearly six days to listen to the tapes, review the entire transcripts and form a preliminary opinion as to what they were dealing with. Adding further, were the additional personal notes and remarks from the head of their Order, Father Beitel.

"Giuseppe, my fellow brothers. Do we have a crisis on our hands? Or is this something special? Estazzi asked

Over the next hour all four men, princes of the Catholic Church sat and systematically went through all before them, in part seeking answers. In essence, their questions and deliberations lead them down paths that ultimately brought them to the depths of their faith, confronting them with one simple question. What happens next? Towards the end, it is Cardinal Mendoza who spoke.

'You're Eminences... Are we looking at a case of undeniable fact here? The man's physical alteration, the episode in the hospital.'

"Perhaps, Miguel that suggests a case of undeniable fact but there is something else. This relic if that is what it is, needs to be tested. It needs some technical forensic analysis. We've done it before".

For a few seconds, no one responded, bringing a sharp look around the table.

"Indeed we have my brother! Bonaire replied with some unease.

"This all started in Geneva. And, if I'm not mistaken, aspects of this scientist's experience originated with an image of the Holy Shroud'

'That's correct Giuseppe, The Dean of the College said.

"It's all in here," He said pointing to the documents in front of him.

"Our brother Francois Burgoyne and Father Provincial spoke at length on this matter, and produced some compelling evidence that the image of the shroud found expression in some aspect of their physics."

"Science! Whispered the Secretary of State.

The others turned to the senior cardinal to sense where his thoughts were. He didn't always share his innermost thoughts, not even to his holiness. Cardinal Estazzi had his reclusive moments but knew sometime:- very soon the face and the man dominating the news would come calling, and it wasn't to see him or his brothers sitting around this table. There was a sharp tap on the door, and three men enter and approach the table. All stand. Three men entered most knew two of them well, the other they only knew about.

"Brothers in Christ, you are all most welcome, please come, and join us," Estazzi announced.

"You all know, Father Superior of course, and Father Provincial Sienna, and this is Father Francois Burgoyne. He added, as the three Jesuits went and embraced each of the Cardinals. Francois Burgoyne knew all of the Cardinals by reputation only, but in an instant he felt the single gray eyes of the Cardinal Secretary Of State gaze over him.

He smiled at the Jesuit but the eyes remained cool. Initially, there was a formality but it quickly melted. Never had Burgoyne been in the close confines and company of such influential men of the church. In turn, each of the cardinals surveyed this intriguing fellow priest. Bonaire allowed his guest to get settled, and then played host, pouring them either coffee or tea.

"How is your brother in law, Francois? He was in our prayers in recent times, Bonaire asked as he poured. Burgoyne smiled gratefully and thought how he would answer.

"He is well your Eminence. Thank you for asking, adding,

"A man who has gone through a renewal in himself, even spiritual renewal"

That brought a few smiles. Then the head of the Jesuit Order pulled his chair closer to the table and noticed the distinctive Papal symbol emblazoned on all their folders sitting on the table. Alphonse Sienna sat on his right.

"Your Eminence's I see you've all received my notes and those of Brother Burgoyne. You must have many questions? He asked.

Cardinal Bonaire got up and reached for the TV remote and flicked a switch. A small TV and recorder came to life and immediately showed the CERN press conference. Central to the display was Du Pont himself. They all watched in silence for about five minutes, and then Bonaire switched it off. Even seeing it again made for compelling and evocative viewing, such was the passion and delivery.

"A remarkable man. Quite remarkable! The Secretary of State whispered to no one in particular. Of particular interest around the table was to first discuss events leading up to Du Pont's episode.

"Tell us, Francois about this young man, who works closely with Professor Du Pont, and his *utterances*. He spoke in Aramaic!

The Jesuit nodded then quickly took the cardinals over the entire Melrose experiences including his use of ancient languages, and of course, what it contained. When he'd finished, each of the men around the table sat back.

"You're sure Francois! The last words of Christ, as he would have cried out! Asked Mendoza.

"Yes, you're Eminence without a doubt. Quite unsettling. Francois replied.

"Indeed". The Cardinals each held dearly to the teaching of Christ. Handed down and written in Scripture, the Gospels that ruled their priestly lives and ordained how the true messages of Jesus were enshrined in human life. They devoted their entire life to an apostolic mission based on faith. Everything before them in the folders posed new dimensions to their beliefs. Aspects of this entire story reached out from the pages almost summoning them to look deeper into a mystical event of staggering proportions. Then, it was Cardinal Misner, The Dean of the Sacred College who leaned forward and looked across at Father Burgoyne.

"You speak here in these notes Francois... "Of the manifestation! The presence in the garden. He asked gently.

"Burgoyne glanced across at his friend Alphonse Sienna, who just nodded his approval. "Indeed your Eminence, I recall it well your Eminence. Not something easily forgotten"

"What form did it take?

"The manifestation itself was a young boy. Burgoyne replied everyone listened. The description of the event was detailed and emotional in parts. The Jesuit described the entity, and it's presence along with identifying that it was they were addressing.

"It was a spirit entity recognised by my brother-in-law. One that knew who we all were including me. It was very non-threatening and invoked God Almighty's name. It also suggested that Doctor Du Pont was... No! Suggested, is not correct. *It announced*, that my family member was highly favoured'.

"On Earth, or in Heaven! My brother?

A voice from behind called out. Standing at the doorway, having entered unheard was the incumbent bishop of Rome, Cardinal Gianelli Agostini. His Holiness Pope Leo the 4th.

Everyone stood as he moved across the room towards the small gathering. All the Cardinals bowed, the three Jesuits clear their chairs and stand respectfully on the spot. He had piercing blue eyes with olive sallow complexion whose skin showed a man who spent quite some time outdoors. Unlike the others, his posture was erect medium build just under six feet. A man at complete ease with himself in his role as Vicar of Christ. His aquiline features hid his age for a man in his late seventy's

'I was passing". He said softly.

Turning and looking at Francois Burgoyne, he did something he seldom did in public he bowed towards the three Jesuits.

"Highly favoured, is indeed a great honour, Brother Francois. "Please continue".

He reached out to his Cardinals, one by one they take his hand and kissed the ring. Then turning he quietly he gave each of them a look, turned and saw himself out, leaving his fellow priests to carry on the work. Work of which, would end up on his desk.

Sal Madere.

The bedroom windows caught the afternoon light just right, causing the room to feel like a personal sanctuary. Du Pont sat upright looking out at the trees enjoying the intimacy of his wife's touch. She moved around him inspecting her work, scissors in one hand a small camel-haired brush in the other. She liked to groom her husband and took it upon herself to trim his hair when the occasion demands.

"It's so strong, my love. When I think of what it looked like in hospital". She said, holding up a mirror for him...

"Not bad! Not bad at all. He teased. She tossed the scissors and brush aside, leaned over him gently cradled his head in her arms.

"When all of this is over, we need to get away somewhere. She whispered. He rose and took her in his arms.

"How about Rome. Ever been? She smiled at his wry humour, his gift for turning serious moments light. Then her expression changed.

"You must go there! Yes? She whispered.

Claudine knew he was still working matters out amid a personal mission. It was something she felt was inevitable, a matter of personal conviction for her husband.

"I have to, my love. I made a promise"

'Yes, I know. Promise me something. Make a promise to *me* you'll remain the man I married.' He took both her hands and cupped them in his.

"What if that man remains the same but wants to do more?"

'As long he wants to do it for all the right reasons, then that's fine by me." She reached up and drew his face closer and stared into his eyes and tried to imagine the things they saw, and then kissed him tenderly.

"You know, I'm still in love with that man I married. She whispered

"Please take care of him for me. I thought I'd lost him once. I never want to go through it again".

Over the next few days, Geneva was caught up in a spree of international conferences. In just over one week, nearly an additional one million people flowed into the Swiss capital. Tourists were in the majority, but a substantial number of the visitors were political and diplomatic personnel. It was a little surprising when Doctor Benni Mocthi got the invite for dinner that evening and at such short notice. It came from his colleague in Obstetrics Dr. Kells. Dinner invite was for 7.30pm at a small restaurant, Sachs Place that specialized in Lebanese cuisine.

A table for two. Out of surprise more than anything else Mochti was happy to comply. A quick call to Kell's extension over in the maternity wing confirming he was up for it and was delighted to accept the invite. All he got was his answering service, so he left a quick message. Later just after 7.30 pm he sauntered into a busy and bustling restaurant greeted by the exotic aromas of lamb and roasted nuts. It was his first time there, the crowd sitting around was mainly suits, and from the look of things, mainly diplomatic. Sitting in an alcove near the bar area, he saw Michael Kells already sipping Arak.

His colleague got up smiling and shook hands. Kells immediately ordered a round of Arak. It didn't take long for Mochti to realize this wasn't entirely social. His colleague looked preoccupied and finally apologized for turning this setting into a bit of a medical confessional. He listened then the drinks arrived. Mochti took his first sip, allowing the arak's aniseed flavour to take its effect.

"What you mean, perplexing Michael? Mochti finally asked. The moment Kells mentioned,Denise Du Pont Mochti stopped and he put his glass down. The conversation turned medical and over the next fifteen minutes, the Obstetrician gave Mochti a detailed overview of his patient's condition as her pregnancy progressed right into the third trimester. They ordered their meal, hardly spending any time deciding on dish selection. Eventually, it became apparent why the obstetrician was so exercised by recent delivery.

"Four different times! Benni. Four! Kells held up four fingers. All the tests, the scans, were conclusive. Denise, oh sorry, my patient was carrying a boy!"

Kells was clearly agitated. Mochti's own conclusions to the sex of the foetus were otherwise, but that was an early assessment and left it at that. Besides, he wasn't in Obstetrics

"How can that be, Michael sounds very odd. How many this year? He enquired.

"Over a hundred deliveries! Everyone textbook, and in every case my gender prediction was spot-on" Kells said

He whipped out some pages from a case next to him and leaned over the table. For a further five minutes, they both exchanged professional opinions.

"You can imagine my surprise Benni during delivery. A beautiful baby girl, healthy in every way. Of course, the couple was over the moon! I was completely taken aback, stunned even. It couldn't be...and yet this child was one special young lady. She should be a *He*! Kells whispered.

Washington DC- The Oval Office

"Yes Prime Minister! We need to respond as a block. Not as NATO per se, but a unified strategy...Agreed. None of us had any warning on this. This came from nowhere, even our Intelligence community here are baffled. Thank you, Prime Minister, Let's stay in touch".

He dropped the phone back in its cradle like it was infected with something. President Cameron Jefferson Douglas, known to his closest circle as *Cam,* was not a happy man and less so, from his call to the UK Prime Minister.

"How is it, guys? With what we spend on Intel gathering, this Shroud Technology blanket was nowhere on the radar. He hissed in frustration. "Even the Brits are in the black! He snapped at no one in particular. Looking around at his inner circle, his Defence Secretary, Secretary of State, and Head of the CIA.

"In the next twenty-four hours, I want to know everything we have on this Professor Du Pont. Everything! Then added quietly "That's not a request. It's an Executive Order!"

Apostolic Palace, Vatican.

His Holiness moved with pace, leaving his four senior Cardinals the task of keeping up. Taking two steps at a time he mounted the ornate marble staircase leading to the Papal apartments and his private chambers. All around him frescoes looked down upon the Vicar of Christ. Pastor, preacher, and priest all in one. Christ's temporal authority on earth and not afraid to use the power of the papacy when he saw fit. For over four days he had listened intently devouring every nuanced expression, each event in all its detail in the report from his brethren Cardinals. Dogma, and church doctrine aside, his focus was on authentic words and deeds. The presence and presentation of undeniable fact. Origination of new truths, and on whose authority did these truths emanate. The liberty of free thought, the expression of free will, or seeking out of deeper truths, must all be balanced to God's will... Our Father who art ... *The will be done. Thy Kingdom come.*

Leo the 4th seated himself behind a simple oak desk, with two candleholders at each end and a battered 100-year-old bible, worn and tattered with dog-eared pages opened on the desk. He possessed an encyclopaedic memory and despite his advancing years, could recite much of the four gospels almost from memory. Once seated, his Cardinals gathered round him like centurions ready to do his bidding. He blessed himself and leaned forward for a few seconds in a moment of silent prayer. His secretary of the Vatican State, his Dean of the Sacred College of Cardinals and two other Cardinals remained standing. Their pontiff was a much-loved man, simple in many ways, who was a reluctant successor to the throne of Peter but once he ascended to that throne, he was one of the most decisive and inflexible Popes in decades. For political and church matters, and essential curial reform, including discipline, he relied heavily on the priests standing before him. On matters involving spiritual or miraculous happenings with his church, it was to Cardinal Bonaire he would instinctively turn to.

"Is World peace, free from nuclear destruction, about to descend on us Giuseppe? He asked quietly to his Prefect Cardinal.

'Not yet, you're Holiness, but the politics of fear has begun. Bonaire replied.

The Pontiff smiled "Mundus sine more'

"Holy Father, do you need to see some of the news briefings? His Cardinal Secretary Estazzi asked.

"No your Eminence! I do not. But thank you. My brothers my heart, and my head speak to me in different ways. My heart deeply wants to believe Christ is reaching out to us, in this most unexpected way and wants us to listen. My head says, watch for prophets who speak in my name and filled with falsehoods. How are we to proceed? How do we determine if this is indeed good fruit. We must know if the fruit itself is good my brothers. Not just determine, but to know within our hearts if this man is pure at heart.' The Pontiff whispered.

The Cardinals nodded.

"There are aspects that disturb me Holy Father. The Dean of the College spoke.

'Yes, you're Eminence I know. The Pontiff replied knowingly. "You refer of course, to a particular testimony in the transcripts.

'Yes? Indeed Holy Father. There are references or revelations as to the true significance of divine birth. Specifically, Church dogma on Immaculate Conception. The testimony related in the transcripts puts an entirely different aspect to our teachings on this. The content and explanation here are quite... extraordinary. As a revealed truth, it presents an entirely new understanding and dimension to our teachings"

"Yes, our teachings. Church Magisterium exercises all authority over divine truths. And yet, how do we reconcile conflicting truths when they confront us? The Pontiff asked

There was a silence as the Cardinals let their supreme leader and successor to St. Peter worked his thoughts through. He was a scholar in his own right, a devotee to Plato and others, but always used Socrates as his guide when asking probing questions. The Socratic method was one, where identifying the right question to ask was prime. When done so it elicited truths and shown light on matters of substance. Leo, the 4th had complete mastery of such technique and armed with an almost elephantine memory and razor-sharp forensic mind, he called up details from all the transcripts with penetrating ease and matched them to the profile of Professor Fletcher Du Pont. There was little he missed.

"It's an interesting use and application of the term, Shroud. He said finally as if posing the question to himself.

"Your Holiness?

"The term Shroud, my brothers. It covers, gives protection, and provides comfort. It covered the entire body of Jesus Christ. Now, it is proposed to cover our planet like a blanket. More interesting still, it seemed, that was the first event on this Professor Du Pont's computer".

They all looked at each other, realizing how true that was. This all started with a simple image, turning up in the most unlikely of places. Standing, the Pontiff gazed around making eye contact with each of them. Instinctively all four crimson-robed cardinals stood erect and return the gaze. Expectant missionaries ready to carry out the wishes of his Holiness.

"For us to know the fruits of this my brother cardinals, we must see for ourselves. We will look into the eyes of this man, and see if his soul is a mirror of God's will. Cardinal Secretary, would you be as gracious as to extend a welcome to this noble and eminent man to join us here, in Peter's house?"

On a damp and unseasonably wet Friday morning, Francois Burgoyne flew into Geneva Airport a little after 11 am on flight SA 105 from Paris. Packed in his briefcase he carried a sealed A4 envelope bearing the symbol of the Papal keys. Summoned the night before, to travel to Paris where a package of significance awaited him. He wasted little time and had a good idea of what it might contain. His overnight in the Jesuit House in Paris gave him and his superior a chance to refresh their thoughts and renew their reflections. Both men were still coming to terms with the revelations they were exposed to and privileged witnesses. The sealed letter from Rome had arrived earlier that day, accompanied by a call from the Father Superior, this was something to be handled expeditiously.

Michelle Du Pont took the responsibility to get to the airport and collect her uncle. On the way back to Sal Madere, the banter was light, and all about Angelina Claudine. Intuitively, she knew there was much her uncle needed to keep to himself. She noticed he carried a more solid case finished in a beautiful walnut edging bearing the symbols of two crossed keys on its cover. After an hour they pull into Sal Madere and stopped at the front of the residence. The Jesuit was tired physically, working off reserves, but mentally he was alert and focused. Once inside, Claudine had prepared lunch but insisted her brother took a nap. He was having none of it. He headed straight into Du Pont's study, to find his brother-in-law surrounded by newspapers and magazines on a reading frenzy to do with Science and military topics. Physics was sexy, again.

Du Pont got to his feet and took the Jesuit's hand.

"Well done Francois, you must be exhausted!

"Not as bad as you might think. Some of that energy of yours must have rubbed off." He joked. He found a chair and placed both briefcase and casket aside. Then he sat. Claudine entered followed by Michelle.

"Anyone hungry? She asked.

"Perhaps black coffee, sister. Her brother shot back.

"Fletch?

"No darling, I'm fine. Du Pont said. He looked at the Jesuit. 'Well, do you have it?

Francois opened the briefcase and gently removed the sealed envelope and handed it to the scientist. The enveloped carried the unmistakable papal symbol was sealed with a dark blood coloured wax seal imprinted by the ring. Du Pont held it then showed it to the others.

"Well, Pops! Go on. Open it! Michelle urged anxiously.

"You open it Sweetie! He said softly to his youngest daughter.

Michelle reached out and gently took it. She picked up a silver letter opener and expertly broke the seal, and handed it back to her father. Du Pont opened the envelope and removed a cream coloured crisp sheet monogrammed with the Papal logo.

My Dear Professor Du Pont. My Brother in Christ.

It would be my most fervent wish to welcome you, to visit us in Rome.

I would be greatly honoured if you accept my invitation. We have much to discuss. It was with much relief and great joy we received the word, on your truly miraculous recovery, and that Almighty God spared you and your family from any further hardship. You have been in recent times uppermost in our thoughts, and our prayers. Recent events, both Political and Ecclesiastical require great Faith and trust in our Heavenly Father no more so when the subject of Nuclear Weapons is involved. We note with continued interest your organization's substantial intervention and pray it will bear fruit. The Church will play its part, as it must, to assist. Other matters of a deeply profound nature need to be discussed in private. I follow in the footsteps of a Fisherman Professor, armed with the teachings of the true Christ, and must follow where these teachings lead, both spiritually and morally.

Hence, my invitation, and as I have spoken already we have much to discuss.

May Christ's blessing be always with you, and your family?

Your Servant, and pastor. Leo

Lex Orandi, Lex Credenda

Du Pont stood for a moment trying to read the mind of the author. Smiling to himself, pleased this was as he had hoped. Personal research and literature review spoke volumes on the short reign of Pope Leo the 4th. A pastoral simple man, with the common touch that put humanity first above all other considerations, although there was nothing common about his intellect. Reports circulated suggested, as a young seminarian, Ginelli Agostini possessed an IQ over 130. The Jesuit took the letter from him and carefully read it. With practiced care, he placed it back inside the envelope.

"It requires your acceptance Fletcher" Du Pont nodded

"Of Course. And respond we will. It's what comes next. What does it mean Francois? He asked casually

"The Holy Father wants you to go to...."

"No.! *The Latin*? What's it saying? Du Pont asked

The Jesuit simply smiled. "It means. The Law of Praying is the Law of believing..."

The American paused for a few seconds. Reaching over his desk, he lifted the newspaper and stared at the ghostly eyes and face of the man he will stand before in the coming days. He thought to himself the supreme Pontiff, following in the footsteps of a Fisherman, and the teachings of a Carpenter.

"Now for the other matter. It must travel with me back to Paris Fletcher and treated as a relic of the church." Francois said

It was a decision taken by Du Pont himself. He needed no reminder or keepsake. The cloth was that last exchange that occurred in a tomb, its image was a mere shadow of the real face he knew and would be forever seared into his thoughts.

"Of Course! Francois let's do that now. Then you rest. Tomorrow you fly to Paris, and then we'll meet with you in Rome'. He said.

Sal Madere-

The following days, Du Pont, spent a little time at CERN, preferring the sanctuary of Sal Madere, and its garden, spending precious time with Angelina Claudine. She slept in the summer shade under the great oak in the garden under his watchful eye. During which time he did some catching up in reading. He could barely recall how old he was before he stopped reading any religious material, but now he became prodigious and reasoned in what he chose to read. Waging through page by page over portions of the New Testament he tried to reconcile the narration of the gospels about Jesus, and those of the man he encountered. He knew him simply as Yeshua, only became known as Jesus, simply because of Hebrew sounding names, struggled phonetically through Greek and suffered further alteration into English, hence, Jesus.

Still, it made little difference. A flutter caught his attention out of the side of his eye a small Pigeon perched on the edge of the cot where Angelina slept. His almost reflex action was to swat it away but stopped.

In its beak was a tiny white feather as it danced from one leg to another, and then almost leaning over the edge opened its tiny beak allowing the petal of the feather to drift down gently, floating until it finally landed resting on the forehead of his grandchild. 'What a clever little fellow you are! He muttered. Then he caught himself, a wry smile crossed his face, instantly recognising the simple metaphor.

'Of course, you are, little fellow. You're a Pigeon, and what are you guys best known for? The bird twitched back and forth perched in one position.

"That's right my little friend. You guys carried Messages".

That night before their departure, the family sat and enjoyed the evening meal. Denise and Paul were beside themselves with Angelina, even though Melrose took the night shift to attend his daughter his weariness did little to stem his joy. In a matter of days, his parents would arrive and spend time as guests in Sal Madere. It was one of those intimate moments when everyone sat around and over a few bottles of wine, fond memories were rekindled and the talk was of family matters. Tomorrow was another day. Thoughts of her husband's impending meeting in the Vatican was daunting. Both daughters sat around their father, each finding solace and strength from his easy composure and seeing for themselves he was at peace as he ever was in their entire lives.

"Dad, whatever happens, tomorrow, we love you. Our love has no conditions. You know that Pops! Denise said reaching out to him.

Taking each of their hands in his, Du Pont smiled

'You two, and the image of your mother was all that kept me sane.

Whatever happens in Rome? We'll be there in spirit Pops, every single step of the way. Leaning over she gave him a peck on the cheek.

The City of Rome the following day baked in temperatures in the high thirties, many of its ancient shrines splendid in response looked down on its citizens with curious indifference. It sweltered in the afternoon heat with little or no cooling breeze, making the entire city feel like an open-air sauna. The vast Basilica of St. Peter basked in the glorious sunshine. The Eternal City opened its ancient arms to the thousands who flocked to its majestic setting, almost surrounding them. Bernini's magnificent extended curved structure embraced all that entered the basilica itself. Stunning structures of imperial power, blending Baroque and Renaissance architecture designed to impress and intimidate in a bygone era. The world and humanity came calling, many from curiosity to inspect and admire its grandeur, others to pay homage to their faith. It was both imperial and imperilled by circumstances of a more intolerant time. As tourists mingled and studied its magnificence in the oppressive blanket of heat, little if any noticed a black saloon drive around its exterior perimeter and head through a barrier into a secluded courtyard to the side of the Basilica.

It was a little after 4.30 pm on a hot afternoon. The car pulled around to the side of the grand esplanade of columns and worked its way into a large cobble stoned courtyard. Swiss Guards resplendent in their distinctive Blue, Red, Orange uniforms stood at the entrance to an arched doorway. Inside more guards stood ready to lead the way. Despite the oppressive heat, they looked impeccable and capable.

Du Pont and Claudine sat for a moment in the back seat.

"Well, so begins the ecstasy, and the agony my love...

This is far as I go my darling. Claudine smiled

"Wha! But I need you to..."

She nodded towards the archway door. Standing in his full Jesuit regalia was her bother, Francois. "He's in charge now my love," She said kissing him.

"Now go my love, follow your heart.

He looked towards his brother-in-law then opened the door and stepped out. As he did, the saloon moved off quickly. Du Pont stood for a moment in the sunshine, dressed in a dark navy blue suit, with a snow-white opened necked shirt. A matching white handkerchief peered over his breast pocket. He walked deliberately towards the archway to his brother-in-law. Francois's demeanour within these settings was sombre, with a hint of ecclesiastic formality. Du Pont paused to survey the surroundings he's about to enter. The massive structure, this imperial rock of Christianity. Glancing upwards he took in its magnificence and instant memories of a small stream came to him.

That magical moment lost in another time where he drank water in that tranquil evening surrounded by meadows and burdened with a potent symbolic message. *Time can be like* a *stream carrying its purity along its journey, twisting, and turning.* A memory laden with enormous significance, and *along that passage, it loses its purity*. The source of refreshing water nurtured all who drink from it, much like truths handed down, the *further it travels from its source, often loses that purity.* Standing in this place two thousand years on, he wondered if the present occupant of this citadel was a drinker of pure water. He remembered something else.

The question! A simple question that was put to him. *"Can you carry water that far!*

"This way, Fletcher. Follow me". Francois said.

Inside the building, everything changed. The physicist felt he stepped into something akin to a medieval palace with its tall marble vertical walls rising around him. So different from his world of particle colliders. His temple, his place of worship lay buried in the earth back in CERN.

Here, he was a pilgrim. Within these cathedrals of polished marble, antiquity reigned supreme. As they walked their footsteps carried echoes. Their passage through enormous porticos of great-carved classical sculptures reminded him of men of another era, men who shaped and created magnificent beauty and striking physiques. The palace of Popes. They came to a wide marble staircase and quickly made their way up numerous flights of steps until they came to a large set of tall teak doors.

"This is where I must take my leave of you, Fletcher. The Jesuit whispered.

"May Jesus Christ infuse you my dear brother" He embraced and held him.

"I am here and ready. Then raising his hand knocked twice on the door, and stepped back.

Slowly, the large teak doors parted, and the figure of Cardinal Paulo Estazzi, the Vatican's Secretary of State stood on the other side. Du Pont took a few steps forward and stopped. The Cardinal did likewise and paused. Smiling the Cardinal extended his hand.

"Professor Du Pont, you are most welcome." "Allow me the honour, I am Cardinal Paulo Estazzi, his Holiness Secretary of State".

Du Pont faced the aging priest. The pale gray eyes returned the inspection. A few seconds passed, as both men gazed at each other. The physicist reached out and took the extended hand. The older man moved closer and looked into the eyes of the American. Estazzi relaxed his hand but felt the grip. He smiled at Du Pont for a second, searching to find the truth behind the man. As he does, an icy cold chill passed through him. A gentle tingling down his back lasting only the briefest of moments, followed by a mild physical sensation.

"Come, my friend, his Holiness awaits" The Cardinal finally gestured. Du Pont released the hand and bowed and then stepped past him. As he does he paused and looked sideways at the Cardinal.

"No more, you're Eminence. No more Pain! It is finished!

The gray eyes light up and shot him the briefest of looks.

"No more Illness your Eminence. Du Pont whispered then touched the other's shoulder.

Stepping inside he looked around and paused. He was standing in a long room glistening murals filled one side of the room, which turned out to be a library. Gathered around an assembly of over fifteen crimson and purple-robed cardinals of the Roman Catholic Church stood in silence watching the American make his entrance. It took a few seconds to absorb the presence and setting. There was nothing only stillness, and an awkward moment of silence as the esteemed gathering studied the tall American.

None of them missed the notable departure in dress code by the scientist. Dark suits and black neckties were the expected decorum with a visit with his Holiness, certainly not open-necked shirts. An old wooden chair sat at one end. Seated, his Holiness Leo IV finally raised himself and stood.

'Holy Father, Your Eminences. May I present Nobel Laureate, Professor Fletcher Du Pont of CERN." Cardinal Estazzi announced.

Du Pont bowed to the Cardinals. Heads nodded. Seats were already arranged into a horseshoe shape around the Pontiff's seat. The Pontiff moved toward him with patrician grace and extended both arms in his customary welcoming gesture. Reaching out he took Du Pont's both hands and clasped them in his. He flashed a broad smile to the scientist.

"Welcome ad Petri mum." "Professor Du Pont, your humble servant. I am truly honoured."

Du Pont took the hand and bowed and kissed the ring of the Fisherman.

"Your Holiness, the honour is entirely mine". The supreme Pontiff looked over the tall scientist, taking in all the small details. If everything he read was true, he was staring into the eyes and face of someone with the most remarkable story in human history. His mind and intellect try to imagine the journey from physics to metaphysics the man standing before him had endured. With unexpected candour, the pontiff asked

"Are you a man of faith, Professor? Do you believe in the living Christ?"

Du Pont paused. There were many ways he could respond. Finally, he bowed slightly

"Yes, I do, Your Holiness! Adding.

"But it would be impossible for me, not to, your Holiness. Not with someone you knew and had spoken with"

The pontiff stiffened and took a more studied interest at the face of the scientist. His eyes grew intense. "You experienced... Spiritual Ecstasy? He whispered rhetorically.

"Yes and more! Wisdom, with blinding truth Holy Father"

They moved towards the Pontiff's throne, where an empty vacant seat was waiting. The words lingered, as each of the cardinals reflected on the scientist's response. The Secretary of State showed the scientist to the chair. The pontiff moved to his seat with deliberate more measured slow strides considering the words of his guest. A steel trolley on casters was wheeled in. On it a casket, almost a meter square with a glass cover.

Inside, the cloth with its image. The pontiff gestured towards the group of Cardinals, then one by one, each of them rose and approached the casket. A silent procession began as each of the Cardinal Bishops made his way to the casket and gazed into its contents. Some faces looked and remained impassive as their eyes fell on the ghostly face, others looked making the sign of the cross. Others, the expression on their face was all it took, placed their hand over the glass, and then moved on. After the last cardinal had returned to his chair, the pontiff stood and made the sign of the cross

In nomine Patris..

When finished with the Lord's Prayer the Pontiff moved to the casket and gazed at its content. Turning towards their guest his expression became intense.

"Professor, we have all listened and read with humble hearts and observed with complete shock at the physical and spiritual transformation of your miraculous experience. Perhaps, you might share with us, the essence of your spiritual journey."

Du Pont looked to the gathering of attentive faces. Men of the church.

"With your Holiness permission, may I stand? The Pontiff nodded and gestured to the scientist with his hand. The physicist moved and takes a few steps into the middle.

"I never believed in a Supreme Being, your holiness, you're Eminences. Nor the existence of an Afterlife, not even the existence of a soul, or spirit. None of these notions meant anything to me. They were convenient crutches, psychological mind games, idle fantasies that people, and religious institutions, churches called... Faith. The Pontiff smiled and merely nodded at the honesty and conviction of the sentiment. My Church was Science! My tools, my articles of faith were experimental thought. To conceive ways to understand all we hold to be a reality. Evidential, meaning all my faith was based on evidence of a fact, how atomic structures exist, its substance, and how it behaved. It's a mysterious church in its own right; it kept secrets, and only surrenders its truths under certain conditions. I believed I knew much and understood my science, the essence of the matter, and how it ordained all order in our reality."

He hesitated for a few seconds choosing his words.

"On both counts, Holy Father, I was so flawed"

He began to pace the short space inside the arranged seats

"Somewhere, and for reasons I barely understand holy fathers, I was brought to a place where the intersection of physics and metaphysics meet.

He then proceeded to describe in some detail his passage into realms, not possible to explain but found himself in the domain of Angels. Over two hours he began to paint a picture of existential circumstances and the manner truths were revealed in such breathtaking beauty. The process in which all physical reality was wielded and recast to explain divine will and providence. The Angelic nature of a creature called Etaanus, the great Keeper of The book Of Seals, and his encounter with the Nazarene Carpenter. Sources of his teaching had become corrupted and impure, like a small stream. In his most collected voice he went on to describe the manner of the river, and its alteration and message contained within. Du Pont moved towards the casket and looked down at the cloth. "

"I was summoned to all of this by an image that appeared from nowhere into my world. At the time it troubled me deeply. An unexplained, impossible occurrence crept into my domain on a simple terminal screen. How utterly unprepared was I, and my colleagues to see and understand its significance? It was merely an invitation. Little did I know? He faced the pontiff, his hand still resting on the case.

"Your Holiness, His injuries were horrific... he faltered and his voice began to break. Cardinal Paulo Estazzi got to his feet and came to the scientist. Du Pont struggled to contain the emotions, realizing for the first time, that it was becoming impossible for him to recall his experiences without reliving its effects. ...In some of our last moments together this vibrant, charming and charismatic man, shared with me his last moments, amid the brutality and bloodlust for violence."

His control started to slip as the emotions surged back over him.

"Yeshua saw his demonic tormentors! He saw them unleash unspeakable human cruelty. They crushed his face' He began to sob and then regained some control. Leo IV was now on his feet, shaken, and moved towards the scientist.

"Nothing exists in all our archives that describes his suffering, my friends. The shroud image is just a hint of his abominable treatment ... but this! He said staring into the casket... .".. This was our last moment, into the tomb. The cold stone of the rock had turned warm from radiated heat from some earlier spontaneous release of energy!

'Divinitatae Dei. Resurrection! The Secretary of State whispered.

"He lived Your Eminences, Your Holiness. He showed me a vision...It materialized into the structure of the tomb wall itself. It was a gathering just like this it looked like Conclave with all of you gathered together. He held me physically, both his arms on my shoulders, my new apostles. He whispered.

"I started with twelve... Du Pont lowered his voice to a hush, turning and faced the Pontiff. He spoke to me directly.

"My truths have become tainted. New Messengers must restore everything."

'Then he placed his hand on my chest, over my heart, Holy Father! He whispered to me. Then, he looked into my heart, and smiled ...and before everything faded, he came closer and whispered" "...Tell them. *Tell them all!* That you knew, Yeshua Ben Yoseph!"

There was a hushed silence as the words hung over each of them. The Pontiff turned and stared into the casket, no one spoke for a number of seconds as the man who inherited Peter's throne disappeared into his thoughts. A moment passed. A hush filled the room. All the cardinals fixed their eyes on the physicist then turned to their Pope. Du Pont gently removed his jacket and placed it on his seat.

"There is more, your Eminences. I was taken and shown spheres where souls languished". He closed his eyes the intensity began to take hold.

..."Realms of unimaginable beauty, occupied by people with great abilities and gifts. Creatures restored to glorious forms to their former existence as Angels. Different aspects of existence opened up to me, vast kingdoms, Dominions of endless beauty... and then to places across the great gulf, to the ultra-mundane, the Abyss".

In living detail, he spent the next twenty minutes casting and painting vivid constructs of the ultra-mundane, the changes each different one represented. Every detail related was the substance that Messenger unfolded for him to see and grasp. Even as he spoke, his senses reawakened all those fearful, and ecstatic moments as if they just occurred.

"... A place of utter horror, where no light or colour exists only eternal gloom". He continued He began to shake as vivid images came rushing back.

Unnoticed by the Du Pont, the cardinals left their seats and moved in closer, around the Holy Father and the physicist.

".. So evil was this realm, so vile, so malevolent, it consumed everything with its choking power. It espoused hopelessness, full of the most hideous of creatures. A realm of depravity both physical mental...Such was its nature I thought I would never survive it... His breathing became heavy. "...The task of Redemption, that task was to build a....

"Enough!" The Pontiff said softly. "That's enough, my dear brother!

He then nodded to his cardinal Secretary Of State. Du Pont stopped and regained his composure. His breathing slowly returned to normal. Looking around he saw, only faces of compassion. Then he heard a voice, he knew well.

Fletcher, come and sit here," said Francois Burgoyne.

Leo IV returned to his seat and sank into it. His Cardinals came closer and gathered around both men. Then, slowly Cardinal Estazzi moved towards him and did something no one remembered seeing him ever doing. With great ease, he got down on his knees and kneeled before his Pontiff.

"Your Holiness, I have no longer any need for these"

He said softly with a quiver in his voice. In a single movement, he reached into his robes, hands showing a slight tremor and removed a pouch with a vile of insulin, with a single syringe and placed it on the ground at the feet of his supreme pontiff. His Holiness and the Cardinals see the objects and are instantly taken aback. They all knew of the esteem cardinal's struggle with his illness. A hushed murmur ran through the gathering of cardinals.

I believe Holy Father. I believe...I am cured. He said, his voice shaking

"Christ teachings your Holiness has lost much of it authenticity! Du Pont cut in.

The Pontiff gave the physicist a sharp look, a flash of anguished expression.

"How can you know this, my brother? Christ's teachings live on, through his church."

"It was conveyed to me in very vivid terms, Holy Father ,like a Stream.

A stream! How is this so, my brother?

'The further from the source, it became less refreshing, stale, and filled with impurities. His teachings, you have to restore that purity. All of you! You're his messengers, Du Pont said quietly.

Cardinal Estazzi moved towards the scientist. Moving like a man touched by some inner flame that began to burn, his eyes had intensity through the tears running down his face.

'Holy Father! He whispered hoarsely.

"Perhaps...we listen to this man now with our hearts. He carries something that perhaps is the good fruit, we so desperately need."

Each of the Cardinals studied the tall American. All devoted and as passionate in their views and beliefs. Their creed brooked no deviation from the orthodoxy of church authority, yet they were compelled to listen. Their logic was rooted in dogma, unflinching in every way possible, and for all of that, this man standing before them carried a strange, almost mysterious authority.

The Pontiff moved and invited the Du Pont to the Papal residence within the apostolic palace. Six Cardinals as well as the Secretary of State, Dean of the Sacred College, Cardinal Bonaire, accompanied them to the apartments. If he thought the library was ornate, nothing quite prepared him for the setting of the palace itself. It was not what he'd expected. Everything was tasteful, paintings by some of the masters full of the history of the papacy itself and yet surprisingly comfortable. They entered a living room area where several plush armchairs circled a rectangular glass-topped coffee table. The walls were the plain lemon-cream colour with two white lampshades casting a soft light giving a relaxed feel to the room. The air conditioning hummed discreetly in the background making the room pleasant contrast to the outside humidity of the city.

Again, without any formalities, the Pontiff asked everyone to be seated. The mood had turned sombre.

"Some aspects of your transcripts, my brother are in deep conflict with Church teachings.' It was the dean of the Sacred College, who broke the mild tension.

"Indeed my brother Cardinal, there are others in the transcripts." Said a Dutch Cardinal. "Your focus...on Redemption, is not entirely... doctrine"

Du Pont sat back in the armchair for a moment and listened as princes of the church opened up issues where they struggled to reconcile matters of dogma, and these new insights. The scientist finally gently raised his hands.

"Your Eminences, you must listen." Listen to me! I struggled as to how I could explain much of...

"Your sincerity, and more to the point, my brother, and your authenticity", The Pontiff injected quietly.

317

Du Pont smiled appreciating the pontiff's choice of words. Reaching into his jacket, he removed a soft cloth wrapped around a small object. Laying it on the coffee table, he unwrapped the cloth, revealing the polished wooden sculpted hand. It's dark colouring catching the Cardinal's attention.

"This was sculpted by the hand of a Carpenter. If I'm not mistaken it's from an acacia tree, and it's very old. Apart from my handprints and those of my eldest daughter, there is only one set of other prints on it... Yeshua Ben Yoseph gave this to me."

The Pontiff studied the sculpted piece, unable to take his eyes off it and felt like the room suddenly close in around them. As they stared at the carving for a few seconds, there was a tap on the door and a young priest entered, and briskly came towards the Pontiff and whispered in his ear.

The Pontiff listened then looked up sharply, a flash of the sharp intellect glanced at the American then gave everyone a curious look. The young priest immediately went and opened out the large window. The warm air from outside rushed in, reminding everyone of the latent heat from the city. They all stood and followed his holiness make his way to the window. The view looked down onto the vast open vista of St. Peters Basilica, where crowds of tourists wandered round. Excitement suddenly began to erupt as the crowds take in the surreal arrival of birds.

From nowhere and from every conceivable direction winged creatures converged into the Basilica causing everyone to stop and look on at something quite out of the ordinary unfold all around them. Hundreds of pigeons had circled the square flying in a pattern similar to swallows, except in the space of a matter of minutes, it swarmed into thousands. The entire scene was a cloud of birds flying almost in unison, and then, spectacularly began to land and perch on the steps of the Basilica itself. Thousands of birds descended on the entrance to the house of Peter. Onlookers stood stunned at the sight. Then from somewhere in the centre of raised voices cried out.

Du Pont looked out and saw a spectacle that caused him to smile. He studied at the supreme Pontiff. He had the look of a man suspended between dogma, and an inner struggle. As they looked out at the sight of thousands of pigeons moving like a sea of feathers, they heard the shouts from below.

The Egyptian Obelisk dominated the centre of the basilica, but to the left and right spaced equidistantly, two granite fountains were located. One built by Bernini, the other older one by Maderno. No sooner had the pigeons perched themselves on the steps, when water from both fountains mysteriously began to overflow. At first, it provoked amusement, as the spray offered bystanders welcome relief from the heat, but then the flow gathered momentum. Like a cauldron, the flow increased and started to create two distinct trickles outwards over the surface of the Basilica itself. In no time, the trickles turned to torrents of water that soon became rivers. People took shelter, as the joyous response faded and everyone became anxious. After only five minutes, alarms and sirens were heard in the distance, as word quickly spread to civil authorities that something was amiss.

Soon two new river flows rolled out of St. Peters and raced down into the Largo Del Colonnatto then flowing on down the Via Dei Corridori. Traffic slowed down as drivers looked on baffled by the unexpected spectacle. The symbolism and impact were stark as it was unsettling. The Holy Father placed both his arms on the railing in part, to steady himself, as he took in all that he had heard, and now witnessed. Below him was a scene that was highly symbolic and laden with meaning. He turned and gazed at Du Pont, and then his fellow priests.

"What are we to make of this my brothers in Christ? He said softly

"Two very powerful symbols Holy Father. Du Pont whispered.

Cardinal Estazzi simply looked on. The cold gray eyes now had tears.

"We've been given a sign, my Pontiff. He said hoarsely "Pigeons, Holy Father!

"Yes, Paulo my friend, I know. They carry Messages! Like us, his new Apostles We must do likewise...and restore its purity..." Like these fountains my friend. We must renew and rekindle Christ's teaching.

Du Pont stood back into the shade of the balcony. Soon the crowds below notice their Pontiff from high on the papal apartment window. Water flowed and cascades everywhere but didn't deter them from turning their attention upwards, and in one spontaneous act, hundreds clapped and applauded their Pope, almost as if they knew and connected with his thoughts at that moment in time. Du Pont slipped back into the shadows of the doorway and simply watched. Then unnoticed he retreated inside to gather his own thoughts, wondering if he was a worthy advocate to a man he hardly believed in up to now.

Deep in thought, he noticed a table sitting to one side. Drawn to it he approached and saw beautifully etched golden keys overlapping in its distinctive x shape.

The symbol of the Papal keys. He stared at them for a few seconds thinking what they represented. As he did, thoughts flashback to the images of another dominion. The domain of Angels, and creatures of unfathomable power. Neither murals tapestry, paintings from the great masters on earth, could come close to depicting what he had seen.

"The keys to the Kingdom Of Heaven, My Brother," Said a voice from behind.

Cardinal Giuseppe Bonaire was standing behind him studying him.

"Indeed you're Eminence. And, I've seen a glimpse of what that Kingdom looks like".

Before the Cardinal could respond Du Pont reached out and took his hand. The Cardinal felt something being pressed into his. Looking down he saw a simple object. A small metal key pressed into the palm of his hand.

"It was my symbol all my life. To unlock secrets! I no longer need it your Eminence. Take it as my gift."

Bonaire stared at the American and then noticed the Holy Father was standing very close to them. Close enough to have heard. Bonaire placed the simple object in the middle of the inlaid table and bowed to the Pontiff. "Symbols can be important, my son. More than you know. The Pontiff smiled

"Take this Shroud Technology for example. Do you think it can work my son? Can it save us from ourselves and, our thirst for power? Also, your choice of description —a Shroud is a most evocative and powerful symbol Professor. No accident I suspect!

He added with a slight touch of irony. Du Pont sensed they moved on from spiritual to pastoral.

"Its potency is in its name, your Holiness. Shroud is passive, it means to shelter and protects. It doesn't threaten. It will work! It's my belief and that belief comes from here." He said placing his hand over his heart.

Belief! It was all he ever spoke about. He feared being forgotten, and people losing faith, no belief, and no sense of hope. It was always about... belief.'

The others, all instantly attentive to the exchange, suddenly joined both Pontiff and Bonaire. His Holiness said little for a few seconds but studied the senior physicist with renewed respect.

"That word requires a great deal. It places a great demand on human beings to understand all that *belief* entails. Your very first exposure to these truths, your journey, began with a certain image on only your computer device if I'm not mistaken. You sure it hasn't inspired you in a certain way of thinking? He smiled.

"If you believe in the man, then it shouldn't be a problem. Du Pont said

No one spoke. The Pontiff locked his fingers and gave everyone around him a caring look.

"We have so much to discuss, my Friend, and perhaps now is not the time. But, remember we are all here, following the steps of a Carpenter."

Du Pont moved towards the Pontiff, and took his hand and kissed the ring, and then slowly rose. Some seconds passed, the scientist was close enough to smell the fragrance of the Pontiff's cologne.

"He was so much more than a Carpenter, I assure your Holiness. I only saw him as a man, but there was a briefest of moments when he appeared before me, as a creature of sublime perfection. His message, his truths are like water." We must carry water that is pure, your Holiness." He whispered.

He stepped back and bowed.

"Your holiness, my work and visit here are completed. With your grace and your blessing may I...?

"Indeed, my brother. Indeed. You have opened our hearts. May I call you Fletcher, He added after a few seconds.

"Of course, your Holiness, I'd be much honoured."

After saying their farewells, each of the Cardinals left the apartments, leaving Du Pont and the Holy Father to themselves.

"I cannot say, or offer you any guidance Fletcher as to what almighty God's plans are for you, for any of us...but in my heart I feel, you have been chosen for some task." He glanced over at the table and saw the small key resting on the Papal keys.

"Are you sure you wish to leave this with us?

"Yes, Holy Father, it's helped me unlock enough secrets for...many lifetimes!"

The Vicar of Christ gave the other man a long knowing look, sensing that everything about him contained truths that had yet to emerge.

"It is my wish, my son that we stay in contact. The Pontiff said, adding "So, my friend, my Brother in Christ, keep your heart open. That's how he talks to us. Now go, and find great peace." He extended his hand; Du Pont took and kissed the ring.

When he left the apartments Du Pont retraced his steps but a more leisurely pace and headed towards the Library taking some minutes to get there. Arriving he finds Francois Burgoyne was standing with Cardinal Bonaire next to the casket. Both men appear formal, their expressions were taught, almost pale. Du Pont approached them buttoning his jacket. Instantly, he sensed something. Both men stood there. He approached and was just about to say something when he glanced down into the casket. His heart almost stopped. The imprint of the face was now clearly more defined than ever. It was stained in blood, with defined scar marks evident, but both eyes were closed. Du Pont stared for a moment and realized it was now almost as it first appeared on his screen. A final reminder if one was needed his ordeal was no figment of the imagination. He also remembered something else. In that alternative existence a place as real and substantive as everything about him now, choices were put to him, and as he recalled those choices if he accepted, would come with conditions and some aids.

Up to now, he hadn't remotely given any thought on what that might entail.

"What does this mean Fletcher? His brother-in-law asked quietly.

There was nothing he could say. It was finally Cardinal Bonaire moved closer to the Physicist and took a moment. Then, placed his hand on Du Pont's shoulder and smiled. He glanced at Francois for a second then back to the physicist. The smile eventually faded replaced with a serious look.

"It means my brother, that whatever the, Lord has done with you so far...

...He's not finished with *you* yet!

The Garden- Sal Madere.

Felix Deveraux and most of CERN's most senior scientists mingled around the garden of Sal Madere.

It was just after 4.0pm on a Saturday afternoon. The garden party was long outstanding and overdue. It allowed friends and family the opportunity to celebrate the arrival of the new family member Angelina Claudine, and also a chanced to mark the closing of a chapter in recent events with Du Pont himself. Two large tables had a variety of cold meats and salads, along with some of the finest choices of wines. Du Pont and Claudine took turns to thank everyone for their friendships and support.

Paul Melrose sat in the shade mastering the art of cradling and keeping up conversations. Denise and Michelle played hosts enjoying the company of their guests, the Melrose's, along with some fellow Jesuits their uncle invited to the gathering. Sitting in one corner of the garden, Du Pont, Deveraux, and Carina Ambrosiana shared lighter moments with Francois Burgoyne.

"...So the Shield technology funding has been approved? Du Pont asked in amazement. "Of Course! Deveraux boasted. "They are queuing up for participation. Better to be in, rather than out"

Francois Burgoyne teased both scientists.

"CERN' funding is increased then...for this new Shield?

"Indeed, Francois. It's good. Investment in peace and knowledge" Deveraux smiled.

He turned his attention to his brother in law sitting holding his malt.

"What about this new, let me think? The Jesuit probed

"Receptor Particle! This mystery particle. Is that not exciting?

Deveraux's expression changed, as did Du Pont's at the mention of this.

Both men and the Governing Council took certain decisions to withhold any publication of results. Its use and application were, if proven and harnessed in the proper manner, enormous. The Jesuit knew he touched on something, but pressed on. He was intrigued and his malt was beginning to unlock his priestly reserve.

"What's so fascinating Francois? Thought you'd little time for such vagaries! Teased Carina Ambrosiana

"It's a fascinating choice of name, *Receptor*. What is that? He teased.

Deveraux's smile returned, his face giving little away to the wily cleric, preferring instead to let his friend respond. "Well, it's just a fancy way to give it, a touch of the mystique, Du Pont said disarmingly.

The Jesuit smiled and looked over towards, Paul Melrose with his daughter in his arms.

"Well, with all that has happened in the recent past, Fletcher, this new Shroud Technology, your Vatican experience, and now Angelina Claudine. Why bother? Leave it to others. You've done more, seen more than most people in a single lifetime. ?

Why?

It felt to the others like his brother-in-law was gently trying to set boundaries for Du Pont. To ward off any further excursions down uncertain paths. To try and rein a thirst that lingered in him after his ordeal. Claudine wandered over and sat next to her husband Du Pont held his glass then looked at his brother-in-law holding his stare, and then at the others. *How do I tell them. How do I explain, this, is just the beginning.*

"You asked why? Well, I'll answer that. It's what comes next, Francois.

"It's all about, what comes next!

Epilogue

"My God Angelina!

...That's quite an extraordinary tale!

The headmistress said taking in everything, still quite shocked at all she heard.

She momentarily thought her young student was full of fanciful imaginings, but something about the details and the way she told it made her take this young Angelina more serious. And given the way events had unfolded in recent times, she studied the twelve-year-old closer. There was maturity a certainty of purpose beyond her years.

"I see you brought your sketches. Your mom tells me you enjoy drawing in charcoal. Says you spend hours drawing great scenes?

"My granddad, says I should take up Art, but I'm not so sure about that. She said smiling

"May I see some of them? The headmistress asked.

The twelve-year-old hesitated for a few seconds and then slowly handed over some rolled sheets to the teacher. Then rolling them out carefully and with deliberate movements, she saw there were three medium white sheets.

The headmistress stopped and stared at the drawings. They were drawings of faces, some male, and female, but what caused the teacher to pause was the nature of the sketches themselves. The detail of the work was quite simply exquisite. Facial features crafted and portrayed by the hand of a master. The eyes that stared off the pages were like princes drawn with such skill and command of shadow and highlights.

There were over thirteen faces, all with great beauty even the eyes themselves almost came to life as if these images were gazing back. Turing, she looked at Angelina carefully. Then choosing her words.

"Did you draw all of these my dear...I mean they're so beautiful. Their expressions they're so delicate and yet so...!

"I even know their names! Angelina cut in.

"This one is my favourite. He teaches me how to draw ...That's Etaanus!

The End.

∞

Next Book by Martin Jeremiah

THE COMING OF AGES

Printed in Great Britain
by Amazon